COMES THE REVOLUTION

Birdie's story

KARL RODMAN

ISBN: 1502399733
ISBN 13: 9781502399731
Library of Congress Control Number: 2014916730
CreateSpace Independent Publishing Platform
North Charleston, South Carolina

PROLOGUE

Birdie's room is flooded with winter's brightest sunlight. Outside, it is bitter cold, particularly cold for New York's Hudson Valley, but inside, the manufactured home feels snug. She focuses on the ceramic bust of Mayerhoff, which she brought home from Russia and has treasured for nearly seventy years. An elongated Jimmy Durante nose accents Mayerhoff's handsome Semitic features. Its vivid green-and-blue glaze brings a smile to Birdie's face.

From the other end of the manufactured home, she thinks she can hear Mimi, her live-in caretaker, moving about. Birdie pushes back her quilt, brings her skinny legs over the side, and eases her feet to the floor. She tentatively stands up and then shuffles to the bathroom, feeling the usual arthritic pains.

Emerging from her bedroom, she ignores the false teeth sitting in a bowl of water. She pays no attention to the hearing aids on her night table. "The batteries are no good anyway."

She drops her frail body into the middle of the living room couch and smiles up at Mimi, who wishes her "Good morning" in her lilting West Indian accent. Birdie's slender hands reach out for the proffered cup of coffee.

Birdie is petite, although that word is seldom used to describe a woman who says that she is only a few months short of entering her one-hundredth year. Most of her life, she has been anything but petite, short, yes, but buxom and robust rather than petite. People who look at her portrait, which she brought back from Moscow in nineteen forty-one, are struck by her facial resemblance to the movie star Ingrid Bergman. But now she is tiny and frail.

Mimi peels an orange, divides it into sections, and puts them on a plate, which she brings to Birdie, who has already finished her coffee.

Mimi takes the empty cup to the sink. When she turns around, she sees that Birdie's head has fallen onto her chest. Birdie is dead.

Within the hour, Birdie's daughter, Joy, calls Isaac, her cousin who lives in Florida, to tell him her mother, his aunt, has died. Isaac responds by recalling the Hebrew legend that it is only the just who are granted a sudden and painless death.

Joy goes on to tell him, "Of course I am relieved. And yes, we are still coming down to visit you next week. Why shouldn't we?"

The following week in Florida, Isaac asks Joy for family tales, believing that she wants to talk about her mother and that talk is good for her, until Joy angrily turns on him, saying, "No more! Don't ask me anything more. You know she could never tell the same story twice in a row. Those years in Russia are a mystery. Was she really married to my father? Why did she leave him? When? And why did she go off with Bryan, abandoning me in Moscow to live with my grandmother for a whole year? Was it really a year? You figure it out. And I couldn't care less about her politics, whatever they were. I don't even know how old she really was. I'm through! She was ready to die. She died, and that's all I want to hear."

ONE

I t was 1929. Nineteen-year-old Birdie lived with her parents and her older sister, Elsa, on the third floor of a Brooklyn walkup. Her Yiddish name, Fagel, means "bird." Her mother lovingly called her by the diminutive form Fagelah, but on the official rolls of the high school she attended, her name appeared as "Birdie." The name change was her own idea. She insisted they alter her school enrollment forms as soon as she became aware of the baggage carried by the name Fagel.

Her family, like so many of her neighbors, had emigrated from rural Russia. Her father, Louie Tillow, came by himself in 1900. He worked, first as a peddler, then discovered his trade: window washing. In six years, he saved enough money to bring over his wife, Clara and their seven-year-old daughter, Elsa. One year later, Birdie was born.

At home they spoke Yiddish, and while Louie cared little about religion, Clara insisted on keeping a kosher home. Clara favored her younger, "American" daughter, Birdie, whom she adored. The plump infant grew into an overweight adolescent. Her mother's devotion produced a daughter who was confident and strong-willed. At the age of thirteen, Birdie realized that it was the slimmer girls who were the popular ones, and she rapidly shed most of her excess weight, going on to have friends and admirers, if not a boyfriend.

There was never enough money, but, like for most of their neighbors and friends, coping with life left the Tillows little time to think of themselves as poor.

Completing high school, Birdie had no plans and no compelling dreams. Absorbing the country's optimistic mood, she was untroubled by questions about her future.

A week after graduation, she took the subway to Macy's department store and applied for a job. She was immediately hired, given a uniform, and put to work as an elevator operator. That was when she joined the Communist Youth League.

She joined because her closest friends were members. Neither of Birdie's parents involved themselves in politics. They had arrived in America well before the Russian Revolution of 1917. Still, everything they were hearing from there was positive. Her mother's cousin Sarah wrote from Moscow at least once a year, telling of her optimism. "Life is still hard," she would say, "but we have our hope. It's better for the Jews now." So it was with her parents' approval that she joined the Communist youth organization.

For the next two years, Birdie's friends were her fellow league members. They marched in May Day parades and vacationed at a camp in the Catskills where they sang the songs of the American labor movement and folk songs from the Appalachian Mountains. They danced folk dances from Russia, Greece, and Palestine.

Occasionally, at the end of those dances in the barn, a comrade would invite Birdie to climb into the hayloft where they would cuddle atop the fragrant and prickly hay.

One evening, following a lecture at the youth league, Birdie walked home, hand in hand with her friend, Frieda, who lived in her building. It was Frieda who had introduced Birdie to the group, and it was Frieda who had convinced Birdie that her role in life was to make the world a better place, specifically by working to bring a Soviet revolution to America.

"Of course, the country isn't ready for that yet, but our job is to educate the masses, to make them ready, to teach them where their real interests lie."

Birdie offered no reply, and they walked in silence for a while until Birdie said, "Did you get a good look at Peter, in the back of the room, at his 'literature' table? He keeps pushing his pamphlets on me. He's a real nudnick, you know."

"He's not a nudnick. He's sharp as a tack. It's just that he's so crazy about you that he doesn't know anything else to say."

"You think so?"

"I know so."

Another lull in the conversation followed. Birdie squeezed Frieda's hand as they passed two roughly dressed men, hunched on a stoop and passing a paper bag back and forth. "Look!" Frieda said, "I think there's a bottle in there. They're drinking."

"Isn't that why we go to these Communist meetings, Frieda? So that people like them can have a better life?"

A moment of silence followed, and when they had passed the men, Birdie said, "I've been thinking. You know the oldest joke around, the one about strawberries and cream?"

"You mean the one where this speaker in Union Square gets up on his soapbox and tells the crowd, 'Comes the revolution, you'll all have strawberries and cream for breakfast every day?'"

"Yeah, that one."

Frieda went on, "Then, when a heckler keeps shouting out, 'But I don't want strawberries and cream for breakfast. I hate strawberries and cream!' the speaker points at him and replies, 'Comes the revolution, you'll have strawberries and cream, and you'll like it! - Good story. So what?"

"It's like this," Birdie said, and she held her palm flat, horizontally, at her waist, at first with the palm down and then she turned her wrist, so the palm faced upward.

"What's that supposed to mean?"

"It means that when I was this high..." she began, palm at the waist, facing down. "...that joke already had a beard this long," she finished, palm facing up.

"So, what about it? What are you saying?"

"Nothing," Birdie answered "I was just thinking."

Birdie had been at Macy's for over a year when, at the end of her shift one day, she was called into her supervisor's office. "Sit down," the older woman said, with an apologetic smile. "I'm sorry, Birdie. We have to let you go. This is your pay for today, and tomorrow, you shouldn't bother to come in." She handed her an envelope.

"How can that be?" Birdie asked. "I thought we were friends. Is there anything wrong with my work?"

"No. Of course not, Birdie. You know how bad it's becoming. There are others who have been here much longer than you. Lydia, for example. I've watched her children grow up. We're saving the jobs that we still have for people like her."

That night, seated around the enamel-topped kitchen table, Birdie reported to her family, "I'm out of work. They fired me."

"I'm sorry, Fagelah, but we'll be OK. You'll see," her father said in Yiddish. "Why are you slumping like that? Sit up straight and proud. Now you're part of the Depression, just like everybody else. You shouldn't be surprised."

"I'm not surprised," she said. "I'm sad. And I'm mad too."

Birdie understood. She knew that nearly a third of American workers were unemployed. Banks were failing. But the *Daily Worker* informed her that in Russia, there was neither depression nor unemployment. Discrimination was against the law. The exploitation of women was ended, and now women took their rightful place in the workforce alongside men. Stalin's ambitious five-year plan was being overfulfilled. Electricity was being brought to the peasants. In Moscow, they were building a subway, which was going to be monumental.

What was more, Birdie had relatives in Russia.

"I'm going to Russia," she announced to her parents, standing erect, to her full height of five feet, two inches. "I want to help build a Socialist society, to do something interesting, something exciting."

She spent the next year selling magazine and newspaper subscriptions door to door. Had she not insisted on offering the *Daily Worker* ahead of her other publications, it might have gone faster, but still, she was a persuasive salesperson, and by the end of the year, she had accumulated enough money to buy a one-way passage on a Soviet freighter.

Birdie's steamship passage was purchased, and Clara was devastated to realize that her favorite daughter was leaving.

"You'll see me again, Momma, I promise. But we'll say our good-byes right here. I'm going down to the boat by myself. I don't want anyone to come with me."

On a June day in 1931, Birdie carried her cloth-covered cardboard suitcase down to the Brooklyn pier where the rusting SS *Igor Checherin* was being loaded with freight.

She offered her papers to a T-shirted young sailor who shook his index finger in a gesture of refusal. The sailor led her to the officers' and passengers' living area where Birdie introduced herself to the other paying passengers. There was a couple: young academics, enrolled in a leadership training course at Moscow's Lomonosov University, and there was Lisa, an attractive thirty-year-old photographer who planned to record the epochal changes taking place in Russia. She and Birdie were to be bunkmates in the second passenger cabin. Birdie was impressed by Lisa's mannish haircut, so stylish, in contrast to her own old-fashioned, shoulder-length brown hair. The tailored slacks Lisa wore left Birdie ashamed of her own very plain ankle-length dress.

Passengers' and officers' quarters were located above deck in the ship's superstructure. Her cabin had windows that could be opened. Quarters for the crew were below deck.

After a simple dinner, the passengers were invited to join the crew below. Descending the metal stairway into relative darkness, they were greeted by the sounds of Russian folk songs and loud accordion music. The rhythm resonated in Birdie's heart. These were the tunes her mother hummed and occasionally sang throughout her childhood. These were the records they played at the gatherings of the youth league. She was acutely aware of happiness rising within her. *I made the right decision. I belong here,* she thought.

She stood at the open metal door while her eyes became accustomed to the low light. The crowded room was illuminated by a single bulb screwed into a porcelain fixture dangling from the ceiling. Also, there were several candles stuck into empty bottles. Through the smoky haze of Russian *papirosi* (cigarettes), Birdie found an unoccupied chair. She saw that the crew included both men and women. Her attention focused on a rotund woman with bright scarlet lipstick and heavily rouged cheeks. Her hair was dyed a shade of orange Birdie had never encountered before.

The woman approached her. "Welcome," she said. "I am Ludmilla Ivanovna. I am communications officer." Her English was heavily accented but good. Birdie was more surprised at her array of gold-capped front teeth than she was to have found a translator.

"I am very pleased to meet you," Birdie said.

"I too," Ludmilla replied. "We will talk all week. Maybe I practice English and I teach you Russian?"

"That will be wonderful," Birdie said.

Ludmilla embraced her and then went off to sit next to one of the two accordion players. Birdie marveled at the strength of Ludmilla's voice, which rose and carried above the general din.

How beautifully she sings! And I'm so pleased that I already have a Russian friend. She was startled by the approach of a wiry, serious-looking young sailor who smiled and then, in Russian, introduced himself as Yuri. He offered her one of the sweet-smelling *papirosi*, cigarettes which, in the coming years, Birdie would rarely be without.

Yuri had no English. Birdie had, at most, one hundred words of Russian, but they communicated, each speaking his or her own language, repeating the same word over and over again, emphasizing different syllables and accompanying their speech with gestures. After a while, Yuri invited her to dance.

"No. Nyet. I'm not ready to dance," she said.

They sat in silence, watching the dancers. Then Yuri gestured an invitation for Birdie to accompany him above deck. He spread his arms and took a deep breath, indicating that the air on deck would be fresher.

Holding her hand, Yuri led the way toward the bow of the ship where he helped her to climb onto a coil of heavy lines. The coil was large enough so they could lie flat, with Birdie's head resting on Yuri's arm. They looked up at the stars and out at the sea.

Birdie was wrapped in bliss. *This is Socialism!* she said to herself. She offered no objection as Yuri rolled over atop her and kissed her lips. She remembered the nights in the hayloft at summer camp. Then, as Yuri began to unbutton her blouse, she reacted just as she had done on all of those other nights. She pushed him off. "*Nyet.* I'm not ready for that. I don't want to go that far."

There was no lack of communication. Her message was clear, and Yuri turned out to be considerate - considerate but also persistent. Every evening, they met out on deck. On each of the subsequent ten nights until their arrival in the southern port of Odessa, Birdie continued to protect her virginity from Yuri.

On the second of those nights when, quite late, she returned to her cabin, she found her roommate Lisa in bed with one of the sailors. Birdie was afraid to undress. She did her best to ignore the two of them as they ignored her. Climbing into her bed, fully clothed, she lay there listening to the activities across the cabin. She didn't disapprove. She was intrigued. She was still excited from her tussles with Yuri, and this excited her further.

Despite the unexpected company, sleep came quickly, and when she awoke in the morning, Lisa and her sailor were gone.

It wasn't until after lunch that she and her bunkmate were alone in their cabin. Birdie lay on her bunk, trying to nap. When she heard Lisa come in, she kept her eyes closed. Lisa sat down on the edge of Birdie's bed.

"Did I upset you very much last night, sweetie? I hope not. It was just one of those things."

Birdie kept her eyes closed.

Lisa took her hand, entwining their fingers while the other hand played with Birdie's long hair.

"I'm sorry, sweetness, but being on the ocean is so exciting, isn't it? This is what happens to me."

Lisa bent forward and kissed Birdie on the lips.

"No, Lisa. Stop." Birdie sat upright, swinging her legs to the floor. "Leave me alone. I don't know what you are about. But leave me alone." Birdie rushed out onto the deck.

For the rest of the voyage, she barely spoke to her roommate or to the American couple, who, she believed, preferred to be by themselves.

On the morning of the twelfth day, the SS *Checherin* reached Odessa. Birdie received a suffocating embrace from the golden-toothed Ludmilla, who had taken it upon herself to give daily Russian lessons to the eager American. Yuri too found time to see her ashore. They parted fondly but with few words. Upon disembarkation, the Americans immediately separated. The couple, who were official guests of the state, were met and quickly whisked off in a black limousine. Lisa was led off by one of her sailors.

A silent, unsmiling soldier led Birdie to the wooden hut that served as "immigration." There was a handwritten sign on the building proclaiming it as such. By then, the Cyrillic script was less confusing to Birdie, and she was able to sound out the words *Passport Control*. Inside was a barricade, solid, except for a small window at shoulder height - not Birdie's shoulders though. She had to stand on tiptoe to push her passport through the small slot beneath the window. She smiled up at the female officer, who never returned her smile. For what seemed to be an interminable period, the woman behind the window would alternately fix a long, inquisitive glare upon Birdie and then spend an equally long time ruffling through a pile of papers on her desk. After four such alternations, she lethargically reached for her rubber stamp and pad. She made the necessary entries in Birdie's passport and curtly mumbled, "Proceed."

Using her growing vocabulary, Birdie inquired and then made her way, on foot, to the nearby railroad station.

It was easy to recognize the station, the elaborate structure was a prerevolutionary temple of commerce, but the crowd outside confused Birdie. She saw people carrying all sorts of bundles. People were coming and going, and many more were simply milling around. *Nobody here is well dressed,* she observed. *The men are all dressed like laborers; the women are drab, depressed.* She was surprised to see so many, standing, sitting, or lying on the steps, on the marble balustrades, or on the few sparse patches of uncut grass. Nearing the station, Birdie had to leave the sidewalk and step out into the street to avoid a group of ten or so teenagers, boys and girls, some with their backs to the high wall, others sprawled across the pavement, and all of them apparently drunk. *Or might they be drug addicts?* she wondered.

More inquiries and at last a woman led her to the line where Moscow tickets were sold. The line extended all the way across the main hall of the terminal. Somewhere ahead, it entered the next room, and Birdie couldn't see where it ended. All through the day, all through the night, and into the next afternoon, Birdie was a part of that line. It progressed in small snatches. Mostly, it stood still. Gradually, Birdie became aware of the communal nature of the line. She realized that one could leave for brief periods to use the station's filthy and foul-smelling toilet or to search for food, although very little food, if any, appeared to be for sale within the station. Fortunately, as her neighbors in the line became aware that the young girl was a visitor from America, she was gradually adopted as a "distant relative." There was much good-natured banter. Everyone in her immediate vicinity had something to say to or about "our little American guest." There wasn't very much to eat, but her neighbors did manage to keep Birdie fed. Mostly, it seemed, they shared various preparations of cabbage - pickled, in a soup, or right out of the garden. Rarely, someone would offer her a boiled potato.

Birdie had read in the *New York Times* that there was famine and starvation in southern Russia. But she had discounted most of what was being written about Russia as straightforward lies. She was more inclined to trust the *Daily Worker*, which told her that Soviet agriculture, having been collectivized, was making great strides toward plentiful harvests.

When she reached the front of the line, on the following afternoon, she bought her ticket to Moscow, but it was for departure three days hence. Now she too was a part of that multitude at the station, which had appeared so strange at first sight.

The afternoon sun was warm. Birdie found a vacant place on a wooden bench and sat down to consider what to do next. The assembled sprawling, vagrant adolescents were still where she had first noticed them two days earlier. One of the teenaged boys approached her and spoke in passable English. "You are American, right? You have dollars. Yes? We can find you food if it is your wish. Come with me."

"No," Birdie answered. She searched in her purse and handed the boy a quarter. "Bring me something to eat. I'll give you more when you come back."

He pocketed the quarter, ambled off, and returned in half an hour with a loaf of bread and two pickles.

"Now I'll show you where you can sleep tonight," he said.

"No, thank you. I'll stay here, with everyone else," she answered.

The boy sneered. "Afraid?"

Birdie didn't answer, and the boy returned to his companions.

At last, she found herself on her train, in her compartment, in her seat, headed for Moscow. For reassurance, she looked again at the Moscow address of her mother's cousin. She wasn't expected. She wasn't even sure her relatives knew she existed. But, as the train rolled forward, Birdie was excited, proud to have come so far. She felt weight-less and unconcerned - no anticipation and no fear. She was tied to nothing, as free as the bird for which she was named.

TWO

The Ford taxi, newly manufactured in Russia, delivered her to the address her mother had written out for her. "Sarah Grossman is my cousin. She'll take care of you," Clara had told her daughter.

It was a little past ten at night, but despite the late hour, the four-story stucco block gave off a glow, reflecting back the northern summer sun, which wouldn't disappear behind the neighboring apartment houses for another thirty minutes.

Birdie was at the right building, but she found that now she had to pass into a courtyard. Entry was through an arch that was three stories high. Affixed to the top of the arch was a plaster shield with the emblem of the Soviet Union. Most of the spacious courtyard was dry and dusty, bare earth with a few tall patches of weeds. In the middle of the yard, a cast-iron fence enclosed a children's playground. There were swings, seesaws, and a wooden playhouse decorated with traditional wooden carvings. Above the fourth entrance to the right, she found the number she had memorized. The door swung surprisingly freely to her tentative pull, and she entered the nearly dark hallway and stairwell. Smells of urine and of cooking fat assailed her at once. Apartment 4-A was on the top floor. Making her way up the gloomy staircase, she saw there were four doors on each landing, three of them protected by thick padding, made of some leather-like material. The fourth door was plain wood. Buckets of garbage stood outside of most doors. The one bare bulb on the second landing gave off a feeble light.

She climbed to apartment 4-A and banged on the door with the palm of her hand. *Can they hear my knock through this padding?* she wondered.

She pounded again. A tiny light shone through an opening well above Birdie's face. "Who is there?" came a woman's voice, speaking Russian.

Birdie answered in Yiddish. "I am Fagelah Tillow. Are you not my mother's cousin, Sarah Grossman? Your mother, Fagel, and my grandmother Rebecca were sisters. I am named for your mother. I've just come from America."

The door was opened by a plump woman in her sixties. She peered down at Birdie and then quickly enfolded her in a suffocating and protracted embrace. The hug was followed by a series of kisses on the mouth, on the forehead, and on each of Birdie's hands.

"Gospodin Pomilo!" Sarah said in Russian. "God have mercy," she repeated through tears.

As she untangled herself from her relative's embrace, Birdie saw that Sarah was dressed for bed, wearing a nightdress and a light cotton dressing gown. Then she noticed the man, standing just beyond. *Is this Sarah's husband? He looks younger,* she thought, appraising his solid body, his dark, curly hair and his bushy mustache.

"Oh," said Sarah, following Birdie's glance. "This is my son, Mordechai."

Mordechai looked at Birdie with an expression she took to be distrust.

"Come in. Come in," said Sarah. She locked the door behind them and led Birdie by the hand to a couch. "Sit down. I'll feed you. You'll tell us everything."

Birdie sat. She examined the small room, which held, in addition to the couch, a stuffed armchair, an oak table, and two wooden chairs. One wall was fully covered by an oversized bookcase, filled mostly with matching sets of books. Sliding glass panels enclosed the shelves. On the wall behind the table hung a photo of Joseph Stalin. It appeared to have been cut from a newspaper and mounted in a thin wooden frame. The one window faced the courtyard, and on the windowsill, she noticed the blue-and-white tin box into which you put whatever small change you could spare for the Jewish National Fund: money to purchase land in Palestine. The box was identical to the ones that most of Birdie's Brooklyn neighbors kept in their kitchens.

Sarah sat next to Birdie and held her hand. Mordechai sat opposite, on the stuffed chair.

"So much to ask, Fagelah. Your parents, their health. Are they living well? And you! You'll tell us why you are here. So much!"

They were conversing in Yiddish.

"I'll tell you everything," Birdie said, "but first, may I please use your toilet?"

"Oy, excuse me. I should have thought. Come."

Mordechai remained seated as Sarah unlocked the front door and led Birdie into the hall. She opened the door that wasn't padded, the wooden one, and led Birdie through a narrow kitchen, past a kerosene stove, an old-fashioned refrigerator, and a small, linoleum-covered table. At the back of the kitchen was another door. Sarah turned the handle and found it locked. She knocked. "Grigor Petrovich! Are you in there? We need it now!"

Sarah was answered by a grunt of affirmation from behind the door. Soon, a toilet flushed. The door opened, and an old man stepped out. He looked at Birdie inquisitively, smiled, cocked his head, and said, "Privet, devushka" (Greetings, young girl).

The cramped facilities were built into the space below the stairs leading to the roof. There was a wooden water closet head-high above the toilet and a small, stained sink directly under the wooden stairs. The space was so tight that to wash her hands, Birdie had to bend her back and bow her head.

"I'll wait for you in the kitchen," Sarah said.

When Birdie came out, Sarah explained, "We are so lucky to have an apartment here in the center. You see, most of the apartments in the center are communal apartments. We share the bathroom and this kitchen with the other two apartments on our floor. Of course, before the revolution, this was one big apartment. But it's much better to be here in the center of Moscow, not in the new flats they are building out on the edges."

Seated again in the front room, Sarah told Birdie, "Mordechai, my son, is forty years old. He was married to a Russian woman, but it didn't work out well, and they have been divorced for ten years already. Fortunately, they never had any children. Oh, even after the divorce, she continued to live here with us because there was nowhere else to go. But last year, she took up with a policeman whose family had rooms, and the two of them went there to live."

Sarah spoke about her son as though he weren't in the room, and he said nothing until Birdie addressed him directly.

"Where do you work, Mordechai?" Birdie asked in Yiddish.

To Birdie's surprise, he answered in good, but accented, English. "I am a translator. I'm a member of the Writers Union, and I translate from English to Russian, mostly children's stories, but also a bit of Jack London too, I translate."

For Sarah's sake, conversation returned to Yiddish and now that Mordechai had broken his silence, he seemed more willing to participate. There were numerous questions about how the family lived in America. Birdie wanted to ask Sarah about her husband, Mordechai's father. Was he still alive? Where was he? But that question never seemed appropriate. It was nearly midnight when Sarah said, "You must be exhausted, Fagelah. Come. You can have my bed tonight. This is Mordechai's room. I'll spread some blankets on the floor in my room. Tomorrow, if you are still here, we can borrow a cot from next door."

Birdie woke up on the floor. She was wrapped in a white quilt, and her head lay on a feather pillow. She recalled an argument over who got the bed and who got the floor. But she remembered nothing more. From down the hall, she could smell the familiar scent of onions and potatoes frying in oil.

Sarah was gone. An orange bedspread covered her bed.

Birdie put on the same skirt and blouse she had been wearing since she left the ship and went looking for the bathroom.

Neither Sarah nor Mordechai were in the other room. In the hall, Birdie saw that the kitchen door was open. The aroma came from Sarah's cooking.

"Good morning, Birdie. You have to bang on the bathroom door. The old man is in there, and he'll be there most of the morning unless he hears you. Then, when you are washed, breakfast will be ready for you."

Sarah brought Birdie's plate to the table in her front room.

"We need to talk now about your plans, Fagelah."

"I don't really have any plans. I'll find a job. I'll find a place to stay. I'll be fine."

"Oy, little one. If only it were that easy. There are no places in Moscow. You will stay here, with us. We'll tell the house manager. Then we'll go to the registration office and make you legal here. Later, you will have time to begin looking for a job."

Those tasks took the whole day. They shuttled from office to office and from desk to desk. But they did very well. Before the workday ended, Birdie possessed Soviet identification papers and permission to reside in Moscow.

Back home, as the two women climbed the steps, Birdie concentrated on ignoring the smells and the filth. On the fourth floor, the kitchen door was open, and seated on a stool, looking out the window, was a middle-aged man, chubby, his blond hair, turning gray, was crew cut. He was dressed in well-used working man's clothing. His shoes were dirty and scuffed. String took the place of shoelaces. On the windowsill stood a nearly empty bottle of vodka. In his hands, he held an empty glass.

Seeing the women, he smiled broadly, stretched out his arms in greeting, and then began a gracious speech in Russian. It wasn't the Russian to which Birdie was becoming accustomed. It was a heavily accented mix of Ukrainian and Russian. But it was impossible not to understand his meaning. He was offering Birdie a drink, and as politely as she could, she refused. "Nu, stakanchick," he kept repeating (just a little glass).

"No, no," said Birdie, and then she added, "Shalom Aleichem," as she and Sarah turned toward their rooms.

"Why did you say 'Shalom Aleichem'?" Sarah asked. "None of them are Jewish. That is Michael, the tenant of the third apartment on this floor. Michael is married to Nina. She'll be home soon. She manages a music store. He is the janitor in the local school. They have two children, Yuri, who is eight, and Marianna, who is six. And that, plus the old man, Grigor Petrovich, makes up our communal. Now you know about everyone!"

Mordechai returned home soon after the women. His dour expression from the night before was gone. He was actually beaming as he came into the apartment.

"Birdie," he said, "I made inquiries at work. We need someone who can proofread the publications we prepare for English-speaking visitors, to check for errors. If you want to do it, you can start immediately. It's a good job. You should take it."

"Take it?" she answered. "I'll jump at it. I thank you so much!"

"Good. It's settled then. Tomorrow morning, at eight thirty, you and I will go to work together. My office is in the Writers Union. They will find you a desk there too. The building is close. We will walk there in twenty-five minutes."

After supper, Sarah took Birdie across the hall and introduced her to Nina Grigoryevna. Birdie was surprised to find her attractive, lively, and apparently intelligent, given the unfavorable impression that she had formed earlier when she first met Nina's husband. This was a case of instant liking that had nothing to do with what was being said, since Birdie understood little of the rapid conversation. Nina's husband, Michael, was there, but he said nothing. Instead of joining in the conversation, he picked up his accordion and attempted a mournful Gypsy tune, frequently interrupting the tempo as he searched for a particular note, which, often as not, he failed to discover.

Nina threw up her hands, said something in Russian, and left the room. "She wants you to meet her children," Sarah explained.

In a moment, Nina returned, leading two sleepy youngsters by the hand.

This time, Birdie was able to understand as Nina explained to her children that they should meet a guest from America!

"This is Marianna, my daughter. She is six years old. This is Yuri, my son. He is eight."

Birdie shook hands with each and repeated the proper Russian phrases she had mastered to express her pleasure at meeting each of them, and then they returned to bed.

Their visit wasn't long. They had come to borrow Nina Grigoryevna's folding cot, which they took back across the hall and set up in Sarah's bedroom on the opposite wall from Sarah's own bed.

THREE

Birdie heard Sarah stir. Bright sunshine filled the room. The folding cot had proved comfortable.

Only my second morning in Moscow, she thought, *and already I have a family and I'm about to go off to work!*

She and Mordechai set off on foot for the House of Writers. Their route took them through the very heart of Moscow, across Red Square, and past the Kremlin. As they walked, Mordechai provided a running commentary on the history and beauty of the area.

Descending a gradual incline toward the Moscow River, they passed several small onion-domed churches and then came to the most ornate of all, Saint Basil's, just outside of Red Square. To Birdie, the site was so familiar from photographs and from newsreels that her first reaction was one of disappointment. *Yes,* she thought, *it is breathtaking. But no more so than I had expected it to be. I feel as if I've known it forever.*

Mordechai, in his role as tour guide, intoned, "There's a legend that when Ivan the Terrible had it built and he saw how lovely it was, he ordered the architect be seized. Ivan had his eyes put out so that he could never produce another church to rival this one."

Birdie made no response, filing the tale away somewhere in her memory, preferring to take in the church's beauty in silence. They strolled uphill, skirting the ornate structure of the Gostini Ryad, a gracious three-story shopping complex. Mordechai, again, intoned, "Before the Soviet Revolution, merchants would set up their stalls here. Each of those arches housed a separate shop. Now, of course, the stores are all state enterprises."

Birdie thought back to her time at Macy's and refrained from asking why there was so little merchandise on display.

They were passing the outer walls of the Kremlin, the fortress citadel of ancient Moscovy.

"That ornate building over there is where Stalin has his office." Mordechai cocked his head, indicating one of the structures behind the Kremlin walls. "He sleeps there too."

Birdie pointed. "You mean that one, over there?"

"Don't do that," Mordechai said hastily. He pushed Birdie's arm down to her side. "It's better not to be seen pointing your arm toward the Kremlin."

They crossed a wide avenue. It was the widest that Birdie had ever seen, but what struck her was the lack of traffic. Only a few cars or small, canvas-covered trucks were visible.

"We built these roads for the future. Someday, we will need these wide roads in our capital."

Continuing, they came upon a massive construction site. *Or is it a construction site?* Birdie wondered. There wasn't anyone working on it. Piles of debris littered a vast pit. Seepage from the nearby river had formed a small lake.

Again in his tour-guide voice, Mordechai said, "Right here stood Moscow's largest cathedral, The Cathedral of Christ the Savior. Enormous! Last year, they dynamited it. Now we are having a competition to see who will design the Palace of Soviets, which will be built here to replace the cathedral. They say that whatever will be built here is going to be taller than your Empire State Building. It will be the world's tallest building."

Birdie didn't know how to respond to any of Mordechai's little lectures. His pedantic speech intimidated her. Instead, she was content to store up her impressions.

"Now, here we are," said Mordechai. "This is the House of Writers. This is where we will work."

The Writers Union was housed in what appeared to be an unprepossessing two-story stucco building. They passed through an open cast-iron gate into a spacious courtyard. There were numerous entrances, and each was overhung by a metal and glass canopy. Mordechai steered them to one entry on the far side of the court. Once inside, Birdie's initial impression was upended. They were in an oak-paneled foyer. Beyond the receptionist's desk, her view took in a series of rooms, one leading to the next, each more ornate than the last.

Bowing his head to the attractive receptionist, Mordechai continued, "This building is described by Tolstoy in *War and Peace*. He used this palace to picture the Moscow residence of the Rostovs. Ah, here she comes. Svetlana Umrichina. She's the one who will tell you what to do, and I'll see you at lunch, Birdie."

Svetlana Umrichina, whom Birdie assumed was of some importance, was a severe-looking woman, perhaps in her forties. She was dressed in a dark suit and wore her hair in a bun. She kissed Mordechai on the cheek and said in Russian, "So I see you have a new girlfriend at last."

"Go on with you," he replied. "She could be my daughter. Besides, we are relatives."

Birdie was pretty sure that she had correctly understood the exchange.

"Come," said Svetlana, speaking Russian. "Come with me, and I will show you what your task is. Do you understand me, or should I try to speak English?"

"Much I understand," Birdie answered, though she wasn't sure she was being truthful.

Birdie was given a seat in the library and left alone with a pile of English proofs to be checked and corrected. Three hours later, Svetlana

Umrichina returned. Interrupting Birdie's concentration, Svetlana invited her to join the staff for lunch in the cafeteria.

The meal was in complete contrast to anything Birdie had experienced since arriving in Russia: plentiful choices—cold salads with smoked fish, deviled eggs, and sausages; a choice of steaming cabbage soup or an enticing fish soup; and a main course of fried cutlets and fried potatoes. Desserts included delicate pastries, as well as bowls of fresh fruit and cream.

Mordechai was not to be seen. Everyone around her was involved in animated conversation so Birdie sat by herself, ate heartily, smoked a Russian cigarette, and then returned to work.

"Well?" asked Mordechai, as they walked home. "How was your first day among the proletariat?"

"Oh, there is so much I want to ask you. Tell me about the food first. Where did all of that food come from?"

"Birdie, we members of the Communist Party are commonly referred to as 'servants of the people.' Servants of the people must be well fed if they are to do a good job for the people."

"So you are capable of sarcasm, Mordechai! Or is it called irony? I never was sure of the difference. Anyway, does that mean that you are a member of the party?"

"Of course I am. It is expected. But now you tell me what they had you doing today."

"So much to do. But I liked it. They gave me the text of one of those pamphlets that are given out to tourists. I was supposed to check the English. This one explains Stalin's point of view on the nationalist question. He certainly spends a lot of time trying to sort out something called 'the Jewish question' doesn't he?"

"You seem to have started right out with one of the hard ones, you did. The Russians have decided that we are a nation after all. On my passport, it doesn't say, 'Russian': it says, 'Jewish.'"

"Yet," answered Birdie, "on the identity papers they gave me, it says, 'American.' It seems to me that I am Jewish and American at the same time. Can't you be Russian and Jewish at the same time?"

"No, not at present," he answered.

Every day that week, they walked together to and from work. Birdie had questions about the coworkers she was beginning to know, and she had questions about the life she was observing. "Why," she asked, "is life so hard here? Where is the joy I expected? When I walk down the street, nobody looks me in the eye. Why is that?"

"Ah, but maybe you expected too much? We are building something new in this world. Perhaps there are mistakes. There are enemies who want to harm us. It takes time."

Then, on the final day of the week, Birdie decided to ask the question she had been so reluctant to ask. "Mordechai, please tell me about your father, Sarah's husband. Where is he? Who is he? Those books on the shelves, they are his, aren't they? What happened to him?"

"No, don't ask about my father. It is better now that we don't talk about that." Mordechai took Birdie's arm, and they continued the rest of the way home in silence.

FOUR

For the next month, well into a hot Moscow summer, Birdie's life was consumed by her work at the House of Writers and by the family arrangements gradually working themselves out with the Grossmans.

Making connections with her fellow workers was challenging. She felt that nobody among the writers wanted to get close to 'the American.' They didn't go out of their way to avoid her, but neither did they seek out her company. As a result, most of her contacts centered on life in the apartment house.

The old man usually kept to himself. Sarah told Birdie that he was a widower and a pensioner and that he had once been a teacher of biology. As far as she knew, he was completely alone now. He gave Birdie a ritualistic, polite salute of his hand whenever they passed, either in the kitchen or emerging from the toilet, but so far, they had never spoken.

On the other hand, she grew closer to Nina, Michael, and their children. Twice before going to work, Nina had asked Birdie to keep an eye on the children after school until she got home. Birdie didn't know where Michael was at those times. "He's out on the street," was all that Nina had to say.

One evening, Birdie, Mordechai, and Sarah sat in the front room conversing in Yiddish. The topic was food and the lack of food.

It hadn't taken Birdie long to note that most store shelves were empty. She learned that a particularly long line of shoppers in front of a store meant that a shipment of goods had just arrived or was expected soon. She also noticed that the food Sarah prepared daily in the fourth-floor communal kitchen was much more plentiful and much better than the food being prepared by most of the neighbors on the lower floors.

"Well," Sarah explained, "sometimes Mordechai does bring something home from the lunch meal. And there is the special store, just behind the Kremlin, where party members are allowed to get special rations."

"So what about Nina and Michael? They eat pretty well too. For a while, I thought of bringing some of my leftovers from lunch for their kids. Then I realized that they were eating just well as we do. How do they do it?"

"Birdie," Sarah explained, "it's like this. Nina is the manager of a music store. While her salary is very small, you've got to understand how things are done here. Nina has a wonderful position. When a new shipment of musical instruments arrives, she puts them into the back room. She already knows who wants just what and what they have to offer in exchange. They are expected to give her something extra. So she contacts them right away. And that's why you almost never see anything for sale in the stores."

FIVE

Birdie finished her fourth week of work, and, as they did every day after work, she and Mordechai walked home together.

"Tomorrow will be a *Subbotnik*," Mordechai said. "Do you know what that is?"

"From the word for Saturday, isn't it? No. Tell me."

Mordechai explained, "A Subbotnik is a day of voluntary labor. All over the country, people will give up their day of rest to work for the country. Tomorrow, you'll see. Our job will be cleaning up the parks and playgrounds in the neighborhood."

"Our job?"

"Yes, you too."

Birdie and Mordechai left the house the next morning at seven thirty. Sarah stayed home. Only when they got to the storage room at the neighborhood House of Culture did Birdie realize Mordechai was in charge. The red arm band he wore identified him as the organizer for the region. From a storeroom full of supplies, Mordechai distributed rakes, sickles, clippers, and metal trash buckets. As neighbors arrived, he grouped them into brigades and gave them assignments.

Birdie set off with three of her neighbors, two women and a young man, none of whom she had noticed before. They were given rakes and a metal garbage can and assigned the task of cleaning up debris from their own courtyard and from the adjoining buildings. At first, they all worked enthusiastically. All three accepted the foreigner without question and assumed she knew enough Russian to take instructions, even if she didn't respond to their constant jokes or comments. Last winter's dried twigs and leaves were raked into piles. It wasn't clear to Birdie who, if anyone, would eventually remove them. They picked up pieces of old newspapers. They raked up sunflower seed hulls that had been chewed and then spit onto the ground. They found a few bones left from picnics that had taken place the previous autumn.

After two hours, the young man sat himself down on a bench. He took a bottle of vodka from his jacket and said, "Enough, girls. Time for refreshments!" The two young women, each a bit older than Birdie, eagerly joined him. They beckoned for Birdie to come, too. Unsure of herself, she thought that she should keep working but was afraid of looking foolish.

At that moment, making the rounds of his workers, Mordechai materialized.

"Comrades," he said, "is this the way you introduce a foreign visitor to a Soviet Subbotnik? Two more hours, for the country and for yourselves. Show yourselves to be good citizens. Then, at noon, come back to the House of Culture. That's the proper time for being merry."

Reluctantly, the young man recapped his bottle and the group resumed work. They kept at it for another hour – one, of the two hours Mordechai had requested. Then the three of them, apparently all at the same time, decided they had done enough work. Birdie, despite their entreaties, held on to her rake and stayed behind to work alone in the courtyard. She felt conspicuous, standing there with her grass rake in her hands. *Who am I*, she thought, *to set myself up as better than they are?* She felt alone and vulnerable. At last, with relief, she heard the chimes on the Kremlin's Spaski Gate ring the hour of twelve and knew that her task was finished.

When she returned to the House of Culture, she realized that nearly all of the tools were already back in place.

Once everything was locked away, Mordechai took Birdie by the hand, saying, "Come. You'll like this."

He led her the few blocks toward Red Square. From every direction, people headed toward the very center of Moscow. Couples arrived hand in hand. Fathers carried toddlers on their shoulders, while others carried musical instruments. As the square rapidly filled, people gathered into distinct groups, often around someone playing an accordion or a guitar. There was singing, and there was dancing. In one corner of the square, a military band played marches.

"Over here! Over here!" The voice belonged to Olga Beglova, the receptionist who presided over access into the House of Writers. She wore her blond hair in pigtails, which were pinned up, encircling her head. She beckoned enthusiastically.

They found her surrounded by twenty or so of their coworkers. Hampers of food and drink lay open. Birdie recognized the tall janitor, who was playing an accordion. Two of the more boisterous authors were strumming on guitars, though soon the guitars passed from hand to hand and Birdie discovered that her daily associates had talents she had never suspected. Mordechai, it turned out, had a beautiful baritone voice in which he delivered traditional ballads. Svetlana Umrichina, Birdie's stern taskmaster at work, danced beautifully to the accordion's wailful Gypsy laments.

Tiring of singing and dancing, the group moved to reciting poetry. People with whom Birdie had shared meals but with whom she had scarcely spoken kept explaining to her, "This is by the great Pushkin," or "This is by Lermontov. It tells of exile and of captivity. It is very sad." Birdie was thankful for the explanations, since she understood practically none of the poetry.

Then Mordechai announced he was going to recite two poems. "The first is Pushkin." He spoke in a strong and pleasant voice. When he finished, the group applauded enthusiastically. "And now," he said, "a love poem by Anna Akhmatova. She is one of today's great ones. It is too bad that her works are no longer published here."

"*Ne kulturnie*," (not cultured) Svetlana muttered. "He really shouldn't be talking of such things in this place."

Mordechai recited the short poem, and this time, his effort was met with an embarrassed silence instead of applause. Quickly, the accordionist filled the silence by playing a bright Gypsy dance. Olga Beglova jumped to her feet and, using two hands, pulled Birdie upright, insisting that she learn to dance. They twirled in place, and seeing how Birdie's long brown hair swirled to the music, Olga loosened her pigtails and let her blond hair be equally free.

Birdie was transported. Finally, she was reexperiencing what she had felt that night, only a month past, below decks on the SS *Checherin* – She was touching the joyous and sensitive Russian soul, which she had always known was there.

At home, in the evening, Birdie reported to Sarah on the day's events. "This was the best day I've had since I came to Russia! Sarah, you should be so proud of your son. He can do everything!"

Much later, when the "white night" had finally turned dark, Birdie awoke in her cot, silently brought her feet to the floor, and barefooted, made her way to the bathroom. She went through the front room, unlocked the door, and passed down the hall. She returned through the front room and relocked the door. As she passed Mordechai's couch, she felt his hand reach out and touch her bare leg. She stopped. His hand caressed her leg. She stood still as the hand kneaded her calf and then gently brushed her thighs. Birdie was confused. First came a moment of fear, then indecision, and then acceptance. Mordechai swung his feet to the floor and sat up on his bed. His face was on a level with Birdie's ample breasts. He buried his face in her chest. She ran her fingers through his thick, curly hair, all the time pulling his face more firmly to her breast. Mordechai gently pulled her onto the bed.

"Fagelah, my dear one," Mordechai said in Russian and then returning to English, whispered, "I am so happy that you fell into my life."

He kissed her lips, and then he bunched her cotton nightgown up to her shoulders. He still wore his pajamas. He explored her breasts with his hands and then with his mouth. He rolled atop and entered her. Mostly what she felt was sharp pain. Mordechai's movements felt distant and quite apart from her own. It was over quickly, and as they lay side by side, Birdie was both astonished at how little time it had taken and satisfied that she could say, "Now I am no longer a maiden."

Soon, Mordechai was breathing steadily, his breath punctuated by occasional snorts. Birdie rose from the bed and returned to her cot.

S I X

Sunday morning, Birdie dressed and went out to an empty front room. Mordechai's bed, stripped of its linens, was already transformed back into a day couch. She found Sarah in the kitchen.

"Mordechai's gone for the day," Sarah said. "You and I will have a quiet day of rest."

Mordechai didn't return until late afternoon, and when he did, his behavior toward Birdie was no different from what it had always been. But in the evening, while Sarah was in the kitchen, Mordechai said, "I hope you will visit me again tonight, Birdie."

She did. Birdie waited until Sarah slept. Then, as quietly as she could, she eagerly approached Mordechai's bed. He stood to meet her, and this time, they removed each other's nightclothes. As Birdie slipped into Mordechai's narrow bed, she felt, more than ever, she belonged to this world. Making love was better this time, though, once again, Birdie was able to look at their coupling with detachment and tell herself, "I had expected more." Too soon, she was back on her own folding cot.

The next morning, she awoke to the sound of Sarah dressing herself, the start of a normal workday. Seeing that Birdie was awake, Sarah plunked down next to her, kissed her forehead, and said, "I am so happy that you will be my daughter-in-law."

That evening, Birdie and Sarah went across the hall to return Nina Grigoryevna's cot. Nina opened her door, saw who was there, and gave Birdie a big hug and a kiss. "*Posdravlayou.* I congratulate you!" she said. Apparently, in a space as confined as the communal apartment, there could be very few secrets.

One night, as they lay together in bed, Birdie hesitatingly asked, "Does this mean that we will be married sometime?"

Mordechai ran his hands through his curly hair, scratched an itch, and finally answered, "Birdie, you put me in a hard place. It wouldn't be a good thing for me to be married to a foreigner."

Birdie felt a coldness in her limbs. Then Mordechai added, "And besides, what is a marriage today? If you will think of yourself as my wife, I will think of myself as your husband."

Birdie was somewhat reassured by this but didn't know exactly what it meant. She never raised the issue again.

Weekdays, Birdie and Mordechai walked together to the House of Writers, usually, hand in hand. At work, Birdie's relationships improved. She felt herself accepted. No longer consigned to solitary lunches, she began to establish real friendships, particularly with Olga Beglova, who took up the task of making the foreigner feel at home.

The long days of summer gave way to the long autumnal nights. Late on one of these chilly nights, Mordechai awoke, startled by the sound of heavy steps echoing up the stairwell. He lay still, listening. Sarah and Birdie awoke to a pounding on the door.

"Open! We want to talk to you. We have questions."

Sarah came from her room, unlocked the door, and opened it just a bit. Three men pushed their way inside. They were neatly dressed in street clothes. One addressed Mordechai directly. "Comrade Grossman, dress yourself and come with us, and we will ask you questions." The other two searched the apartment, opening every drawer, pulling books from the shelves, riffling the pages, and flinging them to the floor. Linens were removed from the beds, and Sarah's bed was overturned.

Through most of the fifteen minutes of mayhem, the three family members huddled together on the couch. Then the chief ordered, "Let's go." Two of the men took Mordechai by the shoulders and shoved him to the steps. Birdie followed out onto the landing where three flights below, she saw the building manager looking up at them, her face white with terror. All other doors remained closed. The two women, numb with fear, remained where they stood, clutching each other as Mordechai was taken away.

"Oi," moaned Sarah, "first my husband and now my son. I knew, I knew."

They didn't attempt to sleep, and in the morning, at first light, they bundled themselves up and set out by foot for the Lubyanka prison. It occurred to Birdie that this was one of the advantages of living in the center; everything was so close. As soon as the thought arose, she realized how inappropriate it would be to share it with Sarah. At the prison, there was a large group of women, already gathered around the window above which was a placard reading "Inquiries." They were all waiting, seeking any word of their loved ones. Some had been there for days, even weeks.

Sarah and Birdie were lucky. At three in the afternoon, a militiaman emerged, called for Mrs. Grossman, and told her, "Your son, Mordechai Grossman, is charged with slandering the state. He will be tried in three days." The militiaman turned and reentered the prison before Sarah or Birdie could ask any questions.

They went home, dazed, Sarah leaning heavily on little Birdie's shoulder. Arriving upstairs, Sarah said that she felt sick and turned to go to the toilet, but finding the old man in there, she turned and vomited into the kitchen sink. Birdie wiped Sarah's face with a wet towel, cleaned up the mess, and then sat Sarah on the couch and covered her with a quilt. "I'm going to make us tea," she said.

Alone in the kitchen making tea, Birdie tried to think about what was happening. Having the resilience of youth, being just twenty years old, Birdie felt interest even more than she felt fear. It was as if she were observing from a distance rather than participating. *What does this mean?* she asked herself. *How am I supposed to relate to all of this? What should I be feeling? What am I feeling?* The only thing she was sure of was that she couldn't answer these questions. She was surprised to feel more like an observer than a victim.

She brought the tea to Sarah. They sat, side by side, on the couch. At first, they sipped tea in silence. Then Sarah took Birdie's hand in hers and said, "Can you believe I feel relieved? Really. When they came and took away my husband eight years ago, I knew, someday, they would come back for Mordechai. Now, no more waiting. Eight years of fear, and now there's nothing left to lose. My husband was an engineer, a good engineer, and a good citizen. They were building bridges. Everybody had to surpass the plan. If the plan calls for the bridge to be built in two months, we must do it in one. If there is no clean sand for the cement, use whatever there is. He wouldn't do it. They called him 'a British agent, a saboteur, a wrecker.' They sent him off to a labor camp. I never heard from him. Not one word. Probably he has already been worked to his death. He isn't strong, and he isn't well. Mordechai is strong though. He will be back."

The next three days, Birdie took Sarah to join the throng of petitioners outside of Lubyanka and then went off to work. At work, no one asked about Mordechai. Even Olga seemed to be avoiding Birdie's eyes.

On the third day, the same militiaman emerged and told Sarah, "Your son, Mordechai, was charged as a class enemy. He is already on his way to Siberia, to a labor camp where he will harvest timber."

SEVEN

Birdie had no doubt that everyone at work knew the reason for Mordechai's disappearance, but no one asked about him, nor did anyone offer any sympathy. Clearly, Mordechai's arrest was a forbidden topic. Work continued, as before. Every day, she carried a sheaf of papers to her accustomed place in the reference room, and every day was filled with eight hours of solitary, uninteresting work.

Two months passed, time enough for Birdie to have finally written to her parents and to have received a reply. Birdie wrote about her "modern Soviet-style" marriage to Mordechai. She neglected to mention his arrest. Their reply, coming surprisingly fast, included a wedding gift of twenty dollars. Birdie immediately spent the money on a heavy winter overcoat. It was gray, double-lined, and reached to her ankles. Its collar and cuffs were finished in curly Persian lamb's wool.

That night, after dinner, Birdie announced, "I am going next door to show off my new overcoat to Nina Grigoryevna."

As expected, Nina was truly pleased with the coat. "It is as if a new resident has come to live in our communal!" she said.

"Thank you," said Birdie, "but I need to speak with you alone. Will you put on your coat and we will walk a bit together?" Birdie's spoken Russian was now functional, though fractured and ungrammatical.

Out in the courtyard, Birdie took the older woman's hand and said, "Nina Grigoryevna, I am going to be a mother. I have not told anyone. You are the first person. What am I to do now?"

Nina led Birdie to the nearest bench. They sat close, sharing each other's warmth.

"Birdie, little one, if you don't want the baby, then have an abortion. It is very easy. I have gone twice already since we decided that Yuri and Marianna are enough children."

Birdie covered her face with her mittened hands. "Oh, but I want this child. I will have Mordechai's child. I came here, and I chose this life. Now I will make a new Soviet citizen who will grow up in a different world...maybe."

"Birdie, you will decide. You are young, and you are strong. Whatever you do will be right. Let's go upstairs. I'll help you to tell Sarah."

"Upstairs, yes, but you go back to your family. I need to tell her by myself."

The two women parted on the fourth-floor landing, and Birdie went into her apartment. Sarah, who had been reading, watched as Birdie removed her overcoat and delicately hung it in the wardrobe. The apartment was suffused with cold outside air carried in by the coat.

"So tell me, what is so important that you had to tell Nina Grigoryevna first?"

"Oh, Sarah, I am so sorry," she said as she sat down beside her and hugged her. "I didn't know how to tell you. I am going to have a baby. Your grandchild. I think in May, six months from now."

Sarah kissed Birdie, first on the lips, then on each cheek, and on her forehead. "I am so pleased. How are we going to let Mordechai know?"

Birdie had no answer.

Two months later, in January, returning from work, Birdie was met at the door by Sarah, who was clutching an envelope. "This came today," she said. "It is postmarked from the central post office in Moscow. No return address. I waited for you."

They sat down on what was now "Birdie's couch" and carefully opened the envelope. Inside was a smaller one, crumpled and smudged, but with Sarah's family name and address written in large block letters. The letter inside was also in an unfamiliar hand but different from the one that addressed the envelope.

Birdie read aloud, "Mordechai exists. Lesnaya Blok. Tikhonkaia, Siberia. Work is hard. Conditions terrible but we persist. Take care. He sends kisses."

There was no signature.

The day after getting the letter, Birdie knew what she had to do. "Sarah, please, you are taller than me. Reach up on top of the wardrobe and find me Mordechai's knapsack. It's somewhere up there. The one we used when we weekended in the country."

For the next several weeks, every day at lunch in the House of Writers, Birdie would discreetly take something nonperishable from the large buffet: salamis, olives, salted fish, preserves, crackers, chocolates, small jars of caviar, and still more. She had no trouble secreting these in her clothing until the end of each workday.

When, at last, the knapsack was crammed full with these treasures, Birdie told her associates that she was not coming back to work; she was quitting. Svetlana Umrichina seemed annoyed but said, "We have come to rely on you, Birdie. If you change your mind, we will welcome you back."

So, once more, Birdie found herself at the train station. The station, as always, was crowded. But, as this time her destination was Siberia and it was midwinter, she was able to secure a coach seat for the very next day. Her ticket was to Tikhonkaia, five thousand miles on the Trans-Siberian Railroad, almost to the Chinese border.

The following afternoon, Sarah accompanied Birdie to the train station. It was snowing tiny flakes. For several weeks, ice had been building up on the sidewalks. In places, it was already two inches thick. Now the falling flakes coated the slick surface, making each step treacherous. Walking, they held each other tightly. At the train platform, Sarah kissed her daughter-in-law. "Find him. Tell him how much I love him. Tell him to..." She stopped and abruptly walked away.

EIGHT

Birdie found her compartment. An elderly couple, apparently living somewhere east of Moscow, sat facing three soldiers returning to Siberia. The young soldiers were slumped in their seats, but upon seeing Birdie, they sat up and became lively.

"Oh, little one, welcome to our den! Are you really going to be ours for this whole trip?" one said.

She glared at them, said nothing, and removed her overcoat.

Seeing her swelling belly, the behavior of the soldiers changed abruptly. "Oh, little mother, forgive us. You're going to see the father, aren't you?"

"Yes, I am," she said and sat in the vacant seat next to the couple and facing the soldiers.

Nobody spoke, but the soldiers' eyes kept undressing Birdie. She shuddered, feeling that she was constantly being violated.

Exactly on schedule, the steam locomotive began to move, gradually increasing its speed. It passed quickly through the outskirts of Moscow and then plunged into the early afternoon darkness of the Russian countryside in winter.

For a long time, Birdie wallowed in her thoughts, exploring the depths of her unhappiness, her loneliness, and her uncertainties. Abruptly, she was recalled to the present, sensing the train had slowed.

Was I asleep?

The wagons proceeded to crawl for a few minutes and then, as the lights of a town appeared, hiccupped to a standstill. The breaking motion noisily transferred itself from car to car. A conductor announced, "We'll be here for a least forty-five minutes. There's a buffet in the station for those who want."

Birdie put on her overcoat and went out onto the platform. It was still snowing and very cold. She hastened along the platform toward the lights. Not far ahead of her were three figures also approaching the buffet, two of them quite tall, the third rather short. They too were leaning into the wind and moving quickly, their heads hunched down as they hurried toward the buffet.

They can't be any worse than the soldiers, can they? Besides, if I'm gonna be afraid of strangers, I'll never make it all the way to Mordechai.

Birdie began to make out their voices. "Holy Shit, it's fucking cold," she heard, or thought she heard.

English? Americans? Texas? Did I hear what I thought I heard?

Birdie entered the buffet a few steps behind the three men, who were heading directly to one of the three tables. All appeared to be in their twenties, and except that they were speaking English, they could have passed as Russians. They piled quilted overcoats, hats, and shawls onto a nearby table. Birdie approached and politely asked, "Is this chair vacant, and do you mind if I sit with you?"

Raucous laughter greeted her question. One of them, the shortest, said, "She's on the wrong train! She thinks this is the Flatbush line." He spoke with a New York City accent not very different from Birdie's own. The three embraced her and welcomed her as if she were a present from home.

"Who are you?"

"What the hell are you doing here?"

"Where are you going?"

Birdie sat, reached into her pocket, and pulled out a Russian cigarette.

"No way. Put that away," said one of the three. "Here," he said, thrusting out a package of Chesterfields. "Smoke a real one."

The short one identified himself as Max Granich. He appeared to be the group's leader. "This is Carl Peterson, and that's Danny North. We're on our way to show the Russkis how to set up an oil drilling rig. We're headed for Biro-Bidzhan. Danny and Carl both worked in the Pennsylvania oil fields, and I know a little bit of Russian, so we expect we'll do OK. Now let me guess why you're here. I look at your belly, and I figure you're going to visit your husband, right?"

"Yes. He's harvesting timber in one of the camps on the Biro River."

"And I guess too that he isn't there out of patriotism. He was sent away, and you are going to rescue him."

"From your mouth to God's ear."

"Well, our story is different. We chose to freeze our asses off for the good of the people. We came out here to contribute."

"Let's contribute to the economy," said Carl. "I'll go up and get us something at the buffet."

"Hot coffee, hamburgers, and French fries for all of us," said Danny.

After a while, Carl returned, balancing an enameled, beautifully decorated wooden tray loaded with the only things that the buffet offered: hard biscuits and glasses of steaming tea. Each glass, Russian style, sat in a metal holder with a metal handle.

"Hot," said Danny, as he quickly put down his drink. After a while, Max asked, "Birdie, you've got to join us in our compartment! You'll tell us more about how you came to this spot, and we'll tell you our dreams. Come! We'll squeeze you in."

"Of course I will. I'll be so happy to come."

Max went with Birdie to reclaim her knapsack. The couple slept. The three soldiers, realizing that she was leaving, glared at the Americans and made remarks Birdie couldn't understand but which, from their laughter, she assumed were crude.

The new compartment, several wagons forward, was already jammed. The oil-rigging team consisted of the three Americans, three Russians, and all of their tools as well as sacks of provisions, enough to last for several months. The three Russian volunteers, all inexperienced young men, were dedicated and eager to learn from their three "experienced" American comrades. Birdie was introduced, welcomed by all, and squeezed in.

Six days and nights, the train crawled eastward. There were stops to load and to unload freight, stops to take on water and coal, and stops to pick up or to detrain passengers. Birdie spent much of those days hearing the stories of her new companions. It became apparent that her command of Russian was better than any of the three Russians' ability to speak English, so Birdie did lots of translating. She told them about herself, and in the process of trying to describe her own motives, she began to realize how vague they were. Adventure? Dedication to a utopian dream? Escape from a dreary life? She couldn't say, with certainty, what brought her to this place. But exploration of this very topic kept them all talking for the duration of the journey.

"Danny and I are Wobblies," said Carl. "Have you heard of us, the IWW, the International Workers of the World? I've been a longshoreman, a lumberer, a factory worker, you name it. I've worked, and I've been unemployed. When I worked, I was underpaid and I protested. Look here," he said, rolling up his sleeve. "This scar is my permanent reminder of how they tried to teach me to be meek and civil."

Birdie told of her experiences in Washington DC with the bonus marchers. "It was the weekend when I graduated from Midwood High School in Brooklyn. My classmates were all excited about the prom. 'Who's taking you to the prom?' That was all anyone thought about. But not my closest friends. Not the people I knew from our Young Communist League. We were all upset about the twenty-thousand veterans camped out in Washington at the Anacostia flats. Remember? The unemployed. They demanded their promised bonuses, now, when they needed them. Not twelve years from now.

"So instead of going to the prom, we all got on the train and went down to Washington for the protest demonstration. It was great. Then, just one month later, Hoover sent in his generals, MacArthur, Eisenhower, and Patton to clear the Communist squatters out of 'Hooverville.' They killed four and injured over a thousand in the process. I really felt it. Maybe that's when I decided to go help Stalin rebuild Russia."

"There," said Carl, "I told you she wasn't a Trotskyite!"

Max kept returning to the subject of Mordechai's arrest and exile.

"Mistakes get made," he said. "Obviously, you love him a whole lot. You've got to hold on. You've got to believe. Maybe you'll bring him back to Moscow. Maybe he'll get there himself in ten years' time. But whenever he does get back to Moscow, from what you've been telling us, I'll bet you a night on the town, that he'll still think of himself as a Communist."

Birdie heard these words clearly. She sucked them deep into her being. But she was unable to formulate a reply that would express her own truth.

An incident, unbidden, popped into her head. She remembered a party, hardly a year past. There were fifteen or so young people. Some had gone to her high school. Some shared her youth activities. All called themselves "progressive" and believed in the rightness of the Soviet system. For fun, one of the boys was going from girl to girl, taking each by the hand, turning the palm upward, and gently stroking the base of the fingers. Ostensibly, he was searching for calluses. "Comes the Revolution," he said, "I'm going to be the one who checks the hands, to see who is a worker and who isn't." His act was greeted with raucous laughter and approval. Birdie remembered laughing along with the others and then, in a different part of her mind, thinking, *That's barbaric, and we know it is barbaric. That's why we are laughing. We know such things happened in Russia; they shoot people because they aren't workers with calloused hands. And it could never happen that way in America.* Now she was in Russia where such things did happen. And still she wanted to hold fast to her faith. *How,* she wondered, *can you hold onto two contradictory ideas at the same time? Is it possible?*

NINE

After six days and nights of companionship and conversation, the train reached Tikhonkaia, recently renamed Biro-Bidzhan. Birdie parted from her new friends, who were going on a bit farther. She detrained and sought her way to the prison camp.

She quickly discovered how apt her preparations had been. The treasures she had appropriated from the lunchroom in the House of Writers and crammed into her knapsack, could achieve wonders. In exchange for a candy bar, a truck driver drove her along the snow-covered roadway to the very gates of the camp. A single guard stood outside the barbed-wire enclosure. His greatcoat reached his ankles, and the flaps of his wool cap were tied under his chin. His rifle leaned against the fence. In response to Birdie's request to see her husband, he responded with just one word, "Perhaps." He never budged. Occasionally, he glowered at Birdie, but mostly he stared into the distance. After twenty minutes of stamping her feet to drive off the cold, she remembered her knapsack and thought to offer him a pack of cigarettes. Without smiling, he took the gift, opened the gate, and pointed to a shed, where he told her to wait.

The shed appeared to be a reception point and office. A cast-iron stove containing the remnants of a log fire offered little warmth.

An Underwood typewriter with Cyrillic letters stood atop a bare wooden table. A single chair stood nearby. Otherwise, the room was bare.

In the late afternoon, fully dark already, Birdie saw the work gangs returning to camp, each group of about fifteen men accompanied by a single armed guard.

An officer entered the office, apparently prepared to find her there. "Aha, another visitor to our hotel in the woods. So whom have you come so far to visit?"

"Mordechai Grossman. I'm his wife."

"Remain here. I'll have him brought to you." He turned and left Birdie alone again.

A few minutes later, Mordechai appeared. At least the man being brought in reminded her of Mordechai. His shape and manner of walking were familiar, but his clothes were unfamiliar—padded jacket and filthy, torn pants. The mustache was now absorbed into an unfamiliar straggly beard. A woolen cap covered his ears and hid his curly hair. He smiled shyly and pulled off the cap. Birdie was astonished by how gray his hair had become. He, at the same time, saw that she was pregnant.

They embraced. Even through the padded jacket, she felt his bones. Bony and yet at the same time, she felt hard, unfamiliar muscles. He released his grip and ran his hands over her belly.

"There was no way you could have told me. No way. I kept sending you messages, and finally one must have reached you. But I never dreamed that you would come here."

Now they were both crying.

"Mother? Tell me how she is."

"Sarah is a rock. She is my rock. We are closer than ever. She is sure that you will survive this and that you will come back to us."

"So we all pray," said Mordechai. "Every day we pray that it will happen."

The door opened, and the duty officer returned. The treasures of the knapsack were again employed. They negotiated, and it was arranged that in exchange for sausage, caviar, and cigarettes, Mordechai was to be granted a two-day furlough. A storeroom, behind the reception room, was theirs for that time.

A pile of dirty blankets suggested that they were not the first couple to use the room. There was even a latrine outside.

They made a bed out of the blankets and put Birdie's overcoat on top of them. Little heat from the wood-burning stove in the front reached back to the storeroom. All of that first night and during much of the first day, Mordechai slept in Birdie's arms. They took comfort in each other, but there was no attempt at sex. Neither of them felt that urge. Time and again though, as they lay together, Mordechai would raise Birdie's dress up to her chest, put his head on her belly, and just listen or try to feel their child's movements. These were happy moments for Birdie. She felt that she had succeeded in bringing Mordechai a significant gift.

Mordechai, at first, was reluctant to talk about life in the camp. Then, gradually, he began to speak of the prisoners he had come to know. "We work hard. We are cold. We are hungry. We have little to say to each other. We survive. From day to day, we survive.

"None of us is sure why he was arrested, why we were sent here. Most of us have been good comrades. Birdie, where did we go wrong?"

"Oh, Mordechai," she replied, "I count on you to tell me such things. How can I answer you?"

Birdie shuddered at the abrupt awareness of how their relationship had shifted. Mordechai was no longer her instructor, the experienced one who would teach her how to live her life. Now she was the responsible one. It wasn't only that he was a prisoner and she was free. *He needs me now. He can't do anything for his child or family. I'm the one who has to be strong, who has to find the way,* she thought.

On the second day, Birdie went from guard to guard, from officer to officer. She distributed bribes, which she hoped might make Mordechai's life a bit easier. Always, she asked questions—about his sentence, about expectations, about possibilities. Always, she was turned away without answers.

Then, on the third morning, when she was preparing to leave, one of the guards took Birdie aside and said that Mordechai's work gang had arranged for her to remain for the rest of the week. A section in the barracks was cleared out just for them and made separate by hanging blankets. The men in Mordechai's work gang promised to surpass their norm, thus freeing Mordechai from four days of work.

Slowly, Birdie began to understand about life in the prison camp. She met the men in his gang who besieged her with messages to carry home to loved ones. She had brought a small camera along, and they took pictures of the two of them, kneeling in front of stacks of freshly cut logs.

Now, when they lay on their improvised mattress, Mordechai was able to talk about his situation.

"You realize where we are, don't you, Birdie? This is the new Jewish Socialist Homeland, Biro Bidjan. Stalin has created an autonomous region for us. He dreamed up a solution to the 'Jewish problem.' He gave us our own territory, where we can speak Yiddish and be Socialists. Unfortunately, he chose a pretty poor place for our homeland.

"We, prisoners in the camp, are wards of the state. But some of the men working alongside of us are Jewish pioneers who came out here for a better life. It turns out that the best work they could find is cutting trees, just like us prisoners. The government paid their transportation to get here and promised them all kinds of things, but from what they tell us, when they got here, they had to build themselves shelter. Notice I don't call them 'homes.' They live worse than what we do."

"I know. I've heard about Biro Bidjan," Birdie said. "Isn't the idea that Jews will come here and become farmers?"

"Yes. A collective farm has been established, and the farmers are hungry. In fact, they're starving. They don't have animals. They don't have tools, and they don't know what they are doing. That's why the 'farmers' are cutting trees alongside us prisoners."

"Terrible."

Another time, as they lay huddled under their blankets, sharing whatever warmth they could offer one another, Mordechai said, "Ten years. Ten years is my sentence. I don't know if I can make it through ten years, Birdie." When she didn't reply, he added, "Well, others have done it. We'll see."

At the end of the week, they separated. Mordechai returned to his work gang, and Birdie was taken, by truck, back to the railroad station. That afternoon, she found herself aboard a Moscow-bound train, her senses dulled. She tried hard to hold on to her memory of everything that had happened the past few days, but it all kept slipping away. Mostly, she slept. On the sixth morning, the train halted. The thump that accompanied the cessation of motion woke Birdie. She looked out the window and was astonished to see that she was in Moscow. She scarcely knew how she had gotten there.

A taxi brought her home. Climbing the stairs, she was struck by the smells, no longer repugnant, now familiar and comforting. Sarah answered the door, flung her arms around Birdie, and sobbed uncontrollably.

Clearly, Birdie thought, *she hadn't expected I'd ever return.*

"Yes," Birdie said, freeing her face from Sarah's embrace. "Yes, I saw him. I spent seven days with him. And yes, it is terrible there. But he is strong. We can hope. I don't know what else we can do. I'm fine. The baby inside of me is fine."

"Come, lie down on the couch. I'll make you a glass of tea. You'll rest, and you'll tell me everything."

TEN

Indeed, Birdie was fine and she was resilient. After a single day of rest, she set out, on foot, to the House of Writers.

Seeing her at the door, Olga rose from her receptionist's desk and embraced her. "Welcome, Birdie. Oh, how I've missed you! Are you coming back? Later, you'll tell me everything."

Even as the friends were kissing one another, Svetlana came up to them and quickly took charge of her, grabbing her by the arm and insisting, "Come, come to my new office. You've returned because you know that we need you here, right? Look, my office. Now I am the chief. I'm head of the Department of Foreign Languages. How do you like that!"

"Good for you," said Birdie. "I've come back because I need to work."

"I thought so."

"But I don't want to work the way we used to. I want to take my work home with me and then bring it here when it is done."

They came to just such an arrangement.

At first, Birdie wrote to Mordechai once a week, sometimes oftener, describing the progress of her pregnancy, telling all the news she could gather about doings at the House of Writers, and conveying Sarah's love.

She never received answers, not even acknowledgment that her letters were arriving, and gradually, the one-way communication tapered off and then ended.

By spring, Birdie could no longer manage the walk to deliver her work or to get new assignments. Her advanced pregnancy made the twenty-five-minute stroll unthinkable. Instead, she took the public bus, which was much more of a nuisance. First with the wait in line and then with the circuitous route, it took her almost twice as long as walking.

On a spring day, when Birdie was delivering a pile of completed work, Svetlana called her into the office.

"There is going to be a party, tomorrow night, at the American embassy. A delegation of American writers is here. One of them we have translated and published. I want you to come with me. It will make a good impression—an American working in our office—and they'll love it that you are so huge and almost ready to deliver."

Birdie's first reaction was elation. Then she was embarrassed to show up pregnant and without a husband. But nostalgia and curiosity prevailed.

"Yes, thank you. I'd love to go with you. It will be fun to meet Americans again, and besides, I never leave the house anymore, except to come here. Yes. I'll be pleased to come. And I have a pretty maternity dress that Sarah made for me."

An American embassy car picked them up at the House of Writers and brought them to the party. It was Birdie's first visit to the embassy, which stood on the Ring Road, one of Moscow's new, wide boulevards. They passed through the doubly guarded gates: first by two Soviet militiamen, who carefully scrutinized their papers, and then by two US Marines, who saluted the car and waved it into the courtyard. Another marine pointed to the proper entrance, which led into the reception hall.

Inside, there was loud music and bright lights. Birdie recognized Alexander's Rag Time Band coming from speakers on two sides of the hall. Two immense crystal chandeliers hung from the ceiling, looking like inverted half grapefruits, but huge! They reflected and diffused the light from myriad unseen bulbs. Wooden tables lined each side of the room. Well-dressed men and women, but mostly men, were crowded in front of the tables. On one side of the room, the tables were loaded with food. In honor of the local guests, there were traditional Russian dishes: sausages, cold cuts, salads, yogurt, caviar, and the ever-present cucumbers. For the Americans, there were mounds of potato salad, miniature hot dogs wrapped in bacon strips, and most enticing for Birdie, several bowls of crisp potato chips.

On the other side of the room, on identical tables, were drinks. There was sparkling water and red and white wines: Soviet wine from Georgia and from Moldavia, as well as French wines. Bottles of Georgian cognac stood by the ever-abundant champagne and vodka.

Birdie quickly realized, from the bits of conversation she overheard, that most of those who were gathered around the food table were Americans and most of those around the beverage table were Russians.

Birdie was entranced by the familiar smells. Even the clouds of cigarette smoke carried memories of home. As Birdie helped herself to a plateful of food, she was approached by a smiling, solidly built American, maybe just a few years older than she.

"Hello there. When you came in I heard you speaking English to our Russian colleague, Miss Umrichina. Well, to tell the truth, I first noticed your shape. It isn't often that anyone so pregnant shows up at one of these affairs. Then I heard you speak. An American!"

Grinning, he held out his hand.

"Yes, I am a pregnant American. And who are you?" she said, putting down her plate, reaching out and shaking his hand. Birdie was immediately pleased by the man's obvious warmth.

"Oh, I'm sorry, I'm Sam Green, correspondent with *Fortune* magazine."

"Birdie Tillow, from New York."

"You must work with Svetlana Umrichina? That's a question. Do you? I interviewed her once."

"Yes, I do. I proofread and correct translations, that sort of thing. She's my boss."

"Isn't your husband with us tonight?"

"No, he's away –out of town."

"Well, please bring your plate and join us," Sam said, pointing toward a man and a woman sitting in an alcove.

Birdie followed. Sam introduced her to his wife, Belle, and to Belle's brother, Bryan.

Belle, a slim, severe woman, wore her hair in a bun. Birdie noticed her habit of pressing her lips together, as if reserving speech until she could make a judgment.

Her brother Bryan seemed shy and spoke little. He had masses of wavy black hair. A Charlie Chaplin mustache gave his otherwise dashing appearance a sense of vulnerability. Birdie liked it that he was smoking a pipe. Mordechai smoked one too.

Bryan stood up to shake Birdie's hand. Then they all sat down, balancing china plates on their laps.

"So tell us, Birdie," Belle asked, "what is it that brought you to Moscow?"

"Well, I got out of high school and I didn't have any particular plans so I decided to come here and make some sort of contribution. You know how it is. It seems funny now, talking about building a better world, and then life gets in the way." Saying these last words, she looked down and lightly massaged her belly.

"We're not so different, Birdie. We came here to see what it is all about," said Sam. "I write for the newspapers as well as for *Fortune*. Belle does occasional pieces on the theater scene. We've been here for almost a year already. It's fascinating. And Bryan here, Belle's brother, he came to visit us, but he never seems to leave."

He said this with a smile, and from the way it was received, Birdie judged that Bryan was a welcome guest.

"Let me explain," Bryan said. "I came to visit. But now I earn my keep, ghostwriting news releases under Sam's byline."

"Enough, you two," Belle put in. "She doesn't need to know our whole family history!"

Throughout the conversation, Birdie nibbled and crunched potato chips that were fresh from the embassy kitchen; they were salty and delicious, though not exactly the potato chips that she remembered from Brooklyn. She also tried a couple of the pigs-in-a-blanket, the little hot dogs with bacon that also carried familiar smells of home.

Sam was starting to tell a current anecdote when Birdie put aside her plate, stood up, and said, "Excuse me. I need to go to the bathroom." As she crossed the crowded reception room, she could feel liquid trickling down her leg. She sat down on the toilet and felt the gush of her water breaking. Having a fair understanding of the process, she had no fear. There wasn't any pain. She took an embassy towel and wiped her legs clean. She washed her face and hands and without any leave-taking went directly out to the courtyard where several cars were waiting. She opened the rear door of the nearest one, got in, and ordered the astonished driver to take her home to Sarah at once. "Otherwise," she threatened, "I'll give birth to my baby right here in your nice clean car!"

The Russian driver unhesitatingly complied.

By the time Birdie climbed to the fourth floor, she was sure she was going to deliver then and there, inside the apartment. But she was very mistaken in her timing. Sarah went across the hall to fetch Nina Grigoryevna, a relatively recent mother. Nina taught Birdie about timing her contractions and how she would know when it would be time to go to the birthing clinic. The three women spent the rest of the night together. Between each of the increasingly frequent contractions, Birdie was aware of the greasy food she had eaten at the party. Nina told her to breathe deeply between pains, but the bacon-wrapped hot dog and the fatty potato chip taste arose in her throat with every deep breath. Finally, Birdie went down the hall to the kitchen where she managed to vomit up the embassy food into the communal sink.

At dawn, Nina woke Michael and told him to take Birdie and Sarah to the nearby birthing clinic. Later that morning, Birdie gave birth to a girl. Her name was registered as Zoya Grossman. Zoya was a popular name, which Birdie chose at the last moment, just because she liked it. Zoya was born on May 12, 1933.

Birdie spent two full weeks in the birthing clinic. She thought it was an unnecessarily long stay, but such was Soviet practice. The midwives and nurses taught her to nurse, and she took immense pleasure in having Zoya at her breast. They also taught her how to prepare baby bottles and how to tightly swaddle the child, Russian fashion. Sarah visited every day and always stayed for several hours. Much of the time, she contentedly sat with the sleeping child on her ample lap. Five of the eight beds in the room were occupied, and Birdie was acutely aware that she was the only tenant of the room whose child had not been visited by its father.

When Birdie and the baby returned home, a drawer at the foot of the wardrobe was pulled out, emptied, and used as a bassinet.

Family life rapidly assumed its own routine. Little Zoya rarely slept through the night, but with two women to look after her baby, Birdie was soon rested, and within a week, she returned to the House of Writers, leaving Zoya in her grandmother's care. The arrangement pleased both women since, with Mordechai gone, Birdie's salary had become essential.

"You see," said Sarah, "now we have become a typical Soviet family. I am a pensioner. I stay home and care for my granddaughter while you, the mother, go to work and while the father is off somewhere else." She tried saying this with humor, but there were tears in her eyes before she finished speaking.

ELEVEN

Returning to the House of Writers to pick up a new assignment, the first person Birdie saw was Olga.

"Look at you," said Olga, slowly getting up from her receptionist's desk. "You're a mother now! I'm truly happy for you."

Olga put her arms around Birdie and was about to kiss her when suddenly she buried her head in Birdie's shoulder and began to cry.

It was a moment before Olga could speak. Then she looked up, and said, "You're the same age as I am, but you have a family now, and I don't have anyone...No. This is your time to be congratulated, not my time for pity." With these words, she finally smiled and delivered kisses on both cheeks.

Before Birdie could respond, Olga released her and threw up both hands, saying, "Oh, I just remembered. Look. A letter came for you. I've been holding it for a week."

"Who would write to me at this address?" Birdie wondered as she took the envelope, opened it, and read:

Dear Birdie,

Congratulations on the birth of your child! You see, the American colony in Moscow is small and news travels quickly.

The three of us enjoyed meeting you at the embassy party last month, despite your hasty departure. It seems I was in the middle of an annecdote when you ran out and I never got to finish it; therefore, we would be pleased if you would join us for supper one night at our apartment. How about next Friday? Give us a call.

Regards.

Sam and Belle Green and Bryan Cantor

A telephone number and an address followed.

Birdie was pleased to have been remembered. She was uncomfortable about asking to use the phone at the House of Writers, so on her way home, she detoured to the Central Post Office and Telegraph building where there were public phones, and there, she accepted the invitation to eat with the Green family at the end of the week.

Their apartment, within walking distance from Birdie's communal, was on the third floor of a new building, number fifteen, Sivtsev Razhek. This was an old and prestigious street. On the way there, as she had learned was customary when visiting, Birdie bought a bouquet from a street vendor. The neighborhood was home to artists, performers, writers, and up-and-coming government functionaries. Number fifteen had several apartments set aside for members of the foreign press.

"Welcome to our Moscow home," said Belle, greeting Birdie at the door. "Oh, what lovely flowers. Asters? Come in. You talk to Sam and Bryan while I put them in water."

The apartment reminded Birdie of what she had always taken for granted in America. Not only was there a private kitchen and bathroom, there was a living room and two separate bedrooms. And there was a telephone!

"I had no idea. How quickly one forgets," Birdie said to Sam and Bryan. "A private bathroom now seems like such a luxury."

From the kitchen, Belle responded, "Someday, everybody will live like this, but the country isn't ready yet."

They sat, drinking wine and making conversation. Birdie showed photographs of her baby. But she sensed a certain awkwardness, momentary lapses in the flow of conversation because of the one big topic no one felt comfortable discussing—Birdie's missing husband.

Do they know he's been imprisoned in Siberia? she wondered. *I hope they won't ask me about him, but how can they avoid it?*

During one lull in the conversation, Birdie looked around and then commented, "This is such a lovely apartment, but, what would happen if you reversed the way this room is set up? If you put the bookcase against the other wall and the couch over in its place, then you wouldn't be wasting so much space as a passageway into the next room. You'll see. It will work better."

"Maybe," Belle replied, pursing her lips, her face clearly expressing displeasure. "Now I'll go and put the meal on the table."

Bryan had no response to the suggestion but looked puzzled, as though he ought to say something.

Sam said, "We'll think about it."

Belle served a fine dinner of roast chicken, crisp string beans, and mashed potatoes. Dessert was chocolate pudding. It was a real American meal, and Birdie enjoyed it thoroughly.

After supper, the table was cleared and they moved back to the couch and easy chairs. Both women began chain-smoking American cigarettes. Sam and Bryan smoked pipes. When they were seated, Birdie had a question for Bryan.

"Tell me, Bryan. I remember, at the embassy you told me that you just graduated from Fordham. I couldn't figure it out. What was a good Jewish boy like you doing in a Jesuit institution in the Bronx?"

Belle answered for her brother. "He won't tell you straight. He was always a good student. He got a scholarship to Fordham. Religion had nothing to do with it."

This was followed by a moment of uncomfortable silence. Then Sam said, "Birdie, here's the story I was about to tell you when you left the embassy so abruptly. It's about the American congressman who was attending a meeting here in Moscow. His room was on the second story in the Metropol Hotel. 'I know,' the congressman said, 'the damned Russkis are bugging my room. Somewhere there has to be a hidden microphone.' He looks behind the pictures on the walls. He moves every piece of furniture. Nothing. He takes off his shoes and scuffs his bare feet along the rug, until he finds a bump. He pulls back the rug, and there it is: a circular metal device screwed in place. 'I've got the sons of bitches!' he says. He bends down and carefully unscrews the device. And as he removes it, the chandelier in the ballroom below crashes to the floor!"

Birdie laughed appreciatively.

She suspected that sharp political arguments and related jokes were a staple at the Green's' table, but that so far, this evening, they had been avoiding politics, out of deference to their guest. Birdie determined that she'd ask Sam about his work.

"Tell me Sam, Aren't you covering the government's purge trials. I hear it's the major topic, now, in the world's press."

Sam put down his pipe, and with his hands on his knees, he leaned toward Birdie and said, "Yes. But we won't talk about that right now. What I want to talk about is your husband. Birdie, we know about his being sent away. Svetlana told me. It must be terribly hard for you. Do you want to talk about it?"

Belle looked at her husband with disapproval. "What do you think she can say? You don't expect her to say, 'I made a mistake and married a man who turned out to be a class enemy.' Do you?"

"No," Sam defended himself, "I mean, how can we give you support, Birdie. You don't have to discuss it at all if you would rather not. That's fine."

"Belle," Bryan said to his older sister, "you don't talk to a guest that way. It's not polite. It's not nice at all. You can't label the man an enemy when you know nothing about him."

"I know what they are trying to build here," she answered, "and that the people who oppose them are on the wrong side of history. You can't tell me what I know or don't know, Bryan." Turning to Birdie, she added, "I apologize for Sam's question. It was in bad taste."

"That's all right," said Birdie, rising from her chair. "Anyway, it really is time for me to get back to my baby. Thank you for a wonderful dinner. Thank you for having me."

The leave-taking was abrupt. As she went into the night, she thought, *Funny people. They love to argue with each other. But I don't owe them any defense of Mordechai. Still, I enjoyed having a taste of the good life - of life as it was before I came here.*

Meanwhile, back in the Greens' apartment, as the door closed behind Birdie, Belle said, "That's a dangerous woman. She gets what she wants."

"Maybe," Bryan replied, "but you have to credit her with having spunk."

TWELVE

A few days later, Birdie returned to the House of Writers, intending to pick up her newest batch of translations for proofing. Before she had fully passed through the wooden door, Olga sprang up from her accustomed place and pushed Birdie back into the courtyard.

"News. Big news! Svetlana Umrichina. They've taken her away. Yesterday. They came in their big black car. Two men. And they took her away."

"Oh my God!" said Birdie. "Speak clearly. Slowly. In simple Russian words, so I can understand you. What does this mean? Do you think that she is an enemy?"

"You know what I think, Birdie. I never told you this, but remember that day when we were all in Red Square together? It was a Subbotnik?"

"Yes."

"And you remember, don't you, when Mordechai recited the Akhmatova poem, how upset she got? I think she's the one who reported him to the authorities. I think she's been watching all of us and she tells stories on anyone who gets in her way. Whatever it is that she's accused of, she deserves what's happening to her. But don't tell anyone that we talked about this. OK?"

Birdie kissed Olga on the cheek. "Of course."

Only then did they enter the building.

With Svetlana gone, no work had been put together for Birdie to take home. It didn't matter. She was hardly able to think about her work. Her hands were trembling. Her thoughts were all about Svetlana's arrest and what it might mean, but she couldn't focus. *Now I know what they mean when someone says, I felt the earth disappear from beneath my feet.* Clear thinking was beyond Birdie's ability that morning.

Nonetheless, without her being consciously aware of it, she had made a decision. By the time she got home and told Sarah the news, she found herself saying, "Sarah, I am sure that it was Svetlana who was responsible for Mordechai's arrest. Now I know what I have to do. I'm going to find out who it was that listened to her stories, and I'm going to make them reopen his case. I'll make them see that Svetlana lied, that Mordechai did nothing against the state, and they will have to free him!"

Her voice was so loud that she frightened the sleeping Zoya, who awoke screaming. Sarah, being closest to where the baby lay, picked up her granddaughter.

"Now, now, hush little Zoyshinka."

"No," said Birdie. "Give her to me. Let me be the one to comfort my fatherless baby." She snatched Zoya from Sarah's arms and paced the floor until the child stopped crying.

That afternoon, Birdie walked to the Telephone and Telegraph Center, intending to call Sam Green. *He must know his way around. He'll tell me where to start.*

"Hello, Sam Green's number. How may I help you?"

It was Bryan who answered the phone.

"Bryan, is that you? Hello. It's Birdie Tillow. May I speak to Sam please?"

"No, I'm afraid that you can't. He and Belle have gone off to Germany - Germany, where the big story is happening. They'll be gone for two months or so. But how are you? And what can I do for you?"

"Oh God! I don't know. Maybe you can help me. I'm not sure. Can I meet you somewhere?"

"Sure. Remember how to get to our apartment? Come now. I'll make coffee."

"I'll be there in less than half an hour. Are you sure it's OK?"

"I'll be waiting for you."

It was a short walk to Sivtsev Rajack. It felt sinfully luxurious to take the elevator only to the second floor, where she was greeted by Bryan, whose first question was about the baby's health.

"Zoya's fine. I'm so lucky to have my mother-in-law, Sarah, to help with her."

"Good. So tell me. What is the crisis that brings you to us?"

"Bryan, my boss at the House of Writers...Oh, I forgot. You know her, or at least Sam does. Svetlana Umrichina. She was picked up yesterday by the NKVD and taken away, and, Bryan, I'm sure she is the person responsible for having Mordechai sent away. This means...I hope this means that now I have a chance to make them reopen Mordechai's case. Now they can clear his name and send him back to me. I have to figure out where to start. I hoped that Sam would have contacts and that he could tell me whom to speak with."

"I see why you are so excited, Birdie. Sit down. Breathe a little bit. Drink some coffee. Then we will make a plan."

Bryan served American coffee with biscuits.

"Now we can think together," he said. "You know, you are not the first wife to be pleading for the return of her husband. There are other voices out there. But I'm pretty sure you're the only American among them. That ought to catch their attention. Yeah, we do have a chance. Believe it or not, the first person you should write to is Stalin. It's a well-established tradition. In the old regime, you would have written to the czar. Everybody does that as a first step, and sometimes it gets results. Then you can write to the heads of various ministries, starting with the NKVD, but even write to your neighborhood police station. Next, you can write to the newspapers and even to the American embassy. And then, once they have a document to look at, you start making the rounds, trying to find somebody who'll talk to you. You're going to be very busy."

"I don't have a typewriter, and I don't have an office anymore. I don't even know if I still have a job. Hah! You know what? I'm quitting my job. I won't go back. My new job is saving my husband, bringing him back from Siberia. Can I use this typewriter?" she asked, indicating the Remington on the desk.

"Yes, you are welcome to use it. It's in English though. No Cyrillic letters. You know what? You've come to the right place because as you write the letters, I can take them down to Novosti, the international press center, and have them translated for you."

Birdie hugged Bryan, kissed his cheek, and thanked him again and again.

"I feel so hopeful now. I want to start right away. May I?"

"Be my guest. I'd say, 'our guest' but for the next two months, I'm the only tenant here. Listen, I need to go out and file a story I've just finished. Over there, on that table, is an extra key to the apartment. If you have to go out—go, come, whatever—feel at home. Do as much as you can for now, and we'll talk about it in an hour or so, when I get back."

Alone, Birdie began typing. *This is a scene out of a comedy,* she thought. *Here I am, Fegelah Tillow, sitting in Moscow, writing to Joseph Stalin, begging him to give me back my husband, Zoya's father. This can't be real.*

She was still working on the letter when Bryan returned an hour later.

"Here is my best effort," she said. "What do you think of it?"

"May I do a little editing, Birdie? This is what I do best, you know."

Together, they revised the letter. The changes were all Bryan's suggestions. Birdie forced herself not to show how upset she was at the number of phrases she had proudly written now being crossed out by Bryan.

"OK. Now it's good. Let me take you to dinner, and then you can start making lists of what your next step will be."

This was Birdie's first restaurant meal since coming to Russia. Restaurants had all but disappeared from Moscow. Those that remained were for weddings and for major commemorations, but certainly not simply to drop into for a meal. The National Hotel, where Bryan took Birdie, was a pre-Revolutionary landmark, offering a full menu and catering to foreigners as well as to those few Russians in power.

Birdie thrilled at the sight of foods she had not seen since leaving America. She consumed a large meal, attentively and appreciatively, and then, when she felt beautifully pampered and as coffee was being served, she said, "Bryan, you are doing so much for me, and I hardly know anything about you. Please, now you tell me your whole story."

"So far, there hasn't been much to tell," he said. "In school, I was always the brainy one. When other kids did sports, I organized a chess club. College wasn't much different, because I lived at home with my older brother and two sisters. At least I managed to graduate in three years. Then I married Tanya. She was the only member of our high school chess team who could beat me. But our marriage only lasted for two months. So then I came here, to visit my older sister, Belle."

"Oh, Bryan, I'm sorry. Sometime maybe you'll tell me what happened to the marriage."

"I can tell you now. I couldn't make her happy. I wasn't man enough for her, so she had the marriage annulled."

Birdie changed the subject. "It's late, Bryan, and my mother-in-law will be worrying about me. May I come to the apartment tomorrow and we'll continue this job?"

"Of course. Come for breakfast if you can."

"No, first I'll go to the House of Writers and tell them I'm through."

"You do that. I'll expect you later in the morning."

They shook hands and parted in opposite directions.

The following sunny morning, feeling both trepidation and relief, Birdie walked to the House of Writers, but got no farther than Olga's desk.

"Nu, Olga? How is it today?" she asked. "Is everything normal?"

"I haven't heard a word. I suppose that's normal, and I have no idea who will take over Svetlana's duties."

"You mean nobody's in charge yet? Nobody is running this den of creative geniuses? Well, I'm quitting. I'm finished. It's been good for me. I love you, Olga. I'll miss you terribly, but now I have something else I need to do. Yes, I'm leaving. Please tell whoever cares not to expect me back."

Birdie turned and raced out of the building before Olga could respond.

For most of the summer, Birdie worked out of the Green apartment. First, she compiled lists of those who should be petitioned. She wrote the letters, and Bryan, after meticulous editing, took them to the press center for translation.

When the letter-writing phase was over, Birdie started the daunting task of trying to personally meet with the recipients of her letters. Most often, she would be stopped by a woman at a desk, the same position that her friend Olga occupied at the House of Writers. The receptionist would usually rebuff her, saying, "He is not receiving today." Birdie was discovering this group of women, apparently, were running the country. She suspected it was they who would eventually determine Mordechai's fate.

After a full day of making her rounds, and before returning to Sarah and Zoya, Birdie would often stop by at Sivtsev Razhek to report to Bryan on her lack of progress. On one of these visits, Birdie, exhausted and demoralized, plopped herself into an overstuffed chair and silently stared at the blank wall.

Bryan, waiting for her to talk, took out his pipe, filled it with tobacco, lit a wooden match, and began to draw on the stem with sharp, quick breaths.

The tobacco caught, and puffs of smoke rose. Only then did Birdie speak.

"I'm close to the end, Bryan. Nothing! No one cares. We've tried everything. Enough! No! That isn't it. I've used up my savings already, and Sarah's pension isn't enough to keep her, me, and the baby alive. I was foolish, walking away from a good-paying job."

"Stop it, Birdie. You'll find another job. You've done everything you can do for Mordechai. Now you'll go back to work."

"But not at the House of Writers. Somewhere, there must be another job waiting for me."

"Let me ask around," he answered. "With your language skills, it shouldn't be hard."

Birdie knew she had picked the right time to go back to work. She had largely exhausted the channels of appeal. She had succeeded in speaking to a few officials, all of whom dismissed her by promising to "look into the matter of your husband's arrest." Even when she didn't get past the receptionists, she always made sure to leave a letter behind. *Maybe a paper record will clog up some pipeline until it is dealt with,* she hoped. *Meanwhile, I'm going on with my life!*

THIRTEEN

Two days later, Bryan arranged through one of his press pals for Birdie to be interviewed at the Moscow film studios, *Mosfilm*. She went and after a fifteen-minute interview was promptly hired to begin the following day, writing the subtitles on films destined for English-speaking countries.

The metro brought her back to the center of Moscow, where, before going home, she stopped at the Postal and Telegraph building to tell Bryan her good news.

"Marvelous," he said. "I insist on taking you there for your baptism."

"Ridiculous. I just came from there. I took the metro to the Lenin Hills station, walked a few minutes, and there it was."

"Yes, but I'm so proud of helping you land the position. I want the pleasure of watching you walk through those steel gates they have there."

Birdie consented.

When she went downstairs the next morning, there was Bryan, sitting on a wooden bench in the courtyard. They rode the metro and then walked along the high esplanade, looking out on a panorama of all Moscow.

"You know this spot, Birdie? Before it was Lenin Hills, these were the Sparrow Hills. It was precisely here that Napoleon paused in his conquest of Russia. His army halted right here, and he waited for the city fathers to come up to him, to symbolically offer the keys of the city. You know what happened next, don't you?"

Birdie was silent, enjoying the view spread out below, of gold-domed monasteries and churches sparkling above the wooden huts, now being replaced by blocks of new apartment houses.

Hearing no answer, Bryan continued, "They never appeared. Instead, the city fathers abandoned the city to Napoleon. Then, in a little while, it was fire, lack of food, and winter's cold that drove Napoleon to retreat, to flee Moscow."

How strange, she thought. *Are all men like this? He lectures me, just like Mordechai did that first day we walked through Moscow. But it was different then. Mordechai has the city bred in his bones. Bryan sounds like he's parroting a lesson he learned somewhere. Still... Mordechai speaks with the authority of a commissar. Bryan is trying to be polite.*

At Mosfilm, Bryan shook Birdie's hand. "You'll do fine," he said and then watched as she passed through the gates.

Now Birdie was working with vibrant, artistic, and bright people. True, there were intellectuals at the House of Writers, but Birdie found them dour and often cynical. *Even Mordechai,* she realized. *He takes himself so seriously. He doesn't know how to have fun.*

That afternoon, Birdie telephoned Bryan to share her excitement. "All the filmmakers, actors, directors, photographers, stagehands, they are all driven by the excitement of making films that will bring the message of Socialism to the people. I feel their enthusiasm. I'm a part of it."

A week later, she told him, "You know, my command of the Russian language still isn't good enough to transcribe a conversation that's being projected, but with scripts, dictionaries, and help from coworkers, I'm doing fine."

A few months after she began working at the studios, she found her coworkers all atwitter at the arrival of the leading stage director, Vladimir Mayerhoff. He had recently staged an acclaimed modernization of Chekhov's *Seagull* and was now coming to codirect a film version of the play. Birdie was fascinated to see that the actors and actresses with whom she worked, celebrities who were recognized everywhere, were just as excited by the presence of the famous stage director as their own young fans became in their presence.

The sound stage where *Seagull* was being filmed was in an area quite separate from the screening room in which Birdie worked. Her coworkers had been talking about Mayerhoff for several days before she first saw the great man at lunch in the cafeteria. He was carrying his tray toward a table where, by accepted practice, only the most senior Mosfilm personnel would sit. She recognized him immediately from his photographs, which frequently appeared in the newspapers and in film and stage magazines. A shock of gray hair, combed forward, and his enormous nose were frequently caricatured in the press. He was not particularly tall, but he carried himself with an air of importance.

Like most of those around her, Birdie was fascinated by him and stared at him through most of the meal. She was sure that, at one moment, she even caught his eye and sensed that he winked at her.

Two days later, again in the cafeteria, she saw him carrying his lunch tray, and to her surprise, he brought it over to where she was sitting.

"Excuse me," he said in British-accented English, "I am told that you are an American. May I please join you?"

"Of course, Mister Mayerhoff. I would be honored."

"Yes. Thank you," he said, sitting next to her. "There is so little chance for me to practice my English. You must call me Vladimir or Volodya. My close friends, of course, call me Volodya. And I'm told that you are Birdie. Is that correct? I would like it if you would correct my mistakes, Birdie. It is so many years since I have been in your country."

"Yes, but I don't believe that you make mistakes, Mister Mayerhoff. Your English is flawless."

They conversed all through lunch. Mayerhoff's formality was replaced by friendliness. He asked Birdie to tell him about herself, and to her surprise, she found herself talking about her husband, his unjust conviction, and her trip to Siberia to see him. Mayerhoff listened attentively but offered no opinion and then asked Birdie if she would like to visit the set of *Seagull*.

They walked across the lot to the film set. She sat and watched as actors and cameramen questioned him about how he thought this particular scene should be staged. After half an hour of fascination, Birdie got up and said, "Thank you, Mr. Mayerhoff. This was wonderful. Now I'd better get back to my own work."

"Oh, don't go yet," he said, taking her by the hand. "I want to show you one more thing."

He led her by the hand. "I want to show you the magnificent office they have given me."

As he spoke, Birdie wondered who on the lot was watching them and just what they might be thinking of her. She looked at herself, as though detached from her own body.

Fagelah Tillow, from the Brooklyn tenements. Look at yourself, sharing in the life of the famous!

Then another thought came to her: *This is corny. I'll bet he's planning to offer me a part in one of his plays, on the condition that I submit to a tryout on his casting couch.*

She wasn't afraid to accompany him; rather, she was feeling an equal mixture of excitement and curiosity.

Mayerhoff led her into a cramped office and shut the door behind them. One small window faced the film lot. It was largely obscured by thick lace curtains. An immense writing desk was littered with books, scripts, and notepapers, covered in handwriting. The presence of a telephone attested to Mayerhoff's status. On the walls were three framed prints, a double portrait of Marx and Engels, one of Lenin, and another of Stalin. A plush sofa covered in green velvet and a pair of wooden chairs consumed the remaining space.

Mayerhoff took her two hands in his and looked into her eyes as though examining her face for the first time. "You are a very pretty woman, Birdie, but you look more Russian than American."

"Not Russian. I'm Jewish. Like you. My parents come from Odessa."

"Ah," he said, "but that doesn't explain your beauty or your softness." He pulled her toward himself, wrapped her in his arms, and pressed his body into hers. He twisted sideways, and the two of them, still pressed together, flopped onto the couch. Birdie felt Mayerhoff's hands pulling her blouse out from under her skirt and then reaching under the blouse to cup her breasts. Her brassiere was pulled down, releasing her breasts, which he kissed and sucked and licked.

Birdie lay still, unprotesting, as her clothes were gently removed. Mayerhoff took off his own shoes, socks, and pants but kept on his blue shirt with its starched collar open at the neck. His lips returned to her lips, to her breasts, and then traveled down to her navel. His hands explored, fondled, and then entered the wetness below. His lips followed and his mouth's exploration of her womanhood was a pleasure she had never imagined. His tongue brought her to the first orgasm of her twenty-three years. His lovemaking was slow, attentive, and aware. This was so new and unexpected. He held her there, at the height of pleasure, for an exquisitely long time, and only then did he enter her.

They lay together, wrapped in each other's arms for a short while, and then he said, "Now, I suppose you must go back to work."

As Birdie walked across the lot, back to the projection room, she was sure that everyone was staring at her. She imagined looks of curiosity, of disapproval, and of jealously. She didn't mind and wasn't embarrassed. She walked with confidence, feeling smug and proud.

When Birdie went home to Sarah and Zoya that afternoon, she was confused. She had no feelings of guilt for having betrayed Sarah's son nor toward her husband, far away in Siberia. She was well aware that she had just experienced something that Mordechai had never been able to give her and that, in truth, she hadn't known that she was capable of—that she didn't even know existed. *But Mayerhoff was using me. I'm sure he'll never speak to me again. And everyone at work is going to think that I am cheap...Or maybe not. Anyway, I'm glad that it happened.*

She was particularly attentive to her daughter that night, bathing her and singing her to sleep.

The following day, on her way home from work, she stopped at a gift shop on Gorki Street. She bypassed the busts of Lenin and of Stalin, going straight to a table closer to the back of the room on which were ceramic busts of the day's cultural heroes: writers, musicians, Arctic explorers, and so on. She emerged carrying a ceramic figure about ten inches tall and somewhat wider than it was high of Vladimir Mayerhoff, with his prominent Jimmy Durante nose and abundant wavy hair. The clay was glazed in brilliant blues, greens, and whites. Birdie would treasure the keepsake for the rest of her life.

FOURTEEN

Months later, a director on whose film Birdie was writing subtitles, offered her two tickets to the Bolshoi Theater. She thanked him and on the way home from work, telephoned Bryan to come share in the all-Tchaikovsky program.

When she arrived home and told Sarah about the two tickets to the concert, her mother-in-law became as excited as she was.

"That's marvelous," she said, "but what will you wear? I know. The maternity dress I made you. You wore it to the American embassy and went into labor wearing it. Go. Find it, and I'll remake it to fit you. It'll be perfect."

Later that evening, as she sat sewing, Sarah said, "I'm glad that you are taking Bryan. He's done so much for us."

Birdie grunted in agreement, not looking up from her book.

"Mordechai never did have time to take you to a concert. Did he?" Sarah asked.

"No. But Mordechai makes his own music. You know what a beautiful voice he has. Someday, we'll hear Mordechai sing again. You believe that, don't you?"

"Maybe. It should only be!"

The night of the concert, in the resewn dress and with a generous application of lipstick, Birdie, before descending to meet Bryan in the courtyard, said, "I'm going to make a bottle for Zoya, for when she wakes up. What will you be doing while I'm out?"

"Don't worry about us. I'll make the bottle myself, and then I'll pick out a book to read. Maybe Turgenyev. You have a good time." They kissed good-bye, and Birdie scampered down the stairwell.

As always, the Bolshoi Theater was full. The steps were crowded with people. Some were waiting to meet companions. Others were loudly requesting "Any extra tickets?" and a few, equally loudly, were offering, "Extra tickets here!" Bryan took Birdie by the hand, and they squeezed their way through the only one of the heavy wooden doors that was open, allowing ticket holders to enter. They turned right, as their tickets indicated. A marble staircase took them up to the dress circle. A door led to their box, a side balcony with three rows of four wooden chairs in each row. They took their seats in the first row. Birdie leaned on the brass railing. First, she needed to overcome a sudden pang of vertigo. Then, gradually, she felt herself being absorbed by the immense theater. A chandelier in the center of the hall dominated the space, but the heavy fire curtain, closing off the stage, was equally impressive. Its design, not immediately recognizable, was a series of Soviet emblems, hammers and sickles, elaborately stitched into the fabric.

"Oh, Bryan," she gushed, "it's so lovely. I could just look at the people all night. Look, army officers in their silly big caps. And everywhere there are children who look so excited. Look there! The little girls with the huge bows in their hair. And all the couples!"

"Birdie, you have to read more Russian literature. That's what the theater has always been about, 'See and be seen.' That's part of the spectacle."

Unseen, the musicians began tuning their instruments. The lights dimmed. The fire curtain rose. Behind were still more curtains. These opened to the sides, revealing the orchestra. Applause greeted the conductor's arrival on stage. The theater became even darker.

The first piece on the program was the waltz from *Eugene Onegin*, a piece Birdie knew and loved. Birdie's bare arm rested against Bryan's. They maintained the pleasant contact. Soon, Bryan took her hand in his, and a thrill ran through her body. *So totally unexpected.* She squeezed his hand in response, feeling a wave of well-being and of pleasure.

When the concert ended and they found themselves out on the street, Bryan took her arm. Arm in arm, without anything being said, they walked in the direction of Sivtsev Rajack.

Upstairs, sitting on the couch, they sipped wine. Shoes were removed.

"That's a lovely dress you have on, Birdie."

"You've seen it before."

"Never!"

"Yes, you have. When Zoya, my baby, was inside me. Right here she was."

"Show me," said Bryan, putting his ear to her belly. "I don't hear anything. Come out, come out, little one." He began to tickle her. "Where are you, baby?"

"Two can play at that," she said as she tickled Bryan's sock-covered feet.

They wrestled, giggled, and teased until they were sprawled together, entwined on the couch. Birdie thrilled at the rigidity of Bryan's erection, poking her belly. They held each other even more tightly. They kissed. Bryan's hands went beneath her blouse. They lay that way for a long time, neither moving, and then both fell asleep.

When Birdie awoke, the room was sunlit.

"Oh shit! Bryan, I have to go back to my baby. And then to work."

Both were still dressed.

"Thank you for a wonderful evening," he said.

"Maybe I'll try to come by this afternoon," she said, kissed him quickly on the cheek, and rushed into the street.

Sarah met her at the door, still in the clothes she'd had on the previous evening.

"How dare you? What should I think? I see now. You weren't raped. You weren't even murdered. I was wrong to think you were. You're not even hurt. You are a hussy. Your husband is in Siberia. Your sleeping baby isn't six months old yet. And you are not ashamed to be out all night like that cat howling in the courtyard every month!"

"Oh, Sarah, you are wrong about me. It wasn't that way. Nothing bad happened. I haven't got time to stay and convince you. Now that I've seen Zoya asleep, I have to change and go to my job." She brushed past Sarah, changed her clothes, and went out to the toilet. She stood by the closed toilet door, banging on it steadily until the old man relinquished the room to her. Then she left for work without either woman saying another word. Sarah just glared at her, furious. This was their first fight, and Birdie felt terrible, but she didn't know what she could say to make it right. Besides, she felt the justice of Sarah's anger.

She didn't stop by to see Bryan that afternoon. She wanted to, but she knew that mending the rift with Sarah was her immediate task.

When she got home, Sarah was feeding little Zoya who was sitting up, propped in a chair, securely wedged in place by pillows. Sarah said nothing to Birdie. Her cold disapproval hurt much more than angry words. Birdie kissed her daughter, who largely ignored her, concentrating instead on each dollop of food her grandmother was spooning into her mouth. Birdie lit a cigarette and sat on the couch, submissively huddled against the armrest, quietly watching Sarah.

Finally, Birdie sat up straight and broke the silence. "Am I really such a terrible person? I support the three of us. I do everything I can think of to bring Mordechai back. And I try to go on with my life. I don't want you to judge me all the time. It's my life, isn't it?"

Sarah put down the spoon, wiped the baby's face and hands, lifted her out of the chair, and gave her to Birdie.

"This isn't easy for me to accept, Birdie. Yes, it is your life, but it is my son's life, too, you are playing with. I know. I know. He isn't here, and you are. Still, we are a family, and I expect more loyalty."

Instead of answering, Birdie put the baby down and went out to the communal kitchen for a wet rag, with which she wiped Zoya's face and proceeded to clean up from her feeding.

A truce was developing, a cease fire, a resumption of their previous life, but not a reconciliation.

On the third afternoon, Birdie returned to Bryan's apartment.

"I was waiting for you," he said. "I've got the name of a new commission you should write to. Maybe it's just more of the same, but we've got to try everything, don't we?"

"Thank you, Bryan," she said, rising on tiptoes to give him a quick kiss on the cheek. "That's good news. But I'm disappointed. You're so matter of fact. Somehow, I'd expected a warmer welcome."

Responding, he put his arms around her, hugging her tightly.

With her head still buried in his shoulder, Bryan said, "I'm sorry, Birdie. Can you stay the night? Tomorrow, Sam and Belle are coming back from Germany. I'd like you to stay with me on my last night as a householder."

She did stay. She felt guilty, leaving her child without first telling Sarah. But she was sure Zoya's grandmother would take at least as good care of the child as she herself would have done.

They cooked together, ate, and then sat down to compose the new letter, seeking to reopen Mordechai's case. Next, they read and discussed some newly arrived American newspapers. Finally, they undressed and went to bed together. Bryan lovingly massaged Birdie's shoulders and her back. Then he held her tightly and still in an embrace, they drifted off to sleep.

Leaving the apartment the next morning, Birdie wondered, *Is he restraining himself because he is honoring my marriage to Mordechai? Or is it more than that? Something is wrong. He is a strange man. He's loving. He's smart. And he's very nice to me. I'm certainly attracted to him, but I don't understand him and I don't understand what's happening between us.*

Birdie had no intention of spending more nights in the apartment once Sam and Belle were back. But twice she went there for supper, and once, the four of them ate in a restaurant. Bryan often met Birdie after work at the Mosfilm studio. They enjoyed strolling under the trees, watching the yellowing leaves, what the Russians lovingly call "Golden Autumn." Then she would return to Sarah and Zoya.

The emotional "truce" between Birdie and Sarah evolved into something that wasn't war and wasn't love. Birdie wondered, *What was it like with Mordechai's first wife? Even though they were divorced, they continued living together all those years. That must have been terribly hard on Sarah. Or is she just used to misfortune? Maybe she doesn't expect any more out of life?*

Still, they shared in Zoya's care. Birdie was quite willing to defer to Sarah's experience whenever there was any difference in approach to the girl's upbringing. Apparently, Yiddish and Russian were becoming Zoya's languages. Birdie made a few attempts to give her some words of English, but her efforts evoked neither interest nor response.

FIFTEEN

On a January afternoon, leaving work, Birdie found Bryan bundled up and shivering outside of the Mosfilm gates.

"It's always a pleasant surprise to find you here, Bryan."

"Let's walk. I need to discuss something with you... that is, I want to discuss..."

Bryan took Birdie's arm and they set off along the esplanade toward the metro, but clearly, Bryan was having difficulty explaining what it was that he wanted.

A brief silence and then Bryan continued, "Ever since I came here to visit my sister, I've been working for my brother-in-law. I can't complain. His contacts, his jobs. I write the articles, and he signs his name to them. I'm just a 'ghostwriter.' But enough! Now I want to see some more of Europe. I want to go to Switzerland, to Germany, to England, and to France. I'll write about what I see. I'll send my reports to Sam, and he'll get them printed. But mostly it will be a vacation. Do you want to come with me?"

"You mean it, don't you? You mean me and my baby?"

"No. I'm no good with children. And it would limit us in just about every way. Besides, Sarah is practically raising the child now. What difference would it make if you went away for a couple of weeks...or a month?"

"It's a great idea, but what about my job? I'm not going to throw it away. I love it." She thought for a moment and then said, "You know what? You cover for Sam. You write his articles whenever he's away. Do you think Belle would fill in for me – kind of hold down my job while we're away?"

Getting Belle to help out was easy. She welcomed the adventure of it. And arranging things at the studio turned out to be simple too. Telling Sarah was the more daunting part of Bryan's proposal. But that night, when Birdie asked her mother-in-law for permission to go, Sarah unenthusiastically agreed to be the sole care for Zoya while Birdie went abroad.

"It will hardly make any difference," she said sarcastically.

Birdie registered Sarah's stab but was too excited to feel either guilt or shame.

Two weeks later, Sam and Belle accompanied Bryan and Birdie to the Belorussia Railroad Station. Birdie was wearing the same overcoat she had worn to Siberia nearly two years earlier. Sam brought a bouquet of fresh flowers.

"Don't stay away too long, Bryan," he said. "I've come to rely on you here. I'll miss you."

They shared a sleeper compartment all the way to Zurich. There, they found a hotel right by the lake. From their down-stuffed double bed, they could look over the lake and at the snow-covered Alps just beyond.

On that comfortable bed, they tussled and they cuddled, but as before, whenever Birdie offered intercourse, Bryan immediately lost both his playfulness and his erection.

On their second day in Zurich, as they lunched in the hotel restaurant, Birdie was enthralled to see sailboats on the lake.

"It's midwinter, we're surrounded by mountains, and yet there are sailboats out there. Amazing! But, Bryan, what's really amazing is realizing how we've become acclimatized to life in the Soviet Union. Can you believe it? It seemed natural, living that way. We began to think everybody lives that way. We forgot what the rest of the world is like. And now, all of a sudden, everything is so different."

"Go on, Birdie. Tell me more about what you are feeling."

"Well, maybe I'm not feeling so much as forgetting. I am forgetting why the Russians have to live the way they do. Sarah, Zoya, and maybe Mordechai and I, we live in a communal apartment because no speculator is allowed to build housing and get rich. Instead of building apartments, right now, Stalin is industrializing the country. Later, when they catch up with the West, then they'll build more housing." She paused, sighed, and continued, "On the other hand, it feels very good to come here and live the life of a European tourist—eating warm croissants and sipping hot chocolate in our bed every morning!"

Birdie spent most of their Swiss week luxuriating, resting, and recuperating. Gradually, she realized how much pressure she had been under since leaving her parents' home. Not once had she taken time to stop, to unwind, and to reflect. Now she found undreamed-of pleasure in claiming a cushioned deck chair out on the hotel balcony, wrapping herself in wool blankets, and gazing across the lake and at the surrounding Alps for hours.

Here I am, she thought, *a mother, a married woman, sort of, and someone who is helping to build Socialism in Russia. But it all happened so fast. Also I'm Birdie Tillow. I'm enjoying myself, right now, in Switzerland. Soon I'll go back to my Russian family and part from Bryan. Is that OK? Do I like being a mother? Do I miss Mordechai? Am I really feeling anything, or am I just acting out a series of roles, like one of the actresses at Mosfilm? And will I ever see Mordechai again? Will anything come of all the petitions I wrote?*

While Birdie was exploring her mind from the comfort of a deck chair, Bryan was busy searching out subjects to interview. One afternoon, when they met in the hotel bar, Bryan told her, "There's a steady stream of German Jews passing through Zurich now. I've met so many of them. They're all running from Hitler's anti-Semitic regime. But very few of them will stay here. Switzerland won't keep them. So they're all trying to find out what country will accept them."

It wasn't until two in the morning, when he finally felt satisfied with his article on the refugees, that Bryan came to bed. The next morning, he wired the article back to Moscow, to be filed under Sam's byline.

Two days later, after spending the day apart, they met again in the hotel bar. Bryan was even more excited this time. "Birdie, today I ran into a *shaliach* from Palestine. That's Hebrew. It means 'one who is sent.' They sent him here to convince the refugees that they belong in Palestine, the Jewish homeland. We are meeting again tomorrow. I'll write it up, and Sam will be thrilled with it. You know, Sam's much more of a Zionist than he ever was a Communist."

"How can that be?" asked Birdie. "Your sister is one of most doctrinaire Marxists I've met. She wouldn't allow him to be anything else, would she?"

"Well, it isn't such a big conflict really. Barak, the fellow I've been interviewing, is sent here by his kibbutz. Do you know what a kibbutz is?"

"Sure, it's a farming community in Palestine."

"Yes, but from Barak's description, they practice a Communism that's purer than anything Russia has come up with. There doesn't have to be any conflict between Sam's Zionism and his belief in Socialism. It's just that he and Belle put the emphasis in different places."

"You're fooling yourself. Belle's gonna bite your head off."

The next afternoon, as they sat on their accustomed stools at the bar, Birdie was puzzled.

"Bryan, you look strange. You keep twitching your mustache. You look as though you want to tell me something but are afraid to. What is it, *milie moi*?" she asked, using the Russian endearment, meaning "my sweet."

"Thanks for being so observant, Birdie. You're making it easier for me to ask. I know I promised you we would do Europe on this vacation: France, Germany, England...but you know the old story about the rube who went on his first visit to the big metropolis? When he got back, they asked him how he liked the city and he answered, 'I dunno, there was so much going on at the depot, I never did get into the city.' Well, I'm feeling that way about Zurich. It's the most exciting place I've ever been. I'm not ready to drop the contacts I've been making. How about we stay right here for the rest of this vacation? We can go to the other places another time."

Birdie visualized herself spending most of the next two weeks reclining on her deck chair, taking in the scenery, meeting Bryan in the bar every afternoon and dining every evening. "Bryan, I've never been as content in my life as I have been for this week. It's a fine idea."

The next two weeks were much like the first week, and then they took the train back to Moscow.

Sam and Belle met them at the station in a hired car. After hugs and kisses, they settled in the car and Belle told Birdie, "I'm so glad that you're back. I went in for a couple of days to cover for you, but they didn't want to teach me how to do your job. They said, 'Just tell Birdie we are counting the days till she returns.'"

"Well, I'm so grateful to you for trying. And I love hearing that I was missed. Now I really feel that I have come home...to you, to my job, and to my baby. Thank you. Thank you!"

They brought Birdie to her apartment block. She kissed them each, and they left. Birdie carried her cardboard suitcase through the building's tall arch, crossed the courtyard, and climbed the three flights to the apartment. As she climbed, she was struck by the smells and by the dinginess. *Strange,* she thought. *It's become so familiar that I've stopped noticing. Now it's as if I'm seeing it and smelling it for the first time.* She reached the apartment and banged on the door.

It opened. With stubble on his cheeks and his now gray hair in need of cutting, there stood Mordechai himself, returned.

Sixteen

"So. You've come back. We wondered when you would come back."
Birdie stared. She stood still, not knowing what to say or do. *Do I kiss him? Do I kneel and beg forgiveness? Can I express joy at his return, or will he think I am lying?*

The seconds during which she just stood there seemed interminable. Then Mordechai, whose face still expressed no emotion, called into the other room, "Sarah, bring the baby. Tell her her momma is back."

Sarah emerged with the wailing Zoya in her arms. Birdie put down her suitcase and reached out for the child, who squirmed, turned away, put her arms around Sarah's neck, and howled her resistance at going to her mother.

"Let's sit down. We'll talk," said Mordechai.

They all sat, Sarah still holding the child.

"Birdie, I know how hard you worked to reopen my case. It is wonderful what you did. And I am not the only one who is free now because of you. You made them reexamine all of Umrichina's slanders.

"And I know about this fellow, Bryan, who has taken my place and taken my wife from me. It wasn't pleasant to come back and be told about him. I came back and found that I no longer have a wife, but that I have a beautiful daughter whom my marvelous mother has been raising.

"I know, also, that you have been working at Mosfilm, earning money and buying our food, and we thank you for that. What I don't know is what happens next. You tell me, Birdie. Are you ready to go to your Bryan? Are you both going back to America? What do you want? What happens now? Let's reason together."

When Mordechai began to speak, Birdie hardened herself. Anger was her shield, but, listening to him, she felt her anger softening. She felt that there might be room for understanding. *Maybe,* she thought, *there is still some ground on which we can all meet.* She desperately hoped there was. But she still didn't know what to say. Instead of answering his questions, she asked, "Has Zoya been healthy while I was away?"

"Zoya is our treasure. Certainly. She is fine," said Sarah.

"And you, Mordechai, did they take you back at the House of Writers?"

"They took me back. And they gave me Umrichina's job. I'm the head of the Foreign Language Group now."

"All right," she said. "Now it's my turn to talk. Bryan isn't any husband to me. It really isn't like that at all. We work well together, very well. We had a beautiful time in Switzerland. But he isn't my husband and he can't be my husband. And I don't love him. I know I've disappointed you. But...but...Oh, I don't know. Can we still try? What do *you* want? Do you want me to stay? I'll be your wife if you want me to."

It was agreed that they would live together, but trust, let alone love, would take a while to be reestablished. The "truce" which had long been in effect between Sarah and Birdie had now become a three-way affair. They would live together; sleeping together was a different matter.

That evening, Birdie went across the hall to reborrow the cot from Nina Grigoryevna. This time, it was set up in the front room, opposite the couch. Its old spot, in Sarah's room, was occupied by Zoya's new crib.

Spring was soon welcomed back to Moscow.

Zoya was a pudgy toddler. She wasn't speaking yet, but understood everything, either in Yiddish or Russian, but nothing in English.

Birdie saw that Mordechai was comfortable with his new role at the House of Writers. He seemed happier and more self-confident than she'd remembered. He said little about the labor camp or about how it had affected his beliefs. Aside from his hair having turned gray, his health appeared to be excellent.

In the first few weeks after Birdie's return from Switzerland, nobody in the family said very much to anyone. Days, she went to work at Mosfilm, Mordechai went to the House of Writers, and Sarah stayed home with Zoya. Evenings, the three of them sat in the front room and read. Birdie and Mordechai read history, memoirs, and biographies. Sarah preferred the classics. And at least two evenings a week, Mordechai had meetings or party work.

Occasionally, after work, Birdie would be surprised to discover Bryan lurking outside the studio gates. Each time, he walked her to the metro station. Other than those "accidental" meetings, Birdie assumed that Bryan was staying away because had no right to intrude on her company.

During the first of those afternoon strolls, he told her that Belle was pregnant and intended to go back to America close to her delivery date.

"You mean," Birdie reacted, "that for all of her beliefs in Soviet superiority, when it's her own body, only America will do?"

"Don't be so hard on my sister, Birdie. We all want what's best for ourselves, don't we?"

"You may be right. At least she has been good to me. Tell her I wish her all the best."

Months went by without Birdie and Mordechai ever discussing their feelings for each other. There was no intimacy—emotional or physical. Then, what finally reunited them was a coupling, not unlike the first time they had lain together three years earlier.

Late into a sleepless night, Birdie rose from her cot and went out to the communal kitchen, where she smoked a cigarette. Upon returning to the apartment, she found that Mordechai too had left his bed and stood at the window, looking into the unlit courtyard. Standing there, he was blocking her from returning to her cot. Rather than step aside, Mordechai reached out and put his arms around her waist.

"Come, little bird of mine. Enough time is wasted." He pulled her toward the bed. She was surprised but didn't object. Once the surprise was overcome, she welcomed the affection and enjoyed the sex. His time in Siberia had made his body harder. His lovemaking was still abrupt. Clearly, Bryan was a more considerate person. Bryan had much more understanding of what a woman wanted. But Bryan was unable to complete the act, and Birdie was aware of how much she welcomed the feeling of her husband's body inside her own.

Mordechai finished and rolled over, composing himself for sleep. Birdie got up and went back to her cot.

It took another three weeks of increasingly frequent encounters before Birdie once more folded up the canvas cot and took it back across the hall to Nina Grigoryevna. She appreciated Nina's good grace in taking it back without any comment.

Life took on an accustomed regularity.

It had been nearly a year since Mordechai's resurrection and Birdie's return from Switzerland. As she left work in the afternoon, she noted how early Moscow's autumnal sunset now came. *It will be dark, even before I get to the metro station.* Her thoughts were interrupted by the surprising apparition of Bryan waiting for her outside of the ornate iron fence.

"I came to tell you, Birdie, that Belle has come back with her newborn, a boy. That makes him my nephew. They named him Isaac. She says that she wants you to come by and visit her baby."

"Oh! I'd love to come. But what about you, Bryan? It's been so long."

After a moment of hesitation, he answered, "I've been in this country too long, Birdie. I'm going back to the States."

Birdie experienced his pronouncement as a physical blow. She was astonished to realize the strength of that blow, the void that his absence would cause. She realized how different Moscow would feel without the assurance of Bryan being somewhere nearby. She took a moment to overcome the feeling of abandonment and then simply said, "Well, that's a surprise. I'll miss you. What do you intend to do with yourself back in New York?"

"I don't know. Something is sure to come along. But thanks for telling me that you'll miss me. I like that. Birdie, if you can come tomorrow, it will be lovely for the four us to be together one last time."

That night, Birdie told Mordechai, "I won't get home tomorrow till late. The studio is celebrating completion of the film I've been working on." It was the first time, ever, that she had deliberately lied to him, but she had no desire to rupture their fragile reconciliation.

When she got to Sivtsev Rajack, she was warmly greeted. Belle showed her the sleeping child, who was lying in a magnificent perambulator, imported from England. Birdie felt a pang of jealousy. *That is something I never dreamed of having for Zoya. What a comfort it would have been for Sarah! But it's so foreign, unheard of!*

"He's beautiful. So healthy! And he looks just like both of you," Birdie dutifully gushed.

"Now," said Belle, "meet Liza Korson. She is Isaac's nursemaid. As soon as Bryan leaves, she will move in with us full-time. Then we will be able to travel again."

"Pleased to meet you," Birdie said in Russian to the pale woman with stringy hair. "Do you speak English?"

"Little bit," she said, "but they teach me." Liza spoke with the same Ukrainian pronunciation as Michael, Nina Grigoryevna's husband.

"I hope you are hungry, Birdie," said Sam. "We're celebrating Bryan's departure by dining royally at that Georgian restaurant on Tverskaya Street. Oops, not Tverskaya. For hundreds of years, it was Tverskaya. Now they've renamed it Gorky Street. Do you know Gorky?"

"Certainly. We film his stories at Mosfilm, and I've done English subtitles. Still, to tell the truth, I haven't actually read him yet. Mordechai says he is definitely worth reading. Someday, I'll try."

"You two are impossible," Belle snapped. "Sam, you know better than to describe our meal as 'royal'...There's no such thing in this country anymore, thank God. And you, Birdie, don't dismiss our greatest proletarian writer so casually."

At this point, the baby woke up.

"Liza, take the baby," said Belle. "We're going out."

Liza picked him up from the crib, but Birdie took him from her arms and began to rock him, gently and lovingly. "You sweet little thing. Are you going to be friends with my Zoya someday? Will you stay here, or will you go back to America and become a Capitalist?"

Birdie kissed him on the forehead and gave him back to Liza. She hastened to put on her coat and meet up with the other three, who were already out in the hall.

The food was Middle Eastern, spicy, and delicious. The atmosphere was festive, the conversation lively; they talked about political rumors, about New York, and about their children. Belle was full of questions about the doings of the celebrities who appeared at the film studios. Sam lifted his large body from the chair and raised his glass in a toast.

"To my brother-in-law. You'll be missed, Bryan. It's not just that I'm having my right hand cut off. Now I'm going to have to deal with your sister all by myself. Truly, you are a good man, and we all love you."

It was nearly midnight when they accompanied Birdie as far as her apartment block.

"Promise me you'll keep in touch with us," Sam said. "Of course, we won't be able to offer you Bryan anymore, but our house is still your house."

Birdie kissed Sam warmly and turned toward Belle. Instead of accepting the proffered embrace, Belle reached to shake Birdie's hand.

Bryan winked, smirked at his sister's aloofness, and, with just a peck on the cheek, kissed Birdie and abruptly turned aside.

He can hardly wait to leave me, she thought. *Well, life is going to be simpler now.*

SEVENTEEN

On a Saturday morning, Birdie was still in her nightclothes, Mordechai having left the house, and Sarah was in the kitchen, when they heard a pounding on the padded front door. She opened it to find Marianna, now twelve years old, holding an envelope.

"It's from America! I wanted to bring it to you before somebody might take it."

Wordlessly, Birdie took the envelope. She recognized her mother's handwriting, quickly kissed Marianna on the cheek, shut the door, and opened the envelope as she dropped into the upholstered easy chair.

A letter from home was a rare treat. Birdie and her parents were infrequent writers, and every time a letter did arrive, she feared bad news. However, this was all good news. After telling Birdie how much she missed her beloved daughter, Clara wrote:

> Your big sister, Elsa, is finally getting married. She has a wonderful fellow. His name is Louie, just like your father's name! Unlike your father, he is big! He has a trade. He fixes radiators in cars. You'll like him. We do! We pray you will come home and we can all be together again. We so look forward to meeting our granddaughter, Zoya!

Birdie thought of the Brooklyn tenement, of the small bedroom she had always shared with her older sister. *Now, perhaps, she's getting the love and approval I always got. Is it possible she chose a man named Louie to please our father? I know I will see them all someday. I have no idea when or how. But I will.*

It was still autumn when Mordechai announced that Birdie should join him on an outing to a friend's *dacha*, or summer house, "It will be our friends from work. You'll remember most of them. They keep asking me about you. We're going to the dacha of Pitor Alexandrovich. You don't know him. He's new. We'll go by train. Next Sunday. It's about two hours from town. You'll like being with us."

Indeed, Birdie enjoyed the excursion into the country. The train deposited them at a small village of one-story wooden homes. Most had elaborately cut out bric-a-brac and scroll work decorating the windows and the eaves, but nearly all the wood was in need of painting.

Behind each house was an outhouse. Each home had its own vegetable garden and a large pile of recently cut and carefully stacked firewood. Birdie noted with satisfaction the electric wires leading to every home.

In the center of the village, next to the well, stood a life-sized statue of a smiling Joseph Stalin. The dirt road leading from the station was named Karl Marx Street. It wasn't clear that any cars ever passed on the road. Certainly none were to be seen at the moment. She did see one horse-drawn wagon though, and they passed a couple of motorcycles leaning against the village store.

It was a twenty-minute walk beyond the village to reach the dacha. They had to step carefully to avoid mud puddles left from yesterday's showers, downpours which seemed to come almost every afternoon that time of year.

Clearly, Mordechai had been there before. He led Birdie straight to the dacha, which was surrounded by a wooden picket fence. The dacha itself was a one-room wooden cottage, lacking electric service. There was an outhouse and a toolshed. In front of the house, several apple trees were laden with ripe fruit. A large bed of blackberries had been picked clean. Behind the house, most of the property was taken up by the garden. There were rows and rows of potato greenery, the underground crop not yet dug. There were extensive beds of green cabbage heads, which would remain in the field through the fall and winter, to be harvested as needed, and there were cucumber vines from which most of the crop had already been taken.

The party was well underway. Blankets were spread beneath a large apple tree, and most of the guests were busily consuming the feasts they had brought from Moscow.

Mordechai introduced Birdie to the host, Pitor. Immediately, he and Pitor began discussing their work, leaving Birdie to greet her old friends on her own. Birdie's warmest welcome was from Olga, whom she had not seen in over a year.

"Olga, mine," she said. "You are so pretty with your yellow hair up in braids that way! You look wonderful."

She and Olga stayed together, ate together, sampled the picnic treats that others had brought, and then stretched out together in the sun. Meanwhile, Mordechai and Pitor continued to talk, apart from the others.

Olga lifted herself into a sitting position, looked at Birdie for a moment, and then asked, "You were abroad, weren't you? Switzerland, yes? I haven't seen you in all that time. It must have been wonderful. Do they really live that much better than we do?"

"What should I tell you, Olga? Of course the rich live so much better than we do. And, yes, I was living like one of them. And the poor people in Europe live worse than we do. Or maybe they live the way we live now. But in Europe, there are always going to be poor people. And here in the Soviet Union, someday, we'll all live like the rich people. At least that's what we believe, that we should all be equal."

"I know, I know. Like the slogan 'It will be better.' Enough politics. Mordechai has told me about your Bryan. But I'm not sure I want to believe him. You tell me, Birdie. Were you in love? Are you still in love with him?"

"So you know about Bryan! It is much more complicated than that. No. I don't think...well, maybe it is love...but love is such a complicated thing. And anyway, it doesn't matter anymore. Bryan's gone back to America. So what did Mordechai tell you? I'm surprised that he said anything to you—to anyone."

"He didn't say very much. Just that you went to Switzerland and that now you are back."

Birdie was sure that Olga knew more about her life than she was admitting but didn't push any further.

Olga undid the braids that encircled her head, let down her long blond hair, and settled down, flat on her back, with her arm protecting her eyes from the sun. She didn't say anything more for a long time. Then Birdie became aware of her uneasy breathing and stifled crying.

"What is it, Olga? Is something the matter?"

"Birdie, I'm twenty-four years old. It's too late for me. Nobody is ever going to take me to Europe. Nobody is even going to marry me now. I don't know what happened to me, how I became an old woman so quickly."

Birdie raised herself up into a sitting position and took Olga in her arms. Olga continued to cry.

Birdie, still holding Olga in her arms, looked up at the heavy clouds, which had begun to roll in from the west.

Mordechai arrived. Standing above their prone figures, he said, "Come, you two. Time for the party to break up before the rain gets here. Olga, you'll ride with us, won't you?"

The three of them gathered up dishes, folded blankets, and started for the station. They were halfway there when a frighteningly close lightning strike was followed, almost immediately, by a clap of thunder, which shook the ground beneath them. The deluge began. By the time they got onto the Moscow-bound train, their feet were covered in mud and they were wet through to the skin.

After walking through three full carriages, they discovered an empty, backward-facing bench. Shivering from the cold and from the wet, the three of them sat, Mordechai in the middle, with his arms around both women, holding them tight to conserve and to share body heat.

As Birdie looked around her, she realized that most of the returning city dwellers carried large bundles of food, which they either grew themselves or purchased from someone's dacha garden. She understood the privileged place she, Mordechai, Sarah, and Zoya, as well as those at the House of Writers, occupied in the Soviet hierarchy. *True, she thought, the working class is in charge now. Is this a classless society?*

Eighteen

It was late autumn. Darkness came early now. Sarah bundled her granddaughter in leggings, a coat, and scarf. "A little bit of fresh air before bedtime," she said and took the toddler downstairs to the courtyard. Birdie and Mordechai were in the living room, he reading, she, with needle and thread, stitching the hem on one of Zoya's dresses.

"Mordechai, listen to me. Put down your book for a minute and talk to me."

Mordechai put down his book, picked up his pipe, and relit it. He drew on it a few times until the flame caught and he was able to produce a satisfying amount of smoke. "All right, now I am listening. Tell me," he said, "or ask me."

"What I want to tell you is that I am worried about my job. I am worried about more than my job. I am worried about you, about us, about this country, about the whole world."

"So tell me, Birdie. What brings such concern all of a sudden?"

"It's Sasha...Sasha Bernstein. They came today and took him away. He's almost finished shooting his film, Dickens's *A Tale of Two Cities*. It's a wonderful film. Now they say that it's British propaganda and that he is in the pay of the British Secret Service. He's probably going to end up like you. They'll send him to Siberia. Or maybe he will confess to being an enemy, and they'll shoot him."

"Go slower, Birdie. You may be right. But after they sent me to Siberia, they did admit their mistake, didn't they?"

"God, Mordechai, you're such an apologist. All around us, everybody is afraid to say what they are thinking. Stalin's closest associates, the very men who made your revolution, are confessing to unbelievable crimes, and they are being shot as 'enemies of the state.' Aren't you afraid?"

"Yes, Birdie, we are all afraid. But what's happening is complicated. Your Sasha Bernstein is producing *A Tale of Two Cities*. You've read the book, haven't you? Dickens was right when he said, 'It was the best of times; it was the worst of times.' That's what we're going through now: the best of times and the worst of times. Hitler's thugs are beating and killing Jews. He is rearming Germany as fast as he can. The rest of Europe and America are still in an economic mess. Isn't that why you came here in the first place? But look at what we're doing here. Look at how quickly we are taking our place as an advanced country. Look at our industries. Look at our schools. Do you realize that all of our peasants know how to read now? Look at our universities, our scientists, our explorers, our artists."

Clearly into his most patriotic mode, Mordechai, warming to his subject, stood up and gestured with his pipe. "Stalin is leading us toward a Communist society. Just look at our steel mills. We opened a metro right here in Moscow that is better than any other in the world. We taught an illiterate population how to read, and now we have as many people in university as America has. Our villages already have electricity. Agriculture is collectivized. I could go on."

Mordechai returned to his chair, puffed on his pipe, assuring himself that the tobacco was still lit, and then he continued, "Birdie, you can't do all of this at once unless you lead with a strong hand. Of course people have suffered. Maybe innocent people. No. I correct myself, not *maybe*. Innocent people have suffered. But look how far we've come and remember where we are going!"

"Stop lecturing me, Mordechai. I know all that. But meanwhile I'm afraid that Mosfilm is going to fire me. I'm an American, and that means that I might be a spy. They are afraid that someone will accuse them of purposely harboring a spy if they keep me."

It happened just as she predicted. At the end of that week, Birdie was called into her director's office and told that her services were no longer needed by the studios on Lenin Hills.

Birdie was prepared. She knew that English teachers were sought after. She wrote notices of her availability to give private English lessons and glued them up on the poles of street lamps, alongside numerous other such cards put up by people who were offering services, looking for jobs, or hoping to trade apartments.

Soon letters of inquiry began arriving at the apartment. Surprisingly fast, Birdie had all the students she wanted. They were mostly young professionals who hoped that knowledge of English would advance their careers.

She met with them individually, evenings in the neighborhood library.

Life, once again, was assuming a pattern.

"Sarah, now that I am home during the day, you can be free again to go out and do things."

"What kind of things? I'm an old lady, a grandmother. Taking care of Zoya is what I do best."

"You're not an old lady. But if you want to stay at home and read your books, who am I to tell you to do otherwise?"

One day, Sarah announced, "Tomorrow, is Zoya's third birthday. Let's have a celebration."

"Who will come?" Birdie asked.

"Oh, you know, all the children who play with her in the courtyard. Let's have the party right there, in the courtyard."

The party, put off until Sunday, was a success. The spring weather was perfect. Michael Karavan brought his accordion, and his children, now teenagers, led circle dancing and singing games for the toddlers. Mordechai arranged for the man with the ice cream wagon to bring it into the courtyard where *marozhenaya* (ice cream) was freely dispensed. Sarah baked sweet rolls, and several of the fathers brought vodka for the grownups. Zoya thoroughly enjoyed being the center of attention.

Birdie went to bed that night, well contented. But she woke up in the middle of the night with a severe pain in her abdomen. She lay in bed for a while, waiting for it to go away. When it didn't go away, she got up and paced between the kitchen and the outside hall until the pain lessened. Finally, she was able to get back to sleep.

In the morning, Mordechai asked, "What happened last night? Did I hear you moaning, or was it a dream?"

"No dream. You heard me cry out in pain. But it went away and I'm fine now. Maybe it was all that ice cream yesterday."

Birdie felt fine all of the next week. But then, in the middle of giving an English lesson, the pain suddenly returned. It was strong enough for her to be nauseated, to go to the library's toilet and vomit into the sink.

Her student, a young engineer, brought her home, and the following morning, Mordechai went to the pharmacy to get medicine for an upset stomach. Birdie stayed in bed all day.

In the afternoon, Sarah said, "Fagelah, your eyes are looking yellow. I think I should bring you to the *medpunct* and let a doctor look at you."

The doctor examined her, and she said, "It might be hepatitis. You certainly are yellow jaundiced. We need to watch you for a couple of days and see if your coloring returns to normal. Take these pills, morning and night, and come back in three days."

But by the third day, Birdie felt so completely recovered that she didn't bother to go back to the doctor.

Then, six nights later, the pains returned. This time, so sharp that Birdie insisted Mordechai take her to the hospital immediately.

She was admitted to the hospital and put onto a cot in the surgery ward. The doctor who examined her, a middle-aged woman, asked, "How long has this been going on? Have you had weight loss?"

"Yes, there has been weight loss."

"What does your stool look like?"

"I don't know."

"Well, soon we will find out."

The next morning, upon examination, Birdie's stool was found to be nearly chalk-white.

This time, she was examined by two senior doctors, men. They conferred, and one of them told her, "We believe that you may have pancreatic cancer. It is a disease we usually see in older people. But maybe you being an American...Who knows?"

"So what will you do? What is the treatment? Will you have to operate?"

"No. If it really is pancreatic cancer, it is inoperable. We will keep you here in the cancer ward and make you as comfortable as we can, but there is very little we can do for you."

Cancer!

Birdie heard the word and reacted not with thoughts so much as with pure fear, which expressed itself first as a wave of intense cold and then as a stabbing pain in her chest. Taking a breath demanded intense concentration. Then there came barely formulated thoughts. *Am I going to lie here in pain until I waste away and die? Is this why I came to Russia? Momma, Poppa, help me. Sister Elsa. Oh, I need you now. Wait for me. I'm coming home.*

The doctors left her. She wept, and then she slept.

In the morning, the pains were gone. Despite the remonstrations of her doctors, Birdie got out of bed, dressed, and left the hospital.

She went straight to the American embassy where she explained her predicament and requested help in securing passage to America as soon as possible. Only then did she return home.

She said nothing about her diagnosis all evening but sat still, watching Sarah prepare Zoya for bed. Birdie went to the crib and kissed her daughter and then returned to the front room and sat in the center of the couch. "Come," she said. "Sarah, sit here. Hold my hand. Mordechai, you too. Take my other hand. Good. Now I'll tell you. The doctors told me what I have is a death sentence. Cancer. I don't believe them. I'm not ready to die. I want to go home, to my parents. I want the American doctors to cure me. I want my mother to hold my hand while I get better. Then I'll come back to you. Zoya will have a good home with both of you until I get back. And I will come back, I promise."

Neither Mordechai nor his mother protested Birdie's decision, and within the week, she was on the train to Paris and from Paris to Le Havre, where she boarded a ship for New York. From the ship, she sent a telegram to her parents: "Arriving on Normandy. July 20. Maybe very sick. Love you. Fagelah."

She spent most of the ocean crossing on a deck chair, wrapped up in blankets. The pain was with her most of the time, but it was bearable. She was treating herself delicately, like a breakable piece of glass.

Was I already sick, that time in Switzerland? she wondered. *I spent most of my time in a deck chair then, too. But it felt different.*

Birdie was overjoyed to be met by her family at the dock. There was her mother, Clara, and her father, Louie, both looking older than Birdie remembered them. And there was her sister, Elsa, accompanied by a big-chested man who towered over her petite sister. It was her husband, "Big Louie."

Clara said, "Fagelah, you look pretty good to me. You look beautiful. What's wrong?"

"Take me home, Momma. We'll all sit down. I'll drink a glass of tea, and I'll tell you everything."

Big Louie hailed a taxi. They all climbed in, Birdie and her parents in back, Big Louie and Elsa in front with the driver. Their conversation, until then, had been in Yiddish. But now Poppa Louie proudly pronounced, in English, "Birdie, if you want, we speak English now. I was in night school. OK, for an old window washer, huh?"

By the time they reached Birdie's childhood home, her abdominal pains had returned. She grimaced as she climbed out of the taxi. She hesitated, and Big Louie easily picked her up and carried her in his arms to the second-floor apartment.

"You'll have your own bedroom now that Elsa is married."

"Oh, Momma, this will be the first time I've ever had a room to myself in my whole life. Let me lie down now. I'll get into bed, you'll all gather 'round, and I'll tell you the whole story. Don't worry; it doesn't feel so bad now."

Birdie told them of the Russian doctors' diagnosis of pancreatic cancer. "He said that it is very likely a death sentence."

Poppa Louis listened to her story with growing alarm. He stood up, saying, "I have a friend whose brother is a doctor. Enough said. I don't believe you're dying." He went right out in search of his friend, who quickly summoned his brother.

Within an hour, Poppa Louis returned with Dr. Kipnes.

Kipnes listened to Birdie's report of the Russian diagnosis. He examined her, and he said, "They may be right, Birdie. But they may be wrong. I want to put you in the hospital right away for a thorough examination."

"Can't she sleep here tonight?" Clara asked.

"No, I want her in Mount Sinai tonight. I am going to use your telephone right now and have her admitted—"

"But," Louie interrupted, "we can't afford a Fifth Avenue private hospital. Impossible!"

"It will be all right, Louie. Don't worry. Mount Sinai has charity beds as well as private beds. I'll arrange it. I know how to do it. You'll see."

That evening, Birdie was brought to Mount Sinai and assigned a cot in a four-bed surgery room. Her family members were all sent home. Nurses hooked her up to various machines, drew blood, and subjected her to numerous tests, including X-rays. They kept her up well into the night.

Finally, Birdie fell asleep, only to be awakened at seven in the morning for still more tests.

At noon, she was visited by the attending surgeon, accompanied by a smiling Dr. Kipnis.

"Not so bad, Birdie," said the surgeon. "It isn't cancer. You have gallstones. We're going to remove your spleen. But you'll be just fine without the spleen. You still have a long life ahead of you. I've sched-uled you for surgery this afternoon."

"Dr. Kipnis, will you tell my parents, please?"

"Of course I will, and when you come out of the ether, they'll be there to see you."

"Thank you."

The operation went without complications. She woke up in the intensive care unit to see her mother and her father by her bedside. They were only allowed to stay for fifteen minutes. Later, Birdie was wheeled back to the charity ward.

The next morning, seeing the surgeon enter her room, Birdie, despite the pain it caused, scrunched up and greeted him with a smile.

"You are in fine condition, Birdie," he said. "We'll leave this tube in you for three days, to drain the incision. The nurse will help you get out of bed now, and you'll just take a couple of steps. Then, gradually, each day, we'll increase the time that you are out of bed. In ten days or so, you should be able to go home. Do you have any questions for me now?"

"No. No questions. But thank you, Doctor. I am very happy. It's such a gift to have my life returned to me."

NINETEEN

On Birdie's eighth day in the hospital, Bryan appeared. He came into the room hesitantly, as if hiding behind his gift of a chrysanthemum plant, which he held out in front of himself.

"Bryan, what are you doing here? How did you ever find me at Mount Sinai?"

"Simple," he said, "but I almost didn't come. I can't stand hospitals." He said this quietly as he glanced at the other three patients in the ward.

"No. Explain to me. How did you know I was in America?"

"I'll explain," he said before kissing her on the forehead and pulling a chair up to the bedside. "It's like a chain, Birdie, how we're connected. Sam was covering one of those cultural events at the American embassy. Your husband, Mordechai Grossman, was there to greet a writer come from America, one of the writers he translates. Somehow, Sam got into a conversation with Mordechai and figured out who he was. So he asked about you and learned you were probably somewhere in New York in a hospital. Nothing about what was wrong with you. Sam told his wife, and immediately, Belle wrote to me, airmail. I got her letter and made a few phone calls. Presto! Here I am. Are you OK, Birdie? You look good. What did they do to you?"

Birdie told the story of her misdiagnosis and of how scared she had been. "I expect I'll spend a while with my parents, and as soon I feel strong again, I'll go back to Moscow. Now you tell me, Bryan, what have you been doing since you left Moscow?"

"Nothing special. A little bit of this, a little bit of that. Sometimes I help my friend Benny write articles—still ghostwriting. Sometimes I help out my father at the movie theater he manages in the Bronx. Oh, I'm living there, at home with my big brother Lee and my little sister Lilly."

It seemed to Birdie they had hardly begun to talk when Bryan stood up, saying, "I can't stay. Give me your address and phone. You get home, then we'll talk."

Birdie was released from Mount Sinai and spent nearly two months with her parents, each day expecting a call from Bryan, which never came. One afternoon, in early spring, Birdie and her mother sat, looking out the living room windows, staring at a late-season snow flurry. Large, moist flakes rapidly covered branches that had just begun to bud. Even parked cars were soon covered in snow.

"I love the way it looks," Birdie said. "You can imagine it's a blizzard, but you know it will melt and disappear in an hour or so."

After a moment of thought, Birdie added, "You know what? It's time for me to go back to my family. I promised them I'd return healthy, and you've cured me. Now it's time."

"But do you really want to go back, Birdie?" her mother asked.

"Yes. Of course. It's so comfortable here. But..."

Birdie couldn't continue. Her jaws shook and stifled sobs made speech impossible. At last, she said, "You've...you've...made..." She thought of the phrase *You've made your bed. Now you have to lie in it*, but she was unable to voice the words.

The next morning, Bryan finally called.

"Birdie, are you all better? Can I see you?"

"Is it really you, Bryan? No. You can't see me. What makes you think you can drop in and out of my life, like a yo-yo or something?"

"Don't be that way, Birdie. I really do want to see you."

"I'm going back to Russia, Bryan, to my family."

"That's good. It's what you should do. I've been thinking about that. Meet with me. I think I can help you get home."

She agreed, and they met that afternoon at the soda fountain a few doors down from the Tillows' apartment. They sat in a booth in the back of the store and ordered coffee.

"Listen carefully," he began. "I've been thinking about what you should do."

"You can't tell me what I should or should not do!"

"Shush. Listen to me. Even in the short time you've been home, Europe has become much too dangerous for you to go home that way. You don't want to go anywhere near Nazi Germany. The only safe way to get to Russia today is from the east. You have to go to California. Take a boat from there, across the Pacific."

Birdie added a second teaspoon of sugar to her coffee, stirred it, and sipped from her cup, without responding.

"Here's my idea," Bryan continued. "I'll drive you to California. I have some money saved up. We've been to Europe already. It's time that we see America. Why don't you and I take a grand trip across the country? I'll buy a car. We can see everything we've ever wanted to see and then, when we get to California, we'll sell the car. You can go on from there by boat, and I'll take a train back to New York. It's a good idea, isn't it? Let's do it!"

"You don't need to convince me, Bryan. It's a wonderful idea!"

Birdie sent a telegram to Mordechai and Sarah saying, "On way home, cured, healthy. Don't know when arriving but hope find you all well. Love, Birdie."

Bryan bought a four-year-old Plymouth—a gray, four-door vehicle with wide running boards.

The day before they set out on their cross-country journey, Birdie insisted Bryan first come by and meet her parents. After a bit of con-versation, Clara told them, "Well, neither Louie nor I understand how you young people choose to organize your lives, but it is clear, Fagelah, you're doing what you want to do. Again, we won't see you for God knows how long. It's a sorrow. But we wish you happiness. And we await your return; next time, it should be with little Zoya, God willing."

When Bryan came for her the next day, there were embraces and handshakes. Her parents accompanied them downstairs where the Plymouth was parked. More hugs, and they were off.

Bryan loved the physical sensation of driving. Birdie loved to watch the scenery go by. Often, they picnicked by the side of the road. Just as often, they ate in the car, Bryan driving and Birdie feeding him, bite by bite. She chose their snacks carefully because Bryan's nervous stomach was bothering him. Most nights, they stopped in one of the private homes along the highway that advertised "rooms to let." Occasionally, they would come across one of the new "roadside cabins for tourists."

Their "grand tour" of America was a voyage of surprises. Mornings, they would seek out a place that served hot coffee, pour several cups of steaming coffee into their thermos bottle, and take it to the car. Once seated, Birdie would unfold one of the roadmaps they picked from the display racks whenever they filled the car with gas. She would study the map and announce, "This is where we are going today. Stay right on this highway for another thirty miles, then I'll tell you what to do."

They managed to visit most of the tourist attractions along their route, which kept altering according to what the day's map suggested as "must-see" attractions.

Along the way, they talked about whatever came into their minds. They shared all the jokes that they had ever heard and remembered. They smoked incessantly. Birdie got into the habit of lighting a new cigarette for Bryan just as the one in his mouth was ready to be snuffed out. But in the evenings, once they were settled in, Bryan would abandon his cigarettes for the comfort of his pipe.

There were days when they slowly made their way across vast, seemingly empty spaces, the Plymouth pulling them along at a steady forty-five miles an hour. Bryan explained that the car was capable of fifty, but that he was afraid the engine was going to overheat and the radiator water would boil away, leaving them stranded. At these times, Birdie would fix her gaze on distant mountain ranges ahead of her and marvel that after driving for several more hours those mountains appeared not a bit closer.

They were two months on the road before arriving in San Francisco.

They sampled the pleasures of that city, particularly enjoying their wine tastings north of the city.

They drove to the magnificent redwood groves in Marin County where the towering trees evoked Birdie's memories of the unending forests of Siberia. Suddenly, like a weight falling on her, she recalled the horrors of the labor camp where Mordechai was enslaved for a whole year. The cold, the fear, the deprivation, and the degradation all came back to her. She wouldn't express any of this to Bryan. All that she said was, "I don't like it here in the woods. It's scary. Let's leave. Now!"

When Bryan suggested that from there they go down the coast and into Mexico, Birdie demurred. "We've reached the Pacific Ocean, Bryan, and I'm feeling the tug of my family in Moscow. Tomorrow, we'll go into the American Express Travel office. You saw it. It's just down the block from our hotel. We'll ask about boat departures."

There was a steamship departing to Vladivostok, USSR, in a few days, out of San Diego. So Bryan got his wish to drive the coastal highway, south, through Los Angeles and into San Diego.

He drove Birdie right to the pier.

"Will I see you again, Bryan? Will you ever come back to Moscow?"

"Maybe I will. It turns out I'm a pretty good foreign correspondent, and I'm not accomplishing very much here. So, likely, I'll come back, but first, it's my little sister's turn to go there. She's dying to take a turn visiting her big sister Belle in Russia. And my big brother, Lee, is getting married soon. I'm going to be his best man. After that, we'll see."

"Please do. Even when I don't see you, it makes me feel good to know that you are in Moscow."

The springtime crossing of the Pacific was calm and uneventful. Arriving at Vladivostok, Birdie was reminded of how easy life in Russia was becoming for anyone possessing foreign currency. She went directly to the special window marked "Foreigners" and bought a ticket for what would be her third journey across Siberia in only six years.

TWENTY

After noon on the eighth day, she was back in Moscow. A taxi brought her to the apartment block. She entered the courtyard, and with her small suitcase in hand, she climbed the familiar stairs.

At the door, Sarah's greeting kiss was proper but restrained.

"Aha, Fagelah, so you made it. Mordechai is out. He'll be back later. Zoya," she called to the four-year-old, who was on the bedroom floor, drawing with colored pencils.

"Zoya, your mother has come back after...feels like a year. Come and greet her."

Zoya continued coloring her picture.

Birdie knelt down and said in English, "I am happy to be back with you again, darling. Did you miss me?"

"She doesn't remember any English," Sarah said in Russian.

Now Birdie took the child in her arms and kissed her, while muttering endearing words in Yiddish. Zoya twisted, squirmed, and struggled to escape from Birdie's grasp. Through tears, Zoya appealed to her grandmother, "Take me, please, *Bubby!*"

"I surrender," Birdie said. "She needs time to become accustomed to me."

Mordechai got home at eleven thirty. Zoya and Sarah were in bed, in the other room.

There was another difficult reconciliation. First, Mordechai needed to get over his surprise. He sat down, stared at her, and said, "I forgot how pretty you are, Birdie. Well, are we still man and wife? I hope that we are."

That night, Birdie had full and satisfying sex. Birdie was pleased to feel how attentive Mordechai was in his lovemaking. *It was good for me to stay away so long. He's become a different man,* she thought. *Now he knows how much he has missed me!*

Family life gradually reestablished itself. Mordechai's duties as a party member kept him out several evenings a week now. Birdie reassembled her small flock of English students. Sarah actively encouraged Zoya to bond with her mother, feeling quite ready to relinquish some of the responsibility for the child's care. Even though Zoya now attended the *yasli* (kindergarten) for most of the day, caring for a five-year-old remained hard work for a sixty-six-year-old retiree.

Birdie's twenty-eighth birthday came.

Mordechai proudly announced, "We're in luck, my love, I was able to get tickets to the new Eisenstein film, *Alexander Nevsky,* for tonight. I think you'll love it, Birdie. Everyone is talking about how good it is."

"Please. Mordechai, I'm not a child. I know how special it is. Yes, I even know that Prokofiev wrote the musical score."

Then Birdie reconsidered her sudden anger. *Maybe he isn't patronizing me. Maybe that's just the way he is,* she thought.

"But thank you for remembering my birthday. And you're right, I will love it."

In the evening, dressed in their best clothes, they set out for the short walk to the movie theater. They walked in silence for a while. Then Mordechai took her hand.

"I have a confession, Birdie. It was Olga who got the tickets at work. She isn't feeling well and gave them to me. I completely forgot it was your birthday."

"At least you admitted it, Mordechai. Thank you for that. It doesn't really matter. Let's pretend it's my birthday present anyway."

Emerging from the theater into the crisp April air, Mordechai began to summarize his reactions.

"Marvelous!" he said. "It's a work of pure propaganda, you know. Those Teutonic knights attacking us in the thirteenth century were wearing helmets just like the German soldiers wear today. They cross our borders, and our blond Slavonic hero, Alexander Nevsky, destroys them. Ah, and the music! Marvelous!"

"Propaganda?" Birdie asked. "Yes. I guess you are right. Are we really going to have to fight Hitler?"

"Who else is there? Do you think the British care about what he is doing to the Jews? America will do anything to stay out of a war. No, it's just us. And besides, he hates everything that we stand for. He's deathly afraid of Communism. And that's why Stalin made this film, to prepare us. You can see it coming, Birdie. We need to be ready when he attacks us."

A year passed, and on August 23, 1939, meeting in Moscow, Vyacheslav Molotov and Joachim von Ribbentrop signed a treaty of nonaggression between Germany and the Union of Soviet Socialist Republics. Within a few days, on the twenty-eighth, a small notice appeared in *Izvestia*, the official Soviet government newspaper, announcing the treaty. For days, it seemed, this was the only topic of conversation.

At supper, on the twenty-eighth, it was Sarah who opened the conversation. "How could he?" she asked. "He has betrayed everything we believe, everything for which we sacrificed, struggled, and went without, everything we have been building..."

"Stop, Mother. Don't be a crybaby. Stalin knows what he is doing. He is buying us time, time to prepare and to build our army. I promise you, Comrade Stalin is no happier with that man Hitler than you are. So many terrible things have had to be done to get us where we are now. And there will be more. Look at the year I spent as a prisoner of the state. I could be bitter. I'm not. You, Birdie, you understand why the pact was necessary, don't you?"

"I understand less and less every day," she replied. "Once, I thought I knew why I came here. Now I'm not sure of anything. I admire you, Mordechai, for being so positive."

The following night, Mordechai told Birdie that he would be out late "... *explaining the pact to my comrades.*"

Birdie prepared to write to her parents. *This is long overdue,* she thought. *It's months since I've written.*

Searching in the desk for writing paper and not finding a blank sheet, she turned to a pile of papers Mordechai had been working on. *Maybe somewhere among these.* No blank paper. At the bottom of the pile was a sheaf of letters, tied together by string. Birdie still had trouble deciphering Cyrillic script, but the signature on the top letter was clearly "Olga." Next, she observed that all of the letters were written in the same hand. She untied the packet and deciphered terms of endearment with which each of the letters concluded.

"I kiss your sweet lips and await our next meeting. With love," read the first one.

The sly little bitch! My closest friend! thought Birdie. *So that's how Mordechai managed to survive my absence. And it was Olga who taught him all those new tricks!*

Anger was the first emotion. Then, in her gut, there came a sickening and painful churning. The world in which she lived was not the same world she had thought she inhabited. *Everything is changed. But how?* Her reason told her not to feel betrayed, even to be happy for Olga and for Mordechai. *Who am I to complain?* she thought. *Each of us has done what he wanted to do. I guess we're even now.*

Birdie retied the packet of letters and put them back where they had been.

There was nothing that she wanted to say to Mordechai. She knew, with no doubts at all, that the life they were living was not the life she wanted or deserved. *Mordechai is good; he is bright. He can't help being pedantic. That's who he is. But he isn't attentive. He doesn't give me the nourishment that Bryan does...And what about him and Olga? Sure, it hurts. It makes me feel that I am less of a woman. But can I find it in my heart to be angry or blaming? Sure, I can. Yes. I'm angry. Even if I do deserve this. Still I'm angry!*

She let her thoughts circle around and then return to the same questions. And she made no effort to talk about her feelings, neither with Mordechai, nor with anyone else.

One evening, having completed a tutoring session in the library, she began her leisurely stroll home. Unintentionally, she found herself walking toward the Greens' flat on Sivtsev Razhek. *There it is. I'll go up and find out if, and when, Bryan is coming back.*

Belle opened the door, gave her a look of surprise, and said, "Well, if it isn't the one we were just talking about!" Belle offered her cheek for a kiss and then said, "Bryan came back last Tuesday. Bryan, come in here. Look who's come to see us!" Belle called toward the kitchen. "Come in. Come in."

Even if she had come with the hope of eventually seeing Bryan, his unexpected presence flustered Birdie.

She accepted Sam's hug and his kiss but was unsure how to respond to Bryan. They stood, looking at each other. Bryan was as handsome in life as he had been in her memory. His wave of jet-black hair suggested mystery and excitement, while the dark mustache made him look like the vulnerable youth that he was.

He held out two hands. She took his hands in hers and began to cry.

"Go," said Belle, pushing them both onto the landing. "Both of you, go outside and talk. There is no privacy in this apartment. Go into the street and say what you have to say to each other."

In the street, Bryan said, "Birdie, I'm so happy to see you. I wasn't sure how I could contact you. I wasn't even sure that you wanted to see me again and have your life disrupted any more than it has been."

Birdie clamped her lips tight, forcing herself to stop crying. She looked up at him and said, "Bryan, I want you to marry me. We'll live here, in Moscow, as long as you need to write for the newspapers, and then you'll take us home, me and Zoya, and you'll be a father to my child."

They kept walking, side by side but not touching each other.

Silence. Then Bryan said, unbelievingly, "You really mean it?"

"Yes, I do."

"But can you see me with a child? I'm not a family man, Birdie. It's been wonderful, all of the time that we spent together. But I can't take on a daughter. You know I can't, don't you?"

They walked further in silence.

"Yes, you can, Bryan. I know what you can do and what you can't do. You'll be a good father. Meanwhile, I'll go back to Mordechai. You come and get me when you are ready."

She stopped, reached up to kiss him on the cheek, and said, "I want you to come for me." With that, she turned, left Bryan, and headed home.

A week later, after working with one of her students, Birdie was leaving the library and there was Bryan, standing on the sidewalk.

"What have you come to tell me, Bryan?"

"Do you still want to marry me, Birdie? Do you understand what you are letting yourself in for? I'm a very unhappy man. I'm moody. I have a bad stomach. I can spend hours sitting on the toilet. And I'm no lover at all. Is this the man you want to marry?"

"Are you saying that you have changed your mind? You're willing? That you'll be a father to Zoya?"

"Yes. I'll try, at least. I'll do my best...How will you tell Mordechai? Do you want me there with you?"

"No. I'll tell him myself. Sarah too. Where will we live?"

"You can move in with us, at Sivtsev Rajack, at least until we find a place of our own. When will we do it, Birdie?"

"Tomorrow. I'll tell them this evening. Then tomorrow we'll go to the marriage registration office, and then I'll move in with you. Zoya can stay with her father and grandmother until we find a place of our own."

"I like that. I don't think that Belle and Sam are ready for a second child in the house."

They parted, and Birdie returned to her family, confident that she would be able to face them and to say what she needed to say. Her resolution was stronger than her fears. Climbing the familiar stairs and smelling the familiar smells, she thought, *This has been my life for nearly nine years. Fascinating. Exotic. But it isn't me. Bryan is going to restore me to myself. My life is going to be more than this.*

Confident in her decision, Birdie found the words to tell Mordechai that she was leaving him, moving out immediately. She told Sarah that she and Bryan would have a honeymoon, and that soon thereafter, she was going to claim her daughter, who, in time, would grow to value her American citizenship. She told Zoya that she was going away again but that she would come back soon.

She didn't allow questions. What Birdie presented was a *fait accompli*.

"Now I'm going across the hall. I'll sleep on the cot tonight, but in Nina Grigoryevna's home."

In the morning, after Mordechai had left for work and Zoya went off to nursery school, Birdie crossed to the Grossman apartment.

"Sarah, I feel terrible asking you to do so much for my child."

"She's my only granddaughter too, you know."

"That's right. And you have been like a mother to both of us, and I love you for it. I know I have been a terrible daughter to you, and I haven't been a very good mother to Zoya. Maybe that is why God has put you in the picture, so that Zoya will grow up knowing that she is loved...I don't know. I am leaving Mordechai. He is a good and a wise man. But he isn't the husband that I need. I know about Olga," Birdie said. "We don't have to pretend that we don't know about that. But

Olga isn't why I am leaving. I can't be a tourist for the rest of my life. None of this is real for me, and Bryan can give me my real life back again."

"I hoped it would be different this time…" Sarah said aloud, more to herself than to Birdie, who knew Sarah was referring to Mordechai's earlier failed marriage.

With this, both women cried. Sarah took Birdie in her arms and rocked her like a child. "Go," she said. "Go with your Bryan. Zoya will be happy here until you are ready to take her to America. We will cry to see her go, but it seems to be written that it be this way."

Birdie gathered up her possessions, all of which fit into the same cardboard valise with which she had arrived from America nine years earlier. The ceramic bust of Mayerhoff was carefully wrapped in a sweater and placed in the midst of her clothing. Carrying the winter great coat over her arm, she kissed Sarah once more and departed.

TWENTY-ONE

S am and Belle signed as witnesses to Birdie and Bryan's civil marriage, and the four of them celebrated with dinner at the five-star Metropol Hotel. Liza, their nanny, was to babysit Sam and Belle's son, Isaac, and then spend the night at their apartment.

When they were seated in the restaurant and served wine, Sam raised his glass, saying, "A toast, Birdie, welcome to the family, and we have a kind of wedding gift for for the two of you. It isn't a thing, exactly. Well, in fact, it is. Belle and I have decided that it's time to go home. We are leaving for America at the end of the month. Sivtsev Razhek will be all yours, you and Bryan. *Na Zdarovia!* To your health!"

Then, turning to Bryan, Sam proposed a second toast. "Bryan, this is your bar mitzvah as well as your wedding! You'll be on your own now. No more ghostwriting. I can see it already. All the important news, gathered by you and printed right there on the front pages with your own byline: Mr. Bryan Cantor, staff reporter, Moscow!"

Birdie was thrilled at Sam's announcement that the apartment would soon be hers and Bryan's. *I'm doing the right thing,* she thought. *It's going to work out for the best.* She took her husband's hand firmly in hers.

From the restaurant, they went directly to the apartment, which Birdie now entered as a married woman. Even though the apartment was much larger than the Grossmans' and even though Birdie and Bryan had their own bedroom, it still felt cramped. Baby Isaac's crib was in with his parents. Nurse Liza slept on the living room couch. Nevertheless, Birdie wasn't concerned that her lovemaking with Bryan might be heard by everyone. She was accustomed to life in a communal apartment, and moreover, she doubted Bryan would come up with any riotous consummation of their marriage vows.

Bryan dosed himself with Pepto-Bismol to soothe his nervous stomach. Then, as he was coming to join Birdie in bed, Isaac began to cry. Belle hollered, "Liza, wake up and take the child!" They heard Liza's steps and then heard Belle telling her, "Walk him till he settles down."

Birdie giggled and then pressed her forearm into her face to stifle her laughter. Bryan, too, began to giggle, and soon, they were wrapped in each other's arms, shaking with laughter. The laughter subsided, and they slept.

After breakfast, the two men left for the press center. Liza dressed Isaac and took him out to the park, leaving Birdie with her new sister-in-law.

"You're going to have your hands full, trying to make a man out of my brother," Belle informed her. Birdie had no idea how to answer. Instead, she invented an excuse to leave, telling Belle that she needed to go to the library to prepare for her afternoon student's lesson.

"Be sure you're back here by six," Belle warned. "Liza will want to serve dinner and get home, you know."

Not having any place she needed to be, Birdie wandered the streets of Moscow for several hours. The October weather, as could be expected, was variable. She started walking in warm sun. Soon, the sky became cloudy. The wind rose and brought sharp, chilly rain. Birdie turned toward the library, and by the time she got there, it was snowing.

When she finished with her student and returned home, the sky was clear.

"You're back just in time," said Belle. "Come sit down. The baby is sleeping, and dinner is ready." They all sat, and Bryan proudly announced, "A triumph, Birdie. There's nothing like having connections! Our honeymoon begins this Friday. We are going to Yalta for two weeks!" Birdie looked at him, astonished, as he continued, "We'll be in the Taurica Hotel. It's stupendous...right on the seaside promenade. It used to be one of the Black Sea's most exclusive resorts. It's where the aristocracy went to vacation. Now it's a workers' sanatorium, but they take private guests as well."

"Very good, Bryan," Belle said, "but give Liza a moment to serve us, then we'll talk about it." She picked up the glass bell in front of her and gently rang it. In response, Liza emerged from the kitchen with the first course.

Anxious to tell the whole story but less sure of its reception, Bryan continued, "Yalta is protected from the wind by the Crimean Mountains. They come right down to the town. That's why there are palm trees growing in the parks. I have the brochure here," he said, taking out a printed sheet from his jacket pocket.

"Eat, Bryan. Eat," said Belle. "Then we'll look."

"Workers' sanatorium," said Sam. "We did a story once about the vacation sanatoria run by the trade unions, didn't we?"

"Indeed, we did. And there's more. Just a few years before the revolution, Czar Nicholas built himself a palace there, in Yalta, Livadia."

Birdie allowed herself to make no comment on Bryan's surprise announcement, of which, obviously, he was so very proud.

They finished the meal. Liza cleaned the dishes and went home.

As soon as Bryan and Birdie retired to their bedroom, Birdie turned on him and angrily, but in a controlled voice, said, "Don't you ever do that to me again, Bryan. Yalta sounds fine, but you are never to make a decision for me without my permission. Never!"

The resort turned out to be even nicer than Bryan had described, and despite her objections to Bryan's unilateral decision, Birdie thoroughly enjoyed the two weeks they spent there. They strolled along the embankment and took excursions into the countryside. The sanatorium offered massages, sauna, steam baths, and mineral mud baths. They let the house physicians give them medical evaluations and were happy to be pronounced "fit." Some Russians still swam in the chilly Black Sea, but Birdie and Bryan were content just to take cushions onto the pebbly beach and sunbathe.

They met most of their fellow vacationers, all workers, who had been sent there for a month's recuperative vacation by their trade unions.

Birdie was treated like a celebrity, not because she was American and not as a newlywed, but because she had once worked at Mosfilm and could tell her new friends stories about their favorite movie stars.

When they got back to Moscow, Sam, Belle, and baby Isaac had already departed for America. Bryan and Birdie—Mr. and Mrs. Bryan Cantor—would be the sole occupants of the apartment on Sivtsev Rajack for the next year.

Five days a week, Birdie tutored and coached students in English. She kept the weekends free to spend with her daughter, who was living with the Grossmans until it would be time to go to America.

Once, she and Bryan took Zoya to the zoo. They tried other "family" expeditions as well, but Bryan was slow to develop a relationship with the child, who apparently understood no English. Despite several years in the country, Bryan was not comfortable speaking Russian. He was well aware of the complicated structure of the language and acutely embarrassed by his grammatical mistakes.

Twice, on weekends, they brought Zoya to spend the night with them in Sivtsev Razhek, but each time, it worked out badly. Bryan was upset at the change in routine, Zoya was frightened, and after the second attempt, Birdie never tried again.

Her relationship with Sarah gradually improved. Birdie suspected that Sarah enjoyed being her granddaughter's primary caretaker, treasuring the time she could be with the child and knowing it would soon end. Birdie, on the other hand, was content to see her daughter only on weekends. *I'll have time enough to raise her by myself,* she thought. *Meanwhile, I'm happy, she's happy, and Sarah is happy.*

Even Mordechai, when they were all together in his apartment, seemed to harbor no ill will. Once, when Birdie brought Zoya back to the apartment after a visit to the puppet theater, Olga was there with Mordechai, and the two of them urged her to come with them to a party that evening. "Bring Bryan. We'll have a good time."

Birdie thanked them but declined.

TWENTY-TWO

Birdie entered the tiny lobby at Sivtsev Rajack, gathered the day's mail, and rode the elevator to their second-floor apartment.

"What's this fancy letter, Bryan? It's in French."

The engraved invitation read: "L'Ambassadeur d' Afghanistan, prie Monsieur Bryan Cantor de lui faire l'honneur de venir passer la soiree chez lui le Jeudi 16 Novembre, a 8 heures."

"Can't you dope it out, Birdie? It's just another chance to dress up, to eat good food, and to rub shoulders with important people. One gets used to it after a while."

"Well, la-di-dah," she said. "Aren't you *tres important*," and kissed Bryan on the cheek.

Bryan was introducing Birdie to a world of society, protocol, and power of which, growing up in Brooklyn, she had never dreamed. It didn't take her long to realize that this world was equally new and foreign to her Bronx-raised husband. Every week, there were invitations, such as the special "foreign press" passes to enter Red Square on "the Day of Celebration of the International Holiday of Workers, May 1." There was a constant round of receptions at the American embassy. Tickets were readily available for the Bolshoi Ballet, for concerts and theater.

An invitation went out to the press corps to attend a reception for the famed architect, Boris Titov, to celebrate the opening of his newly built exhibition hall.

It was a ten-minute walk from Sivtsev Razhek to the gleaming land-mark structure. They set out, wrapped in coats, gloves, shawls, and hats with earmuffs tied below the chin—protection against the December cold.

Arriving in front of the white-marble edifice, Bryan remarked, "Well, we've watched it go up for over a year now. Let's se what's inside."

The brightly polished wooden doors brought them downstairs to the well-lit cloakroom. An attendant took their outer clothes, gave Bryan a receipt, and hung their wraps on racks, which stretched the width of the basement. Birdie, seeing the opposite wall was completely mirrored and that the female guests, having taken off their coats, were primping themselves, did likewise. She refreshed her lipstick, straightened her new dress, and with sideways glances, compared her attire and appearance with those of the other women. She was satisfied with the comparison, pleased with how she looked.

They climbed the marble staircase to the main exhibition floor. The space was cavernous and well lit. Attractive draperies obscured the windows. The bare white walls, were still devoid of exhibits; that would come later.

In the middle of the hall were rows of tables laden with food and drink, to which Birdie and Bryan steered directly.

Soon, balancing plates overloaded with hors d'oeuvres and pastries, as well as cutlery and napkins, and each with a wineglass in hand, Bryan and Birdie crossed the room in search of a place to sit.

"Come, Come. Follow me, over there," Bryan said, raising his head and pointing with his chin, indicating vacant tables far in the back.

"No," came a voice in English, calling from the nearest table. "You are Americans, are you not?" asked the scarcely accented voice. "Sit. Join us, please."

It was a large, fleshy, well-dressed fellow, perhaps in his mid-thirties, who stood and welcomed them to his table. He was with a woman, probably his wife, also plump, of a similar age and with shoulder-length hair dyed an unusually bright fuchsia.

"Let's become acquainted. This is my wife, Luba. She teaches mathematics at Moscow State University. My name," he said, "is Igor Svaboda. I too am an architect on the staff of Comrade Titov. I work with him on this edifice. I assist him."

"Then you have reason to celebrate tonight," said Birdie. "We're the Cantors. I'm Birdie. This is my husband, Bryan. You must be very proud, Comrade Svaboda."

"Not Comrade Svaboda. You must call me Igor. Igor and Luba. But do you really like it, our project?" asked Igor.

"Impressive. All that marble," Bryan said.

"You mean you don't really like it. Too much pandering to accepted styles. Well...what is one to do?" Igor shrugged his shoulders and threw his hands widely to the side in a gesture of helplessness. "No," he continued, "You've seen our work. Now tell us about yourselves."

Conversation was easy. They found so many subjects of mutual interest that they were constantly interrupting one another, even finishing each other's sentences.

The only impairment to their conversation was the constant interruption by well-wishers coming up to Svaboda, shaking his hand and telling him what a marvelous structure he and Comrade Titov have produced.

Before they parted, arrangements were made to meet again. Bryan and Birdie were invited to come to dinner at the Svabodas' apartment the following week.

The Svaboda's apartment house was an imposing structure, known to house the elite of Moscow's rulers, as well as a number of its most celebrated intellectuals. An armed doorman stood at the entrance.

"Whom do you wish to see?" he asked. "Papers please."

They were passed through, and on the way up, in the elevator, Bryan said, "At least, this time I'll be prepared for her hair color."

"Hush, Bryan. She's a professor. Mathematics. If she wants to make a statement, that's fine!"

They were greeted with hugs and kisses and escorted into the spacious and tastefully furnished apartment, where Luba introduced them to an older man whose gray beard hung to his chest.

"Bryan, Birdie Cantor, meet my father, Victor Kramer. He lives with us. My father is an artist."

"A famous artist," Igor added. "A superb painter! He is an Honored Artist of the USSR!"

Kramer sat with them at the dinner table, but then retired from the company. The couples again found that their conversation flowed easily and continuously. They shared enthusiasms and were interested in each other.

"Luba is half Jewish," Igor said. "Not me though. My family is German. We've been here ever since Catherine the Great invited us to 'Westernize and civilize' the Russians. We've been trying hard to do that ever since."

"Have you had any luck?" Bryan asked.

"Well, we try," he said, smiling and shrugging his shoulders.

"Too bad our son, Vladimir, isn't home," Luba said. "He's in Leningrad this year, studying at the Academy of Music, he plays the cello. This is him," she said, lifting a framed photograph from atop the upright piano and proudly showing it to Birdie.

As the visit was coming to a close and Igor Svaboda was retrieving his guests' coats, he asked, "By the way, Bryan, do you like to play chess?"

"Do I! All my life I've played. I've been looking for a fellow chess partner. If you're the one, we can be friends for life... Unless, of course, you are far too good for me. I'm a duffer, a pure amateur."

"Not at all. Next time you come over, we'll play a game."

The friendship progressed, and they frequently visited one another. Bryan now had a chess partner he could sometimes beat. This pleased him. He considered himself to be a decent player, but most of the Russians he played with seemed to have a deeper understanding of the game, which completely eluded him. He consoled himself, saying, *They all spend hours and hours memorizing the great games. I'd rather play instinctively and not turn a game into a formula.* Now, at last, he'd found a Russian against whom he felt comfortable playing chess.

A letter came for Bryan from his kid sister, Lilly.

> Dear Bryan (and Birdie too),
>
> First of all, congratulations on your marriage! Since this time around your marriage was hatched in the land of Socialism, I expect that it will be successful, eh, big brother? Anyway, now that I've finished high school and earned a little money, I'm ready to take the big step. Expect me to arrive on your doorstep within the next few weeks. (Maybe even before this letter gets to you?) I sail for France this weekend, and then I'll make my way, by train, to Moscow. (They say Germany is a bitch right now, but I'll just stay on the train and pass right through, I guess) Can't wait to see you and Russia.
>
> Love, Lilly.
> P.S. Family is fine.

Lilly arrived just a week after her letter. Birdie, at first, was struck by how much she resembled her older sister, Belle. However, as Birdie compared them, Lilly's features were softer. Where Belle appeared severe, Lilly seemed childlike and self-effacing. It quickly became clear how different they were in temperament. Birdie found her to be sweet, not a bit aggressive. Birdie decided that she might be described as harmless and a bit vacuous.

Bryan was content to have his sister as a house guest, provided it didn't interfere with his routine and his work, so it became Birdie's task to show Lilly the sights.

After two days of sightseeing, Lilly announced, "I know somebody at Moscow University. A girl who's here, taking a course in Marxism. Tell me how to get there, and I'll look her up tomorrow."

The next day, Lilly set off for the university and didn't return to Sivtsev Razhek until eleven at night, just before the busses stopped running.

"What kept you, little sister?" Bryan asked.

"What an exciting day! I met so many people. My friend Lauren isn't just here to study Marxism. She's part of a whole delegation of kids who are learning to be youth leaders, community organizers. There are twelve of them, like me, all in their early twenties. And some of them are Negroes."

"OK," said Birdie. "Tomorrow, you'll tell us all about it. Now, it's bedtime."

In the morning, Lilly reported, "The nicest part of it is how well they welcomed me. I don't have to attend the classes, but they want me to come and spend the evenings with them."

For the next several evenings, she did just that, coming home just before the buses stopped running for the night. And then, on the night when she didn't return home at all, Birdie and Bryan didn't worry. They assumed, correctly, that she was spending the night in the student dormitory.

For two nights, they heard nothing from her. On the third evening, as they were preparing for bed, a pounding on the door announced her return.

Bryan, in pajamas, opened to Lilly, who stood there holding hands with a light-skinned Negro, who stood about an inch shorter than she.

"Chris, this handsome man is Bryan, my brother. Bryan, meet Christopher Brown. He's from Pittsburgh."

"Come in. Come in," said Bryan.

"Yes, sit. I'll be right out," Birdie called from the bedroom.

Birdie emerged, tightening her bathrobe belt.

"We're always happy to meet fellow Americans here in Moscow," she said. "Tell us all about yourself."

They sat and talked. Christopher, sitting on the couch next to Lilly and holding her hand, seemed relaxed, confident, and well-spoken. He explained he would be returning to America soon. "When I get there, I'll take a job in the steel mills and organize the workers, grow the union—better working conditions, better pay, all of that."

"Tell me, Chris," Birdie asked, "how does it feel, as a Negro, to be here, in a country where Jim Crow is against the law?"

"Strange," he answered. "Maybe they don't have Jim Crow here, but they don't have Negroes either. When I walk out in the street, strangers come up, take my hand, and rub it to see if the color comes off, or they run their fingers through my kinky hair, like it's something they've never seen before."

"That must have been an unexpected blow to you." Birdie said.

"Well, when I walk down the street in Pittsburgh, the people may not like me, but at least they know who I am and what I am. Yeah..." He nodded. "It isn't what I thought I'd see."

Birdie went into the kitchen to make tea for the four of them. Lilly joined her and whispered, "The dormitories are a terrible place—noisy, crowded, and of course the men and the women aren't even in the same building. So, is it all right if Christopher spends the night here with us?"

Birdie had just a moment of conflict, but she overcame it and assented, "Am I supposed to make up a bed for him in the living room, for looks, or is that unnecessary?"

"It's unnecessary."

"Well, Lilly, I'm happy for you, that you found somebody you like."

The next morning, Lilly and Christopher went to the university for the day but returned, together, each of the next three nights. Then Chris, with his delegation, departed for America.

The morning after Chris's departure, Lilly was slow to get out of bed. Birdie, losing patience, finally went to her door and called, "Awake, little one. Time to get up! We've had our breakfast already."

"There's nothing I want to do," came from behind Lilly's door.

"Yes, there is. It's Saturday. Today, you're finally going to meet my daughter. We'll pick up Zoya at her grandmother's, and we'll all go to the Moscow Zoo. It's one of her favorite places."

Lilly found Zoya to be amazingly noncommunicative. She tried, speaking in Yiddish, to introduce herself as Bryan's little sister, but seven-year-old Zoya, at this stage, refused to respond even to Bryan, let alone Bryan's "little sister."

That evening after the excursion, Lilly decided she had seen enough of Russia and was ready to go home.

Two days later, Bryan and Birdie accompanied her to the railroad station, wished her bon voyage, and waved good-bye as the wagon departed. Then they fell into each other's arms in a silent expression of release.

TWENTY-THREE

Nineteen forty was a productive year for Bryan. There was no shortage of material to write about, but always, he needed to walk a narrow line. His articles had to be sensational enough to grab valuable space on the front page of his American newspapers, yet they had to be calm enough to be passed through by the Soviet censors. Bryan received commendations from his New York editors, first for his coverage of the Winter War between Finland and the Soviet Union and then again for his analysis of the incorporation into the USSR of Latvia, Lithuania, and Estonia.

It was April, 1941. They were at home, discussing Bryan's latest article, which reported on the neutrality pact, just concluded, between Japan and the USSR.

"So what do you really think, Bryan? Are we any safer than we were before the pact, or is the war coming here too?"

"I'm not a prophet, Birdie. I'm a reporter. But at least we are witnessing history. It's exciting being in the middle of it," he said. "Sure, I'm scared. But it's fascinating. Don't you want to watch it happening?"

"No, Bryan. I've already witnessed enough history for one lifetime. I've seen the NKVD come and take away my husband. I've traveled into

Siberia. When I got there, I saw men being treated like beasts, and I've seen them survive that treatment, some of them; some didn't survive. Enough already, Bryan. If war finds us here, we're trapped. Life is going to be hard—harder than you can imagine. And if Hitler gets here, God forbid, do you think we will be spared? Let's go home, Bryan. We'll take Zoya, and we'll go home now."

Accustomed to following Birdie's lead, Bryan settled his affairs and concluded his relationships with his various publications. The foreign press office was told that the apartment would be vacated.

Igor Svaboda came to the Sivtzev Rajeck apartment for what had become a weekly chess game: one week there, the following week at Igor's. Birdie opened the door to his knock, kissed him, and said, "It's good you are here. This may be for the last time. Very soon we are returning to America."

"No! ... Well, maybe, for you, it's time."

That evening Luba telephoned, inviting them to come for a for a farewell dinner.

Five of them sat around the Svaboda's oak dining-room table: Birdie and Bryan, Igor and Luba, and Luba's father. The candelabra in the center of the table blazed. They completed their meal. Igor stood up, walked around the table to pour cognac, and said, "Tell them now, Luba."

"We have a parting gift for the two of you," Luba said. "My father, Kramer, "Honored People's Artist," wants to do a charcoal portrait of each of you. Don't worry; all he needs is that you sit for him, half an hour, at most. Then he'll photograph you and finish up from the pictures. He'll have it all done before you leave for America."

"I'm dumbfounded," Birdie said. She turned toward Kramer, who understood no English, threw her arms wide apart, and opened her mouth wide in a gesture of surprise. "That's like visiting the Vatican and taking home a sketch by Michelangelo!" She stood up and kissed Igor, Luba, and then the old man. Luba translated Birdie's remark for her father, who chuckled, shook his head, and put out his palms as if to deny her words.

Birdie went alone to the Grossman apartment to make her pronouncement that it was time to claim nine-year-old Zoya. Climbing the familiar staircase in the Grossmans' flat, she wondered how it would be received. She rehearsed her speech, stopping on each landing to find the most acceptable way to announce that she was taking her daughter to America.

When Mordechai heard that Birdie was taking their daughter away, he responded in character, much as Birdie thought he would. He remained his normal, contemplative, pedantic, and emotionally withdrawn self. "Yes," he said. "We knew this day would come. She is my daughter too, remember. But, yes, there is a better life awaiting her in America. And you are right, Birdie. When the war comes, none of us knows what will happen."

Sarah, on the other hand, was devastated. She cried. She moaned. She took the child on her lap and began to rock her.

Zoya had been following the grownups' conversation passively. She remained quiet until Sarah enfolded her. Then she stroked her grandmother's hair and crooned to her, "Don't cry, Babushka. Don't cry, little Babushka. Everything will be OK. You'll see."

It was settled.

"Next week, at this time, we will be on our way. Bryan and I will pick up Zoya and all her things the night before. She'll sleep at our place, and we'll leave the next morning."

Two steamer trunks containing the accumulated treasures, belonging both to Bryan and Birdie, as well items left behind by Bryan's sister and brother-in-law, were shipped ahead, addressed to Bryan's parents in New York. Among these treasures, carefully swaddled in a hand-embroidered tablecloth, was the ceramic bust of the stage director, Mayerhoff—colorfully exaggerating his Semitic features and his flowing mane of white hair.

A taxi deposited the three of them at the Yaroslavsky station, each carrying just one suitcase. The station, as always, was jammed, but there was no need to stand on line. Through Bryan's diplomatic connections, they had already obtained three reserved seats in the "soft" carriages.

Despite the press of the crowd, pushing them first this way and then that, they held hands tightly and squeezed forward to the large clock in the middle of the concourse. There, as planned, Igor and Luba were waiting: to send them on their way. Luba carried their farewell gift - Kramer's portraits - carefully spindled and packed into a cardboard tube.

"Hello, dear friends," said Igor. "You arrived in plenty of time, I see. Let's find your compartment and deposit your baggage, and then we should have time for a glass of tea before we see you off."

"Yes," added Luba. "Before we wave good-bye and hope that you don't notice the tears in our eyes."

"We'll never get anything to eat in this madhouse," Bryan said.

"Don't you worry," Igor said. "We're what you call 'very important persons.' Aren't we? I'll show you where the canteen just for party members is hidden."

They located their compartment and stowed their luggage.

"Open your presents now," Luba said.

Bryan untied the string securing wrapping paper around the cardboard tube, carefully slid out the two portraits, and began to unroll them.

The first to be unrolled was of Bryan.

"Exquisite," said Birdie. "You look debonair, mysterious, handsome."

The second portrait was unrolled, and Bryan said, "You are so beautiful, Birdie. It's you. Absolutely you. Look, Zoya. Do you like it?"

Zoya didn't react at all until Birdie repeated Bryan's question in Russian. Then she replied, *Krasivie,* declaring the portrait "pretty."

"Now let's go for something to eat, something for the journey," said Igor.

They sat in the private canteen, well insulated from the turbulence outside the door. A dour-faced waitress brought them tea and assorted confections.

"Ach, I wish we could come with you," said Igor.

"Hush!" his wife scolded.

"Really," Igor continued. "Life is going to be much duller in Moscow with the two of you gone and with our avant-garde theater a thing of the past."

"What do you mean?" Bryan asked.

"You haven't heard, have you? Mayerhoff's work has been judged to be 'antiparty.' His crime was an inability to accept Socialist realism. He was declared a secret enemy, and some say he's already been shot."

These words were addressed to Bryan, as Birdie had her back to the conversation and was fussing with Zoya, brushing away the powdered sugar that was accumulating on her daughter's dark-blue pinafore. But Birdie heard every word. Her first reaction, shock, was immediately followed by a tingling and a throbbing, which she felt between her legs as a quick, pleasant recollection passed through her mind, followed by a desire to escape, to run and never come back to this place.

She said nothing but continued to fuss with her daughter.

Forty-five minutes later, Birdie, Bryan, and Zoya were on their way home.

TWENTY-FOUR

It was late April 1941, when the newly constituted family departed Moscow, traveling east, away from the European turmoil. A steamer took them from Vladivostok to Yokohama. From Yokohama, they sailed for San Francisco on an American liner. The passengers were mostly businessmen of many nationalities. The second day at sea, a steward delivered a note to Birdie, inviting her family to dine at the captain's table that night.

As they sat, the captain turned to Bryan and said, "What a lovely family you have. Introduce yourselves, please. Tell us a bit about yourselves."

"Pleased to. Yes, I am Bryan Cantor. I'm a foreign correspondent, or I was one. Now we're returning home after several years in Moscow. This beautiful woman, sitting next to me, is my wife, Birdie. We were actually married in Moscow, which is the reason that our daughter, Joy, speaks no English."

The table guests were left to figure out the logic, if any, of Bryan's statement.

Birdie was flabbergasted at the sudden renaming of her daughter. *From where in the world did he dredge up that American name, Joy? No more Zoya?* But "Joy" she became, and Joy she remained.

From the west side piers in Manhattan, a taxi took them directly to the home of Bryan's youth, to the Cantors' apartment in the Bronx.

Their door, on the ground floor of the brick building, was opened by Bryan's father, a balding man, somewhat shorter than his son. The two embraced and kissed each other. *Russian style,* Birdie thought. *Why not? His parents are immigrants from Russia, just like my parents. I'm glad to see them so close.*

Birdie liked the man right away. She noted his dark suit and neat tie. *This is a man who is warm and accepting,* she thought.

A slender, graying woman stood silently behind the two men.

"Inside everybody. Inside," said Bryan. They all pushed into the narrow hallway where Bryan kissed his mother's cheeks and did the introductions.

"My father, Morris, and my mother, Rose, meet your daughter-in-law, Birdie. You might figure out how she came to be Birdie. She used to be called 'Fagelah.' And this seven-year-old lady is your granddaughter, Joy."

Kisses all around.

"You are even prettier than Lilly described you," said Morris, speaking in unaccented English. "Lilly told us so much about you. She said we would love you immediately. And we do!"

Rose turned to Bryan and asked in Yiddish, "Does she speak our language?"

Birdie answered her in Yiddish, "Of course we can speak Yiddish. Zoya...I mean Joy speaks Yiddish too."

Birdie didn't know what else to say to her mother-in-law. She saw that Rose was a thin, pale woman. She had probably been attractive when she was young but now seemed oppressed by growing older and perhaps, from living in a country she barely understood.

"Where is Lilly?" Bryan asked in English.

"Your little sister is all grown up," answered Morris. "She's gone off to Pittsburgh to be with her union organizer. I expect they'll be getting married just as soon as he gets out of prison."

"Prison?"

"He and his comrades were sent away for five years. 'Criminal syndicalism' was the charge. That means trying to start a revolution."

"That sweet little boy!" Birdie said. "A real revolution?"

"They've raised lots of money for an appeal, and Lilly thinks that he'll get out next year at the latest. Then they plan to get married."

Rose knew barely enough English to follow the conversation. Instead of trying, she disappeared into the kitchen to put some food on the table.

They sat down at the enamel table in the kitchen, where Rose served a luncheon of stewed pears, followed by reheated matzoh-brie.

"Bryan probably warned you, she's not a great cook," Morris said. "But you won't be hungry while you are living with us. Lee and Becky will be here soon; then you will have met our whole family. Too bad our oldest isn't here. Belle's living in Washington. But you already know Belle and Sam, don't you?"

They were drinking tea, Russian fashion, out of glasses. Joy was looking out the window at the newly opened greenery in the park across the street when they heard rhythmic knocking of knuckles against the front door.

"I still know that knock. That's my brother. That's Lee and Becky," Bryan said as he got up to answer.

Still sitting at the table, Birdie got her first look at her brother-in-law Lee. He was the same height as Bryan but heavier, built like the athlete he was. His open and honest face was made more interesting by the flat nose, which had been broken in a boxing match during one of his two terms at City College. The brothers stood in the doorway, face-to-face, looking into each other's eyes. Neither moved. Suddenly, Bryan reached out and gave Lee a resounding slap. His hand came away leaving a red splotch on Lee's cheek. Lee blinked and just as forcefully slapped Bryan. They each delivered a second slap. Then they embraced.

"That's something they like to do in front of strangers," Morris whispered to Birdie.

Joy, frightened at their behavior, ran to her mother and buried her head in Birdie's lap.

From behind, Becky pushed the brothers into the apartment.

Birdie was struck by Becky's twinkling, mischievous eyes. Birdie remembered Bryan telling her that the two of them met while working as lifeguards at one of the city pools. Now Lee sold liquor and Becky was teaching first grade, there in the Bronx. Teacher that she was, Becky went straight to Joy, knelt, stroked Joy's dark hair, and said, "Don't you pay any attention to those grown men still pretending they are little boys."

Whether she understood Becky's words or not, Joy responded with a shy smile.

The next day, they visited Birdie's family in Brooklyn. Bryan drove the three of them in the family car. It was a second homecoming. Everyone was there, waiting for them: Birdie's parents, Clara and Louis; her sister, Elsa; Elsa's husband, Big Louie; and their son, Ernest, who was just one year older than his cousin, Joy.

Clara and Louie remembered Bryan from his brief visit when he picked up their just-recuperated daughter and carried her away, all the way to California. But now he was their son-in-law! More important, here was their granddaughter, Joy!

From Joy's point of view, too, it was a homecoming. Unlike Bryan's mother, who was apologetic and self-effacing, Birdie's mother, Clara, was effusive, warm, and cuddly. She wasn't heavyset and buxom like Grandmother Sarah, back in Moscow, but she spoke in similarly accented Yiddish. She had Sarah's warmth, and Joy bonded with her instantly. Again, Joy felt, she had a caring grandmother.

Late that afternoon, returning to the Cantor home in the Bronx, Birdie said, "Thanks be to God! She was so taken up with Joy, she's finally letting up on me. I love her, but she can be suffocating, you know."

With Lilly gone off to Pittsburgh, there was plenty of room for the family to live comfortably with Bryan's parents.

The first place that Birdie went in search of a job was Macy's, where, twelve years earlier, she had operated the elevators. Now she became a saleslady, in one of the perfume counters located on the ground floor. Bryan accepted his father's offer to help at the photography studio he had recently opened.

Joy was enrolled in the local public school. "Momma," she said in Russian, after her first week in school, "they don't like me. They laugh at the way I try to speak."

"Hush, Zoya. Soon, you'll talk just the way they do. Be patient."

Joy wasn't satisfied with her mother's answer but knew that Birdie considered the matter closed.

TWENTY-FIVE

Becky asked her sister-in-law to talk to a meeting of her teachers' union chapter. "It's just for people in our school, well, in our union. There's another union too. But we're the good guys. We'll want you to tell us about life in Russia. We'll have singing. We'll eat a little bit. You don't have to give a speech. You can just answer questions."

It was a pleasant evening in late May when Birdie accompanied Becky to the fortress-like three- story school where her sister-in-law taught third grade. They climbed one flight, went down a cavernous hallway, and entered the teachers' lounge. There were about twenty-five attendees, all members of the teachers' union. Most were young people, in their twenties and thirties. A few were gray-haired veteran teachers. The women outnumbered the men. Some teachers were seated on stuffed furniture. Others were on wooden folding chairs, facing a large desk, which served as a stage. A woman with long dark hair was sitting atop the desk, her legs dangling, as she strummed her guitar. Birdie recognized the song they were singing, "Hey Dzhankoye." It was a Yiddish song exalting the deeds of Jewish collective farm workers in Biro Bidjan, Stalin's Autonomous Jewish Republic where Mordechai had spent years as a prisoner, harvesting timber. They sang in English:

Aunt Natasha drives the tractor.
   Grandma runs the cream extractor.
   As we work, we all can sing our song.
   Who says that Jews cannot be farmers?
   Spit in their eye, who would so harm us.
   Tell them of Dzhankoye, Dzan!

When the song was over, Becky walked to the desk and announced, "One more song. OK? Then we'll hear from my sister-in-law, Birdie Cantor, who just returned from the Soviet Union."

"Very good," said the woman with the guitar. "Here's a new one. I learned it off of a record by The Almanac Singers. You know, Pete Seeger's group. Here's how the chorus goes..."

Oh, Franklin Roosevelt told the people how he felt.
   We damned near believed what he said.
   He said, "I hate war and so does Eleanor,
   But we won't be safe till everybody's dead.

The audience laughed and cheered. "Now, all of you try the chorus." The teachers quickly picked it up and sang along.

Then Becky came forward and introduced her sister-in-law.

Birdie stood by the side of the desk, the fingers of one hand splayed out and pressed hard into the wooden surface, steadying her and limiting her chances of swooning and dropping to the floor.

"I'm happy to talk to you," she began. "Excuse me if I'm nervous. Very nervous. It's because this is the first time I've ever been asked to speak to a group. A group like this. Any group! But I'll do my best. That's a nice song you just sang. And, yes, we all hope there won't be any more war. Not for America. Not for Russia. But you can't be sure, you know...I don't have a speech for you. I'm told that I can answer questions instead. How about you ask me a bunch of questions, then I'll know what you are interested in?"

Many voices rang out, all at the same time.

"Is it really a worker's paradise? Describe it."

"Tell us about your life there."

"What about the purges? How did they make those people confess to things they couldn't have done?"

"How could Stalin have signed a friendship pact with that monster, Hitler?"

"Whoa, one at a time. OK, thanks. That's enough questions for me to think about. I can tell from your questions that most of you support the Soviet Union but that you've been hearing things that bother you. I'll try my best to tell you what I saw."

Birdie started by describing her daily life in Moscow. She told of her marriage to Mordechai and of Joy's birth. "Later," she said, "the brother of your associate, Becky, he came along and rescued me from what had become a bad relationship. He married me and brought me and my daughter back to America."

At this point, one of the men, a bearded fellow, hunched into one of the overstuffed lounge chairs, interrupted her. "Enough about you. Enough about privileged Americans. Tell us about the Russians."

"Hush!" came a woman's voice. "Let the woman talk already."

"OK," Birdie continued. "I'll tell you about the Russians." She began to describe how it was to live in a communal apartment, sharing a kitchen and bathroom with at least two other families. She described the primitive living conditions she had seen in the countryside.

Another interruption, this time from one of the veteran teachers, a gray-haired lady seated in the front row: "You're telling us how bad it was. Tell us how good it is."

Birdie hesitated for just a moment. "I can do that," she said and began to speak of the country's achievements—electrification, industrialization, and construction, as well as the mass education. She talked about her honeymoon in Yalta, describing the social welfare achievements of free health care, recuperative vacations in sanatoria, and preventive medicine.

Gradually becoming more sure of herself, the ideas came readily, and she was soon speaking with ease and fluency, no longer bracing herself against the desktop.

"One of you asked about the Hitler-Stalin pact," she continued. "I want you to know that it didn't cause controversy only here in New York City. Even in Moscow, everybody has an opinion about it."

As she spoke, Birdie watched herself, as if from afar, and realized that she was censoring her words, talking about all that was good and skipping over everything that troubled her. *This audience is composed of people with unshakable convictions. They don't want to have their beliefs disturbed, and I don't want to be the one to do it.*

That was why she refrained from saying anything about Mordechai's arrest and time in Siberia. *I'm afraid they couldn't deal with it,* she thought. *It won't fit into their neat picture of the way things are.*

In response to the question about the purge trials, she said, "You know, sometimes it's hard to make correct judgments. My brother-in-law, Sam Green, was a correspondent in Moscow. He attended most of the trials, and he came away with the belief that they were fair and open and that the confessions were truthful. His judgment may have been clouded by wishful thinking, but what about the American ambassador, Joseph Davies? He also thought that the trials were genuine. What do I think? I'm not sure. I am sure that there are enemies who want to destroy Socialism. I am sure that those enemies are being supported by the Capitalist countries. And like most of you, I do want to see this experiment succeed."

She concluded, and was gratified by the applause and approving smiles.

Becky embraced her, thanked her, and suggested that she might not want to remain for the boring business meeting to follow.

When Birdie got home, she told Bryan, "That's the last time I'll let anyone trot me out as an expert on Russia. I hate having to tell people what to think."

TWENTY-SIX

"The phone's ringing. Pick it up, Birdie," Bryan called out from the living room where he was immersed in his newspaper. Birdie, who was in the kitchen, helping her mother-in-law prepare supper—actually, watching more than helping—went to the phone.

"It's about time somebody in that home answered the telephone!"

Birdie had no trouble recognizing her sister-in-law Belle's voice.

"How are you, Belle? Yes. I know you still want to know when we're coming down to Washington to see you."

"No, I'm not asking. I'm telling you. You're back in America for a month already. Come this weekend."

"It so happens that I'm going to have the weekend off. Wait just a minute..."

She called into the living room, "It's your sister, Bryan. We can go down to Washington this weekend, can't we?"

"Sure."

"I heard him," Belle said into the phone. "Wonderful. This will be the first time your Zoya meets my Isaac. And they're almost grown up already."

"Joy. That's her name now. No more Zoya. We'll explain it when we see you this weekend."

During the four-hour train ride to Washington, Birdie coached Joy, telling her what to expect. She explained that Sam and Belle settled in Washington to be near Sam's younger brother, Morris. Similarly, Bryan filled in his wife's knowledge. "Morris is the rich brother. Years ago, Sam helped put his brother through school, to study pharmacy. Now, Morris has his own drugstore—a couple of drugstores, in fact. It's become his turn to try and set Sam up in business."

"You mean no more writing for the newspapers?"

"No, Sam is one of those people who thinks he can do anything he sets his mind to," Bryan explained. "Back when he paid for Morris's schooling, he was a Hebrew teacher. His college degree is in social work. He tried that for a while, then newspapers (mostly because he wanted to see Russia), and now he's gone into business."

They arrived at the terminal in Washington. Passing through the rotunda, nine-year-old Joy was entranced by the arched roof soaring overhead. Outside, they found a taxi, which took them to the newly built complex where the Greens lived in a two-bedroom, second-floor apartment.

After greetings and introductions, Belle said, "Isaac, you take Joy into your room. See if she wants to play with your blocks."

As Isaac led his cousin away, Sam asked, "Is she speaking English yet? Will they understand one another?"

"She's been in school for a month already," Bryan answered. "Her English is quite serviceable. Remarkable! But she says that in school she still gets teased for her accent."

The grownups spent the evening catching up and reminiscing.

"How are you finding the business world?" Bryan asked Sam.

"Slow. The Laundromat seemed to be a good investment at the time. But I don't think it's getting me anywhere. Tomorrow, I'm going to take you downtown and show you a store that I'm interested in. It's a grill and a newsstand. It's on a busy corner, just around the block from my brother's store. I'll show it to you, and then we'll do some sightseeing."

In the morning, while Belle prepared breakfast, Sam went downstairs for the Sunday newspaper.

Soon, Birdie heard Sam's heavy steps, clumping up the stairs at a rapid pace. He flung open the door and then slammed it shut behind himself. "What's the matter, Sam? You look terrible."

He didn't say anything but spread the newspaper on the table. The headline read, "German Troops Invade Russia." There were few details, other than the report of a massive crossing of the Russian borders on that morning, June 22, 1941.

Instead of the excursions they had planned, they remained, all day, by the tabletop radio. New bulletins came agonizingly slowly, always describing the progress of the rapidly advancing Nazi army.

Toward evening, Birdie said, "Let me tell you something. A couple of weeks ago, Becky invited me to talk to some of her teachers union comrades, to tell them all about Russia. When I got there, they were singing protest songs against Roosevelt, against our intervening to save Britain. Now they're going to forget they ever sang that song. They'll change their thinking. I can see them, turning around on a dime and clamoring for Roosevelt to get us into the war. I can't stand it! Hypocrites!"

"Oh, Birdie," Belle answered her. "You lived in Russia for ten years, but you never understood what was going on in front of you. It's because you lack a basic knowledge of Marxism. You're limited. You think like a bourgeois reader of the *New York Times*. Becky's fellow teachers will understand exactly what they have to do and why."

"Enough, Belle. Stop it," said Sam. "This has to be a hard day for Birdie. It's a hard day for all of us."

"It's not as hard for those of us who have a scientific understanding of where history is taking us," Belle replied.

Shortly after this exchange, the three Cantors were on the train, traveling back to New York.

Nearly six months passed. Then Japanese bombers all but destroyed the American fleet at Pearl Harbor. Within a day, Congress declared war on both Japan and Germany. Suddenly, America and the Soviet Union were allies.

Bryan was pleased to discover that his ulcers would keep him out of the army.

"I'd make a lousy soldier," he told Birdie. "I'd be worried all the time, and I doubt that I could ever bring myself to shoot anyone. My brother Lee's got a good idea, for him at least. He's joining the merchant marines. He may get torpedoed and drowned, but at least, he won't have to shoot anyone."

Bryan's friend from college days, Bernie Matz, telephoned to say good-bye. "I'm leaving for Washington DC. My part in the war effort is to be a propaganda analyst for the Office of War Information. Pretty good, huh?"

"Pretty good, Bernie. Sharpen your pencils, and write those fascists to hell!"

"Listen, Bryan, why don't you come too? I know that they're hiring—anybody who is still out of uniform and who owns a copy of Strunk's *The Elements of Style*."

Bryan presented the suggestion to Birdie.

"What do you think? And notice, please, I'm asking you first. Before I tell you what I think."

"Are you being sarcastic, Bryan? Are you testing me? If Bernie is right, if they'll give you the job, I say we jump at it. We can't camp out here in your parents' apartment for the rest of our lives, can we? And it will be pleasant to live near Sam and Belle. Joy will have Isaac as a companion, I would hope. Try them. See if the job really is yours for the asking."

It was, and Bryan accepted it.

The family moved into a garden-style apartment complex, much like the one that the Greens had been living in. It was close to the new home into which Sam, Belle, and Isaac Green had just moved. For Birdie, the move to Washington meant that, for the first time, she, her daughter, and her husband would live together in their own apartment. Five days a week, Bryan went to work for the Office of War Information. Joy was enrolled in the public school, and Birdie stayed home and relished the idea of being simply a "housewife."

TWENTY-SEVEN

They frequently visited back and forth with the Greens. One Saturday, they arrived for lunch and found that eight-year-old Isaac had spread most of the family's record collection on the floor in front of the phonograph. The powerful bass voice of Paul Robeson filled the room, singing the popular Soviet anthem "Native Land."

As soon as greetings were exchanged, Belle addressed her son, "Isaac, enough. We have company. Put the records away. Now." He began to reinsert the shiny shellac records into the sleeves of their albums. Joy sat with him on the floor examining a large set of twelve-inch records enclosed in the sleeves of two elaborate red cardboard cases.

"What are these?" she asked. "They have Russian writing on them."

"Those," said Sam, "are something special that we brought back from Moscow. The whole album is one speech by Stalin."

"It was spoken in Red Square, on a May Day," Belle added.

"I remember when you bought those," said Bryan. "Someday, they'll be a collector's item. You'd better treat them carefully. There are sixteen records in that collection, and the first three records are entirely devoted to applause. Isn't that right?"

"Bryan," Belle said, "your sarcasm is wasted on the children."

"Still," he answered, "can you imagine what would have happened to the recording engineer if he had dispensed with all that applause?"

"That's enough, Bryan."

The records were returned to their shelf beneath the phonograph.

Sam indeed had taken out a lease on Henderson's Grill, in downtown Washington. The city was full of wartime workers, and the store was thriving.

Bryan thoroughly enjoyed his job editing "morale-boosting releases" for the Office of War Information.

Birdie often helped Belle at the newly opened Russian War Relief storefront downtown. RWR was a depot for the collection of clothing and foodstuffs that could be bundled up and shipped to needy Russians. Its other function was to make known and to give meaning to the fact that the Soviets were now our allies.

Most afternoons, Birdie would return home in time to greet Joy on her return from school, but occasionally, the eleven-year-old would let herself into the apartment with her own key and await her parents' return.

Once, returning late from a day of preparing RWR bundles, Birdie found Joy and Bryan together, in the kitchen, preparing super.

"This is a rare treat!" she said.

"We got hungry," Bryan said and kissed Birdie on the lips. "How did it go today?"

"Your sister is a something different! What can I say? I love her... maybe, but she isn't very easy to work with. You can be sure of that."

"I know," Bryan said. "She's very short on praise, to say the least. Still, you're doing good work, both of you, and I'm proud of you."

"True. It's good work, but sometimes, I think Belle and I are there for two different reasons."

"What do you mean, Birdie?"

"I mean, Belle is there for a cause, because she's a true believer. She actually thinks she's educating the working class, teaching them about Socialism. And me, I'm there to help my Russian family and friends—Igor and Luba, and the Karavans, who lived across the hall. My God, little Yuri is big enough to be in the army by now. It's terrible, not knowing how anyone is doing." She turned to Joy and said, "Not a word from Granma Sarah. Nothing about Mordechai..."

Joy looked up, but didn't respond to her mother's words. Neither Bryan, nor Joy, knew that Birdie had been writing letters to Sarah weekly, always posting them at the Central Post Office, never sure whether or not they would arrive, and never receiving any reply.

She wrote letters to Sarah and Mordechai in Moscow, posting them at the Central Post Office, always unsure if they would arrive and never receiving an answer. Never sharing this information with Joy, who never asked about her Russian family.

One Friday evening, Birdie hosted a meal for the Greens. It was November, almost a year since America entered the war.

When the Greens arrived, the blackout curtains were tightly drawn. The two families had pooled their remaining ration stamps, and Birdie managed to obtain a not very large pot roast.

"Well," said Sam, as they sat down to supper, "this is a pleasure I won't be repeating for a while."

"What do you mean?" asked Birdie.

"I'm going to be in uniform after all—not an army uniform. I'm joining UNRRA. That stands for United Nations Relief and Rehabilitation Administration. We're going into the newly liberated countries to administer UN relief supplies."

"You mean you're enlisting?" asked Bryan. "Really?"

"Indeed I am! They're going to ship me abroad somewhere. I have no idea where I'll be needed."

"Good for you!" said Birdie. "If that's really what you want to do. But you just started a new business, and you say it's doing well. How can you just up and leave it like that?"

"I was waiting for you to ask, Birdie. That's where you come in. I need you to manage Henderson's Grill while I'm away."

"Me? What do I know about managing a store?"

"Don't pretend you're just a poor housewife," said Sam. "You know as much about running a store as I knew when I started. I'll teach you, in no time, whatever I've learned. The rest, you'll figure it out."

It was agreed. Birdie quickly learned to manage Henderson's Grill, and Sam Green, in uniform, flew to North Africa.

Sam's time with UNRRA was an experience in bureaucracy. His assigned task was to administer relief to newly liberated Yugoslavia, but Tito, so far, wasn't allowing Westerners into his country. Therefore, Sam was sent to Cairo, Egypt. He was given a desk and papers to study and told to wait until they could send him on.

It was Birdie's third week at Henderson's Grill when Belle dropped in one morning. They sat at a booth and drank coffee.

"It's been a while, Belle. Now you can report to Sam. Look! It's still here. Just the way he left it."

"No, Birdie. He isn't worried about you and the store. Neither am I. But I want you to know, we do miss you at Russian War Relief. Oh, and I thought you'd enjoy this letter that Isaac got from his father."

"Will Isaac mind my reading his private letter?"

"Don't be foolish. Read." Belle handed over the folded sheet.

Dear Isaac,

I love you and miss you very much, but I'm sure that you know why I have to be here. The Germans are killing our people, the Jews, and we are now killing the Germans. The war has to be won, and I believe we are winning it! It seems that my part in the operation is insignificant, so far, but I'm happy to be doing whatever is asked.

Here I am in Cairo, where the streets are full of camels and Jeeps. Before I tell you my adventures, I need to take you back in history.

I don't know how much you know about the previous war, "World War I." It was thirty years ago. Even before I met your mother, that was the first time that the world had to fight Germany. I did my part by joining the Jewish Legion. It was a part of the British army. I was a recruiter. We got Jewish youth to join the British army to help liberate Palestine from the Turks (who were aligned with the Germans). Anyway, in case you don't remember my stories, I finally shipped out to go and fight. But the end of the war came while I was still on the ocean. So when I got to Palestine, instead of fighting, they had me guarding Turkish prisoners of war.

Finally, I was demobilized and I chose to stay in Palestine for a year. Well, here's the exciting part. Last week, on leave, I took a train to Tel Aviv, the all-Jewish city in Palestine, and I visited with some of my old comrades from the Jewish battalion who have settled nearby. My old buddies are farmers now, and they are extremely proud of their Jewish community.

I hope that someday I can take you and your mother to visit the Jewish land of Israel.

I kiss you lovingly. Your father, Sam

P.S. Hug your mother for me, also hugs for Birdie and Bryan.

"Nice," Birdie said, folding the letter and returning it to Belle. "Sounds like he's having a good time over there. – Well, I'm glad we had some time together, but I've got to get back to the cash register and let poor Mr. Rubin go home to his family already."

TWENTY-EIGHT

After a month of managing Henderson's Grill, Birdie was confident in the job. She enjoyed the responsibility. Whatever self-doubts she'd once had were gone.

From behind the cash register, right by the door, she could observe customers at the soda fountain, perched on circular revolving stools. Other customers sat in the row of booths along the opposite wall or at the wooden tables in the middle of the room. The girl she had recently hired, right out of high school, stood just outside the door watching the racks of magazines and newspapers and collecting money.

Two men entered and asked Birdie if they might speak with the manager. They were neatly dressed, each wearing a sports jackets and a fedora. Both were young. One of them was considerably taller than the other. Birdie sensed something out of the ordinary. *They aren't dressed like government workers, and aside from government workers, almost all the other men are in uniform these days. The taller one has curly hair. Jewish? Clearly not intellectuals.*

"I'm the manager," Birdie answered.

"Glad to meet you. What's your name, Miss Manager?"

"Mrs. Birdie Cantor."

"Miss Birdie, as I look around, I see you have a good business here. Very good. And we think we can help you make it better." This was said by the taller of the two.

"Tell me how," said Birdie.

"Pinball machines," he said. "There's lots of money in pinball machines. We'll install them. We'll maintain them. And it's a simple deal. We split the take."

Birdie pointed to the row of booths and to the three round tables in the middle of the store. "I don't think we have any more room. Look for yourselves. Most of the tables are already filled, and it's only eleven o'clock."

"No problem about space," said the other man. "We take out all them booths along the wall there. You'll see. It will work out fine for all of us."

"I don't think so," said Birdie, "but let me think about it."

"But we are here for your sake too," said the taller one. "Remember, it's a *mitzvah*, a good deed, to help out a fellow Jew."

"OK," said the shorter, younger man. "You think about it tonight. Tomorrow, we'll come back for your answer."

Birdie didn't think enough of the offer to bother mentioning it to Bryan.

At midnight, the store had already been closed for two hours and Birdie was asleep. Bryan was in the living room, reading, when the telephone rang. "This is the Fifth Precinct calling. There's been vandalism at your store. Somebody poured paint all over your news racks, and they threw a brick through your plate-glass window."

"Wait," said Bryan. "You need to tell that to my wife."

Birdie, by then wide awake and alarmed, snatched the telephone from Bryan, listened to the officer repeat his report, and then said, "I'll come right now. Will you still be there?"

"I'm coming with you," said Bryan.

"No, sweetheart, you stay here with Joy. There is nothing for you to do there, and tomorrow, you have your own work. I'll take care of it.

It's probably nothing more than a couple of drunks on their way home from bar closing."

Two police officers were waiting for her on the sidewalk outside the store. They never went inside. All they wanted was confirmation of the particulars regarding ownership of the property so they could fill out their report. They never asked Birdie whom she thought might have done it. She was astounded at how abruptly they left her alone.

Birdie examined the damage—a broken plate-glass window and shards of glass all over the floor and on some of the tables—then she sat at one of the counters. She was angry, but when she thought about what she was feeling, she realized that she was not at all afraid. *I've gotten through worse than this.* She telephoned Igor, the Russian émigré who did her maintenance. The act of speaking in Russian again somehow calmed her, allowing her to look around as if from outside herself. Igor promised to come first thing in the morning to paint over the vandalized racks and to replace the window. Birdie swept up the broken glass. She opened a large carton of paper napkins, put the napkins on a shelf, and flattened the cardboard, which she taped over the broken window. Then she went home to sleep for a couple of hours.

At nine in the morning, Birdie was back at the cash register when the same two men appeared, smiling politely.

"Hello, Birdie, I guess you thought over our proposition, huh?"

"How much choice do I have?" Birdie asked.

"Well, from what we see, with that guy out front repairing your window, I'll bet your sleep got interrupted last night, and the last thing we want is that you should sleep badly."

"Then I guess we have to be partners. Are we going to sign papers or anything?"

"No. No papers are necessary. Our engineers will remove the booths sometime next week. Then they'll install the pinball machines. Maybe eight or nine of them. You'll see. We'll both make money on this. You'll be very happy."

They left, and Birdie considered.

I suppose I've done the only thing I could have done. Now what? Do I tell Bryan? No. He'd only be upset. Do I tell Belle? No. Sam left me in charge, and he never asked me to involve his wife in running the store. The police? They scare me; they seemed so uninterested in the whole thing. So where does that leave me? I don't think I'm guilty of any crime. All I can do is cooperate with them and see what happens.

Monday, a crew of three men arrived. The outdoor news racks remained open all day, but the grill was closed, and by the end of that day, a row of nine electrical pinball machines stood along the wall where five booths had been. Three round dining tables remained in the middle of the room, and the soda fountain still ran the length of the opposite wall.

Birdie wasn't sure what to expect, but she clearly saw that there were a multitude of wartime Washingtonians who had plenty of change in their pockets and who were eager to play the pinball machines for five cents a game.

To Birdie's satisfaction, the owners of the machines did show up regularly at the end of each week. They opened the machines and scooped the nickels into a cloth sack. Then, in cash, they gave her the store's half of the previous week's take. It averaged around two hundred and fifty dollars a week.

The new machines were a particular pleasure for Joy and Isaac. Whenever either came to the store, as long as their money lasted, they were allowed to play to their hearts' content for two and a half cents per game. They were thrilled by the bright lights and by the bells ringing as the balls ricocheted off of the bumpers. They were especially pleased at knowing they were playing for half price!

Then, a couple of months after installing the machines, Birdie's two "associates" came back one afternoon and said, "You know we've been watching your store, and the machines are doing fine, but we think you can do even better."

"What do you mean?"

"We've been watching what's going on, and we see how this city is buzzing. Washington's become a twenty-four-hour-a-day operation.

There are people on the streets all night. And we think you should stay open around the clock. We're sure that the pinball machines will keep ringing for most of the night."

"I've thought of that too," said Birdie. "But I'd be nervous. It's a different neighborhood after midnight. I'd be afraid to be out on the streets at those hours."

The two men looked at each other and laughed.

"Oh, you've got nothing to be afraid of. Security is our specialty. That's one thing we can promise you. We take care of it. You'll have nothing to worry about, ever."

"I'm not sure," Birdie said.

"Yes, you are," said the taller of the two. "Certainly, Mrs. Cantor, you don't doubt the word of a couple of fellow Jews, do you? We think that you should do it, for your own good. Here's the offer, Miss Birdie. You keep the store running all night. You'll make lots more money. We'll protect you and the store, and all we want for our services is three hundred dollars a week. We'll both do well. You'll see."

Again, Birdie refrained from telling Bryan why she was instituting new hours. *He is so pessimistic and nervous already. If I tell him about the associates, he'll just fall apart,* she thought.

Having the grill open twenty-four hours a day required Birdie to hire a third shift, a cashier, a short-order cook, a waitress, and a dishwasher. The newsstand remained closed on the late shift. She found the additional staff, but every so often, one of them—and most often, it was the nighttime dishwasher—would fail to show up. Whenever one of the crew failed to show, Birdie had to fill in.

Wartime Washington, indeed, was busy. Despite her weekly payments to the "associates," the store was making more money than ever, and Birdie was delighted to think of herself as a successful businesswoman.

The war news, which Bryan and Birdie followed closely, was going from disastrous to hopeful. Finally, a letter arrived from Sarah, from Moscow. She sent hugs and kisses to her granddaughter, Zoya. She said that Mordechai was somewhere at the front, but she had heard nothing from him for several months. She spoke of the difficulty of obtaining food but expressed optimism that things were finally going well.

It was the last letter that Birdie was to receive from Sarah.

Igor and Luba Svaboda wrote twice during the war. They wrote of the utter destruction in Nazi-occupied territory, and they wrote that Igor, instead of fighting in the war, was already at work drawing up plans for postwar reconstruction. "Everything has to be rebuilt," Luba wrote. "Housing, factories, bridges. Right now, everything goes to the war effort, but we are confident of victory and busy planning for that day."

Furthermore, she wrote, "Our Volodya is fortunate. He is a member of the Red Army Band and spends his time entertaining our warriors. He is near the front, but neither shooting anyone, nor being shot at."

It was during these war years that Bryan's father, Morris, suffered a stroke. His recovery left him unable to operate his photography shop.

Rather than sit home with nothing to do, he found a job assembling cardboard boxes for a jeweler friend. He worked at home, assembling the boxes slowly and carefully, despite the pain in his arthritic hands. A year later, he died in his sleep. Rose, unwilling or unable to live alone, was placed in a Jewish old age home, where she lived until her death two years later.

With the Soviet offensive at Stalingrad, the war's momentum had clearly shifted, but it took another two years for the Allies to achieve victory. Once Yugoslavia was liberated and Tito assumed control of the government, it became doubtful that he would ever allow United Nations personnel into his country. So Sam's waiting was over. He came home, bearing a large assortment of gifts, including Egyptian scarabs and wall hangings.

Sam was pleased to see Henderson's Grill doing so well. Then Birdie told him the whole story of her "associates."

"That scares me, Birdie. Somehow, we need to end this 'association.'"

For a month after Sam returned, he and Birdie worked together, running the store. At the same time, Sam investigated partnering with some of his old friends who were starting a new venture, prefabricated aluminum housing for the returning veterans.

They found a war plant in Ohio that could be converted. "I want to sell my lease," Sam told Birdie. "There's money to be made out there. Excitement too!"

The next time the two "associates" arrived to take their bag of nickels, Sam told them that he intended to end their arrangement.

"You can't do that," they said.

"Yes, I can."

They turned and left the premises.

That night, Sam left work as the midnight-to-eight shift arrived. He crossed the street and walked toward the parking garage where he kept his car. Crossing the street, he saw a black sedan materialize, as if from nowhere, and come straight upon him. It knocked him to the ground, and his leg got caught by the rear bumper. He was dragged the length of the block.

Belle got a telephone call that he was in the hospital. He was there for two weeks, while Birdie ran the store. When he got out of the hospital, he told Birdie, "That's it. The war is over. Eisenhower's won, Stalin's won, and our war with those criminals is about to be over. We'll lock the door, and Henderson's Grill goes back to the landlord. End of story."

TWENTY-NINE

The war over, Bryan's job with the Office of War Information was terminated and the family returned to New York, to the Bronx, where they found a rental apartment in one of the new city projects.

Birdie returned to Macy's. Her old manager was gone, but her excellent work history with the store was enough to secure a job, despite the competitive, postwar job market. Now she was stationed on the ground floor, at a kiosk in the middle of a main aisle. There, her task was to demonstrate clever ways of folding and wearing an assortment of colorful scarves. Birdie was a good entertainer, a crowd pleaser, and her station was usually surrounded by shoppers.

It was a tiring routine, even for the energetic thirty-five-year-old, but necessary, as she was now supporting her family.

Bryan was unable to find a full-time job, but occasionally, friends did come to him with editing work.

Twelve-year-old Joy, enrolled in the public schools. Having shed her Russian accent, she felt herself to be less of an outsider.

They had been settled for a month when Birdie's father, Louie, had a heart attack and died within a few hours. It was Birdie who made the funeral arrangements. When they returned from the cemetery to the

Brooklyn apartment of Birdie's childhood, her sister, Elsa, took her by the hand and said, "Momma will come live with us, with Big Louie, Ernest, and me. I'll stay here tonight, and tomorrow, she'll come to us."

"But you don't have room for her, do you?" Birdie asked. "Ernest is already a big boy. He's fourteen, and he needs a room of his own."

"He'll do fine on the couch. You'll see."

Birdie embraced her sister and through tears, squeezed out, "I love you, Elsa...You're such a good person."

The autumn weather turned cold. It was after six in the evening when Birdie got home from Macy's and took the elevator to her sixth-floor apartment. Joy, having fixed her own supper, was downstairs visiting her friend Doris. Bryan, as expected, was waiting for Birdie to feed him.

"Birdie, you won't believe it," Bryan said.

"Shall I sit down?"

"No. I'll tell you right here. The phone rang, just an hour ago. It was Igor Svaboda! They're here, in America, in New York. Luba and Igor!"

Birdie sat down anyway and peered up at Bryan.

"Explain, Bryan. How could that be?"

"He didn't tell me. Tomorrow. We'll find out everything. We're meeting them tomorrow evening."

The two couples met in a Manhattan restaurant. There were Luba and Igor, looking just as they had looked five years earlier, before the war, except that Luba's shoulder length hair was no longer that eye-stopping shade of fuschia. Now she appeared as an attractively plump brunette.

They embraced warmly and sat down. Bryan reached across the table to take Igor's hand. In his other hand, he held Birdie's. She, in turn, reached for Luba's, and the four of them, holding hands in a circle, joyfully beamed at one another.

Birdie broke the spell. "Nu? So tell us how this comes to be?"

Igor answered, "Once Germany was divided into zones of occupation, I was sent to Berlin to begin rebuilding. A month later, Luba came to visit. They wouldn't let our son come along, but Luba came."

"And your father?"

"No, Kramer stayed behind, in Moscow. Well, anyway, once Luba got to Berlin and looked around a bit, we simply crossed over into the American sector, and here, we are. HIAS, the Hebrew Immigrant Aid Society, is helping us and soon—"

"Tell them the truth," Luba interrupted. "It wasn't that simple," she continued. "Igor's projects have always been in the capital. When they sent him to Berlin, it wasn't as 'chief architect.' He was assistant to an old rival—a competitor."

"Now you're giving the story a plot," Igor said, flushing and looking angrily at his wife. "That was part of it, maybe, but a small part."

"But why?" Birdie voiced her puzzlement. "Whatever disappointment you may have had, you both had such good lives in Russia. You are respected and successful. You live comfortably. Your son is at the beginning of an exciting career. You have important work to do. I never heard you express a single word against your homeland. Why did you do it?"

"Let me answer," Luba said. "We did live well, particularly because of my father's status. He's an 'Honored People's Artist.' And, of course, they liked our work, I'll admit. But it won't last, Birdie. It's dying. They had a marvelous dream but not anymore. Today, nothing but fear. Everybody looks out for himself. Now that we don't have the Germans to fight against, it's going to fall apart. You Americans don't see it yet, but I speak the truth—"

Igor, again, interrupted his wife. "So we came here, to make buildings and to teach mathematics and live by reason."

The friendship was resumed. Bryan once again had a frequent chess partner. Birdie and Luba went to concerts together. Luba took it upon herself to educate Birdie's ear and to teach her to appreciate string music.

"After all," she said, "our son Volodya already has a position with one of Leningrad's finest and best-known quartets. Someday, God willing, you'll hear him, and I want that you should understand what you're listening to."

THIRTY

Apart from her job at Macy's, Birdie's time was taken up by a full social life: exploring Manhattan with Luba and Igor Svaboda; becoming close with their downstairs neighbors, whose daughter was now Joy's best friend; and finding her life particularly entwined with Bryan's three siblings'.

Bryan's big sister, Belle, with Sam and Isaac, was four hours away, in Washington DC. They remained in close contact. Birdie and Bryan followed the trajectory of Sam's new and prospering career in real estate development.

Bryan's kid-sister, Lilly, with her husband, Christopher, and two small daughters, had left Pittsburgh and settled in Harlem, where Christopher was writing a novel based on his eighteen months in prison, charged with "political syndicalism."

Brother Lee and his wife, Becky, who lived in Manhattan, were less frequent visitors.

Birdie and Bryan were dining with the Svabodas in a Chinese restaurant they often visited.

Examining the menu, Igor said, "I can't get over it. This is a plea-sure we never had in Moscow! You know what? Tonight, I'm feeling good. Let me order, and tonight's meal is my treat."

Igor tried to order, but the waiter had to caution him that he was requesting much more than four people could possibly eat.

"You must have good news to tell us," Birdie said. "You are so full of yourself tonight."

"Indeed," Luba said. "Igor has a job, with a big-shot developer. He's an architect again!"

"Wonderful," Bryan said. "So America is the land of opportunity after all."

It was spring of 1949. Becky telephoned her sister-in-law Birdie invit-ing herself and Lee to dinner. "I need to talk with you," she said.

When they arrived at the Bronx apartment, sixteen-year-old Joy opened the door. Her uncle Lee took her in his arms and kissed her, sticking his tongue into her mouth.

Joy was upset but said nothing.

Becky glared at her husband, and then she turned her dazzling smile on Joy and said, "Here's what we brought for you. Chocolate-chip cookies, fresh out of my own kitchen."

Birdie came to the door just in time to pull the box of cookies from Joy's hand. "Becky," she exploded, "you don't give cookies to a teenage girl who is trying to watch her weight!"

"Mother, for God's sake, can't you be nice? And it's my business what I eat!"

"Enough!" said Birdie. "Come inside. Seems we haven't seen you in months. Tell us how you've been."

At the supper table, Birdie asked her sister-in-law, "So tell us the news you're withholding."

"No," said Becky. "First, we'll finish this wonderful meal. I don't want anything to interfere with your pot roast."

When the adults moved to the living room where Birdie served coffee, Joy announced, "I'm going downstairs to Doris's." She kissed

Becky and thanked her for the cookies. She ignored her uncle and left.

Downstairs, Joy was surprised to realize that she was unable to tell Doris about Lee's deep kiss. Normally, the two girls shared everything, but Joy was upset, confused, and said nothing about it.

Settled on the couch, holding her coffee cup, Becky spoke. "OK, here's what I came to tell you. I lost my job. They took it away from me! I saw it coming long ago. We all had to sign loyalty oaths. They wanted us to swear we'd never belonged to any subversive organizations. Even if I hadn't been part of the teachers union, I couldn't sign the damn thing, because next they'd be asking me, 'Do you know anyone who has been a member?'"

"Becky, that's terrible," said Bryan. "When did this happen?"

"Yesterday. At the end of the day. He told me to clean out my desk and not to come back...My principal, for Christ sake. I groomed him to take the damned principal's exam!"

Birdie left her chair and went to the couch, where she squeezed herself between Becky and Lee, put her arms around her sister-in-law, and held her tightly. "You must feel terrible!" she said, rocking her.

"I do. It is. I..." Becky sniffled and then allowed herself to cry.

"Horrible! What about your job, Lee?" Bryan asked. "Will you be all right?"

"I'll be all right," he said. "They like me at work, and as long as I don't sell whisky to minors, I guess I'm nobody's security risk. We'll be OK, but it's Becky's life – teaching. She's great at it, and she loves it. Such a waste."

"The bastards!" said Bryan. "But remember," he added, "at least, we love you both."

"Thanks. Screw them," said Lee. "In fact, we're still going ahead with our plans to buy a summer cottage up in Croton."

"Good for you," said Bryan.

Becky detached herself from Birdie's embrace, shook herself, took a deep breath, and then joined the conversation. "It's more of a shack than a cottage. But it will be our little baby. We'll love it, and we'll grow it. It's only forty-five minutes from our apartment, door to door. And it's cheap enough so even without my salary, we can do it."

That summer, Birdie's whole family found their way to the northern suburbs of New York, close to Lee and Becky's cottage in Croton. They rented the big house in a modest bungalow colony that had a small pond, well stocked with sunfish.

The house contained three suites, a common room, and a shared kitchen. Birdie, Bryan, and Joy occupied one suite; Lilly, Christopher, and their daughters, another; and Belle, Sam, and Isaac came up from Washington to occupy the third.

Another of the bungalows on the property was taken by Birdie's sister, Elsa; their mother, Clara; Big Louie; and their eighteen-year-old son, Ernest.

It was a summer of comings and goings.

Birdie commuted to Macy's five days a week, leaving her husband and daughter behind. She loved the forty-five-minute train trip twice a day, as it was a completely private time, with no responsibility.

Lilly and her girls stayed all summer while Christopher spent five days a week in the city, editing a Communist magazine and working on his novel. Belle was uncomfortable with the crowding, so she made only a few visits during the summer. Sam was involved with his construction business so his visits were even less frequent. This left Isaac with a suite to himself where he was doted upon by his two aunts. He was as happy as his cousin Joy was bored and unhappy. Joy constantly fought with her mother, who had no patience with her complaints that there was nothing to do.

Louie found a job nearby as an auto mechanic. Often, he brought along his son, Ernest, to whom he was teaching the trade. Elsa stayed in the cottage most of the time, caring for her mother, Clara, who, at eighty-six, was nearly blind.

In August, Belle phoned from Washington. Birdie was in the kitchen and picked up the receiver.

"Hello, Birdie; it's Belle. Are you sitting down? You won't believe it! They served me with a subpoena—Congress. They're out to get us."

"What are you talking about?"

"I mean it. The House Un-American Activities Committee ordered me to come before them and testify."

"Are you going to do it?"

"I have to."

"When?"

"Next Wednesday. Here's the thing, can you and Bryan come down and hold my hand? It'll be a big comfort to have you here."

"Of course we'll come. Tomorrow? Tuesday? What are you doing about it? What are you feeling?"

"Tuesday will be fine. Let's not talk any more on the telephone. I'm sure my line is bugged. We'll talk on Tuesday. You'll leave Joy up there with Isaac?"

"Lilly will watch them both. And don't worry about Isaac. You have enough to think about. Your son will be fine."

Bryan and Birdie rode the train to Washington and took a taxi to the Greens' home where they arrived to learn that Sam, too, had been subpoenaed.

"Belle, you look terrible," Birdie said. "I guess you both feel terrible."

"It's a media circus," Sam explained. "Our phone keeps ringing with hate calls, but I'm afraid to miss anything important."

"Nothing's that important," Bryan said. "Unplug the damned phone! Let's have a drink and see if you can explain what's happening."

"They aren't looking for anything they don't already know," Sam said. "They're seeking publicity. The newspapers have been full of it."

"It must be terribly hard, not knowing who is still your friend and who is going to turn against you," Birdie said.

"It's pretty bad," Belle agreed.

"What do you think they'll ask you?" Bryan asked.

"They aren't looking for information," Sam said. "They want to scare us. They're after me because I contribute to causes they don't like. Our lawyer tells us we can't answer anything, because if we do, we've waived our rights against self-incrimination. In other words, once we start talking, they can ask us for names of other people who have contributed money or even gone to meetings, and if we refuse to answer, we're in contempt of court."

"So what are you going to do?"

"We'll respectfully refuse to answer, based on our Fifth Amendment rights protecting us against self-incrimination. How's that for a mouthful?"

Wednesday morning, Birdie helped dress her sister-in-law. "Your best dress. You're going to be beautiful. Show them you've got nothing to be ashamed of and you're not afraid of them."

"Even if I am scared silly?" Belle replied.

The hearings went much as Sam had predicted.

Bryan and Birdie remained another night. The phone was left off of its cradle, and there were pictures of the Greens on the front pages of both morning newspapers. Belle's picture showed her wearing a string of pearls and looking quite attractive.

"Enough of this," said Birdie. "Get on the train with us. Come back up to the colony."

"No, not yet," Belle answered. "You go. Be nice to Isaac. Explain what's happening and tell him we'll come up soon."

THIRTY-ONE

Summer was almost over. Joy was thrilled. Her cousin Ernest had just gotten his driver's license. Here was an escape from boredom. Together, they explored all the back roads in the neighborhood.

He even invited her to attend a concert nearby. Ernest's junior permit didn't allow him to drive after dark, but this was an afternoon concert at Lakeland Acres. Paul Robeson was going to sing.

Paul Robeson was a cultural hero to Joy and all her friends. She had been raised on his songs and on his legend. She knew he had been an "All-American" athlete in three different sports during his college career at Rutgers, even if she didn't know what it meant to be "All-American." She knew that he had been a scholar, but he left scholarship to become a world-famous singer, a movie star, and a Shakespearian actor. She knew he was an advocate of racial equality, and she also knew he had lived for a time in Russia, just like she and her mother. He lived there, Joy was told, because he believed that Soviet Russia was a land free of racial prejudice.

She also understood his fight for racial justice had led conservative America to reject him, despite his celebrity, to deny him an audience, and even to revoke his passport, thus denying him access to foreign stages.

Now, for the first time, she was going to hear him, in person!

Ernest drove carefully. They had plenty of time to reach the concert grounds only a few miles away.

Exiting the Taconic Parkway and entering the two-lane local road, they saw that both sides of the road were lined with people waving their arms and yelling frantically. Their faces were flushed with anger. Their words jumbled together, and Joy couldn't make out what they were saying. Then Joy recognized the teenaged girl who served her ice-cream sodas at the Rexall store. The girl caught her eye, stuck out her arm, and, with a fierce look, extended her middle finger at Joy. As they got closer, there were more and more people lining the road. A rock hit the hood of the car and bounced off to the side. Another rock hit the passenger window on Joy's side. It was the rear window, but some of the shattered glass went over Joy's shoulder and onto her lap. Joy was surprised to realize that, having survived the broken glass, she was less afraid than before, more intent on what was happening to them.

Now, through the shattered window, they could clearly hear the cries from those standing only a few feet away.

"Go back to Russia, you dirty kikes."

"Nigger-loving Jew bastards."

Ernest tried to give his full attention to the car. Ahead, there was a crossroad. The corner was full of angry people, but further up the road, he didn't see anyone. He turned right as quickly as he dared. A volley of stones bounced off the back of the car.

That was their full experience with the Peekskill concert. Ernest drove home, shaken, still fearful, but driving very carefully.

Arriving back at the colony, Ernest went right to his family's bungalow. Joy found her mother in the summer house's spacious kitchen, peeling potatoes.

"You're home already? Was it good?"

"Mom, it was terrible," Joy said, and in a trembling voice, she proceeded to relate all that had happened to them en route to the concert.

By the time she completed her telling, Joy felt herself quite composed, but Birdie was terrified.

Everyone in the house soon gathered around the radio and gradually constructed a coherent story of the afternoon's events. They found out that Paul Robeson had not even gotten onto the concert grounds. His car was stoned, but lying on the floor of the car, he was unhurt. Hundreds of others had not been so lucky, but no serious injuries were reported. The concert had been canceled.

The concert organizers vowed to reschedule. "It is our right, as Americans, to meet and to listen as we choose."

Now, those opposed to the concert organized themselves. They adopted the rallying cry, "Wake up, America. Peekskill did."

The concert was held, as rescheduled, for September 4. But by this time, Birdie's extended family had completed their summer vacation and moved back to their homes. The children were back in school. None of them made the trip up to Peekskill for the concert, which was held at a disused golf course.

On the Sunday of the second concert Birdie and Bryan spent the afternoon close to the radio, which was tuned for news broadcasts. Reports began arriving well before the concert was scheduled to begin. Neither left the apartment, and by evening they were able to have a semi-coherent picture of what was taking place

A contingent of self-appointed peacekeepers, veterans and union members had linked arms in a circle around the grounds to prevent violence from erupting. The concert proceeded without incident.

It was only as the thousands of concert-goers were making their way home that violence erupted. There was just one dirt road leading out of the concert grounds. The road was lined with rock-throwing, self-styled "patriots." Windows were broken, cars were overturned, and people were beaten and hospitalized. The police were there but made no effort to halt the rock throwing. Rather they told the drivers who were appealing for help to "keep on moving."

As far away as the New York City line, protestors stood on the over-passes, dropping rocks onto cars carrying Negroes.

"Enough, Birdie. Let's go to bed. It's horrible, but we can't listen all night. All that's left to say is 'thank God that we weren't there'"

"Don't be foolish, Bryan. Thank God that Joy and Ernest weren't there. But I suspect that I'll always regret not being a part of it."

THIRTY-TWO

One result of the summer at the bungalow colony was that Birdie, for the first time, felt close to Lilly. Christopher, she found more difficult. As she explained to Bryan, "He's a good Communist, and he's a Negro. Maybe he's a Negro first. I'm never sure. But one thing I do know. He's got Lilly right where he wants her, waiting on him hand and foot."

"Well, he's becoming an important man. He's one of the intellectuals who explains to the faithful what they should be thinking, and it doesn't hurt the cause that he's a Negro...well, one-eighth probably, but in this country, that makes him a Negro."

"Sure, he's an intellectual, Bryan. But Lilly has to show him how to wipe himself. Do you know what he said to her when we all went to the diner one night? He looked at the menu, and he actually asked his wife, 'Lilly, do I like Brussels sprouts?' Can you believe that?"

June 25, 1950, was a Sunday. Bryan, Birdie, and Joy were at home in the Bronx. The radio was turned on, and all three were listening. They heard that troops of the People's Republic of North Korea had crossed the border into South Korea. Bryan and Birdie remained by the radio most of the day. They heard the United Nations Security Council vote unanimously to engage in a police action to halt the North Koreans. Two days later, President Truman announced that American forces were going to the aid of South Korea.

Bryan still had no regular work. While Birdie was demonstrating scarves at Macy's and Joy was at school, he sat home listening to the war news. When Birdie came home at six, he poured two glasses of Chianti. They sat next to each other on the couch.

"Birdie, I'm terribly worried," he said.

"You are always worried, Bryan. What is it?"

"I'm not always worried," he objected. "I'm always depressed. It's not the same. Worry is entirely different. Aren't you worried about this war, Birdie, about what can happen to us?"

"No, Bryan, I'm not really worried. We are living in terrible times, sure, but we've seen worse. We'll make it through this one too."

"No, Birdie. This is different. President Truman has built camps out west for people like us. He is going to round up everybody J. Edgar Hoover thinks is disloyal. You saw what happened to Belle and Sam, called before Congress, their pictures spread over the front pages of the newspapers."

"What are you saying, Bryan?"

"I'm thinking something. I'm thinking that this is a good time for us to leave the country again."

"You can't be thinking of going back to the Soviet Union, can you? We already tried that. It wasn't what we expected it to be. Was it? At least for me, it was much harder being there than I'd imagined. And, anyway, if it does come to a war between America and Russia, how long do you think we would last over there? Not one minute. They'd round us up in a second."

"That's why I think that maybe we should go to Israel. Now that the Jews have their own country...our own country, we should at least go and see it. Besides, Israel hasn't taken sides in the Cold War, has it? They are friends with both America and Russia."

"You're out of your mind, Bryan!"

"No, I'm not. Besides, you know how much we have always enjoyed traveling. The war's over now. The dollars we've saved are like gold abroad. Think of it as another adventure. We'll go, and we'll see what happens?"

"I can't leave Joy behind again. She's about to start her senior year in high school. What would she do over there?"

"For God's sake, Birdie, they have schools, just like we do."

Birdie spent three days thinking over Bryan's idea. Bryan spent those three days at home, sitting by the radio, sulking. Every hour, he listened to the news broadcasts over WQXR, and on the half hours, he had the news from WNYC. On the third day, he didn't bother to get out of his pajamas.

"All right, Bryan. We'll do it. For you, we'll do it. I figured it out, and I asked some questions. I called Sam in Washington. He has friends over there. And I have a cousin in Tel Aviv. Sam even suggested we put Joy into a kibbutz boarding school."

When Joy was informed of the decision to pick up and move to the two-year-old state of Israel, she was furious.

"No way! You have no right to do this to me. You did this when I was a little girl. You can't do it now. I'm not going!"

"Yes, you are," her mother said. "We're still responsible for you. One more year, we decide. Then you'll go off to college. Now, we're the ones in charge."

There was much yelling back and forth between mother and daughter. Bryan tried to be the peacemaker, explaining why it was the right thing to do. Joy was unmoved. But she was overruled.

Becky found a tenant for their apartment, a woman with whom she had taught, who agreed to sublet it for at least a year.

Bryan figured that they had best leave through Canada. "They're taking passports away from people they consider 'subversives,' but we won't have to show our passports at the Canadian border, and we can go on from there without problems."

Sam and Belle came from Washington to wish them farewell. They booked into a Manhattan hotel, and the night before Birdie, Bryan, and Joy were to depart for Israel, Sam hosted a supper for Belle's siblings. They were all there, in one of the hotel's private dining spaces—all except for Joy, who was expected but was still sulking and refused to leave the house.

It was fortunate that a private space had been secured because conversation around the table was loud and even more heated than usual.

Christopher opined that the Cantors, by leaving, were shirking a responsibility. "The fight for a better world is here," he said. "You can't just duck out of it."

"Of course they can," Becky responded. "Look at what's happened to us, sitting at this table. I've had my job snatched away. Sam and Belle were paraded in front of Congress. You, Christopher, you were locked up in prison."

"Wait. It's my turn to talk," said Belle. "Maybe fascism is coming to America. Maybe it's here already. But in either case, why do we think Israel is the answer? That tiny postage stamp of a country? Christopher is right, I'm sure. Bryan, you're my little brother, and I love you, but Israel? You'll see. You're going to be squeezed to death over there by the same Cold War you're running away from. You can't run away."

"Enough, Belle," Lee interrupted. "Birdie and my brother are going off on an adventure. Let them go peacefully."

As the discussion became particularly loud, Sam picked up his knife and rapped it against his wineglass. When, at last there was silence, he stood up. "A toast," he said. "To my *meshuganah* (crazy) in-laws, two wonderful people about to set off on an adventure, perhaps necessary, perhaps mistaken, but nonetheless, an adventure. May God preserve you in his very own land, and may you soon return to a better America."

Igor and Luba Svaboda appeared early the next morning, to help them load the car and to wish them well.

"It won't be the same city without you two," Luba said.

"Nonsense," said Bryan. "When all this foolishness passes and we come back to New York, I expect that you, Igor, will be building skyscrapers on Park Avenue, and you, Luba, will certainly be head of the math department at Columbia University."

"From your mouth to God's ears," said Birdie. Anyway, it seems you two are always seeing us off to somewhere. And yet we always manage to get together again. Now we'll see what comes next."

The suitcases were loaded. The adults embraced. Joy, still furious at her parents, turned away from Luba's attempt to hug her. She refused even to acknowledge the Svabodas' presence.

They drove, north, toward Montreal. Joy sat, sulking, in the back-seat, feeling sorry for herself, while Birdie fed grapes and brownies to Bryan, as he drove.

In Montreal, they sold the car and boarded the *Empress of Canada*, for England. Bryan and Birdie had their own cabin. Joy had an adjoining one. The second day out, the weather became rough. Both Birdie and Joy were terribly seasick, and each spent a full day and a half in bed. Bryan, on the other hand, despite his nervous stomach, felt fine and appeared in the nearly empty dining room at all the appointed times.

On her second day abed, feeling a little better, Joy got restless. She decided to try out the upper bunk. She climbed up, got under the covers, and went back to sleep.

The following morning, after a light breakfast in the dining room, Birdie was approached by the cabin steward.

"You'd better check on your daughter. Somebody's been sleeping in her upper bunk."

Perhaps the steward was just joking. Or maybe he resented having to make up the second bed. But Birdie took him to be serious. She questioned Joy, "Have you had somebody in your cabin, Joy? You aren't ready for that. Tell me. What happened?"

"Mother! You're being ridiculous!"

The ensuing fight went on with Birdie defending herself as being concerned only with her daughter's well-being, and Joy insisting that her mother was talking nonsense about things that were none of her business. "Mother, I refuse to listen, and I'll not say another word to you."

It wasn't until they approached Southampton that Joy consented to speak to her mother again.

From London, an El Al flight brought them to Tel Aviv. As they deplaned onto the tarmac, they were smacked by a wave of stifling heat. Birdie noted a group of black-frocked orthodox Jews who had descended just ahead of her kneeling down and kissing the tarmac.

THIRTY-THREE

Birdie's cousin, Yehudit, met them at the airport.

"She may be a second or third cousin. It's hard to keep the relationships straight, Bryan. But we all started out in the same place: Odessa."

There she was, standing just outside of customs and holding up a cardboard sign with "Fagelah," Birdie's long abandoned name, printed on it.

Birdie embraced her and said, "Even without the sign, Yehudit, I'd have picked you out from the crowd. You're my mother, thirty or forty years ago."

Yehudit was ten years older than Birdie. She had been in Palestine since 1920, arriving as a twenty-one-year-old pioneer.

"I'm considered an old-timer," she told them, "even though I'm only in my fifties. My generation is running the country now. Me? I'm just a bookkeeper. I work for the Trade Unions, all my old comrades. I let them tell me what to do, and in general, they seem to know what they're doing. I never did get married. Like most of them, I tried agriculture at first. I was one of the founders of my kibbutz. I lived there for fifteen years. But that was enough. I moved to Tel Aviv, and I watched the country get born. I'm so glad to see you three, my own family, returning, from America, no less. We need you here, and we are so happy that you came."

Yehudit's English was excellent. She spoke endlessly about what the country meant to her. She didn't stop until they arrived at the Katey Dan Hotel, the Cantors' destination on the Mediterranean seashore.

"Check in, eat, relax, and I'll pick you up tomorrow morning at nine and begin to show you Israel."

In the week that followed, Yehudit introduced the Cantors to her country. First, she showed them how to find their way around Tel-Aviv. Later, in her small Hillman Minx, imported from England, they drove out of the urban bustle, through the agricultural fields of the plain, and up into the hills of Jerusalem, passing Arab villages—some still inhabited and others that remained abandoned since the fighting two years earlier. Along the road were rusting vehicles, burned-out relics of the war. The new state was leaving them as they sat, memorials of the War of Independence.

The bare hills clearly showed the remnants of terraces, dating back to Roman days and even further.

Yehudit tried to convey the ecstasy she felt every time she "went up to Jerusalem," the rose-stone city, but the emotional depth of Yehudit's love of the land was not something Bryan and Birdie were ready to share. Love of Zion and the urge to return to the Jewish homeland had not been a part of their upbringing. Still, they were finding the country congenial. The people they were meeting seemed the same people whom they had known in Brooklyn, in the Bronx, and even in Moscow.

They spoke no Hebrew, but with English, Yiddish, and Russian, it was very easy for Bryan and Birdie to make their way. Most Israelis spoke at least one of those three languages, as well as Hebrew. Joy, by then, had quite forgotten Russian and Yiddish, which she had spoken fluently until the age of six, so she was left only with English.

Joy was working at holding herself in an emotional state of suspension. She convinced herself that she was "having an experience." *There's nothing so special that I've left behind,* she thought. *Whatever is coming will probably be at least as good as the life I've left.* What she wouldn't do, was to admit, out loud, that she had accepted her situation.

With Yehudit's help, the Cantors found a furnished, second-floor apartment in Tel Aviv, a one-bedroom apartment in a residential district. The day after they moved in, Bryan borrowed Yehudit's car and they drove Joy to Mishmar Haemek, the kibbutz, in whose boarding school she was already enrolled.

They drove past the cultivated fields of the coastal plain and entered hilly country dotted by small Arab villages. The homes were mostly one-story and flat-roofed. Sunlight brightly reflected off the stucco. A band of deep-blue paint around each doorway softened the light and cooled the homes.

There was a noticeable contrast between the picturesque Arab villages, which seemed to grow right out of the earth, and the recently thrown together immigrant settlements housing Jewish refugees. These were canvas tents or tin huts - jarringly ugly.

Then they entered the Emek, a large plain, most of which had been a mosquito-infested swamp until it was drained and brought back to productivity by Jewish agricultural settlers. As they drove past some of these villages, Birdie felt that she had returned to Russia. Clearly, these pioneers were Russian Jews who had brought their architecture and style of living with them.

Palm trees lined the dirt lane approaching the kibbutz. The high school stood on a hill just above the settlement, consisting of a two-story, cement, flat-roofed dormitory; a dining hall; and several classrooms. Over the crest of the hill was the school's farm, which the high school students operated.

They located the head teacher, Ben-Ami Gordon, a short, rotund forty-year-old, wearing sandals, short pants, short sleeves, and a "kibbutz" cloth sun cap. In his excellent English, he assured Birdie that Joy would be well cared for.

"I'm sure she'll be fine; otherwise, we wouldn't be leaving her here," Birdie said to Ben-Ami Gordon.

When Birdie tried to kiss her daughter good-bye, Joy turned her face so that Birdie's lips only brushed her ear.

"We'll visit you on your free Saturdays," Bryan said. "Once we settle ourselves."

Joy had little idea of what to expect, but whatever trepidation she felt about the unknown surroundings was balanced by curiosity and anticipation. She felt ready to try out a completely new life.

None of her classmates spoke enough English to explain anything, but through gestures, they showed her to her room, where she stowed her few belongings in her very limited private space. The room held two double-decker beds, two dressers, a few built-in shelves, and nothing more.

Soon, an attractive girl wearing very short shorts, led her across the campus, to the dining hall where the choices were limited—all vegetarian, but tasty. In the evening, unable to follow any of the conversations, Joy lay on her upper bed reading. Two boys and the girl in short shorts sat on a lower bunk, talking. Joy wanted to go to bed, and she waited impatiently for the two boys to leave. Only as they undressed and put on their pajamas did she realize that they were roommates—not only the girl who had shown her around, but the two boys as well.

When one of the boys, by gestures, indicated she should come brush her teeth, she was equally surprised that the bathroom, with open showers, was also coeducational. Her final surprise of the night was the discovery that in the bathroom, the only toilet paper was old newspapers and torn-up pages from *Life* magazine.

Back in her room, the conversation continued. Unable to understand a word, Joy faced the wall, pulled her pillow tightly over her exposed ear, and fell asleep.

Having settled her daughter in boarding school, Birdie spent the next two days turning the apartment into a home. First, she scrubbed. Then, with Bryan in tow, she shopped for foodstuff. Only a block away, they discovered a shop selling brightly colored cushions, which, they agreed, would greatly enliven their small living room.

After two days of organizing the apartment, still in pajamas and drinking coffee, Birdie told her husband, "Today, I'm going out to find a job."

"You can't just go out and expect a job to fall into your lap, you know. It doesn't work that way. You don't even speak the language."

"You wait and see. Even here, in Tel-Aviv, they've all heard of Macy's. I'm good. Somebody will hire me."

She put on a newly purchased red dress with white polka dots, descended into the sunshine, and began walking toward the center of the city. It was Birdie's plan to go from store to store, offering her services.

As the day went on, Birdie's optimism gradually evaporated.

At the very first shop she visited, her English greetings were answered by an angry command, "Jew, here we speak Hebrew!" The Hebrew language was completely foreign to her, but Birdie had no trouble grasping the woman's meaning.

That was the nastiest of the morning's rebuffs, but in store after store, it was essentially the same, "No work."

Late that morning, a more sympathetic storekeeper, a gray-haired man in a tailor shop, explained, in Yiddish, that, "Israel, today, is full of people just like you, newly arrived and unemployed. I'm sorry. Would you like a glass of tea at least?"

"Thank you very much. Yes. I would like that...and a chance to sit down."

He took her to the back room, and while he prepared tea, they talked.

"I'm one of the lucky ones," the tailor said. "I left Germany before the war. May I tell you a story that will explain the job situation?"

"Please do."

A certain sparkle in the man's eyes told Birdie that his story was not to be taken seriously.

"It is this way," he began. "A newly arrived immigrant, much like you, went out looking for a job. He saw a construction site a few blocks away. *I'll try there,* he thought. As he neared the site, he heard a rumbling sound. As he got closer, the sound grew louder and appeared to come from a crowd of workmen. Still closer, he saw that they were unloading a truckload of bricks, passing them, brick by brick, from hand to hand. The sound was deafening, but it was not until he reached the site itself that he was able to tell that the noise was conversation. As each laborer received a brick, he would say, 'Danke, Herr Doktor,' and as he passed it on to the next worker in line, he would say, 'Bitte, Herr Doktor, and then, turning to accept the next brick, he would repeat, 'Danke Her Doctor.'"

Birdie laughed and said, "I think I get your point."

She parted from the tailor, encouraged by his shared humanity and less sure of her own job prospects.

It was early afternoon when she found herself downtown, at Dizinghoff Circle, in front of the impressive structure that housed the city's major drama theater, Habima. Remembering her association with artists and actors in her Mosfilm days, she climbed the concrete steps and entered the lobby. The box office was closed, but just inside the next door was a desk occupied by an older woman with bright-orange hair. Birdie hadn't seen hair that color since she left Russia. She approached her and asked, in English, if there was anyone available to whom she might inquire about a job.

"No, nothing available," she was told. "The country is full of unemployed actors looking for work. They are willing just to sweep up the place if we will let them. Sorry. Go away."

Just then, a middle-aged, buxom actress burst upon them and shouted at the receptionist, in Russian, "Look at my costume!" In her hand was a brightly colored jacket, which she waved angrily. "It's falling apart. Who was the butcher who stitched this rag?"

Birdie immediately spoke up, in Russian. "Here, give it to me. Give me a needle and thread, and I'll fix it for you in no time."

The orange-haired receptionist opened her desk drawer and produced needle and thread. Birdie sat on one of the lobby's stuffed couches and performed the required mending.

"You are American," the actress observed. "I can tell it by your accent. How do you know Russian?"

Birdie told her of her time in Moscow, emphasizing her work at Mosfilm.

"We have actors here who have performed in Soviet movies. Are you almost finished with my jacket? Come with me. I'll introduce you."

Birdie discovered that she and the Habima actors had friends in common. They enjoyed reminiscing about the old times in Moscow.

And so, a job was found for Birdie. She was not an accomplished seamstress, barely competent in fact. But there was always some task that needed doing or something to be gone for or looked after. She was resourceful and quickly made herself valuable.

Bryan spent much of his time at the American Information Agency library. At first, he went to keep abreast of the news from America; then, surreptitiously, he observed the operations of the library, trying to ascertain if there was some job that he might be able to perform. There wasn't. Afternoons, he often spent in the park, befriending the local chess players, all of whom were recent refugees from Europe. Bryan's frequent games with Igor Svaboda had increased his confidence, if not his skill, but he soon realized that here in the park, as in Russia before, he was hopelessly outclassed.

THIRTY-FOUR

It was three weeks before Bryan could, again, borrow Yehudit's car to visit Joy.

It was a Saturday. They found Joy waiting for them at the bottom of the palm-lined lane, at the entrance to the kibbutz.

"Let's drive into town," Joy said, climbing into the backseat of the minicar. "I need a break!"

All through the twenty-minute ride to Haifa, the normally taciturn girl babbled, detailing her strange life. "I'm liking my work as part of the kitchen crew OK, but one more week and then we change. My new job, I'll be in the farm group. And, you know what I do a lot, since I can't talk to anyone? I do lots of reading. Especially, I'm loving John Steinbeck! Jack London too! In English, in our library. But you know what? The kids treat me pretty good. We get along. It's OK...except for the evenings when everyone goes to chorus and I feel kind of left out."

"What do you mean?" Birdie asked. "Why don't you go with them?"

"Mom, you know you're always telling me I can't carry a tune. And besides, I don't know any of the words they all know."

Halfway to Haifa, they passed a tent colony, temporary housing for newly arrived immigrants.

"Oh, that reminds me," Joy said, "we've got a community of Yemenites right next to the kibbutz. It used to be an Arab village, and when the Arabs ran away, in the war, it was given to the Yemenites. Do you know what Yemenites are?"

"Of course we know," Bryan answered, not turning around, but keeping his eyes on the road while Birdie put a freshly lit cigarette into his mouth.

"They are Jews who come from Yemen," Joy went on. "They don't look at all Jewish. They look like Arabs. Anyway, we got invited to a wedding there last week. It was fantastic. All the men were dancing on one side of the yard. The women were on the other side. They're not allowed to touch each other. We never did see the bride."

Three hours later, arriving back at the Kibbutz, Joy said, "Don't bother to come up. You can let me off here, by the road. I'll walk up to the school."

As they drove back toward Tel Aviv, Birdie said, "You know, I think we did the right thing. She is going to be happy here. I feel that."

"God knows she's never shared so many words with us," Bryan answered. "Not ever."

A month passed before they visited again. This time, Joy wasn't at the road awaiting their arrival, so they parked by the kibbutz dining room and walked up to the school, looking for her. They came upon her, sitting on a bench, in conversation with a slim boy dressed in sandals and shorts.

"Hello, Mom and Dad. I wondered what time you'd get here. This is Peter. He's in my group. He knows a bit of English, and I can say a few things in Hebrew already."

Peter and Joy stood up. Peter shook hands with Birdie and Bryan and said, in English, "Is good, talk to your daughter. Good-bye." He left.

Bryan and Joy kissed. Birdie hugged her daughter and then asked, "So, who is he?"

"Peter's like me. He's a new student here. He isn't a kibbutznik. He lives on a cooperative farming village. He's only half Jewish. His mother is German, and they got out of Germany in nineteen-thirty-four, when he was a one year old. He has relatives there, and he speaks German with his parents."

"Is he a boyfriend?" Birdie prodded.

"You know what?" Joy went on. "It's very different being with boys on a kibbutz. We're raised together, our group, like brothers and sisters, and they tell me that when it's time to get married, we always find somebody from somewhere else, maybe another kibbutz, certainly not someone from our own group."

Birdie glanced at her husband, who raised one eyebrow, signifying doubt.

"Come," Joy said. "It's time I give you a tour."

The first thing Joy showed them was the bomb shelter, which had been dug in the middle of the courtyard between the dormitory building and the dining hall. They went down into the underground excavation and found it clean, with nothing other than benches lining the walls. They visited her classroom. They passed the woodworking shop and went on to the children's farm.

"In here," Joy said, leading her parents into a low, wooden shed. "This is the goat house where I work every afternoon. She reached across a wooden slat fence to stroke the back of a black-and-white goat that had floppy ears and a wispy beard.

"Meet Ruth. She's my favorite. She's a Nubian. I milk her every day at five."

"Oh, Zoyshinka, I'm so happy that you are fitting in so well. I'm so proud of you," Birdie said.

"And another thing, Mom, Dad, do you know how they punish you here if you are really bad? The worst punishment is that they don't let you go to work! On the assignment board, next to your name, they write 'forbidden to work' and that's your shameful punishment!"

Birdie was satisfied with her work at the national theater. It wasn't all-consuming. It wasn't terribly challenging. But it was work. She met interesting people, and her salary enabled them to keep some of their savings securely deposited. Mostly, it consumed her days.

Bryan had still found no work. His days were taken up by visits to the US Information Agency, chess games in the park, and long walks along the Mediterranean Sea embankments.

One blustery afternoon, Bryan brought home the international edition of the *Herald Tribune*, and as Birdie returned from the theater, even before she could remove her sopping jacket, he told her, "How's this, Birdie? It looks like 'our friend,' Joseph Stalin, isn't really our friend after all."

As he said, "our friend," he held up his first two fingers on each hand, indicating that the designation of 'friend' was meant to be sarcastic.

"I guess," Birdie said. "But wait a minute. Let me take off my coat and catch my breath, at least."

She draped her wet coat over a chair, took a towel, and patted her long dark hair dry. Then she sat on the couch.

Bryan waved his copy of the *International Herald Tribune* in front of her.

"Damn, I wish I could read the local papers," he said. "Here's a report on a series of stories that have been running in the Israeli papers on Stalin's anti-Semitism. And by the time we hear about it, it's old news."

Neither Birdie nor Bryan had trouble accepting the image of Stalin as an anti-Semite. Both remembered, from their years in Russia, how deeply ingrained anti-Semitism was. True, the Soviets, long ago, had outlawed expressions of hate, but the law, as they well knew, did little to alter deeply held prejudice.

The kibbutzniks found it harder to accept the news. The realization that they were not loved by those whom they venerated required some adjustment. But it wasn't Communism that the kibbutzniks turned away from. It was Soviet Russian Communism, which rejected them and which they, in turn, must reject. In its place, they felt, was their own, more successful and more pure Communism.

Joy's understanding of the Hebrew language had become sufficiently good so that she was able to follow some of the discussions about Stalin's viciousness. But there wasn't that much time to think of politics. The school year was coming to a close, and to mark the beginning of summer recess, the two oldest groups were preparing for a five-day hike across the northern shoulder of the country, from the town of Safed to the Sea of Galilee.

They set out by truck, driving to the northern hill country. Joy found it beautiful, reminiscent of family excursions into the Catskill Mountains. Joy's backpack contained a part of the group's foodstuff. Her sleeping bag was tied atop the pack. She saw that her teachers had rifles slung across their shoulders.

On the second day of the hike, they passed by a stream from which Arab farmers were scooping buckets of water. Others, Joy saw, had already carried their buckets up the terraced hillside where they watered their plants. The scene was indelibly fixed in Joy's memory. The thought came, unbidden, that these people were going through the necessary motions, not as farmers, but as servants to their crops. She felt that these Arabs were there to serve their plants, at least as fully as the plants were there for the people's sake.

On the third night, as they were about to unroll their sleeping bags, they were informed that in order to reach their buses at the appointed time, it would be necessary to hike a few more miles that night. So off they went, for three more hours, walking by flashlight or sometimes in the dark, the trail lit only by starlight.

On the fifth day, they reached the shores of the Sea of Galilee. As they approached the lake, Joy heard the chilling sound of helicopters—three of them. Joy knew that helicopters overhead usually signified the evacuation of wounded, most likely from a battle or from a terrorist incident. Fear was never completely out of Joy's mind. In New York, if she heard a sudden, unexpected noise, there was always the possibility that it might signify the start of nuclear war between America and Russia. Here in Israel, the fear was different. She was acutely aware that she and all her friends were surrounded by eighty million Arabs who wished them ill.

I'm not going to live the rest of my life this way, in a place where someone wants to kill me for no reason, for nothing I've done—just because I'm me.

Her fellow students, however, paid no attention to the helicopters. Instead, they approached the lake joyously, plunging, fully dressed, into the refreshing waters. Joy hesitated just a moment and then waded in after the others.

When she next saw her parents and enthusiastically reported on the hike, Bryan said, "You realize, don't you, that this is the beginning of your army training? They are preparing you to be a soldier."

By then, Joy was quite sure that, somehow, she would soon go home, to America, to college, but she kept the thought to herself.

Bryan and Birdie were attending a gathering at Cousin Yehudit's house. There were distant relatives, friends, and coworkers of Yehudit's in attendance. In deference to the Cantors, much of the conversation was in English.

Yehudit's grown niece asked, "How is your daughter doing in the kibbutz?"

"Very well," Bryan answered. "She loves it. She's becoming a real kibbutznik. She's so proud to have been taken into the youth movement."

"Well," remarked one of the guests, a young woman who taught sociology, "I've been reading about Mishmar Haemek in the newspapers. It seems they've come to an ideological crossroads, haven't they?"

"You mean the brouhaha about hiring workers for their plastics factory?" asked Birdie.

"It's good to see that you know about our problems," said the teacher's husband, one of the few in the room who was native-born. "Our ideology is being overtaken by reality. What have you gathered from your visits to the kibbutz?"

"Here's the way our daughter explains it," Birdie said. "They are socialists. That means that there is no money involved in their labor. Everyone works, and nobody gets paid. Everyone is given what they need—at least what the kibbutz can afford at that moment. It's what the Russians claim is their ultimate goal, from each according to his ability to each according to his needs."

"We all know what socialism is," said another guest. "What's the big issue in Mishmar Haemek?"

"It turns out that in winter, when the fields are idle, there wasn't enough work for everybody. So they opened a plastics factory where they make molds for various things," Bryan explained.

"Also," Birdie cut into the conversation, "it provided work for the older generation, for those who can no longer go out to work the fields."

Bryan continued, "The factory did well. There are lots of orders, more than they can handle, and now they are talking about hiring outside workers, at least in the summertime when they don't have enough people to work the fields and the factory at the same time. The problem is, their political view is opposed to hiring workers. That would be capitalist exploitation."

Yehudit's niece observed, "This is—what do you call it in English?—a slippery slope. Once they start making a profit, they'll be just like us, the city bourgeoisie, whom they look down on."

"Ah," said the sociologist, "but they are giving work to unemployed immigrants. They are building our economy. In that sense, they are behaving like good Zionists."

"No," said a bearded professor of oncology. He puffed a couple of times on his pipe and through a haze of tobacco smoke continued, "Hiring outside labor would be the death knell of the kibbutz movement. The kibbutz is based upon sharing, on equality. You, Birdie, from America, you've already stated Karl Marx's formula. If they do otherwise, you'll see. In twenty years, the kibbutz will be a thing of the past."

The discussion in Yehudit's living room went on.

At the general meeting of the kibbutz membership, a week later, a majority vote approved hiring paid labor.

THIRTY-FIVE

I t was spring. As described in the Old Testament, "The rain was gone with the wind."

Tucked away in a corner of the Tel-Aviv USIA reading room, Bryan settled into his accustomed easy chair, opened the *Herald Tribune* international edition, and read:

New York, April 4
Soviet Spies Arrested

The FBI, today, announced that Luba and Igor Svaboda, who came to America from Russia five years ago as refugees have been arrested and are being held at an undisclosed location. The bureau charges the pair have been secretly reporting to the KGB in Moscow.

Igor Svaboda, an architect, is self-employed. His wife, Luba Svaboda, a mathematician, is employed by Columbia University. Her father, Boris Kramer, a highly regarded portrait painter, as well as their son, Vladimir, a musician, remain in Moscow.

Since arriving in this country, according to the charge, the Svabodas have befriended a number of prominent and well-connected people. Their Manhattan apartment has become a gathering place of businesspeople, scientists, and Russian émigrés.

The Svabodas, apparently, have been keeping tabs on the local Russian community as well as reporting on scientific and mathematical progress in this country. It is still unclear whether or not Luba Svaboda had access to state secrets through her work at Columbia University.

A trial date has not yet been set.

After reading the article through three times, Bryan was torn. *Do I go to the Habima Theater and tell Birdie immediately, or should I wait till she comes home?*

He left the reading room and walked toward the theater. Along the way, he purchased his own copy of the *Herald Tribune*. The day was lovely. *It shouldn't be this way. The way I feel, it should be storming. I should be pulling up my collar to protect myself from the elements.*

Bryan found a bench outside of the theater, sat down in the sun, and waited the two hours until Birdie finished work. He sat there, reviewing his relationship with the Svabodas. He attempted to dredge up every detail, first of their chance meeting in Moscow, of their deepening friendship, up to the time he and Birdie departed Russia, of the Svabodas' sudden arrival in New York, and of the close bond he had been feeling with them for these past five years.

I won't be able to sort this out till I talk to Birdie. It doesn't make sense.

Emerging from the theater's front door, Birdie saw her husband and immediately suspected that he had come with terrible news.

"Bryan, my dear," she said. "Why are you here? What's wrong?"

"Read," he demanded, standing up and thrusting the newspaper at her. Birdie sat and read. Before Birdie could finish the article, Bryan asked, "Is that why they befriended us, way back in Moscow? Is that why we played chess together, so that Igor could report on anything I was saying or thinking?"

"Oh hush, Bryan. Poor Luba. How terrible for her—for both of them. Wait, Bryan. Don't assume anything until we know what's really happening."

She stood up, saying, "Let's walk home now, Bryan. We can think while we walk."

For several minutes, they walked, hand in hand, in silence. Then Birdie spoke, as much to herself as to Bryan. "This explains so much. If it's true, it explains why they were willing to leave Vladimir behind to pursue his career...and how she could abandon her father, Kramer. It means that they were much more important people than we ever suspected. It means that they weren't 'turncoats' after all. They were loyal Soviets who had a job to do."

"Loyal to what?" Bryan replied. "Loyal to a system built on lies and terror? Certainly not loyal to the friends whom they reported on. Not loyal to me. It makes me queasy, Birdie, sick. I feel terrible! You know how I feel? I feel as though a cement mixer backed up, raised its tail, and dropped an entire truckload of wet cement on me!"

"You always feel terrible, Bryan. Soon, we'll get home. You'll lie down. There's so much here that I need to understand. It won't come to me all at once."

They walked in silence. Then Bryan said, "I'm listening to you, Birdie. I'm reading your thoughts. You want them to be good Soviet citizens after all. Don't you?"

"Stop it, Bryan! You know life is more complicated than that."

That night, they lay in bed, holding each other, unable to sleep.

"I still don't know what to make of it," Birdie muttered. "I can't find it in my heart to fault them for being true to their beliefs."

"Maybe," Bryan answered. "Let's see what happens next."

For the next two weeks, they followed the story as closely as they could. They didn't dare phone Igor or Luba. There was nobody they could telephone. They assumed that the FBI was tapping the phones of anyone likely to be connected with the Svabodas, and they were unwilling to enmesh friends or relatives back home in an espionage case, however peripherally.

After two weeks, the *Herald Tribune* reported there wouldn't be a trial after all. Luba and Igor Svaboda were to be deported back to Russia. At the same time, a Moscow reporter for *Time*, whom the Russians had arrested and accused of espionage, was to be released and returned to America. Nobody claimed that this was a quid pro quo, but so it was assumed.

THIRTY-SIX

Bryan was home, sunk into his easy chair, eyes closed, listening to the radio. The Hebrew language remained a mystery to him, but he was developing a taste for Middle-Eastern music and especially liked the afternoon broadcasts of *The Voice of Israel in Arabic*. He stood up as the apartment door opened and Birdie returned.

"How was work today?" he asked, even before Birdie had time to put down the bag of groceries she'd carried up the single flight of stairs.

"More of the same...Do this. Do that. Would you please go for this or for that? Actually, it's not all bad. In between, there's always time for gossip. Everybody in the theater, it seems, has a story to tell."

"OK. But before you tell me anyone's story, here, read this," he said, thrusting out a newly arrived letter. "It's from Belle."

Birdie put down the groceries, sat on the couch, and read the letter twice.

> Dear Brother,
>
> You've been away long enough. Come home. Nothing terrible is going to happen. It seems that Truman's firing of General MacArthur was a turning point. The war drags on, but people are getting fed up with it. Senator McCarthy is still finding Reds under every bed, but people are beginning to see through him as well.

Meanwhile, our big news is that we have moved back to New York! Washington, you know, in essence, is just a small town. Ever since the hearings, it's felt unpleasant to us both. We're living in a hotel on West 78th St. until we get settled. Sam's looking for a real estate investment. Isaac is off to summer camp in Vermont, where he is a counselor!

Lilly and Christopher and their girls are fine. Becky is still unemployed, but looking. Lee is unchanged, still a charming pain in the ass.

Sam says to tell you that we miss you and we think it is time you came back.

Your sister, Belle

Birdie was hurt that Belle had not addressed the letter to both of them and had not even offered her a greeting, but she kept the feeling to herself.

"So?" she asked. "Are you going to do what your big sister tells you to do?"

"I don't need you to be nasty to me. Let's talk about it—without sarcasm."

"You talk. It's been an interesting time. I think it's been wonderful for Joy. But I've had enough. You haven't found anything that you can do here. The theater won't fall apart if I leave. Maybe Belle is right."

By the next day, it was settled. Birdie phoned her daughter in the kibbutz to inform her of the decision.

Whatever may have been in Joy's head, her instinctive reaction was always to oppose her mother's dictates.

"Mother, you can't do that to me. This is my home. I'm part of a group. I can't just get up and leave!"

"No, Zoyshinka. It's time for you to go back to America. All your friends will be starting college in the fall. Your friend Doris is going upstate, to New Paltz Teachers College. You could go too. You'll come home and become a teacher. Prepare yourself to earn a living. We're taking you back to the Bronx. You'll go to college, and when you graduate, you can make your own decisions."

Sam and Belle were there to greet the three of them at Idlewild Airport. Sam had warm embraces and kisses for each. Belle hugged her brother and gave a cool peck to Birdie's cheek. She shook Joy's hand.

"Where's my cousin Isaac?" Joy asked.

"He's away, at camp. In Vermont," Belle answered.

Sam drove them to their Bronx apartment, newly vacated by the temporary tenant, who, to their pleasure, had left the place sparkling clean, with all their furniture still in place.

Joy immediately went downstairs to her friend Doris's.

"Now let's, the rest of us, go out for supper, to celebrate your return," Sam said. "My treat!"

They chose a Chinese restaurant within walking distance.

Seated at a round table and having ordered their food, Birdie said, "This is a treat Bryan and I haven't experienced in over a year."

"Maybe no Chinese food over there," Sam said, "but looking at you, the three of you didn't lack for food."

"No," Bryan answered. "Simple food, Lots of tomatoes and eggs. Not much meat.

"Let's not talk about food," Belle interrupted her brother. "From the little bit Joy told us in the car ride, I see that she's swallowed the whole kibbutz mystique. What about you two? Have you gone Zionist?"

"No," said Birdie. "I don't think Joy really believes it all either. But I'll tell you an interesting observation. When we were driving our daughter home from the kibbutz, we passed the Nesher cement plant, a big piece of industrial ugliness. You know what she said to us? She said, 'Look, a Jewish cement plant! It's ours. It makes me so proud to feel that it is ours!' I liked hearing her say that. We don't get that feeling in America. At least I've never had it."

"Didn't you feel that way in Russia?" Belle asked. "That everything belongs to the people?"

"No. I may have felt that way for a little while...at first. But 'the people' were struggling so hard just to survive that they hardly felt like 'owners.'"

Sam, who had been struggling to pick up chunks of his orange chicken with chopsticks, put them aside, unwrapped his plastic knife and fork, and said, "OK, OK. Enough idealism. Did you read the newspapers this week? Just as you were leaving Israel, the dock workers in Haifa went on strike for more money. The Jewish government said, 'You are not allowed to strike,' and Jewish policeman, for the first time, beat Jewish strikers with clubs. That's what it means to have our own country!"

"What you're saying," Bryan offered, "is that it's all bullshit. The world stinks!"

"I'm saying, at the very least, that the world is too complicated to be wrapped up in a few slogans."

"No, it isn't," said Belle. "The world isn't that complicated. But you need a broader understanding than any of you seem to have. It is inevitable that the world moves in the right direction. But none of you understands Marxism well enough to see what's really happening."

"Enough philosophy," said Sam. "Birdie, are you planning on going back to Macy's? What are your plans?"

"Well," she answered, "I'm forty years old. Bryan will be forty next year. I think we are ready to do something serious in this world, but I have no idea what that should be."

"Good!" said Sam. "That's the answer I was hoping to hear." He put down his knife and fork, pushed his chair just a bit away from the table, and turned his full attention to Birdie. "You know that I made some money building homes in DC. Now I've bought a brownstone on West Eighty-Eighth Street. One family used to occupy the whole house. I am going to remodel it and make eight apartments. I want you, the two of you, to be my contractors. Your timing couldn't be better. Here you are, just when I need you."

"But we don't know anything about construction," said Bryan.

Sam shifted his attention to Bryan. "What did Birdie know about running a store before she came to Henderson's Grill? You do it, and that's how you learn. Here's what we'll do. Tomorrow, we'll get together and go over all the numbers. Then, do you remember Dick Stein, the architect who lives in Croton? He's drawn up plans already, and he's filed for a building permit. So we are ready to go. What do you say?"

"We just might," Birdie said. "Thank for your confidence in us. It's a wonderful opportunity, a challenge, and we are thrilled that you want us. Will you give us a day to decide?"

Bryan said nothing. He just looked across the table at his sister, and his expression said, "What in the world is she getting us into?"

Belle, equally silently, answered his stare with a shake of her head and an expression that said, "They are both out of their minds!"

It was agreed that Birdie and Bryan would come to the Greens' hotel the next morning to talk details.

That night, as they got into bed, Birdie said, "Don't look so down in the mouth Bryan. It's a wonderful opportunity. You'll see. If Sam can build apartment houses, don't you think we can remodel one single brownstone?"

Instead of answering, Bryan turned his body toward hers. He pulled her to himself and tightly embraced her. Birdie felt the unfamiliar sensation of her husband's organ stiffening and pressing into her crotch. He freed one of his hands from around her body and began to stroke and squeeze her pendulous breasts.

"I don't know how I could exist without you, Birdie. You truly are a marvelous person."

"Hush," she said returning his embrace. She took hold of his rigid member and felt it go limp in her hand. They fell asleep.

The next morning, as arranged, they met with Sam in the Greens' two-room hotel suite. He described, in detail, how much money he had put down on the property, the size of the mortgage, how much rental he expected the house to bring in, his estimate of what the remodeling should cost, and how long he thought the job should take.

"Since you are new at this, it's probably best that you work for a salary rather than do the job for a fixed amount. But if you do manage to complete the job in time and within my estimates, then I'll give you a substantial bonus."

Belle sat in the second room during the whole conversation, distancing herself from the proceedings. She was invariably intimidated by each of Sam's financial ventures. She was positive that a return of the Great Depression was imminent, and besides, she had no confidence in Bryan and Birdie's ability to make themselves into contractors.

She remained behind while Sam took Bryan and Birdie to West Eighty-Eighth Street to look at the brownstone. Birdie admired the wooden paneling in the parlor, as well as the gracious bay windows on the second and third stories. The building stood on a residential street, only a block from the Hudson River. Birdie told Sam she thought he had made a wonderful purchase and that they would be glad to do the job.

"One thing we have to do before we start work though. We are renting a car and taking Joy up to New Paltz College tomorrow. We hope that they will give her full credit for her time in the kibbutz school. Then, if she is accepted…You said you are going to Vermont this weekend, to visit Isaac on visiting day, didn't you?"

"Yes," Sam answered, "but not just to visit our son. Our nieces, Bridget and Lauren, are there too. Campers. Christopher decided he can't get away this weekend. He's almost finished his novel, and he wants Lilly to stay in the city and take care of him while he writes. So we're appointed to bring them sweets and see that they don't feel completely abandoned."

"Here's what I've been thinking," Birdie said. "In the time before college, maybe there's something for Joy, up there in Vermont. May we come too? Then, on Monday, we can start work," OK?"

"Of course!" Sam answered.

THIRTY-SEVEN

As hoped, Joy was readily accepted into the state college. The admissions officer actually gushed, "Your experience on the Kibbutz sounds exciting. You'll be a marvelous addition to our freshman class."

Bryan held the rented sedan through the weekend. On Saturday morning, the Cantors drove into Manhattan and picked up the Greens. The five of them set off for Vermont, Bryan driving, Belle and Birdie beside him, and Sam and Joy in the back.

"So tell us," Bryan asked, "tell us more about this camp, Higley Hill. Strange name. How did you find this place?"

"Friends," Belle answered. "And don't call it 'this place.' It's a very special place. Also, you shouldn't be put off by the name, 'Higley Hill.' It's just an old Vermont family name. Isaac's been writing to us from camp, and he explained that Dan Higley used to own the place."

"What friends? People I've never heard of?" Bryan asked his big sister.

"It's run by a couple, Grace and Manny Granich, old party people. I knew Manny even before I met Sam. No, Bryan, I didn't used to introduce you to all the men in my life. But it's maybe twenty years since I've seen him. Isaac got the counselor's job on his own. I can't wait to see how Manny's changed."

"Interesting," Birdie said. "I won't ask how well you knew him. Especially with my daughter in the backseat. But tell us more."

"He's another one who spent some time in Russia, helping out the revolution. Then, back home, he met Grace, and together, they went off to China to help edit an anti-Japanese newsletter. It was the Chinese Communists who were backing it. When they came back to America, they moved up to Vermont to become homesteaders. They thought they could live off the land. A couple of years later, Manny's brother, who ran a children's camp in the Catskills, got cancer and asked Grace and Manny to take the campers off his hands. So Manny converted his barns into dormitories, and that's the story."

Birdie thought the name was familiar, but she couldn't place it.

The highway crossed the spine of Vermont's Green Mountains and then, after a few miles on a dirt road they reached the children's camp.

The main house, white clapboard and three stories tall, was built right by the road, New England style, placed there to minimize snow shoveling. For the same reason, the out-buildings spread into a chain of interconnected structures: woodshed, then workshop, then a series of barns, all tied together and winding around to enclose a large barnyard. In winter, one could reach all the buildings without going outdoors. Now these buildings had been converted into dormitories, a social hall, and activity rooms.

Some children sat under sugar maples, apparently conversing, but in fact, anxiously scanning the road for the arrival of their parents. Others stood by the road, waiting for the appearance of a familiar car. Isaac was there with his little cousins, Bridget and Lauren. He recognized Bryan at the wheel of an unfamiliar, rented car and waved wildly. Then he indicated where to park on the grass.

There were embraces all around.

"What do you want to see first," Isaac asked. "I know. Let me show you my bunk."

Sam took one of his nieces by the hand, and Bryan took the other. The group tromped behind Isaac across a mown hay field and out to a wooden cabin.

"This is where I'm in charge of my eight 'seniors.' They're thirteen-year-olds," said Isaac, the proud sixteen-year-old.

The small cabin held four double-decker cots and Isaac's single cot, all with tightly tucked-in linens.

"Here," said Belle. "We brought you treats." From a large cloth bag she had been carrying, she shared out boxes of candies, chocolates, and cookies.

"Now take us to the directors. We should pay our respects to them before we do anything else."

Bridget and Lauren went off to stash their treats in their own bunk.

Led by Isaac, the five visitors trooped into the main house, where, in the living room, they met Grace and Manny Granich. Grace was a short, round, cheery woman in her late fifties. Manny, about the same age, was muscular, of medium height with gray hair and a bushy, gray mustache. His most prominent feature was his high cheekbones, which gave him a distinctly Oriental or Slavic appearance. "Scratch a Russian, and you'll find a Tartar," he liked to say. He might just as well have said, "Scratch a Russian Jew, and you'll find the genes left behind from one pogrom or another."

The Granichs stood in front of the brick fireplace, conversing with another set of parents who excused themselves as Manny, recognizing Belle, gave her a warm embrace.

"Manny! At last. It's been so long. I won't say 'you haven't changed a bit.' You have changed, for the better, I believe. Grace seems to have made a man out of you." She said this with a laugh, and Bryan sensed a rare softness in his sister's voice.

"You haven't changed a bit, Belle. You still say the first thing that comes into your mind. Anyway, we're certainly enjoying your son, Isaac," he said. "Slowly, we're putting a little steel into his spine. So, who have we got here? Who are all these people you brought us?"

"My husband, Sam, whom you've never met, I think. My brother Bryan; his wife, Birdie; and their daughter, Joy, who is about to enter college."

"Welcome! Welcome," said Grace. "Let's celebrate," she said, turning to the table on which was a large punch bowl, cookies, and potato chips. "Here, let me pour you a welcome drink. I know who you are, Belle. Manny's told me all about Isaac's mother, the lovely Belle, née Cantor. But tell me something about the rest of your family."

Birdie began to speak about Joy's experience of the past year in a kibbutz. Grace turned to Joy and said, "It sounds like you belong here. Why not stay here for the four weeks left in the season? We can't pay you anything, but you can certainly earn your keep. We'll put you in with the senior girls. Isaac will introduce you to everyone, and you'll feel like part of the place right away, I'm sure."

Birdie and Joy exchanged glances, shook heads, and wordlessly agreed.

"Do it," said Isaac, clapping his hands. "You love it here."

Other parents were constantly arriving by car, so the Granichs excused themselves, leaving Isaac to show them the camp. They went through the barns and the chicken coop full of black-and-white Wyandotte hens. Then they were taken to see the small swimming hole. "It's always leaking, and Manny's always patching it," Isaac said. "He can do anything."

"Oh my God!" Birdie muttered. She put her hands to the side of her head. "I don't believe it! Now I know why his name sounded familiar. I know him! Quick, take me back to the house. No, you don't have to. I know the way."

"What is it, Mother? What's the matter?" Joy asked.

"Later. You go off and explore some more with Isaac and his parents. Bryan and I will go to the farmhouse." She turned and set off at a fevered pace. Puzzled, Bryan followed, unquestioning.

Birdie found Manny in the living room in conversation with two of the parents, an interracial couple. Grace was elsewhere. Birdie ignored the young couple and placed herself directly in front of Manny. She took his two hands in hers and stared at him. "It is you! Isn't it? That was you on the train to Biro-Bidzhan twenty years ago. Wasn't it? Don't you remember me?"

Manny's look of puzzlement gave way to a smile of recognition. He put his arms around Birdie and gave her a bear hug. "Little mother, *matroushka*, you made it! Welcome to Vermont! And this is the man you went there to save?"

"No. Bryan came later." She turned to the couple, whose conversation she had interrupted. "Excuse us. This is the strangest kind of meeting. No. It isn't. We had a stranger meeting in 1933 on the Trans-Siberian Railroad. I was pregnant then. And now I'm going to leave my daughter here!"

"It's a good place to leave your daughter. She'll like it, I'm sure," said the woman.

"Oh," said Manny. "Excuse our behavior. Let me introduce you. Marilyn, Paulie Robeson. Their two kids are somewhere outside. This is Birdie and, it's Bryan, right? Cantor, you said?"

Paulie turned to Birdie and said, in Russian, "Interesno. Dolzhen buite vui govoritye porusski?" (Interesting. You must speak Russian?) Then, in English, he continued, "I went to school in Moscow while my father was touring and singing in Europe."

"Yes, I speak Russian," she answered. Then, turning back to Manny, she gave him another hug. "We have so much to talk about," she said. "Not now. Today, you have your hands full. But after the camp season. When we come back to pick up Joy, we'll swap stories. You'll tell me all about your time in Siberia and then how you got from Russia to Vermont."

"Right, little mother," Manny said, embracing he once more. "Now we're really buddies."

As Birdie and Bryan went out to find the children, Birdie's legs wobbled. Her body, unsteadily reacting to her head's being back in The Soviet Union.

The night was spent in a nearby guesthouse, and the following day, the Cantors and the Greens returned to New York, promising to ship Joy a trunk of clothes immediately.

Thirty-Eight

On Monday morning, by subway, Birdie and Bryan went to the labor exchange in lower Manhattan to hire a demolition crew.

The first man they interviewed was a fifty-year-old Jamaican, whose accented English they could barely understand.

"Motley is my name. Clement Motley." He went on to say that he had many years' experience in all the construction trades and that he could put together a three-man crew of relatives and friends right away. Bryan had misgivings because it was so hard to communicate with the man, but Birdie liked him and insisted they hire him on the spot.

Riding in Motley's station wagon, they drove to Eighty-Eighth Street to look over the project. Motley expressed enthusiasm and said that he and his three-man crew would show up the next morning at nine. "Yes, Mrs. Cantor. We will bring our own tools."

Bryan returned to the Bronx to purchase an automobile, a six-year-old Pontiac sedan. Birdie stayed behind, studying Dick Stein's architectural plans. After communing with the building for an hour, she walked up to Broadway where she purchased a box of crayons. She returned to the house and began to write on the walls, "remove" or "save."

Early the next morning, Bryan and Birdie drove from the Bronx to Manhattan. At nine o'clock, Motley and his crew arrived.

"Did you order a dumpster, Mrs. Cantor?"

"How do I do that? Should it be any special size?"

Motley led her to the pay phone on the corner. He told her what to order, and, after calling "information" for the right numbers, she had a dumpster promised for delivery the next morning.

Motley and his men set to work. By midmorning, Birdie decided that coffee and doughnuts would be appropriate. She sent Bryan up to Broadway to fetch them. When the men finished their coffee break and returned to work, Birdie realized that, in effect, this was going to be "home" for the next several months. "Bryan," she said, "go back and buy us a percolator. And you know what? See if the hardware store has one of those tiny refrigerators—No, what am I saying? This house already has a kitchen. We'll keep it for a while. We won't get rid of the stove and refrigerator until we have to."

Since the dumpster was scheduled to arrive the next morning, Bryan left his car overnight in front of the building to hold a space for it.

It arrived on time and was properly situated in front of the house. Then, in the afternoon, only a few hours later, they were visited by a building inspector, a cheery Irishman.

"Hello," he said in a heavy brogue. "I see that you've started work already. Can I see your building permits now?"

Birdie took him into the old parlor where Dick Stein's plans were spread on a wooden table. "Here's the permit," she said.

"And the permit to put a dumpster out on the street?"

"Doesn't the building permit include doing what has to be done?"

"And you're gonna tell me that the company left a dumpster here, and you without a permit?"

"Oh, I really didn't know I needed a special permit. You couldn't expect me to pile up the rubbish in the street, could you?"

"By gosh and by gee, if this isn't a new excuse. I'm going to have to give you a citation, you know."

"What does that mean, Officer?"

"I'm no officer. I'm a building inspector. And it's going to cost you one hundred dollars each and every day that thing stands there without permission. And from what I hear these days, it takes weeks before the city's going to get around to granting you a new permit."

"Excuse me, sir, I never asked you your name."

"It's Patrick O'Dowd."

"Now, let's think for a moment, Patrick O'Dowd," Birdie said. "I can hear from your accent that you've not been in this country all of your life. My workers are from Jamaica. It's a new life for them too. I just got back from Israel, and I have to learn the ropes here. We're all in this together, aren't we? All trying to make a living here?"

"Yes, we are," said the Irishman. "And a bloody poor living it is. I've got a two-hundred-dollar repair bill on my Cadillac that's sitting out there, and I don't know how I'm going to pay it."

"Well, maybe I can help you," said Birdie. "I can't pay all of it now, but I'd be happy to help you out at fifty dollars a week until it's paid for. And meanwhile, you could help me out by teaching me the ropes because I have absolutely no idea how to steer my way around the city's bureaucracy."

"You mean I should help you out of your predicament and you'll help me with my Cadillac?"

"I mean you'll come by once a week and teach me how I'm supposed to deal with the city."

"I suppose I can be of help to you. Sure."

"Good. We're all about to take a coffee break. Will you have a cup?"

"Certainly. With pleasure."

Patrick O'Dowd showed up on each of the following four weeks to collect his fifty dollars. Then, it appeared, his Cadillac kept on having unexpected problems, which necessitated continual payments, always fifty dollars. Nonetheless, it turned out that he was, in fact, quite helpful at keeping the work moving without interruptions.

The work progressed, and Birdie learned quickly. Besides being a good worker, Motley was a talented teacher. He taught unobtrusively, managing to suggest changes in such a way as to imply that the ideas were actually Birdie's innovations.

Bryan was there, at her side, always ready to purchase lumber, nails, or a missing tool; to bring in pizza or doughnuts; or to deliver forms to the building department.

THIRTY-NINE

Joy was away at college. Birdie and Bryan were on their way to a party at Lilly and Christopher's apartment in Harlem to celebrate the publication of Christopher's novel *Steel Town*.

Bryan found a parking place a block away, and as they began walking uphill, hand in hand, Birdie whispered, "I can't help it, Bryan. I'm always nervous when we come here. I feel like an intruder. We're the only white people on the block. I'm sure they all look at us and wonder what we are doing here.'"

"Nonsense!" Bryan said. "My sister lives here, doesn't she? We won't be the only white people. Sam and Belle are coming. Lee and Becky too, I think. Lots of others too. You'll see."

They climbed to the third floor, and even before they entered Lilly and Christopher's apartment, they could tell it was already overflowing with people. The air was thick with cigarette smoke. Several couples stood out in the hall, conversing. Among these couples, Birdie recognized Manny and Grace Granich.

"Max, I mean Manny!" she said, hugging him warmly and then kissing Grace. "What are you doing here in New York?"

"We came to honor Christopher, of course. Remember, he's the father of two of our favorite campers," Grace answered.

"We'll go inside and pay our respects; then we'll talk," Bryan said as he pulled Birdie into the apartment.

Inside, they recognized and greeted Paulie and Marilyn Robeson. Joseph North, the beloved columnist for the *Daily Worker*, was there as a friend. He too was a Higley Hill parent, as, apparently, were many children of the Communist Party leadership.

Birdie was torn, so many people she would have wanted to sit down with for a long conversation, but with all the drinking and storytelling the noise was deafening.

Then someone tapped a knife against his wineglass, ringing for quiet. "Speech, speech!" and cries of "Let the man talk!" were heard. Once relative silence was achieved, a heavyset fellow, with an air of authority, stood in front of the window and spoke.

"Christopher's novel is a masterpiece. The story of how the comrades, locked in jail, were able to agitate for the freeing of a youth sentenced to hang on a framed-up charge...Christopher, it was worth all the time you spent in jail to have produced this book."

This proposition elicited considerable laughter and some cheering. The speaker waited for quiet and then resumed, "And now, Christopher, I have an announcement that will be news even to you. Our press, Masses and Mainstream, is pleased to have you as one of our authors. But, I'm afraid, the next time you write a book, there may be some conflict of interest involved in our choosing to publish it. That's because we are, as of today, appointing you to our editorial board!"

Applause, cheers, and whistles followed the announcement.

It was Christopher's turn to speak.

"I want to thank you all for coming. Comrade Aptheker, I am thrilled at my promotion and I sincerely thank you. It is customary for an author to thank those who made it all possible, and I want to do just that. First comes my lovely wife, Lilly, who encouraged me all of the way; my daughters, Lauren and Bridget, who had to be as quiet as mice while Daddy was writing; and all of those comrades who did time with me in Pittsburgh. What an experience that was! What you'll read in the book is..."

Belle turned to her husband, Sam, and whispered, "Isn't he going to say anything about your contribution? About your keeping the family fed and housed while he wrote the book?"

"No," Sam answered. "And I wouldn't expect him to. He considers it to be no less than he deserves. I earn money while he works to make the world a better place."

At the same time, Birdie, who was standing by the door, was invited out into the hall by Paulie. "Let's practice our Russian," he said in that language.

"Gladly," she answered in Russian. "I can't stand all of the noise."

They talked about camp. They talked about work. Birdie learned that Paulie was a trained engineer who translated technical papers from Russian into English. "Except, that is, when I'm helping my father, organizing his concerts or speeches."

Gradually, the guests began to leave.

Bryan sought out Manny.

"So, you spent some of the same years in Russia that I did!"

"Yes, but I understand that you were a correspondent. You led a privileged life. I was roughing it, trying to build things in the most primitive conditions."

"Sort of like Vermont today?" Bryan joked.

"No. Not at all. I'll tell you how primitive it was. We were setting up oil rigs. The trucks were old. The mechanics were all peasants, ignorant peasants. When the time came to change the spark plugs, it was so cold they could hardly hold a wrench. So instead of screwing the spark plugs into the threads on the engine block, they preferred to keep their gloves on and to drive those plugs into place by pounding them with a hammer!"

"I've never changed a spark plug," Bryan said, "though I'd know better than that! But let me tell you, I've come across Soviet bureaucrats who came from the same peasant stock. I can tell you stories too."

Birdie came up to them. She felt real affection for Manny, but had no desire to talk with him about her own years in Russia. She was quite content to let the men swap tales while she listened.

Once they were seated in the car, on their way home, Birdie apologized to Bryan. "I was so wrong to have scary feelings about being in Harlem. It was a wonderful afternoon. Exciting people. Imagine, me talking Russian with Paul Robeson's son!"

"And Manny Granich," Bryan replied. "What a life he's led."

"Hey, Bryan, us too. We've led ourselves quite a life."

"You have, Birdie. My life feels kind of empty."

"Oh, Bryan. Stop feeling sorry for yourself. You know that those thoughts don't get you anywhere."

FORTY

Sam was pleased with the way his proteges were learning their new trade. He was so happy with the results of their work, that in early spring, with the job nearly completed, Sam and Belle announced that they would move into the lower rear apartment.

Before the job was finished, Dick Stein, who periodically checked on the work, stopped by to say that one of his Croton neighbors had just bought a home in Brooklyn Heights and wanted to convert it into apartments. "I'm drawing the plans, and I recommended that you do the job. Maybe you know him?" Dick said. "Sy Goldman? Lee and Becky know him well. Seems he doesn't have much money to pay you, but maybe you can get together and work something out."

On that weekend, Bryan and Birdie drove up to Croton to meet Sy Goldman at Lee and Becky's cottage.

When they got there, the first thing they noticed was that the three small windows on the south-facing wall had been replaced by two enormous plate-glass windows and that with the trees still bare, one could look out across the valley and see the Hudson River, perhaps three miles away.

"It's magnificent! I approve. You've transformed the cottage," said Bryan.

"Yes," Becky said. "It's like this. You have a daughter. Lilly has two of them. Belle has a son. And we have a place in the country. How about that? But I've got exciting news to tell you, even more exciting than our new windows. I've been offered a job teaching at a private school up here in Croton. I start in September."

"Good for you," said Birdie. "First, you'll turn this place into a palace; then you'll abandon the city and move up here for good."

"Yes—" Becky began to answer, but stopped when she heard someone knock on the front door.

Lee opened it.

It was Sy Goldman, who arrived alone. Lee introduced him and said, "Birdie, Bryan, you guys go ahead and talk. Get to know each other. This might be a marriage made in heaven. We'll see. While you're talking, I'll bring in an armful of wood and get a fire lit."

They learned that Sy Goldman was an accountant, about the same age as Bryan.

"Let's start right in. I'll explain the whole proposition," Sy began. "One of my clients needed to sell his building, a great location, Brooklyn Heights. His parents lived in it. In fact, he was born there. Now his parents have moved to Florida. He came to me with all his records and asked me how much I thought he should ask for it. I went over the man's figures and decided I'd like to buy it myself. I told Dick Stein what I was thinking and he said that he'd be happy to draw up the conversion plans. Then he recommended you two to be my contractors."

There was another hour of discussion, the result of which was that Bryan and Birdie agreed to become partners in the deal. Bryan and Birdie were to buy into the deal for half of Sy's down payment. They would do the remodeling for no salary. Sy would advance the construction costs, and they would become equal partners.

Sy offered to have his lawyer draw up a contract. Birdie insisted that, as part of the arrangement, a new deed be drawn up, making Bryan and her half owners of the property.

"Now, hold on," said Sy. "Suppose that you walk away or that you aren't able to finish the job. Why should you own half of the house?"

"Right. Good," said Birdie. "Here's what we'll do. Let the deed take effect when and if we do finish on time and at an agreed-upon cost. I'm sure your lawyer can figure out how to do that. OK?"

"It sounds right. Let me discuss it with my wife, Sylvia, and then run it past my lawyer. It's a pleasure to have met you both, and I think that we have something good here. I'll call you tomorrow evening at the latest. And thanks, Becky and Lee, for getting us together."

As Sy left, Bryan turned to Birdie and said, "Are you sure about what you're getting us into? The down payment comes to just about everything that we earned in the last six months at Eighty-Eighth Street. Are you willing to risk everything we have?"

"Yes," Birdie said. "I think we should do it."

Becky said, "I don't know anything about the numbers, but I know that Sy and Sylvia are good people. You'll like knowing them, and you'll probably like working with Sy."

"Make me a drink, big brother Lee. Scotch," Bryan said.

"I'll make it," Becky said, "then I'll make us dinner."

"Come outside first," said Lee. "I want to show you where we think we can dig a pool."

"You two go," Bryan said. "I need to stay here with Becky and drink while I adjust to the idea that we just gave away all the profits we made on Eighty-Eighth Street."

Birdie and her brother-in-law put on their coats and stepped out into the pleasant April dusk. Lee led Birdie to a spot where the ground sloped down from the house. A split-rail fence separated the cut lawn from a pasture all overgrown with brambles, sumac, and cedars. They leaned up against the top rail, and Lee said, "That's where we plan to excavate and put in a pool. Pretty, huh? Nothing but woods and fields for miles."

Lee moved behind Birdie. He pressed his body against hers. He reached around her and slid one of his hands inside her coat. He held her breast while pressing her against the wooden railings and grinding his crotch into her backside. For a couple of seconds, Birdie absorbed the closeness of his body. Then she removed his hand, freed herself from his grip, and said, "Stop it, Lee! Don't be foolish."

"You want me, don't you, Birdie? I know that my little brother doesn't give you what I can give you."

Birdie slapped Lee, and as she did, she remembered the first time she had met Lee, when the two brothers greeted each other with resounding slaps to the cheek.

Lee smiled back, pleasantly.

"You're incorrigible, Lee. We're going back to the house. Stop acting like a child. No. You are a child. Enough. No more of this."

The working relationship with Sy Goldman proved to be pleasingly free of conflict. He kept the books and wrote out the paychecks. Motley and his crew worked easily with Birdie, still teaching her the ropes, but by then quite willing to take her suggestions seriously. Bryan was always at her side, ready to do whatever was asked of him.

Birdie was discovering that she had a good eye for layout. It was a family joke that as soon as she walked into a room, she began rearranging the furniture. Now Birdie found herself rearranging Dick Stein's placement of walls or closets. Generally, he accepted her changes, if not with approval, then always with good grace.

FORTY-ONE

They came home on a Friday evening, tired but pleased at the progress being made on the Brooklyn Heights conversion. Birdie prepared a simple supper from a box of noodles and cheese, which they ate, listening to the radio news.

An ending to the saga of Julius and Ethel Rosenberg seemed to be near. Accused of spying for the Russians, the couple was awaiting execution at nearby Sing Sing Penitentiary. New developments in the worldwide attempt to delay their electrocution seemed to offer hope, only to be denied or ignored.

Birdie and Bryan were still at the supper table when the front door opened and Joy let herself the apartment, accompanied by a young man.

"Mom, Dad, meet Eric Dean. I hoped you would be home when we got here. Eric drove me down from college. We want to crash here for the night, and then early in the morning, we're driving to Washington for the demonstration.

"You could have phoned, you know," Bryan said.

"Yes, but we were coming anyway. I have my own key. Why waste money on a phone call?"

"You know what you should have done?" Birdie said. "You can let me know you are coming without wasting your money on the telephone.

Next time, you should telephone collect, person-to-person. Ask for 'Joy Cumming.' Then, when I say she isn't here, you say, 'I'll try again at seven.'"

"Anyway," Bryan interjected, "I'm glad that you are going to Washington." He turned to Joy's young man, whose heavy glasses contrasted with his tight crew cut. "And I'm glad to meet you, son," he said. "Are your intentions toward my daughter honorable?"

"That's his sense of humor, Eric; you aren't expected to answer him. And welcome," said Birdie.

In conversation, they learned that Eric was five years older than Joy and employed as a courtroom stenographer in Queens. He had previously spent a few years in the merchant marine. Joy and he met in one of her college hangouts when he was upstate, visiting his older brother, a chicken farmer. Eric noticed the chessboard all set up and offered to play a game with Bryan. They played two games, and Bryan was pleased to win both of them. Having beaten Joy's young man twice, Bryan began to look upon him with much more favor, despite a suspicion that Eric had not been trying his best to win.

Joy slept in her room, and Eric slept on the living room couch. They left the house early, while Bryan and Birdie were still in bed and by eight in the morning were driving south on the New Jersey Turnpike. Many cars displayed placards reading "Clemency for the Rosenbergs." Coming in the opposite direction were a few cars with hastily scrawled papers saying, "Fry 'Em."

The car radio was tuned to WQXR for the hourly news reports. The first thing they heard was that while they slept, the night before, Supreme Court Justice William O. Douglas, while on a mountain-climbing vacation in the west, had granted a stay of the execution.

"Oh my God!" Joy felt herself filled with pleasure. "Two days before their electrocution. Can you believe it?"

Approaching the outskirts of Washington, their mood went from exaltation to despair as the radio reported that Chief Justice Vinson had called an emergency session of the entire court. All the justices, except for Douglas, returned from their vacations and overruled his stay. The execution was to take place the following day.

Eric parked in a lot, and they headed for the demonstration in front of the White House. It no longer felt like a demonstration. Rather, it had become a vigil. Joy was handed a placard with Picasso's dove of peace. Eric picked up one that said, "Innocent." A large banner read, "The Pope urges clemency."

They remained in front of the White House until the warm June sun had set, and then they drove back to New York.

"Don't make up the couch tonight, Mom. Eric will sleep in my room."

Birdie didn't object.

"Our little girl is grown up, I guess," Bryan said as he and Birdie got into their own bed.

"But do we like him? I can't make up my mind," she answered.

"Well, this is only the first fellow she's brought home. Maybe he's not the last."

In the morning, Birdie cooked her specialty, matzoh brie with apple sauce and sour cream. They all sat around the apartment until early afternoon, listening to the radio for any new developments. There weren't any, except that they heard about protest demonstrations taking place around the world.

In recognition of religious sensibilities, the execution was being delayed until sundown, the end of the Jewish Sabbath.

At four o'clock, the four of them went by subway to Union Square, site of a final vigil. Birdie, Bryan, Joy, and Eric were surrounded by a large crowd of likeminded folk of all ages. Joy recognized Susie North, who had been a counselor with her at the summer camp. They hugged each other, and Susie told her it was her senior prom night, but she and her friends were here, in Union Square. "Dancing? You've got to be kidding," Susie said.

The sun sank lower toward the Hudson River and behind the Palisades of New Jersey. It was a glorious evening. The sky was a blaze of red, orange, and yellow. It was all over. Silence. Everyone went home. Eric drove Joy back to New Paltz.

It was nearly midnight when Joy got back to her dormitory, one of the temporary prefabricated structures that had been put up to house the flood of GIs returning from the war and now showing every sign of becoming a permanent fixture on the campus. Her roommate, Doris, was out. Her other roommate, Eloise, the daughter of an upstate dairy farmer, greeted her sarcastically. "So you weren't able to save them, were you?"

"Do me a favor, Eloise. Go bugger yourself."

"They were spies, you know. Someday, we all may be dead, just because they gave the bomb to the Russians."

"Eloise, you're full of shit. I told you and I told you again, it isn't that simple. First, there isn't any such thing as 'the secret of the bomb.' And if there was, the Rosenbergs wouldn't have understood it anyway. And nobody has ever been killed before for spying in peacetime. The only reason the government killed them is because they wouldn't back down and give the names of other progressives. Now we've got the whole civilized world cursing us. And I'm going to bed. To hell with what you think!"

The day of the Rosenbergs' funeral was damp, windy, and cold. All day, the rain fell, paused, and then fell some more.

Eric and Joy drove down from New Paltz, first to the Cantors, and then all four drove to the grave site on Long Island. They arrived early enough to watch the hearse pass through the cemetery's iron gates. They followed, parked along the lane, and found themselves quite close to the open pit. They watched the attendants lower the two coffins, simple pine boxes according to Jewish tradition. They stood close enough so that they could clearly hear the rabbi recite Kaddish, the prayer for the dead. Prayers were not a part of Joy's heritage, but the Hebrew she had learned in Israel remained with her and though Kaddish was recited in the ancient Aramaic tongue, when the rabbi came to the part where he spoke of the cause of death, Joy clearly understood the Hebrew words that he used *"Sh nisrafu al yaday ha rotschim,"* (who were burnt at the hands of the murderers).

The first shovelfuls of earth were thrown onto the coffins. Ethel Rosenberg's mother tore herself away from those who had been supporting her and threw herself, wailing, onto the pile of loose earth. Birdie thought that she looked just like her own, tiny, frail, and blind mother, Clara.

Aside from the mourners in attendance on that blustery, wet morning, there must have been agents of the government, keeping track, taking pictures, and recording license numbers because, a week later, Eric received a letter from the city informing him that his job as a court stenographer was terminated.

FORTY-TWO

Sy Goldman, their partner in the Brooklyn Heights remodeling, was thrilled to see the work finished on time and profitably.

Birdie's nephew Ernest was about to marry his high-school sweetheart, Bridget.

"Let's take them on a vacation. It will be their honeymoon. We'll drive together to Florida and rent a cabin on the beach."

"Birdie, you're being silly. Ernest and Bridget don't want us to come with them on their honeymoon."

"Of course they do, Bryan. You'll see."

It turned out that she was right. It was an enjoyable trip, and for Birdie and Bryan, the first of many visits to Florida.

When they returned home, Birdie decided that they were ready to work for themselves. "I'm going to find us a building that we can remodel just for ourselves. We've got to keep Motley and his crew busy, or else we'll lose them. And who knows? Maybe we'll even want to live in it."

Within the week, she had located a town house on Thirteenth Street, just off of Fifth Avenue. She negotiated a low down payment and a manageable mortgage. The work went well, and even before the project was finished, Bryan and Birdie moved out of their Bronx apartment and into the rear ground floor. Their bedroom opened to a sunny, south-facing yard surrounded by a seven-foot wooden fence.

They had been living there a week when a building inspector arrived. He expressed horror and indignation that they had moved in before a certificate of occupancy had been issued.

Birdie argued with him.

"What do you mean when you say we are 'living here'? We aren't 'living here' yet. We are still building the house. We are working here. There's a difference."

"I'm sorry, lady; the law doesn't recognize the difference. You can't live here without a CO, and you can't get a CO until the job is finished and I've inspected and approved it."

"But the work can't get finished unless we are here to finish it. Certainly, you understand that, don't you?"

"It doesn't matter what I understand. I'm going to write you up, and if you aren't out of here right away, you're going to jail."

"Now, hold on a moment. Take a deep breath. I see from your wedding ring that you are a family man. Do you have children?"

"What are you trying to say?"

"My daughter is about to get married. Her wedding is next month. It's going to be right here, in the garden. Do you know what kind of incredible pressure we are under? Have you ever married off a daughter?"

"Three of them!"

"Then you do understand. Listen, we want you to help make the wedding possible, not to put us in jail. Not now, of all times. We want you to come to Joy's wedding. You'll see how nice the place is going to be. And you shouldn't bring her a present. Instead, we want to buy a nice wedding gift for each of your three daughters. Is that reasonable?"

"It's reasonable. I'll be there. You tell me when."

The afternoon wedding between Joy and Eric took place, as scheduled, in the sunny garden behind the nearly completed home. The building inspector did attend and was pleased with the size of the gift Birdie gave "for his daughters."

Bryan was upset by Eric's refusal to wear a tie, but Eric insisted that it was too warm for that.

The rabbi wrapped a cloth napkin around a wineglass and had Eric stamp on it. "This is so that at the moment of your highest happiness, you shall not forget the destruction of the temple, nor our people's sufferings," he said.

Sam whispered to Belle, "Maybe. And maybe it signifies the breaking of the hymen and man's dominion over woman."

"Hush!" she whispered back.

As soon as Joy and Eric were declared "man and wife," twenty-one year-old Isaac gathered up the glass shards, intending to save them for his cousin, but Joy refused to accept the gift, saying, "Foolishness. I couldn't care less."

Isaac, reasoning that someday Joy would feel different, preserved the pieces of glass himself, throughout the five years that the marriage lasted.

More jobs followed. People heard about Birdie and Bryan's work and sought their services. They undertook to renovate a second brownstone in Manhattan, again in partnership with Sy Goldman.

That was where they were, in the afternoon, waiting for news of Joy's imminent delivery, when Birdie got the phone call from Eric, calling from Mount Saini Hospital. "It's twins, just as we thought, boys, both of them, but not identical. We named them Carlo and Jeffery."

"How's Joy? Is she awake?"

"She was awake. Now she's sleeping. She's fine."

"Don't go anywhere. We're coming right away."

That night, Bryan seemed moody, even more so than was usual for him.

"What's the matter, Bryan? Do you think that you're old, now that we are grandparents?"

"Hold me, Birdie," he said, sitting on the side of the bed.

She held him tight and then began to rock him in her arms. "We have such a good life!" she said. "For the first time in our lives, we have enough money, we have each other, and we have a family. We have this beautiful home. Why are you so unhappy, Bryan?"

He wasn't able to answer her. But over a number of days, it came out that Bryan felt the need to escape.

"Escape from what, Bryan? Do you want to escape from me?"

"No. From all this pressure. From the city. Maybe something like what Lee and Becky have. A place we can go to, but with water. A place that feels far away."

Lee introduced them to a real estate agent who promised she could find them, "Just what you're looking for." On their second excursion, she brought them to a lakeside bungalow colony, outside of Peekskill. The property had everything they were looking for on one-third of an acre: a two-bedroom cottage and sixty feet of waterfront, a short wooden dock, and a garage that could be converted into living space. As the agent led them toward the water, Bryan whispered to Birdie, "Tell her we'll take it!"

"Hush, Bryan. It isn't done that way. First, we make an offer and they reject it but come up with a counteroffer. We say, 'That's the best we can do. Take it or leave it.' Then we see what happens."

Bryan was in agony for the three weeks that it took to reach an agreement. The final price was not much higher than Birdie's first offer.

Motley came out, without his crew, to renovate the garage. Bryan busied himself planting beds of geraniums and impatiens in every likely place. He dug up masses of wild-growing day lilies, which he replanted by the water.

Bryan spent most of his time there, puttering, planting, and fixing things. He built stone terraces to create additional flower beds.

Birdie, meanwhile, spent her days in the city. She finished the paperwork on their latest project and interviewed prospective tenants for vacancies in the three remodeled brownstones they now managed.

Most days, Bryan drove Birdie to the bus in the morning and picked her up in the afternoon, but there was a prospective tenant who sounded promising, whom she could interview only in the evening, so one morning, Birdie said, "I'll stay in the city tonight, Bryan. There is fried chicken and potato salad in the refrigerator for your supper. In the morning, you can poach an egg, or there are hard-boiled eggs that you might want. Why don't you eat lunch out? I'll see you tomorrow afternoon."

The interview went well. Birdie offered the lady a two-year lease, providing her references checked out.

Back in the Twelfth Street apartment, Birdie lit herself a cigarette and scanned the bookshelf for something to read. Bryan had been reading *Mission to Moscow*, a memoir by Ambassador Davies, written in the thirties. She took it to a stuffed easy chair, and as soon as she opened the book, she found a long note, written by Bryan.

Thoughts...in an hour of severe indigestion...

I would like to wail and scream, beat my breast, and tear my hair. I would like to let my agony show and not suffocate it. And I would want this expression of myself to be communicated to someone who is away from me, who will not respond, not comment, not weigh and measure, correct style and punctuation, not even know me at all. Simply read and feel and be a receptacle for me. But a receptacle that will feel exactly in proportion to my feelings. Someone, or better, thinking thing...better thing, than person, because no person can act this role. What person can know my pain without relating it to his own, and thereby diminishing mine? This is not what I need, because my pain is too enormous to be diminished. *My horror of life is too real and true.* I resent having this truth distorted by the occasional optimism forced on me by occasional good feeling, good health, good spirits, and other deceptions. I know that life is more worthless than worthwhile, more ugly than beautiful, more cruel than kind, more insane than sane. I know it with certainty. When I see that men are mad and always have been mad, then I understand that every other judgment about this fact is made to hide this fact. I know and resent, that I too, having as many or more weaknesses as others, make such lying judgments in order to bear living. This I do and everyone does to suppress the truth, to shove it back.

She read the note with growing horror. She reread it. She cried.

That poor man. I knew he was unhappy. I had no idea how unhappy. Oh, he needs me. I'll never understand the world he is living in. Thank God! But how he needs me!

This thought, how much he needed her, comforted her somewhat. She put the note back into the book and returned *Mission to Moscow* to its place in the bookcase. Then she picked up the telephone and dialed Bryan.

"Sweetheart, I got everything done. I can still catch the late bus. You'll come pick me up at the bus station?"

FORTY-THREE

On a Saturday in February, Belle and Sam drove out to the Lake Mohegan cottage where a well-laid fire was blazing in the newly constructed brick hearth.

Bryan and Birdie were outdoors, gathering additional firewood.

"Welcome. *Zdrastvuitye*, hello!" Birdie called out as Belle and Sam emerged from their little Nash automobile.

"Don't you dare speak that language to me," Belle hissed at her sister-in-law. The words were spoken in anger, but at the same time, her eyes sparkled and there was a tinge of sarcasm in her voice.

"Yes," said Bryan. "We read Khruschev's speech denouncing Comrade Stalin too. Read it this morning." He said this with an injured grimace that was not at all masked by his mustache.

"Does your anger mean that now, all of a sudden, you are willing to believe what we read in the *New York Times*? Are we accepting it as gospel?" Birdie asked.

"Yes...No! Maybe this time they are telling the truth," Belle answered. "I'm afraid Khruschev really did say it. Every bit of it. But, you know...truthfully...we knew most of it ourselves, all along. So Stalin really was a tyrant—a monster—out of control. But still, he was on the right side. You can't forget that for a moment."

"Not here in the cold," Sam said. "Are you going to invite us in, or do we have to settle our politics before we go inside?"

Not moving, Belle continued to express her thoughts. "Khruschev's speech can't be a good thing. It's going to take me time to sort this out."

Soon they were seated in front of the fire, and Bryan took up the evaluation where they had left off.

"We all knew this, most of it at least, twenty some years ago, in Moscow. We didn't want to know it. But we knew most of it."

Sam observed, "This is going to be an excuse for a lot of people to turn tail, to say they were misguided all of these years and that the Communists really were the bad guys all along."

"If they do, they'll be terribly wrong," Belle said.

Birdie had nothing to add to the topic. She never liked to talk about those days. "Get it out of your systems," she said. "The kids will be here soon, and once the babies arrive, nobody's going to have time to talk politics."

Before noon, Joy and her family did arrive. She and Eric wheeled the twins in their matching carriages to the front of the house. Even when sleeping, the difference in the twins was apparent. Carlo looked like his mother, Jeffery like his father. Awake, the difference was even more striking. Carlo was placid. He was quick to return a smile, while Jeffery, the image of his father, was colicky, frustrated, and unresponsive.

Bryan held the front door open, making way for the perambulators and the other relatives gathered close to greet the newcomers. Joy put her finger to her lips, signaling for silence. "They're sleeping," she whispered.

Only when Joy and her mother pushed the two carriages into the bedroom and disappeared behind the shut door did talk resume.

"You're looking well, Eric," Sam said. "Have you found a job yet?"

"Yes. Sort of - a job here and a job there. Nothing permanent. I have a buddy who is doing a book about diving in the Florida Keys, and he wants me to go with him and take the pictures. I'll be going down with him next week."

After lunch was served, Eric put on his jacket and headed for the dock where he spent the rest of the afternoon fishing for sunfish, while the others fussed about with the twins.

Within a few days, Belle returned to her old ways and could once more hear the Russian language without feeling discomfort.

Lee and Becky moved into their upstate home to live year-round, passing their two-bedroom, rent-controlled apartment on to Joy, Eric, and the twins. Soon, Eric began to disappear for longer and longer stretches, always telling Joy, "I'm going off with my friend to help him with his latest project. We'll be back in a day or so." He stayed away a bit longer each time and often failed to come home when he promised.

Finally, returning a full week late, without ever having called home, he found that Joy had changed the locks on the door.

"No more, Eric. We're finished! I want you out of my life," Joy shouted from behind the locked door.

Eric banged on the door and kicked at it for almost an hour. Terrified, Joy called her parents, who came right over and found Eric still banging on the door.

"Do we call the cops right now?" Bryan asked him. "The station house is only a few doors away. They'll take you away and charge you with abuse. Or will you go away for now? Then we'll go in and see if we can find out what Joy is up to. But not until you start down the stairs, Eric."

Eric considered Bryan's words and left, saying, "I'll be back later."

Joy opened the door, just a crack, and gestured for her parents to come in quickly. They entered, and from behind the closed door of one of the bedrooms, they heard crying. Birdie went through the door and a minute later came back carrying the howling Jeffery.

"Carlo is sound asleep," she said.

Joy brought a bottle from the refrigerator. She put Jeffery into one of the carriages, propped a nipple in his mouth, supported the bottle with a throw pillow from the couch, and then sat down on that couch, glaring at her mother.

"Now what?" asked Bryan. "What does this mean, Joy?"

"It means that I can't live with him another minute. He's out. I'm here."

"How will you get along?"

"Daddy, do you know how many of my neighbors are on welfare? Do you know what food stamps are? I'll make it. It's OK."

"No, Zoyshinka," Birdie said calmly. "Our family doesn't need welfare and food stamps, thank God. We are doing well, and we can take care of you—if you can take care of yourself. Enough of your Eric. You brought him home, and we accepted him, but good riddance. Now, if you want to, you can tell us. Has he been hitting you?"

"You knew all the time, didn't you, Mommy?"

"And now I'll tell you what is going to happen. You are going to go back to school, here in the city. You'll finish your degree, and you'll be a schoolteacher. Until then, we'll take care of you and the babies."

"Mother! Stop telling me what to do with my life!

"I'm telling you, and I will tell you until you finish what you started. When you finish school, I'll stop telling you."

It worked out much the way Birdie willed it to happen. Joy transferred her credits to New York University and completed her course.

Her parents meanwhile paid living expenses, hired a nanny, and spent a great deal of time with the grandchildren.

Twenty-year-old Isaac threw out the glass shards he had been saving since his cousin's wedding.

Frequently, Birdie was approached by friends or by friends of friends, who offered her real estate deals. Bryan was ready to undertake another remodeling project, but Birdie demurred. "Enough, Bryan. We've done it, and we've made some money. We have rent checks coming in every month. Now it's more important to figure out what to do with that money."

That was when Birdie began investing in the stock market. She started out by getting advice from one of her Croton neighbors who was the economics editor of Christopher's Marxist magazine. He told her, "The coming depression is right around the corner. It will be sooner rather than later." Therefore, he insisted that her money be placed only in ultra-safe bonds. "Take no risks."

But his was not the only advice she got. Birdie had a large circle of friends, and she was constantly listening for tips. Soon, she was buying and selling stocks on a regular basis and doing very well at it. After a while, she had no more use for her Marxist advisor.

FORTY-FOUR

Joy completed her degree and began teaching at a private school in Manhattan. She also acquired a new husband, Richard Johnson.

When Joy and Eric took over Uncle Lee's apartment, Richard Johnson was already living in the adjoining apartment with his wife. Coincidentally, about the same time Joy threw Eric out of the house, Richard was in the process of divorcing his wife. Within a few months of the two divorces, Richard and Joy had become a couple. At the end of the year, they were married, and soon thereafter, Richard cut a passageway into the wall between their two apartments, resulting in one spacious apartment. So, by the time the twins turned six, each had his own private bedroom and an attentive stepfather who radiated sweetness.

On a summer afternoon in 1959, Birdie and Bryan were at their cottage, sitting on their dock, on wooden Adirondack chairs, when, from the house, they heard the phone. Bryan went in to take the call. "It's from Vermont!" he yelled out to his wife, then, into the phone, he said, "Of course you can come. You are always welcome. What time will you get here?...We'll be thrilled to meet her. Bye."

"Was it Isaac? Were you talking to our little nephew?"

"Not so little anymore. He called from the summer camp, Higley Hill. It's his day off, and he wants to come down with a girlfriend. They should be here by ten."

"Good. It's about time he had a girlfriend to show us."

Just before ten, their guests arrived.

"This is Annie O'Neil. She's our assistant cook this summer."

"You're welcome to our home," Birdie said. "Anyone who is a friend of our wonderful nephew is a friend of ours."

Birdie brought out a snack, cold fried chicken and potato salad, which the newcomers ate with the gusto that comes from escaping a summer of institutional food. Then they settled in the living room, Isaac and Annie on the couch, holding hands. Isaac told how it felt to be head counselor. He went on to say, "Grace and Manny are getting old. Tired. Ready to retire. I think they're hoping that soon I'll run the camp for them."

"You'll be good at it," Bryan said.

"Well, by the end of next year, I'll have my teacher's certificate. It's possible."

"What about you, Annie? Tell us about yourself," Birdie asked.

"Not much to tell. A good Catholic education. I was just graduated from Hunter with a degree in home economics, and when I saw the advertisement on their bulletin board for 'assistant cook in a summer camp,' I jumped at it. That's how I met Isaac," she said, squeezing his hand and smiling at him.

"Have you met his parents yet?" Birdie asked.

Isaac answered for her, "No. You're easier. Soon though."

Bryan scratched his mustache, ruffled his dark hair, and said, "It won't be all that hard. Funny how things work out. Now, suddenly, we have a Catholic son-in-law. We love him. It works. I don't think Sam and Belle will have any problem with you bringing home a non-practicing Catholic. After all, they believe in the brotherhood of man, you know."

"But are you a non-practicing Catholic?" Birdie asked.

"Interestingly, my mother didn't want me to go to Hunter College. She said I'd lose my faith if I did. Actually, there wasn't much faith left to lose by then."

Bryan was right about how well Annie would be received by Sam and Belle. They embraced her warmly, and within a year, Annie and Isaac were married.

Both found jobs teaching in the city.

The first summer after their marriage, Annie was again assistant cook, and by then, Isaac was functioning as program director.

By the end of that summer, it was arranged. Grace and Manny would retire and sell the property to the newlyweds. Grace and Manny would stay on as tenants through the winter while the Greens finished their teaching commitments, then, by the following spring, the Graniches would be gone and Isaac and Annie would quit their jobs to become year-round Vermonters.

Birdie was thrilled by Isaac's new career—camp director, amateur farmer, and country dweller. She couldn't wait to become part of the undertaking. The day the deed was signed, Birdie asked Isaac and Annie to supper. "Come by this evening. Can you make it by six o'clock? We've got a ton of ideas we want to discuss with you."

That evening, before supper, at the table, and after supper, Birdie overwhelmed her guests with ideas.

"You know," she said, "how I love that camp. The summer Joy spent there may have been the best summer of her life. And I'm so happy that now, you'll be the ones running it. But you have to admit that it's been a long time since Manny did anything to spruce the place up."

"Yes. You're probably right," Isaac said. "But we can't go up there and start rearranging things all of a sudden. Not while Grace and Manny are still living there."

"OK," Birdie submitted, "but let's go up there for a weekend real soon and study out what has to be done."

A week later, on a Friday, after Isaac and Annie finished teaching school, the four drove up to camp in Bryan's car. It was ten at night when they arrived.

"Welcome," Manny said. Hugs and kisses were exchanged. "Welcome to your new home," Grace said. "Just think of us as squatters. We'll be leaving when the weather turns warm. Supper? Can I fix you anything?"

"No. But thanks," Birdie said. "We stopped and ate on the way up."

"Well, let me pour us drinks," said Manny. "Wine for the young folks? I'm gonna pour vodka for those of us who shared a time in Russia, yes?"

"Not me," said Grace. "I've never been there, remember, Manny? It must've been some other woman you're remembering from those days. I'll have wine."

When they were all seated and with drinks, Birdie said, "I hope, Grace and Manny, that we aren't making you uncomfortable, coming up here and suggesting changes, after all the years you've become accustomed to the place."

Grace and Manny exchanged glances. Manny hunched his shoulders and shrugged, as if to say, "What will be will be." Instead, he lifted his glass and proposed, "A toast. In with the new, out with the old."

The next morning, after wandering from room to room in the main house, Birdie developed a list of suggestions. "I have a pretty good idea of what we have to do," she said. "After lunch, we'll start on the outbuildings and look at the bunks too."

Sunday, after breakfast, they thanked their hosts and parted for New York.

In the spring, as planned, Grace and Manny packed their belongings and departed. That weekend, Birdie and Bryan again accompanied Isaac and Annie to Vermont. The plan was for Birdie and Bryan to remain there for a couple of weeks. Sunday, the young Greens would take the train back to the city, and the following day, Motley would arrive. Isaac would be paying Motley's salary. This time, Birdie felt no constraints at taking out her crayons and marking up the walls.

"Look, here, just where I planned it. See? It's all drawn out. Motley can open up two pass-throughs, one for the platters that get carried to the tables and the other for dirty dishes coming back; that will be a great start," she said.

"And what you really need is a little washroom, right here in the pantry, as you come in."

"No," Isaac demurred. "We have enough toilets in the place. That's low on our priorities."

"Think about poor Grace. All these years, she worked in this kitchen, and every time she needed to go to the bathroom, she had to go up the stairs or outside to one of the other buildings."

"Maybe you're right, Birdie. It was hard for her. But not this year. There are much more important jobs ahead of that one," Isaac insisted. "No toilet!"

Birdie and Bryan remained at camp while Isaac and Annie returned to their last month of teaching.

Motley came up by train the next day to work under Birdie's direction. When the young Greens returned two weeks later, Birdie proudly showed them the completed work, including the new toilet, neatly crammed into what had been waste space in the pantry.

Isaac saw immediately what an immense improvement had been made, but he never did swallow his pride to tell Birdie that she had been right to go ahead and build the toilet.

Camp opened with fifty-five campers enrolled. Among them was eight-year-old Carmelita Motley, whose tuition was partial payment for her father's work.

The summer went well, and halfway through it, the local camp doctor confirmed Annie's belief that she was pregnant.

FORTY-FIVE

The sugar maple leaves were just beginning to turn when Joy phoned her cousins.

"Hello, Isaac. Are you hearing the news?" she asked.

"No, what news?"

"Turn on your television. President Kennedy just announced that the Russians have put missiles into Cuba."

"Joy, we've got a TV set, but the picture's so bad up here it's hardly worth using. I'll turn on the radio. But what about it?"

"You'll see. It's important. Just listen! Bye-bye."

They turned on the radio, and it stayed on for most of the next week.

On the third morning of the "missile crisis," Joy called again to say that Bryan and Birdie were driving her and the kids up to camp.

"Richard is staying at work, but Birdie doesn't want me and the kids in the city, in case the bombs start falling. I think she's cuckoo. But she insists."

At four that afternoon, Bryan drove up the dirt road. Joy's twins sprang out of the car and ran straight toward the chicken coop. The hens, who had been pecking in the grass, scattered at their approach. One rooster stood his ground and advanced menacingly toward five-year-old Jeffery, who ran back to his mother.

They all gathered in the living room where the radio was now reporting on cables that had gone back and forth between Khruschev and Kennedy.

The latest news was about the "quarantine," which the Soviets insisted they wouldn't respect, calling it a violation of international law.

"You know," Bryan said, "a blockade is an act of war. But 'quarantine' is Kennedy's way of blockading Cuba while he pretends he isn't. He's playing word games."

"We'll talk about it...soon...later," Annie insisted. "First, let's get organized. Joy, I'll show you where your rooms are. Isaac, help your cousin carry her things up. Bryan and Birdie, you'll have the same room you stayed in last time. OK?"

Annie took Joy upstairs to one of the bunk rooms where they made up beds for the children.

Only after the children were put to bed did they have time to talk about what was happening.

Seated at the nearest of the many tables in the camp dining room and helping themselves from the platter of spaghetti and meatballs that Annie had just put on the table, Birdie said, "Now it's quiet and we can think. So? What does it mean?"

"I don't think it means anything," Joy said. "I think it's foolishness and our running away from the city was more foolishness. They're not going to commit mutual suicide. Neither of them."

"Bahh. Just shows how little you know about how the world works," her mother answered.

"It seems to me," Isaac said, "that we Americans have surrounded Russia with our army bases and our rockets. Now Khruschev wants to even things out. I can't get too excited about what he's doing."

"That's because you live in Vermont," Bryan said. "You'll probably be among the survivors of the next war, if there are going to be any survivors."

"OK then. What do you think is going to happen?"

"I'm going to have another helping of meatballs. We'll just wait to see who blinks first, the president or the general secretary of the Communist Party."

After coffee, Annie and Joy took over the dish washing while the others started a game of Scrabble. Birdie proudly put down her tiles and made the word *excited*. "How's that!" she said. "And it's on a triple word score!"

Bryan, not to be outdone, placed his letters, going up from Birdie's "x"—"T-R-A-C-T-E-D. Xtracted," he said.

"Bryan, you can't build a word going up. You're only allowed to read them going down," Birdie said. "You know that, and besides, you can't make 'extracted' without another 'e.'"

Bryan glared at his wife. "Never mind," he said, "I can't concentrate. I can't even see the board properly. I'm going out for some air." He stood up from the table, left the game, and went out onto the porch where he sat smoking cigarette after cigarette.

The next morning, the radio announced that Walter Lippmann, in his morning column, was suggesting a possible way out of the impasse. "We Americans," he said, "should offer to withdraw the fifteen Jupiter missiles we have placed in Turkey if Khruschev agrees to withdraw his missiles from Cuba."

"You know what that is?" Bryan said gleefully. "I can tell you, as an old reporter. That's what you call 'a trial balloon.' We are looking for a way out of this without shooting."

At lunchtime, Bryan told Birdie that he wanted to go home.

"But it isn't over," she said.

"No, but I don't feel good and I want to be in my own home no matter what happens. Leave Joy and the kids here. Richard can come for them at the end of the week. Let's go home, now."

"Bryan, we aren't leaving yet. We came here because it's a safer place to be than New York City. Let's not put ourselves in danger if we don't have to."

"Birdie, I've done what you've told me to do for thirty years. Now I'm telling you. Get in the damned car." His voice rose steadily, and his final words were shouted.

Birdie looked in amazement. "All right, Bryan. Calm down. We'll go."

It was three more days before Khruschev announced that he was dismantling the missiles and returning them to the Soviet Union.

On Saturday, Richard drove up to camp. He spent several hours helping Isaac nail shingles onto the roof of a new cabin, and then, Sunday afternoon, he drove his family home to the city.

FORTY-SIX

S am and Belle drove to the Cantors' town house for dinner.
In the years since Bryan and Birdie renovated the house and moved into it, the block had been gentrified into one of Manhattans more desirable locations.

"She's done very well for herself," Sam observed.

"They've done well," Belle corrected him.

Sam didn't comment. He circled the block twice until he saw someone pull out, opening up a parking space.

Birdie mixed martinis and served shrimp cocktail. They sat on couches facing each other, and Birdie said, "Bryan has been having spells where he sees double."

"Do you know what it might mean?" Belle asked.

"Not really. We're going in for tests on Monday.

"*Oy,*" was Sam's first response.

"*Oy vey,*" Bryan replied as he stubbed out the butt of his cigarette, reached for a new one, and winked at Sam.

"We won't speculate," Bryan said. "We'll wait and see what they tell us. You tell us, instead. How is the pregnancy coming? You'll be grandparents any day now, won't you?"

Bryan's grandnephew was born three days later. A note was delivered from "Uncle Bryan." It was a page ripped out of a women's magazine, a full-page photo advertisement. A mother gorilla held up her infant gorilla, and in Bryan's clear handwriting were printed the words, "Beauty is only in is only in the eyes of the the beholder."

Isaac showed the page to Annie, who was lying in her hospital bed.

"Nice, huh? He's sick, but he still has his sense of humor."

"But look, Isaac. Read the words again."

"'Is only in is only in'...and then 'the the'...Oops. Do you think that's part of it?"

Bryan by then was being treated for a brain tumor and for what the family members guessed was widespread cancer. But Birdie refused to divulge any information. She alone took Bryan to all of his doctor's visits, administered his medicines, and never discussed what his illness might be, not with Bryan, not with others.

It was clear to her that this was the way Bryan wanted it, pretending that nothing was happening.

Then Birdie decided to take her ailing husband to Florida, to escape from the cold. She drafted Isaac, Annie, and their six-week-old son to vacation with them and to drive there in Bryan's car while they flew down.

They met at the airport, as planned, and drove to the motel where reservations had been made. They checked in and went up to their rooms on the second floor, and while the advertised "ocean view" was there, it was minimal, being cut off by high-rise condominiums and by a highway, US 41.

Birdie took a look at the rooms and immediately said, "This won't do."

Isaac tried to talk her out of moving. "We're all tired. There's nothing wrong with this, and it's high season already. You won't find anything better."

"You guys stay here with Bryan. I'm going to look."

An hour later, Birdie returned triumphant. She had gone to a real estate agent with her tale of a dying husband's last good time. The agent was suitably sympathetic and booked her a two-bedroom bungalow directly on the beach. It was only a hundred sandy feet or so to the Atlantic Ocean, depending on the tide.

They stayed two weeks. Bryan's formerly wavy black hair was now just tufts of short bristles, gray mixed with the black, but his energy was good. He swam, he read, he painted, and he spoke of things he planned to do when he got better. There was never any acknowledgment that he was dying.

At the end of the two weeks, Bryan and Birdie flew back to New York while Annie, Isaac, and the baby drove their car north.

In the months that followed, Birdie protected Bryan's privacy like a mother hen. Visitors were turned away, even visits by Joy and the grandchildren.

By summer, Bryan was bedridden. Joy's twins were put into the summer camp so that they could be spared the troubled times. Birdie finally acknowledged her need of Joy's presence.

In July, Bryan died. He was fifty-two years old, one year younger than Birdie.

FORTY-SEVEN

August 15, 1967

Dear Diary,

It is exactly four years since Bryan died. In three more years, God willing, I will be sixty. It is four years that I have been keeping this diary. It is two weeks since I moved into this sunny apartment on 106th Street. I can look down and watch the people walking along Broadway. I can look between the buildings and see a bit of the Hudson River. There is less space here and no garden. But they offered me so much money for Twelfth Street, how could I refuse?

So...let me take stock of these years.

I am terribly lonely. True, I have Joy – Richard too - and I have two wonderful grandchildren. Though I do worry about them, Joy is so strict. Thank God for Richard! He is so much more forgiving. I have my sister, Elsa. And there are Ernest's four children and Isaac's two. I have friends; I go to concerts with Rachel. I visit Molly on Cape Cod, and I help her arrange the knickknacks that she sells to the tourists. Is that enough?

It hurts terribly that so many of Bryan's friends have completely left me. Belle has not spoken to me since Bryan died. Even at the funeral, she never once said a word. She is willful, tactless, and narrow-minded, but she's been a huge part of my life and I don't dislike her the way she seems to dislike me. Sam still calls, but he won't talk about Belle. Neither will Isaac. Bryan's pal, Benny, cried at the funeral and promised to look after me. But I've never heard from him either.

July 19, 1968

Back from the dentist. The pain was real, and I did need to go after all. *Bozhe Moi* (my God), is my mouth a mess! Every one of the teeth that I had capped in Moscow is rotted and ready to be pulled. The dentist tells me that he will make a bridge for me and that my mouth will look just like a movie star's. It will cost a fortune!

August 18, 1969

Now Sam is gone too. A heart attack. Sudden. While he was looking at land to purchase. Isaac phoned and told me the whole story. It happened in Maryland. According to his wishes, he was cremated and the ashes were spread. *Gospodin pomilo* (God have mercy), he has been such a friend to me and to Bryan—ever since our very first meeting in Moscow. He was as warmhearted as Belle is cold. How can I go to her apartment for his memorial gathering on Sunday? And how can I not go? Not for Belle's sake, surely. But for Sam, for Isaac, and for me too.

September 30, 1968

Rachel and I saw *Carmen* last night at Lincoln Center. Marvelous!

Next week, she leaves for Florida, and she is urging me to buy a unit near her, in Shelter Harbor. It might be nice?

December 19, 1968

Last night was the first snowfall of the winter. Broadway was just beautiful from my window, big flakes falling slowly and catching all the lights on their way down. And the muffled sounds of traffic. Lovely. Then I went to bed and had the most horrible dream. I had just arrived in Moscow, nineteen years old, without a word of the language. Sarah found me wandering in the street. She took off her overcoat, put it on my shoulders, and took me to her apartment. When I was asleep, her son Mordechai approached my bed, pulled up my nightgown, and raped me. The next morning, I went to the police and, in fluent Russian, denounced him. They came and sent him away to Siberia. Sarah was furious at me.

"Ungrateful bitch," she called me. She started hitting me, and that was when I woke up feeling upset, scared, and guilty of something that I didn't understand.

It was morning already. I am going to be afraid to go back to sleep tonight, lest I find myself back in Moscow.

FORTY-EIGHT

On a May morning, Joy called her mother.

"Mom, I want you to know, I've told Jeffery not to come home anymore."

"What are you talking about, Joy?"

"You know he's been skipping school to hang out with his buddies in Washington Square, smoking dope and playing guitar. Sometimes he comes home, and sometimes he doesn't. Well, he's made his choice."

"Zoya, he's only fourteen years old!"

"Mommy, I've been Joy for thirty years already. Remember? My name isn't Zoya anymore. And I've raised Jeffery for fourteen years. If he doesn't know how to behave by this time, it's completely his decision."

"When did you tell him that he couldn't come home?"

"Let's see...Monday, three days ago, when he stopped by and said he was going right out again; he just needed to pick up some stuff. Already, he hadn't been home for two nights straight. It was the middle of the morning, and he should have been in school. That was the end for me."

"Do you know where he is now?"

"Mommy, I'm trying to tell you. I don't care where he is now. He's his own person. He'll decide for himself what he wants to do."

Birdie hung up. Depressed, she went to the glass-fronted cabinet in her foyer and took out one of the wooden shot glasses she and Bryan had brought back from Russia. It was hand-painted with an elaborate folk motif. She poured vodka right up to the rim and drank it down, Russian style, in one full swallow. She put on a light sweater and set off to find her grandson.

The subway was on a straight line to Washington Square, where she went from bench to bench searching for Jeffery. Whenever she came upon someone who appeared to be close to his age, she asked, "Do you know Jeffery Dean?"

Finally, one sullen boy said, "Yeah, So?"

"Where is he? When did you last see him?"

"I haven't seen him for days, lady."

She went into every bar in the neighborhood. Twice, once with a wink and once with a sneer, she was told, "Lady, if you're looking for your husband, he said to tell you he hasn't been here," and on two occasions, she was invited to sit down and have a drink.

After giving up on the bars and taverns, she went back into the park for one more look. There was Jeffery, sitting on the edge of the fountain right in the middle of the park, easily recognizable by his immense afro. He was strumming a guitar, experimenting with new chords.

"Jeffery, thank God you are OK."

A warm smile lit up Jeffery's face. "Hi, Grandma. What are you doing here?"

Birdie took Jeffery home, made him take a bath, and fed him warmed-up fried chicken and powdered mashed potatoes.

"Now let's talk, young man. Explain what you're trying to do."

"Aw, Grandma. I'm not made out to go to school. That's all it is."

"What do you mean, 'Not made out for school?' I was so proud of you when both you and your brother passed the test and entered Stuyvesant. You know, your grandfather Bryan got into the special high school too. In his time, it was Townsend Harris. You are smart Jeffery, both you and your brother. You've already proved that."

"Sure, Grandma. But they kicked me out of Stuyvesant, remember? That's not where I go now."

"I remember, Jeffery."

"And how can I be expected to go to school when I spend all my time at home fighting with my mother. I've got a lot of things on my mind, you know."

"Listen, Jeffery, you can stay here with me as long as you want to. But only if you promise me that you'll go to school."

Jeffery finished out the school term, traveling from Birdie's apartment. Then in the beginning of summer, he decided to live with his father on Long Island. Eric was now working as a general contractor, and he got Jeffery a job with the drywall crew that he used. Before the summer was over, Jeffery considered himself a master of a trade. "I'll always be able to find work, hanging sheet rock," he proudly reported to his grandmother.

FORTY-NINE

Birdie dragged her suitcase to the elevator, the start of a two-week visit to her cousin, Yehudit, in Israel. During the nineteen years since Birdie and Bryan had been there, she and her cousin had corresponded sporadically. Now she was off to visit her.

Cousin Yehudit, when she reached the age of fifty, had finally married, but for the past two years, she, too, had been a widow.

The day was sunny and warm. Birdie descended to Broadway with her suitcase, handbag, and an over-the-shoulder carry-on. The limousine she had ordered was already there. As he opened the back door for her, the uniformed driver, a white-haired Negro, perhaps Birdie's age, gave her a big smile. Seated, Birdie noted the people on Broadway, some strolling and some hurrying along. She remarked to herself how brilliantly the colors of the women's dresses shone in the bright sunlight. "New York is a beautiful city on a day like this," she said to the driver.

"It certainly is!"

Within thirty minutes, they were at the Pan Am terminal. A sky-cap brought her and her luggage to the check-in desk. More than two hours remained until departure. When she reached the head of the line, a young woman took her tickets and passport, looked at the passport, frowned, and said, "I'm sorry, but this passport is outdated. Do you have your new one in your bag?"

"What do you mean, 'outdated'? Show me. It couldn't be."

But it was.

"Well, can't you let me fly anyway, and I'll fix it when I get to Tel-Aviv. You already know I'm a citizen. You can tell by the old passport. And I'm too old to be a troublemaker."

"No, madam, I'm sorry. We can't let you fly with an outdated passport, and even if we did, the Israelis won't let you into their country without a current passport. I'm afraid you'll have to reschedule your trip now."

"No," Birdie said. "Here, you hold onto my luggage. I'll be right back."

"We can't do..."

Birdie was gone, already outside, at the cab line. A young couple carrying backpacks was about to enter the first cab. "Excuse me," she said. "It's a real emergency. I don't have any time." She squeezed herself between the young lady and the open door, sat down, pulled the door shut, and told the driver, "Rockefeller Center, and fast. As fast as you can and I'll make it worthwhile for you."

As they drove, she explained her predicament. The driver assured her that there was no way on God's earth that she could go to the passport office, fill out the forms, stand on the line, and get a new passport in time to make her flight.

"I'll tell you what," she answered him. "You drive fast. I'll worry about the passport."

The trip into the city was quick. Then, approaching Rockefeller Center, on Fifth Avenue, traffic crawled. Gradually, they approached the imposing tower in front of which hunched the bronze figure of Atlas, holding the world on his shoulders.

"You stay right here! I'll be back," Birdie commanded.

"I can't, lady. I'll get a ticket."

"Yes, you can," Birdie answered, and she left the cab without paying. She climbed the steps to the mezzanine where the passport office was located. The line of applicants reached from the far end of the room all the way to the door through which Birdie had entered. She went to the head of the line.

"Excuse me."

"Lady, you gotta wait your turn," said the man about to present his papers at the window."

"Sorry. No time," Birdie said. She turned to the clerk. "My plane leaves in an hour. My bags are already checked in. I need a new passport. Please. Here's my old one."

"Where's your application and your two photographs?"

"I don't have them. You'll have to fill it out for me. The information is still all the same. Use the old photo."

"No, lady, but I'll tell you what we'll do. You go downstairs, get your picture taken, fill out the applications, and then, seeing as you have to fly today, we'll let you come back here to the front of the line. OK? Now step aside and let this man have his turn."

Birdie ran to the lower level where instant photos were taken. She scribbled a few indecipherable words on the application and returned to the front of the line, where she was given a new passport. She ran outside and found her cab still waiting for her.

"How'd you make out?"

"Go. Go. Go...I'll tell you on the way."

They got back to the Pan Am terminal two minutes before scheduled departure time. Birdie paid the taxi driver generously and ran to the gate. She was pleased to see her suitcase and shoulder bag next to the station where boarding passes were collected.

"You're here!" the attendant said. "We were about to close the doors. We'll put your bags up front. Go! Find a seat. Anywhere."

Birdie took the first vacant seat that she came to, in the fifth row, first class. All the passengers were seated and buckled. Somehow, her story had spread, because when she sat down, held her passport aloft, and said, "I got it!" the cabin exploded into applause.

Birdie's cousin Yehudit had noticeably aged in the nineteen years since she and Bryan had lived in Israel. Yehudit was stooped and walked slowly and carefully, but her eyes shone and she still had her old pioneering zest for Israel.

"It's a different country from the one you left, Birdie! You'll see. We have breathing space now. Remember when you used to visit Joy at the kibbutz, the convoluted paths you would follow to stay within our borders? Now, if you want to go from her kibbutz to Jerusalem, you just go straight. You drive right through the West Bank."

"Aren't you afraid to travel through those territories?"

"Not in the daytime, I'm not. The last time I made the trip through the West Bank, I was going with a friend. We were on our way to Jerusalem. We stopped and picked up a hitchhiking soldier who was heading home on leave. He carried his Uzi, of course, and that made us feel completely safe."

On the sixth day of her visit, they took an excursion up to the Golan Heights. The road followed the shore of the Sea of Galilee and then climbed the hill on the lake's eastern bank. Until the war of '67, two years earlier, this had been a part of Syria. Their driver parked at an overlook. "There, on the other side of the ravine," he narrated, "there on that hill, stood the city of Gamla, the chief city of the region." He pointed toward a hillside, which was bare, save for occasional scrubby bushes and clumps of cactus. "Josephus tells us it was the last northern holdout of resistance to the Romans during the revolt of the year 67. Six years before Masada. Here, even after the Romans destroyed the temple, our people still held out, until the Romans built a ramp right up to the top of the city walls. When they finally captured the city, its inhabitants were massacred. We sometimes call it the Masada of the North."

That night, back at Yehudit's apartment, the cousins argued over where the legitimate borders of Israel should be drawn. Yehudit felt that the afternoon's trip made it self-evident that wherever the Jews lived two thousand years ago, that land should belong to them today. Birdie felt that the issue was much more complicated. She spoke of the rights of the Arabs, of international law, of her desire to see all men brothers, instead of a world divided by religion.

Yehudit said, "Birdie, I love you. But you are an ignorant dreamer."

"I like the 'dreamer' part anyway, not the 'ignorant' part. Because if we are getting up early tomorrow for our tour, then we'd better call it a night."

They met their tour group at eight the next morning. The Egged coach took them south, through the Negev Desert to Elat. That afternoon, they checked into their hotel and took the elevator up to the fifth floor. "Look," Birdie said, as they entered their room, "we're facing the Gulf of Aqaba! It's beautiful!"

"We prefer to call it the Bay of Elat," Yehudit responded. "It's our access to the Red Sea."

They showered and dressed for the evening's program at a restaurant that catered to tour groups. The restaurant, three steps down from street level, was crowded and dark. A string of red bulbs illuminated the raised stage beyond the dinner tables. Yellow beams focused on the band, which played a medley of American show tunes, old Yiddish standards, Russian folk tunes, and popular Hebrew songs. It was impossible to talk above the loud music. The tour guide led them to their two rectangular tables, already loaded with bottles of vodka, red and white wine, and champagne. There were platters of cold cuts and salads and dishes of herring, anchovies, and smoked salmon. Birdie immediately felt herself transported to some of the restaurants she had known in Moscow, restaurants that catered to foreigners and to the well connected. Birdie, once she was accustomed to the light, looked around. She saw some whom she took to be Israeli tourists but more Americans and Europeans. There were a few local couples, and a number of swarthy, dark-haired young men gathered around the bar. The men appeared to be in their twenties or thirties and were certainly locals, not tourists.

After a serving of highly spiced soup, the main course was brought to the table, *shish kabob*, skewers of lamb chunks, alternating with onion, green and red peppers, and tomatoes. Birdie now recalled the first meal she had had in Moscow with Bryan, Sam, and Belle. That had been in a Georgian restaurant, and instead of calling it "shish kabob," the identical dish was known as *shashlik*. By this time, Birdie had sampled enough of the drinks on the table so that her memories of those days were all warm and fuzzy.

Now the band gave way to the performers. A husband-and-wife team sang numbers from *Fiddler on the Roof.* A buxom middle-aged woman in Ukrainian dress sang a medley of gypsy tunes and then an operatic aria. Next, she was joined by two young men in Cossack dress, and as she sang Russian tunes, the two young men danced. Then the band struck up the hora tune, "Hava Nagila." The performers went into the audience and pulled reluctant participants onto the dance floor. They held hands and danced in a circle. Soon, there was a larger circle going around the inner circle. Birdie and Yehudit were content to watch.

Next the band turned to dance music, slow fox-trots.

Birdie saw one of the dark young men from the bar approaching her table.

"May I have the pleasure of a dance with you?" he asked her in good but accented English.

"Oh no," she said. "I've had much too much to drink for dancing."

The young man passed Yehudit, who was sitting next to Birdie. He turned to the woman on the other side of Yehudit, bowed his head, and held out his arm. The woman accepted, and they went onto the dance floor.

Another of the young men, somewhat older, approached Birdie. "That was my friend Yoram," he said. "Yoram is a *nudnick*. You need a real man. Me, I'm Aaron. Come!"

Not waiting for an answer, he pulled Birdie to her feet and led her to the dance floor. He held her tightly as they moved slowly to the music of "Some Enchanted Evening." Birdie, who hardly ever danced, shuffled her feet in time to the music and tried to match Aaron's movements.

"You know, I could be your grandmother," Birdie said.

"That would be so nice," he answered, pulling her tighter. "Where I was born, grandmothers were old ladies. Not sexy women like you."

Birdie said nothing. She felt his stiffness through the material of her dress, pressing against her belly. For a moment, she allowed herself to take pleasure from his nearness, then, emphatically, she created a distance between their bodies.

"What hotel are you staying in?" he asked. "May I visit you there?"

"Don't be foolish."

The song ended. Birdie was escorted back to her seat, and Aaron disappeared.

As they walked back to their hotel, Yehudit told Birdie, "Those men are Sephardim. Most of them were born in Arab countries. Either they or their parents came here as refugees. They give us a bad name. But they were cute, weren't they?"

The following afternoon touring on a glass-bottomed boat, cruising over shallow coral reefs, and marveling at the varieties of fish, they motored practically to the Jordanian border, by the city of Aqaba.

A day later, they were back in Tel Aviv.

"So, Birdie," Yehudit asked. "For two years you lived here. Now for two weeks you have come back. Why don't you stay for good? Have you learned anything about us that you didn't know back in the fifties? Doesn't the Hebrew language comfort your ears the way it does mine?"

"Whoa, slow down. Too many questions. No. I haven't learned much Hebrew. No disputing that. But you know what my favorite phrase is? Well, I have two of them. *Bevakashvet* is one of them."

Yehudit grimaced as though she had sucked on a bitter lemon and then laughed. "How would you translate that mangled phrase?...Plz to be sit? OK, what's the other one?"

"The other one is *rachoosh-natoosh*. I love the way it slides around my tongue."

"Do you know what it means, Birdie?"

"Of course I do! It's 'abandoned property,' or to be more accurate, 'wealth that has been fled from.' This country is full of 'rachoosh-natoosh,' and that's one of the reasons why I can't live here. Because someday, those who were driven out are going to come back and demand what they believe is theirs. No way could I live in a country that's constantly at war."

"You're so foolish, Birdie. You live in America. I read the newspapers. People are being shot dead, just for walking across the streets in America. There is more violence in your country than here in ours. Riots. I'd be afraid to visit you in New York. You've been here two weeks, and nothing nasty has happened...Oh well. We will never agree about this. But you said that 'rachoosh-natoosh' is just one of the reasons that you won't stay. What else?"

"Yehudit, I know what your generation sacrificed to create this country. I understand your dreams. But I don't share them. That's all it's about. Your country is based on the idea of being Jewish. For you, 'Jewish' is all kinds of things—religion, nationality, language. It's too much. Stalin tried to put me into that kind of a box too. 'The Jews are a separate people,' he said. Well, I'm an American who happens to be Jewish, whatever that may mean. Not an Israeli. Tell you the truth, I'm not even sure that I'm an American. I'm a person. That's what I am. I live in this world...freely. What you made here is a ghetto, a place with walls around it, just for the Jews. I would suffocate if I had to live here for the rest of my life."

"Birdie, I love you, but we see the world differently. Still, I'm so happy that you are visiting me."

She kissed her cousin's cheek. And when they parted at the end of the week, it was with hugs, kisses, and hopes of being together again at some unknown time.

FIFTY

They met for lunch, as they often did, in a Broadway delicatessen, only a block from the apartment house in which they both lived.

"You really ought to come down too, Birdie."

"Rachel, you're out of your head."

"No. I'm not—"

"You want that I should become a 'snowbird' like you and run away from the city, just because it's getting cold here."

"Yes. That's what I want you to do!"

"What in the world for, Rachel? What would I do with myself in Florida? It's for old people; you should excuse me."

"Like you and me, Birdie. No, seriously, it's for people fifty-five and older. You qualify. You'll love it. There's swimming, and there's a community house with every activity you can think of. Listen, I'm going down in two weeks. You come with me. Stay for a while and see if you don't like it."

It was October 1970. Birdie and her friend Rachel flew to West Palm Beach. A taxi brought them to the gate of the Shelter Harbor complex. Rachel identified herself and the barrier was raised, allowing them to continue on to her condo.

That night, a group of neighbors gave Rachel a welcome-back party. The next afternoon, they swam in the pool and went out to a Chinese restaurant for supper. The following evening, they attended a current-events discussion in the community house, at which Birdie was thrilled to hear vehement dispute on Nixon's promise of peace talks in Vietnam. "Was he serious, or wasn't he?" appeared to be the matter of debate. Then, one of the residents who had spent many years in Egypt, working for the United States Information Service, reported on the construction of the Aswan high dam. His thesis was that the Russians had scored a major diplomatic coup and that within a few years, unless we did something about it, most of the Middle East would be looking toward Russia, rather than toward America.

Birdie was thrilled by the life she saw going on around her, and the next morning, she went right to the sales office. They showed her a number of units, and by the afternoon, she had written a down payment on a two-bedroom, third-story unit with a small balcony overlooking a man-made lake. Birdie was now a snowbird.

Joy's twins were young men now. Carlo was becoming a prosperous businessman, but he still managed to visit at least once a year. Jeffery, who was now fully reconciled with his parents, was a more frequent visitor. Jeffery never managed to hold onto a job for more than a couple of months, and each time he became unemployed he would come south to "regroup." Often as not, Joy and Richard would accompany him. Nephew Ernest, Bridget, and their four children came for at least a week every year. Annie and Isaac, with their two children, came. Only her sister, Elsa, considered it "too far to travel."

When the number of visitors overflowed the apartment, Birdie found extra sleeping places among the neighbors.

Summers, to escape the heat and to avoid possible hurricanes, Birdie returned to the New York apartment on Broadway, but, increasingly, she considered Florida to be her home.

Elsa, she thought, was a problem. She saw her sister as a responsibility. Even though Elsa was the older one, by eight years, Birdie felt that she understood nothing.

"Elsa, you have to let me take you shopping. You have nothing to wear, and if I let you go by yourself, you'll come home looking like you're color blind or maybe like a streetwalker."

Elsa did not feel herself to be as incompetent as Birdie assumed her to be. But Elsa loved the attention and accepted her little sister's ministrations.

Then Louie died of a heart attack.

Louie and Elsa had driven to Ernest's on Long Island. Ernest wanted his father's help at tuning up his old Studebaker. Elsa saw the two of them working on Ernest's car, which had been pulled into the driveway. The hood was up, and the two of them were bent over, tightening a pulley, when Louie was seized by a sharp chest pain. He called out something, which Ernest didn't understand, and slumped down onto the engine block. Ernest pulled his hefty father onto the grass and attempted to resuscitate him. Nothing.

Within a year, Birdie had convinced her reluctant sister that it was no good for a single woman to live alone in New York. "Come," she said. "I found you a unit here in Shelter Harbor. I'll look after you."

In these years, Birdie acquired three new financial advisors, apportioning a part of her capital to each one. She was a frequent buyer and seller of stocks and of bonds. She followed the suggestions of friends, carefully read the newspapers, and primarily, trusted her own intuition.

Sister Elsa had lived in Shelter Harbor for only four months when Charles Keller, a fellow resident, also recently widowed, began to court her. Keller was almost as short as Elsa. He had been a graphic designer in New York, and when he retired and moved to Shelter Harbor, he began painting watercolors. By then, he was teaching a course in water coloring at the community house. Elsa joined the class, and within a month, they were married.

They married at the local courthouse. Five people participated: Birdie, witnessing for her sister; Birdie's friend Rachel; and a fellow-painter whom Keller had brought.

Birdie disapproved. *Why is she rushing, pell-mell, in such a hurry to be married? Has she had time to know who this man really is? And does he know who she is? How could she have got a man so quickly? She's not as pretty as I am. She's practically helpless, naive, clueless. Maybe that's what men want. Somebody to take care of. And that grin of hers! Those sparkling eyes. It's as if she is flirting all the time. Well, at least she has somebody else to watch over her now.*

Despite her misgivings, Birdie made all the arrangements for the wedding dinner to be held in the community house. She took Elsa on a shopping spree. Together, they selected a whole new wardrobe for Elsa, which Birdie paid for as a wedding gift.

FIFTY-ONE

In late summer of 1974, Birdie's friend Rachel invited a few friends to her apartment on Seventy-Fifth Street, overlooking Central Park.

"You'll know most of the guests," Rachel said, "but there's one man I especially want you to meet."

"Oh ho, and who would that be?"

"Aaron. Aaron Kraus. He spends his winters in Shelter Harbor too. He is an accountant. He lives in Queens, with his daughter, for half of the year. I think you'll like him."

When Birdie arrived, soon after dark, Aaron had not yet come, and she was surprised to realize how anxious she was, how impatient to meet the man Rachel had picked out for her. She tried to join the conversation, but her eyes kept straying from her friends' faces to the front door.

A stranger did arrive. Birdie saw that he was a short man who greeted Rachel at the door with a kiss on each cheek. His silver hair was sparse and stringy. His nose came to a sharp point, and his upper teeth jutted out. She hoped this wasn't Aaron.

But it was.

Rachel introduced him to the room, "My friend from the outer borough of Queens, my friend from Florida, Aaron Kraus." Then she brought him to Birdie. "You should get to know each other. You're neighbors, practically, at Shelter Harbor."

"Glad to meet you," Birdie said, "but you'll have to excuse me. We're in the middle of a hot discussion."

Aaron went to the sideboard and poured himself a drink. He sat in a straight-backed chair, the only unoccupied one in the room, and tried to pick up the discussion occupying everyone. He gathered the topic was Russia's expulsion of the Nobel Prize–winning author Alexander Solzhenitsyn.

"'Thaw' my ass, you should excuse me," said Rachel's current lover, a teacher who had written a book on Khruschev and the changes in Russia since Stalin. "It's still a one-party state. The clique in power still makes all the decisions."

"What do you think, Birdie? You've been through it all," Rachel asked.

"No," Birdie answered. "I don't ever try to explain what the Soviets are about."

A writer of children's fiction, a sixty-year-old woman said, "Still, the man, Solzhenitsyn, was sent abroad into exile. He wasn't forced to recant his writings. He wasn't shot or even sent back to prison. That has to count for something, wouldn't you think?"

Aaron, from his chair on the opposite side of the room, a glass of scotch in his hand, joined in. "Don't make excuses for the Russians," he said. "They are evil. Solzhenitsyn is a great writer, and he knows the difference between good and evil. That's why he is coming to America to live."

Birdie thought to herself, *It must be marvelous to see things so simply.* Then she mused on the etymology of "simpleton." *Poor man, to be so limited,* she thought.

The talk went on and then shifted to a more pressing topic, the newly established national speed limit of fifty-five miles per hour. Everyone had a strong opinion on this topic, except for Birdie, who had never driven a car in her life.

Birdie was among the first of the guests to leave the gathering. As she went to the door, Aaron approached and said, "Did Rachel tell you that I have a place in Shelter Harbor too? Maybe I'll see you there this winter. When do you go south?"

"I really have no idea," Birdie answered, and she went out into the hall.

Soon after Birdie's return to Florida, in November, Aaron telephoned.

"Hello, Birdie, it's Aaron Kraus. You remember me, don't you, from Rachel's party? Welcome back to Florida."

"Yes, I remember you, Aaron. You live here too, don't you? What is it that you are calling for?"

"My, you certainly aren't one for making small talk, are you?"

"Aaron, don't play games. What do you want?"

"All right, I'll tell you right out. There is going to be a chamber music concert in the community room on Friday night. We are playing Mozart and Schubert. Rachel told me that you and she go to a quartet series in New York. I'd like you to come hear us, and then, afterward, we can have a drink together."

"What do you mean 'we are playing'? Are you one of the players?"

"Yes. I play cello. We've been playing together for years. Ever since I got to Shelter Harbor."

"That's very nice of you, Aaron, to ask me to come and listen. Yes, I'll be there."

"That's so good of you, Birdie. I look forward to talking to you after the concert. Till Friday, then."

She walked to the community room and found nearly every seat taken. She took a seat on the side.

When the concert ended, Birdie went up to the stage where Aaron and his fellow players, two men and a woman, were all beaming, slapping each other on the back, and accepting congratulations from friends and from listeners.

"Aaron, it was marvelous," Birdie said. "I loved all the music, but what I liked best was seeing how much pleasure you were taking in each other's playing."

"Thank you, Birdie. I think you grasped the essence of playing in a quartet." He introduced her to his three associates, saying, "This is Birdie Cantor. She's a friend from New York City."

"You never told us you had a friend in New York City," said the woman who played the violin. "You've been keeping secrets, Aaron."

Instead of answering, Aaron took Birdie by the shoulder and turned her away from the group.

"Come on, Birdie; let's go out for a drink and if you are hungry, a snack too."

They drove in Aaron's Buick, through the twenty-four-hour manned gate and out onto the main road.

"How's about China House? They have a good bar, and it's quiet."

"Anything you want, Mister Musician."

They found their way to a high-sided booth.

"So tell me something about yourself, Birdie. I know that you travel a lot. I know that you are a competent businesswoman, and that's about it—except I also know that you are very attractive."

"I hope you know how little flattery will get you. Do you? There's very little to tell. No, very little that I'm willing to tell. My husband, Bryan, and I renovated brownstones in the city and in Brooklyn. Bryan died ten years ago, and ever since then, I've been making investments and paying attention to my two grandchildren and a whole lot of nephews and nieces. What about you?"

"My wife died a year and a half ago. We had been married just one year short of fifty. I was an accountant for all of those years. Last year, on my sixty-ninth birthday, I retired. I'm very proud of my daughter, Lauren, who is a surgeon. My two grandchildren are extraordinary. Ellen is a mathematics whiz and just won a full scholarship to MIT. Larry is a musician, and I expect great things of him when he finishes high school."

"But tell me more about you, Aaron. What are you interested in besides your music?"

"Computers. Yes, computers and Israel. Have you ever been to Israel, Birdie?"

Before she could answer, a waiter came and took their orders, white wine for each of them. Birdie didn't want anything to eat, but Aaron requested a dish of dumplings anyway. "To share."

Drinks were brought promptly, and they conversed on various topics, quickly discovering that they disagreed on most of them.

Aaron was a firm advocate of the Israelis holding on to all the lands they had ever captured. "It was theirs in the first place; in biblical days. Why shouldn't they keep it?" Birdie's belief was that saying Israel should be a Jewish country was no different than saying the United States should be a Christian country. "What has religion got to do with running a country?" she asked.

"Don't you consider yourself Jewish, Birdie?"

"No. I'm an American. Judaism is a religion. Religion was for my parents. I'm American."

This was so far from Aaron's thinking that he didn't try to pursue it further.

"What about Russia?" he asked. "I know that you spent a lot of years there."

"What should I tell you? Do you want me to tell you that I like them? That they are on the right track and that we are wrong? That the Cold War is America's way of trying to hold back the tides of history?"

"Do you believe any of that, Birdie?"

"Oh, God, Aaron. It's much too complicated. I've lived through too much to tell you what I believe now. Yes. I believe a little bit of all those slogans. And at the same time, I know that nothing turns out the way we think it should. Don't let's talk about politics. You said you are interested in computers. What does that mean?"

Aaron explained that the world was on the threshold of utilizing a marvelous new tool. "I just bought myself the newest hand-held calculator available. I'm using it to produce amazing charts that can track the ups and downs of my stock market holdings. And I expect that soon I'll be able to make vast amounts of money on my investments, all because of what the calculator tells me."

"Now you are telling me something that really interests me, Aaron. Would you be able to show me what you are doing, to teach me?"

"Of course I would. I'd be happy to."

Aaron drove Birdie home. He kissed her lightly on the cheek and left her at the elevator, having made an appointment to show her his calculator the next afternoon.

Aaron arrived at Birdie's door, carrying his calculator, several days' worth of *New York Times* business sections, and a yellow note pad. Birdie served tea and biscuits. They sat on the couch. Aaron spread his materials on top of the coffee table and began explaining his theories and methods to his willing pupil. After some time, Birdie asked, "But does it work, Aaron? Are you making money this way? More than you'd been making before, when you just followed your intuition?"

"I don't know yet. It'll take a while. But it seems to me that I'm on the track of something important."

They had been working intensely, huddled over pages of figures, Aaron punching numbers into the hand-held calculator. They sat close, their legs touching.

Then he put the calculator down on top of the pile of papers, put his arm around Birdie, drew her to him, and kissed her on the lips.

She sprang up and lurched away from the couch, painfully scraping her shin on the coffee table.

"No, Mister Kraus. That isn't what I invited you here to do. Too many ideas, you have, and besides—well, never mind—it's inappropriate."

"I'm sorry, Birdie. It was something I wanted to do. I was hoping you wanted me to kiss you too. All right. I suppose our lesson is over. I hope you'll be able to use some of what we have been talking about." He gathered up his papers and stood..

"Now you are angry at me, Aaron. Don't be. Nothing terrible happened. I hurt my shin a little," she said, rubbing it, "but I'm not angry at you. In fact, you know what? I'm having a group of friends over tonight after supper. We sit around, and we talk about interesting things. Maybe you know some of them. Maybe not. Anyway, I want you to come too. At seven thirty. OK?"

"Maybe."

He did come, and though he did not know any of those gathered, he was not at all shy about disagreeing with most of the viewpoints expressed by Birdie's friends.

Everyone, except Aaron, was thrilled that President Nixon had resigned, rather than face impeachment. Only Aaron defended Nixon. "I think he'll go down in the history books as the man who brought China back into the family of nations," he said.

Everyone felt that President Ford's pardon of Nixon was a prearranged deal and that it was shameful—everyone, that is, except for Aaron, who felt that it was the right thing to do in order to heal controversy and then move on to deal with the nation's business.

Discussion shifted to the global recession taking place, to the horrors of 11 percent inflation and to the gasoline shortage, which had already driven the cost of gasoline up to fifty-five cents a gallon. Aaron, again in the role of odd man out, said, "True, true, but look at how well each of us is living in Shelter Harbor. We're going through a cycle. But the very meaning of cycle is that this too will pass and we will still be living comfortably in the richest and most successful country in the world."

Birdie's friends heard him out, politely, but condescendingly.

Talk about gasoline shortage led to a discussion about the proposed Alaska pipeline. This was where people really got angry at Aaron, who defended construction of the pipeline as the proper thing to do. Everyone else was shocked that he could defend the desecration of pristine Alaskan wilderness.

It had been a lively evening. By ten o'clock, most of the guests went home to bed. Aaron was the last remaining guest.

"Thank you, Birdie," he said. "Your friends are quite a radical crew. They gave me a workout."

"I think they rather enjoyed your baiting them, Aaron. Don't go yet. Will you have a drink?"

Birdie took down two of her painted Russian shot glasses and filled them with vodka.

They sat on the couch, again close to each other.

"Let me show you how the Russians toast to *Bruderschaft*...brother-hood. Here, hold out your arm, this way, link your elbow around mine. Now we each drink, with our elbows still linked. Bottoms up! Good. Now we are on familiar terms with each other. We can call each other by the familiar 'ti' rather than the formal 'vui.'"

This time, she didn't object when he kissed her.

The kiss lasted for a long time, Aaron's tongue exploring her mouth. But when she felt his hand go between her legs, she stood up abruptly.

"Again. You're being inappropriate, Aaron. I think you had better go now."

"I'm sorry, Birdie. I don't want to upset you. And I certainly don't want to insult you."

"Go, Aaron. It's time you went home."

"May I still see you?"

"No, Aaron. It isn't a good idea. Don't call me either."

And Aaron didn't call her.

As the winter progressed, Birdie found herself wondering, *Why did I tell him it isn't a good idea?*

In the spring, she called him on the telephone.

"Aaron, it's been a long time since we have spoken. I am really sorry. I was just beginning to know you. Anyway, I am having some of the neighbors here for the Passover seder next week. I'd like it a whole lot if you could come too."

"I'll be there, Birdie."

The Passover table was set for nine: Rachel and her male friend, two other widow ladies, the retired couple from Chicago who lived in the next apartment, Aaron, herself, and finally, as tradition demanded, a place for the Prophet Elijah, should he chance to pass that way. None of the guests were observant Jews. Most would have described themselves as atheists. But the seder was family tradition for all. It turned out that Aaron was the one who best knew the service, so he quickly took over, leading the group through the prayers, tales, and songs that made up the saga of the Israelites' escape from Egyptian bondage.

At the appropriate time in the service, Birdie got up and opened the door to welcome the Prophet Elijah, who failed to appear. Aaron led the group in singing the traditional Passover songs.

Birdie refused all offers to remain and help her wash the dishes, but she did accept Aaron's invitation to cook a supper for her the following night.

They saw each other every day that week, driving to the ocean at Palm Beach, sampling waterfront restaurants along the intercoastal waterway, or strolling together around the ponds in their development.

Birdie was pleased that Aaron, despite earlier behavior, was able to be a patient and attentive suitor. He didn't rush Birdie, and by the end of that week, after dining in a restaurant, Birdie asked him, please, to spend the night with her.

After lovemaking, lying in bed next to Aaron, Birdie replayed her memories of the time, forty years earlier, when Victor Mayerhoff, the famous theater director, lay with her on the couch in his office at the Mosfilm Studios. *Not since then,* she mused, *so many years. Not since then has anyone given me that much pleasure. I'm nearly seventy. But I'm the same person I was then. I'm not sorry for the life I've had or not had, but I'm happy to be here with Aaron at this moment.*

With that thought, she turned toward him, put her arms around him, and pulled him tightly toward herself. "Thank you for reminding me that I'm still a woman," she said.

FIFTY-TWO

They were lovers, and they were snowbirds. When Florida turned hot and humid, they went north.

Birdie found a rental cottage in Westchester County, not far from her brother-in-law Lee's place. It was an aging bungalow colony with a small lake that, halfway through every summer, became choked with a film of green duckweed. The cabin Birdie selected overlooked the lake.

She and Aaron spent the next several summers sharing the cottage.

They maintained their separate condominiums in Florida for just one more season, after which Aaron moved into Birdie's unit.

Nephew Ernest, with some financial help from Birdie, bought Aaron's unit.

Birdie continued to gather interesting people around her. The condo became a salon, where her contemporaries held forth. There was more declaiming than listening. Most of the regular attendees shared the politics that Birdie had grown up with. They saw the Cold War is a travesty fostered by the Unites States, an attempt to stifle Russia's progress toward an economy of plenty for all. Fidel Castro, they took to be a wonderful fellow, under whose direction illiteracy had been eliminated from Cuba. Martin Luther King Jr.'s vital and unfinished work was of paramount importance.

Victor Kantrowitz, a regular participant in the group, loved to cite statistics about relative production of steel between the Soviet Union and the United States. He liked to quote Brezhnev, who said, "When we produce more steel than the Americans do, we will have demonstrated the superiority of Socialism."

"That day is upon us, my friends," Victor proudly proclaimed.

Opinion was somewhat divided about Communist China. Some felt that China was assuming the mantle of leadership within the Socialist camp. Others remained hopefully loyal to the Russians.

Aaron, at these gatherings, sat and listened. He said very little. He knew that most of the guests considered him to be politically illiterate. He, in turn, regarded them as misguided and fixated on a belief system based on faith, unpersuadable by facts.

After a few years of such discussion, there came a night when politics was never spoken.

Victor Kantrowitz came into the apartment leaning on his wife's arm. She led him to a stuffed easy chair and helped him lower himself, slowly and carefully.

"What's wrong, Victor?" Aaron asked. "You're walking like an old man."

"Oy!" Victor answered. "It's been ten days since my hernia operation, and it still hurts like hell every time I strain myself."

"Who did your operation?" asked Max, who had been in conversation with Birdie on the other side of the room but, nevertheless, had picked up the reference to a hernia operation.

"Krivda did it. They told me he's good. I don't know, maybe he's a butcher after all."

"You know what you should have done?" Max replied. "When I needed one, I saw that billboard just outside of town. A clinic in Jersey where they don't do anything but hernias. I figured that if they do nothing but hernias all day long, they must be good at it. And you know what? I was dancing in a couple of days, good as new within a week!"

Stanley and Helen walked in just as the conversation was turning to a discussion of high cholesterol. Stanley immediately joined in.

"I finally went and got mine checked," he said. "The doctor told me not to worry. The number was high, but it was the good kind, rather than the bad kind."

"You mean HDL rather than LDL," Victor said.

"Right. Now I have to worry, do I eat eggs or don't I? I'm hearing lots of conflicting theories."

For the rest of the evening, the conversation never strayed far from everyone's health problems.

Soon after moving into Birdie's apartment, Aaron made a pronouncement: "Birdie, it's time you learned how to drive a car."

"Why? Is it really that hard for you to stop playing with your computer and take me shopping once a week?"

"No, but I think that you're old enough to learn now."

"Aaron, I'm sixty-nine years old. What a crazy idea!"

The next day, Aaron began teaching her to drive. His car was a ten-year-old, four-door Buick with a four-speed manual gear shift. Once she got her learner's permit, he taught her how to make it go. Propped up on two pillows, she carefully inched the car forward and backward around the parking lot. It took almost a year, including two failed attempts at passing the driver's test. But at age seventy, Birdie got her driver's license.

Aaron encouraged her to drive, alone, to the supermarket, even after she had her first fender bender, coming out of the market's parking lot. Then, one year later, Aaron had a stroke. He was in the hospital for several weeks. Birdie drove to the hospital every day. Upon his release, for months, she drove him to therapy sessions. His wheelchair weighed nearly as much as she did. But she learned to fold it up and manhandle it into the trunk of the Buick, singlehandedly.

Aaron recovered most of his functioning. He could walk but with halting steps. He used the wheelchair whenever they went out. His speech was slurred but understandable. However, he could no longer drive. What he missed most though was that he could no longer play his cello.

He could still spend hours on his computer, and he still had Birdie.

FIFTY-THREE

It was winter when Isaac telephoned Birdie.

"So how's the weather down there?" he asked

"Terrible! Cold! We're walking around with sweaters on."

Isaac laughed. "That must be hard," he said. "I'm calling you while I take a break from shoveling out from two feet of new fallen snow, and the flakes are still drifting down."

"Marvelous," Birdie said. "But you're not calling me just to tell me there's snow in Vermont, are you?"

"No, I'm calling to invite you to come on the tour I'm leading this summer. A cruise on the Volga River, Leningrad to Moscow."

Isaac described the trip and told his aunt all the reasons why he felt she should come. Birdie said she'd think about it. "I'll discuss it with Aaron right now. I'll call you back by evening."

She joined Aaron out on the screened porch where he sat, wrapped in a blanket.

"Look!" he said, pointing to a great white egret, standing by the edge of the pond. The egret darted its long neck and head into the water, spearing a passing pin fish.

"Listen, Aaron..." She reported Isaac's offer. "I've never intended to go back there. Never in my life. But this is something I can hardly refuse. You know all about my nephew's summer camp and how, when he sold it, somehow he got into the travel business, don't you? Of course you do. He'll take good care of me. What do you think? Will you be OK without me? It'll be no more than two weeks."

"I wouldn't go near that godforsaken place. But I can understand your wanting to. Yes. Go, and come back healthy!"

That summer, Birdie and Aaron didn't rent the cottage in Westchester County. Instead, they stayed at Birdie's Broadway apartment while Birdie prepared herself for the journey. Then, the week before her departure, Aaron went to stay with his daughter in Queens, where he was to remain while Birdie was away.

The country they were visiting was now called "Russia." No longer was it "the Union of Soviet Socialist Republics," to which Birdie had traveled at age twenty. Now she was eighty-two years old.

They flew on Finnair, with an overnight stop in Helsinki, which provided time for some sightseeing and a comfortable stay in a hotel operated by the airline.

The next morning, they were taken to the Helsinki airport where, it appeared, though their tickets were written by Finnair, the flight was aboard a Russian-built Tupulov operated by Aeroflot, the old Soviet, now Russian, airline. Birdie noted the bald tires on the plane but said nothing about it. *If this is going to be my last flight anywhere, I'm ready,* she thought. *But what about the others? Are they willing to trust this old plane?*

No one else seemed to take notice of the tires.

Birdie and Isaac sat together in the no-smoking section, that being the left side of the plane. On the right side of the aisle were the smoking seats, mostly occupied by returning Russians, who all lit up immediately upon taking their seats. The engines started, and the cabin was engulfed with swirling white clouds. "Don't worry," Isaac assured his thirty passengers. "It's only the air conditioning. It'll clear up in a moment."

Birdie was given a customs form to fill out. It asked her to attest that she carried no firearms, no narcotics, and no letters or packages to be delivered to Soviet citizens. Isaac warned her, "You have to be careful to declare how much money you are bringing in. Also your jewelry and valuables. You'll fill out another declaration when you leave, and if there's too much discrepancy, they won't let you take your money or your stuff home with you. And notice," he added, "it's been over a year since the USSR ceased to exist. Now it's just 'Russia,' but we're still using the old Soviet forms and the rules haven't changed a bit."

After an hour and a half in the air, the Tupulov began its descent into Leningrad's Pulkovo Airport.

It had been fifty-one years since Birdie had last seen Russia.

Sitting by the window, she saw fields and villages at once give way to blocks of residential apartments. There were no suburbs separating city from countryside as in America.

"Are you excited?" Isaac asked.

"That's a foolish question, Isaac. Of course I'm excited, and I'm also scared...and to tell you the truth, sad. So many memories that I haven't touched for years."

"Have you spent much time in Leningrad?"

"Hardly any. Bryan and I came here twice, each time for just a weekend. I scarcely know the city."

From the airport, a bus took them directly to the River Port, where they embarked on the cruise ship that would be "home" for the next two weeks. The itinerary called for two days in port and then a cruise up the Neva River into Lake Ladoga, the Volga, and then the Moscow-Volga canal. The final three days would be in Moscow.

Birdie noted at least fifteen cruise ships tied up at the docks, each with a large red star affixed to its prow. Many were moored side by side, two and even three abreast. They were practically identical, and she had heard they were all built to similar plans, some in East Germany, some in Austria, and a few in Russia. Originally, the fleet had been built by the Soviets as vacation palaces for Soviet workers. *Here, at least,* Birdie mused, *the Soviets' boasts of caring for the workers was true.* She shared the thought with Isaac, who said, "That was then. But now, Boris Yeltsin's new country is strapped for foreign cash, so the newer boats all cater to us, to foreign tourists."

As they stood in line to board the cruise ship *V. M. Molotov,* the group was serenaded by a pair of musicians, one playing an accordion and the other a balalaika. Just inside the door, a rosy-cheeked woman dressed in a colorful peasant costume held out an enamel tray, offering everyone the traditional welcome of bread and salt.

At the reception desk, Birdie presented her passport. She took her key and went to her cabin. She found it to be small and tight but adequate. The toilet, just behind the door, was tiny. *Why,* she wondered, *is there a shower curtain, but no shower.* Eventually, she discovered that the room itself was the shower stall; she could convert it into a shower stall by lifting the faucet from the sink. The faucet, she discovered, was fed by a flexible tube. By hooking the faucet to a peg on the wall, the whole room become a shower stall. Careful arrangement of the shower curtain, she found, was necessary to keep the toilet seat dry and to avoid soaking the roll of toilet paper.

Birdie unpacked her suitcase and went exploring. Every chance she got, she conversed with the crew members. Gradually, her tongue loosened up and she began recalling long-forgotten Russian phrases.

Exhausted, she went to bed right after supper, but sleep eluded her. Partly, it was the excitement of being in Russia, but more so, it was the time difference. Her body told her that it was early afternoon while her fold-up alarm clock said it was almost midnight. Moreover, this was the period of Leningrad's "white nights." The sun didn't dip below the horizon until eleven thirty and within a few minutes, it popped right back up again.

After a fitful night with little sleep, Birdie went to breakfast where she told Isaac she was going to skip the day's tours.

Right after breakfast, she walked to the metro, where she paid the three-kopek fare, equivalent to two cents, American. She marveled at how deep the escalator descended, getting down below the Baltic mud. The ride down into the depths of the metro system allowed her time to stare at the faces of Leningraders ascending toward the street. People were better dressed than she expected. The women's clothes were stylish and colorful. The younger women wore remarkably short skirts. Nobody met Birdie's eyes. Instead, she felt as though everyone was wrapped inside a personal cocoon.

A twenty-minute metro ride brought her to Nevsky Prospekt, the main thoroughfare of the city. In the underground passageway leading from the train platform, there were a few old ladies, nearly as old as Birdie, begging for coins. Teenaged boys and girls performed Beatles' songs. In front of them, on the ground, was a cloth cap, slowly accumulating copper coins. Folding tables were piled high with booklets. Mostly, Birdie noted, these were girlie magazines. Also, there were science fiction novels and books about the occult. *None of that would have been permitted two years ago,* Birdie realized.

She emerged into the bright sunlight. The sidewalk was crowded with pedestrians. There were many whom she took to be out-of-town tourists. There were ordinary soldiers and officers wearing military hats with ludicrously immense brims.

A short stroll brought Birdie to the philharmonic hall, directly across the street from the Evropaiskaya Hotel where Birdie and Bryan had stayed for a weekend before the war.

Birdie climbed the steps and opened the heavy wooden door. She found herself facing a stern-looking receptionist. *Nothing has changed,* she thought. *These women still control the country, just the way they did in my time.*

In carefully rehearsed Russian, Birdie said, "I'm a tourist from America. I'm looking for a certain musician. He is the son of two of my dearest friends. I don't know where he plays. I don't even know for sure that he is still playing. But he plays, or he played, the cello, here in Leningrad."

"Don't keep me waiting," the woman interrupted. "Who is he?"

"Vladimir Svaboda. Have you heard the name?"

"And why wouldn't I know the name? Of course I do. He plays here, in our philharmonic orchestra. Also, he plays in a string quartet. He's quite well known."

Birdie shivered.

"Is he here now? May I talk to him?"

"Let me see. It's only ten o'clock. He should be here by eleven. You can sit and wait for him. Or you could go across the street to the Evropaiskaya, drink coffee, and come back at eleven. Leave your name. When he comes, I'll tell him that you are looking for him."

"Thank you. You are so wonderful!"

Birdie had not finished her first cup of coffee when she saw the gray-haired, tall man enter the room and begin to search faces. Immediately, they knew one another.

"Volodya. It's really you!" Birdie said in Russian, using the diminutive form of his name.

"Birdie! It's amazing that we've never met. I feel that I know you and Bryan so well, through my parents. But when you lived in Moscow, I was already here in Leningrad, studying. When my parents came back from America, in 1950, they spoke of you often at that short time and with love. And now, here you are! Is Bryan with you?"

"No, Bryan has been dead for thirty years already. But your Luba? Igor? Tell me. I haven't heard a word since they were...what? Expelled? Exchanged? They are old now. Are they living?"

"Come," Vladimir said. "Let's find a quiet corner in the lobby where we can talk privately."

When they were settled, Vladimir asked, "Do you really know nothing of what happened to my parents?"

"Nothing. Not a word since they were returned to Russia. I'm embarrassed to tell you we never tried to contact them. It seemed too dangerous."

"I understand. The Korean War was underway," Vladimir said. "I'm sure, at least, that you know that the Americans arrested them, called them spies, and then instead of putting them in prison, they were exchanged for one of your American spies, whom we had arrested. That much you know, right?"

"Yes. We were in Israel at the time so we didn't even have a chance to say good-bye to them."

"Well, they were back in Moscow for no more than two years before the KGB arrested them. They were given a secret trial, and they both were shot. 'Enemies of the people,' we were told. Double agents."

"My God!" Birdie said. "Am I understanding your Russian? Shot?"

"Yes. You understand me."

Birdie shivered as a wave of cold went through her body. The cold was immediately replaced by a sense of emptiness. She realized that her hands were numb, totally beyond her control.

"Are you all right, Birdie?"

"But how am I to understand this? Who were they, then?"

"Hah," Vladimir replied. "Don't you think I've asked myself that question every day for the past thirty-nine years?"

"Oh, you poor man. It must have been terribly hard. But why did the state leave you alone? They did leave you alone, didn't they? Why did they permit you to continue performing?"

"What can I say?" Vladimir answered. "Always, I was waiting to be questioned, to be arrested myself. But they never came for me. It's impossible to understand how they thought. But all of that is long past. And today I still can't tell you what my parents really were. I just don't know. When they went to America, did they go there as spies for the KGB? Or maybe they promised to spy as a way to get out of the Soviet Union without meaning it...or did they really send back secret reports? And if they did, when the Americans caught up with them, did the Americans turn them and send them here, this time to report for your country?"

Birdie interrupted. "But can't you find the truth? Maybe when they returned to Russia, some jealous person accused them of spying and they were framed. We both know it has happened that way."

"Yes. My mother told me about your husband, Mordechai. See how much I remember? I know how hard you worked at uncovering his truth..."

Vladimir stubbed out his second cigarette, stood, combed his delicate fingers through his longish gray hair, and sat down again.

"No, Birdie, I have my music. I have a family. Two grown children. I'm not going to go digging. Probably I'll never know the truth. I can admit it to you, I'm afraid to investigate. Were they American agents? Were they Soviet agents? Were they working for both sides? Who is to know if I, their only son, don't know?"

"Volodya, Luba was a woman who did mathematics and who loved her friends and loved good music. Igor was a man who delighted in creating new buildings. He liked to tell or to hear a good joke. The rest of it is nothing but games that little boys like to play. In English, we call it 'cops and robbers.' Foolishness, meaningless. Such a waste. Barbaric! All I know is that they were my friends and that I loved them."

"Maybe you're right," Vladimir answered. "Your country executed the Rosenbergs. We Russians executed my parents. And it goes on."

After a moment's silence, Birdie managed to inquire politely about Vladimir's life. Then she said, "Volodya, please bring me out to the taxi stand. I have a horrible headache, and I need to go back to my boat."

She stayed in her bed until the boat sailed two days later. Isaac brought food to her cabin each day. She told him nothing about Igor and Luba. She simply said, "I'm not feeling well. Don't worry about me. It will pass."

Never would she tell anyone about her encounter with Volodya Kramer—not Isaac, not Joy, not Aaron.

En route to Moscow, the boat stopped each day for shore excursions. Mostly, they visited ancient churches and monasteries, and after the first day, Birdie was content to remain on board, resting and practicing her Russian with the housekeeping staff.

The day before reaching Moscow, the vessel made what was billed as "a green stop." The landing to which they moored was the only building in sight, a rickety wooden structure. Behind the landing was a grassy field surrounded by woods, mostly birch and young pines. Was this an island? A park? In any case, it was a wilderness.

Birdie was in no mood to picnic, but Isaac went to her cabin and insisted that she come ashore.

On shore, they found the crew members gathering fallen tree limbs and feeding an already large bonfire. Folding tables were placed just outside the landing, and the kitchen crew was busily laying out a traditional feast. There was caviar, both black and red, to spread on buttered white bread. There was plenty of smoked salmon, herring, and sardines. All the drinks to which the tourists had become accustomed were there for the taking—red and white wine from Georgia; Armenian brandy; several varieties of vodka, including herb-flavored; beer; and soda water.

The musicians who entertained every evening in the ship's lounge were already leading the passengers in the Russian-language folk songs they had been teaching them all week.

Singing soon gave way to dancing. The shipboard staff started out, dancing in a small circle. Then they began reaching out for the ship's passengers, pulling them, one by one, into the circle. Birdie, refusing invitations to participate, stood watching.

Isaac was caught up in the whirl of music and motion when he realized his aunt, in the midst of all the gaiety, stood apart, her face registering nothing, her attention somewhere far away.

He abandoned the dance and went to her. Saying nothing, he stood behind her and massaged her shoulders.

Birdie was fully immersed in the past. She was reliving her first night aboard the *Checherin*, so long ago, her first meeting with Russians, unrestrained, completely given over to the songs and dances that embodied their Russian souls. She saw herself going below deck to the dimly lit crew quarters, being overwhelmed by all the sounds and by the unforgettable, sweet smell of Russian cigarettes. She remembered the embraces of her Russian sailor, Yuri.

Isaac stood there with his hands on her shoulders. Neither spoke until she said, "Take me back to my cabin now, will you please, Isaac?"

That evening, they docked at the Northern River Port in Moscow. At supper, Birdie told Isaac, "Don't expect me to come on the tours tomorrow. I'll go off exploring on my own. Now I'm going to bed. I'm exhausted."

FIFTY-FOUR

Right after breakfast, Birdie stepped onto the cement pier, where looming over the *MV Molotov* was the terminal, built in the 1930s, in the same gingerbread style as the seven downtown skyscrapers favored by Joseph Stalin and emblematic of his reign. Its tall spire was topped by an immense red star, similar to the red stars on the prows of all the cruise boats tied up in dock. The sparkling white crispness of the building was diminished by crumbling cement and by dangerously eroded holes in the steps leading up from the river.

Instead of climbing the wide staircase, Birdie followed the gentler ramp of the roadway around the building and up the steep banks of the Moscow River. Once on the top, she followed a footpath through manicured gardens where masses of tulips were dropping the last of their petals. Bright-red poppies, not yet at their peak, competed for attention. The flower beds were well tended. But beyond the flower bed was a grassy field leading toward a stand of birch trees. Here, the grass was neglected, overgrown, and had become a tangle of brush.

The footpath emerged at a busy boulevard choked by three lanes of traffic in either direction. Birdie stood for a moment, undecided how to cross, until she noticed the shelter that covered a passageway, leading pedestrians down, across, and up on the other side of the traffic.

A short stroll through another park brought her to the metro.

A thirty-minute ride took her to the center of Moscow, which she remembered well.

She easily found her way to the apartment where she had lived with Mordechai sixty years earlier. She went into the courtyard, found the proper entrance, and climbed the familiar stairs. The stairwell was even dirtier and more cramped than she remembered. The scent of urine mixed with smells of cooking was immediately familiar. *My God,* she thought, *I actually lived here, five years of my life.* The darkness was intimidating. The steps seemed steeper than she remembered. She paused at each landing to regain her breath. Before knocking on her old door, she found herself repeating the Russian prayer, *Gospodin pomilu* (God have mercy). No answer. She knocked again. The door across the hall opened, and a stooped, gray-haired woman asked if she could help her.

In her passable Russian, Birdie answered, "I'm looking to see if I can discover anything about the people who lived here a long time ago, the Grossmans. Did you know them?"

"Yes. They have been dead, all of them, for a long time. Who are you? Why do you want to know about them?"

"It's not important. Thank you." She turned away and began to descend the stairs.

"Stop. Are you the American? You're Birdie, aren't you?"

"Yes."

"Don't you remember me? At least a little bit? I'm Marianna. You used to take care of me. You played with me in the park. Then when I got older, I took care of your Zoya."

They embraced.

They sobbed.

"Come in," Marianna said. "We have so much to catch up on. So many years are gone by. Let me put up the teakettle." She brought out crackers, jam, and cheese. They sat next to each other on the living room couch.

"Tell me. Tell me everything," Birdie asked. "Your mother, Nina, is she living?"

"No. She and my father moved back to Father's village in the Ukraine, and they both died there. My brother, Yuri, was in the army. An officer. He died in Afghanistan. I live here with my husband, who is at work now. He's an engineer. I taught school until I retired. We never had any children."

"And my family? Tell me everything."

"You know, don't you, that Mordechai married Olga soon after you left him?"

"No, I didn't know. But I'm not surprised. I know nothing. Sarah sent a few letters, early in the war. And then nothing. But she never talked about Olga."

"Then you don't know that Mordechai died in the war. Somewhere outside of Stalingrad. After the war, Sarah went to live with a cousin in Krasnodar. That's where she died. Olga stayed on in the apartment until maybe ten years ago when she traded it to a family with a smaller apartment. She took their apartment and got some money too. I suppose they can tell you where she lives if you want to see her."

"No, not really," Birdie said.

Marianna insisted on hearing everything that had happened to Birdie since she left Russia in 1941. She brought out boxes of photographs. Many were of Birdie in her twenties. "So many memories," Birdie said.

All day, they talked about their lives. At last, Birdie said, "I must go back to the boat soon. For supper. Or else my nephew will worry about me. Tomorrow, I can be free all day. We are supposed to tour the Kremlin and then the Pushkin Art Museum, but I'd much rather spend the time with you, if you are available. I'd like to take you to lunch. Is it possible?"

The next day, they met at noon at the National, where, more than once, so many years ago, Birdie had dined with Bryan. They sat beneath the elaborate skylight with its Victorian stained glass. At lunch, Marianna said, "This is a marvelous meal, Birdie. Back when you knew me, I never could have imagined eating a meal like this, nor eating here, in the National. But you know, almost miraculously, the minute they dissolved the Soviet Union, overnight, the shops had all kinds of food that we hadn't seen for years, if ever. Food I had never seen. It was amazing, the transformation. Expensive though. Too expensive for simple people like me and my husband. Even today, I would never, not for a moment, allow myself to spend this much money just eating. Thank you, Birdie. It is truly a miracle. The miracle isn't that we're eating in the National. The miracle is that you are here!"

They strolled, arm in arm, through downtown Moscow.

"So tell me, Marianna, now that it's all over, were you a believer? You went to Soviet schools. You studied their lessons. You joined the Young Pioneers. How much of it did you believe?"

"How shall I answer you? We never talked politics at home. But it seems I always knew that what they were telling us in school was fairy tales. Even without talking about it, we knew the difference between the government's slogans and the truth that we weren't supposed to hear. Do you remember those huge messages on top of the buildings, saying things like, "We will fulfill the plans of the Twenty-Third Congress" or "Glory to the Party"? They were always there, but mostly we ignored them. You know, like a fish swimming in water. He isn't aware of the water; it's just there. Our life just happened. We never expected it to be different. But what about you, Birdie? You came to Russia expecting so much. You left. You never came back until now. Were you terribly disappointed with what you found here in those years, before the war?"

"It's complicated, Marianna. Remember, I lived pretty well when I was married to Mordechai. He was a party member. That meant a lot. By the way, you lived well too, because of your mother's contacts. For a Russian, you lived very well. Then, when I married Bryan, I lived as a foreigner. It was relative luxury."

They strolled a bit in silence, and then Birdie continued, "I saw that you Russians were doing marvelous things. You made me proud. But I also saw how brutal the regime was. You were sacrificing your people for a better world that would come soon. It never did come, did it? But the sacrifices were horrible. All I could do was to remain silent. I didn't want to be counted among the enemies of the state. But neither could I approve of what was happening. That's why I couldn't come back until now—as an old lady."

Birdie declined Marianna's invitation to come to supper and to meet her husband. They parted at the metro station.

FIFTY-FIVE

The tour was over. Aboard the bus to Sheremetyovo Airport, Birdie told her nephew, "I'm so ready to go home, to Aaron, to Joy and Richard, to my life."

Luggage was checked in. The group passed through security, took seats by the boarding gate, and awaited the flight to Helsinki where, again, they would spend the night before flying on to New York the next morning.

Birdie sat facing the board, which, in Cyrillic and in Roman letters, announced that the flight would board in fifteen minutes.

Ten minutes later, the message disappeared from the board. Isaac inquired and then told his group, "Here's what I found out. Good news and bad news. The local baggage handlers are on strike. The flight is now delayed twenty-four hours. Sorry. But the good news is we're spending the night at the Novotel Hotel, right here on the airport grounds. We're guests of Finnair, and they'll put us on a flight tomorrow afternoon."

In contrast to the ship they had just left, the hotel felt luxurious. The restaurant was thoroughly European. There was a swimming pool and a health spa, but Birdie wasn't interested. She was tired and not at all hungry.

She slept well, but when she awoke in the morning, she felt queasy and decided to skip breakfast. Even though she hadn't eaten the night before, whatever was still left in her stomach seemed to be repeating on her, coming up into her throat, bitter pieces of undigested food entering her nasal passages. She felt herself close to vomiting. *Good,* she thought, *I usually feel much better after I throw up.*

Birdie put her feet onto the floor. The first step that she took toward the bathroom was accompanied by a sharp pain in her abdomen. She cried out as she collapsed to the floor.

A housekeeper heard her scream. She unlocked Birdie's door and finding her barely conscious, moaning on the floor, put a pillow under her head, covered her with a blanket, and went for help.

Coming upstairs from breakfast, Isaac saw Birdie's door was open. Three figures, dressed in white, stood above her. He watched them kneel down and slide Birdie onto a stretcher. She groaned as they shifted her, allaying Isaac's fear that she was dead.

"What is happening?" he asked in his limited Russian.

"We don't know. We're on our way to the hospital."

"I'm going with you."

Ambulances, with prominent red letters proclaiming "First Aid," were a common sight in Moscow. They boasted a three-person crew—a doctor, an aide, and a driver. Equipment was minimal, and as they drove off, it was clear to Isaac that this vehicle was in need of new springs.

Birdie groaned each time they hit a bump or a pothole, but she said nothing.

The twenty-minute ride brought them to a large concrete hospital, surrounded by blocks of identical nine-story apartments. The hospital was of unknowable age. It was drab and in want of maintenance. As Isaac had pointed out to his tourists, Soviet construction was generally shoddy. "You can look at the bare bones of some project," he told them, "regard it carefully, and you won't be able to tell, is this a new building under construction or an old building being demolished?"

Birdie, on her low stretcher, was wheeled down a dark hall with high ceilings. As Isaac's eyes grew accustomed to the lack of light, he saw that the hallway was lined with cots. There was a patient on each one. Many of the patients had family members in attendance.

The aide and the driver rolled Birdie's stretcher down the hall until they located an unoccupied space. Beckoning a hospital orderly to come help, they lifted the stretcher up to the level of the cot. Two of them held it in the air while the orderly unceremoniously pulled Birdie across. She screamed in pain.

The ambulance crew departed abruptly. The orderly, a slim, dark-haired man of forty or so, wearing an embroidered *tubateka* on his head, immediately turned his attention elsewhere. The occupant of the third cot down from Birdie's was trying to get onto the floor. Every time he swung a leg over the bed, the orderly would kick that leg and push the man back onto his back. "You're drunk!" the orderly said. "Lie down, drunkard." The man tried again to get up, upon which the orderly punched him in the stomach. Isaac realized that the orderly was as drunk as the patient.

It took half an hour before Birdie and Isaac were brought into an office, where Isaac answered questions and Birdie's information was entered into a ledger. By then, Birdie had regained sufficient awareness of her surroundings to know she was in a hospital and that Isaac was there with her.

Looking around the room, she saw a discolored sink from which rusty water continuously dripped. An overhead light fixture dangled from an exposed electric wire, and the room's tile floor looked even dirtier than it was because of loose tiles, which had come unglued and were simply swept into a pile against the wall.

Isaac was told to remain while Birdie was wheeled into an adjoining room and given an internal examination. Several times, Isaac heard her scream in pain.

At last, Birdie's cot was wheeled back to the anteroom and then out into the hall.

"Wait here. The doctor will come," they were told.

Birdie held Isaac's hand firmly and looked up with fear in her eyes. "He hurt me very much," she said. "Terribly."

The doctor came and tried to explain Birdie's condition. Isaac understood little of what he said but did understand that the doctor wanted to operate immediately. He thought for just a moment and then asked the doctor, "Will she die tonight if you don't operate?"

"No," the doctor answered. "She isn't going to die tonight."

"Then we are leaving."

An ambulance, no better than the previous one, returned them to the airport hotel in time to meet their group for the afternoon flight to Helsinki.

With difficulty, Isaac procured a wheelchair from Finnair and wheeled Birdie from the hotel to the flight deck. One member of the tour group, a nurse, wrapped her in a blanket and hovered over her during the entire flight, "lest she go into shock."

The flight crew radioed ahead, and an ambulance met them at the airport, taking Birdie immediately to the nearest hospital.

Isaac accompanied the group to their hotel in Helsinki and, first thing in the morning, went, by taxi, to the hospital nearest the airport. There, he was informed that Birdie's condition was sufficiently serious so that in the middle of the night, she had been transferred to the University Hospital, downtown.

When he reached her bedside at the University Hospital, Birdie appeared calm and alert.

"Hello, Aunt Birdie. You look much better. Do you know where you are?"

"Yes, Isaac. I know where I am and who I am," she answered in a clear voice. "And I know who you are too. Maybe, I even know what's wrong with me."

"You look so much better than you did yesterday," Isaac said, bending down and kissing Birdie on the forehead. "What did they say?"

"Diverticulitis."

"Whatever that means," Isaac said. "I can't stay, but I'm so glad you're better. I'm off to the airport. I'll put our group onto their plane and come right back to you, Birdie. Don't go away."

"Not likely."

Birdie was held in the hospital for treatment and observation.

Isaac, who kept his room at the hotel, visited every day, and each day, she appeared to be a little bit better.

On her third day in the hospital, when Isaac came, bearing fresh gardenias, Birdie was able to give him a clearer report.

"Do you know anything about diverticulosis and diverticulitis?"

"Almost nothing. You tell me."

"Well, I have a serious case of diverticulitis," she said, propping herself up in bed and adjusting her pillow so she could sit upright. "Diverticulosis isn't as bad. It means you have pockets in the wall of your colon where stuff can get trapped. Not stuff—stool. Well, if that happens, and the stuff gets infected, you've got diverticulitis. I've got diverticulitis. They're treating me, mostly with antibiotics, and I'm getting better."

"Yeah," he said. "That's a pretty good summary of what the nurses already told me. Also, if all goes well, we should be able to go home by the end of the week."

On the following day, when Isaac visited, Birdie reported, "I'm thrilled with the care I'm getting. The food is wonderful, and what's best is that all of the nurses, the volunteers, and even the orderlies, they all speak English. You know, Isaac, when your uncle Bryan was dying in New York City, at Mount Sinai, it was all I could do to find anyone on the floor who spoke English. But here in Helsinki, everyone does. Go figure!"

Every day, Isaac telephoned Joy and Richard. Each day, he was able to tell Joy that her mother was better. Then, on the sixth day, he was told that Birdie would be released and could return to New York the following morning. There, her own doctors could decide on further treatment.

On the seventh day, Isaac brought a plastic bag containing clean clothes for Birdie to wear on the flight home.

He went to her private room and found the bed empty. "Where is she?" he asked the floor nurse.

"It's OK. She's in intensive care. We had to operate in the middle of the night. Her intestine ruptured. She was given a colostomy. Do you know what that means? It means we cut out the ruptured section of her colon and put a hole into her abdomen. She'll have to wear a bag into which she evacuates her bowels. But she will be fine, otherwise."

"How long will it be before she can fly back to the States?"

"A week or two."

Birdie was still in the recovery room when Isaac phoned Joy and Richard, who were expecting to meet Birdie at Kennedy Airport that afternoon. He reported to Joy on her mother's condition. Then he said, "Now it's your turn. You fly out here this afternoon. It's time I get back to my own family."

The following morning, Joy and Richard were at Birdie's bedside and Isaac was on his way home.

Two weeks later, the day before Birdie was to be released from the University Hospital, she was visited by a social worker, an attractive, graying woman wearing a suit. In fluent English, she advised Birdie that many people were living full and satisfying lives, even while evacuating their bowels into plastic sacks suspended from belts. She held Birdie's hand as she spoke. Birdie smiled back at the woman, but she thought to herself, *Not me. As soon as it's possible, I'll find a New York doctor who can reverse this operation.*

The next day, Birdie was presented with a bill and released from the hospital. The bill totaled two hundred dollars, mostly for incidentals, such as international telephone calls.

That afternoon she, Joy, and Richard flew home to New York.

FIFTY-SIX

Broadway - Riding up in the elevator, Joy told her mother, "Your two valises will be happy to see you. They've been sitting here in your apartment for almost three weeks."

Even as Birdie inserted her key into the lock, she could hear the telephone ringing.

"Quick! You get it, Richard."

He twisted the door handle, entered ahead of Birdie, and rushed for the phone.

"It's Aaron," he said, offering the receiver to Birdie.

"Yes, sweetheart, I'm back. We just this moment got here...Yes. I'm OK, more or less. I can get about...No, I won't be out there, to Queens, to see you. That would be too much for me...We'll talk on the phone every day...No, you shouldn't have them bring you here. I don't want you to see me in this condition...You know how much your letters helped me while I was in the hospital, don't you? I went through terrible bouts of loneliness, and each time I got a letter from you, I felt strong and happy again."

Aaron stayed with his daughter in Queens for the remainder of the summer. Birdie relented a bit, allowing him to visit once a week, driven and accompanied by his daughter. During each of these visits, Birdie was intensely conscious of her colostomy bag and consequently disliked having him in her home. During this time, she rarely went out and she saw no one except Joy.

"I'm not going to let any of my friends see me like this," she told her daughter.

By January, she was well enough to go through a second operation to undo the colostomy. Only then, once normal bodily functions took over, would she allow Aaron to move back in with her.

They didn't go to Florida that winter, and when the warmer weather began, Birdie told Aaron, "If it's still available, let's see if we can rent the bungalow on the pond one more summer."

They rented it, and Birdie hired a carpenter to construct a ramp, making it possible for Aaron to get in and out of the house in his wheelchair.

In late summer, Birdie told Aaron, "I've decided to host a reunion picnic for the people who were on the tour with me last summer. I want to see them all again. After all, they helped save my life, didn't they? Besides, I'll bet not one of them expected to see me alive again."

It was a happy gathering. The weather was perfect. Photographs were shared and stories swapped. Isaac took over the grill, preparing hamburgers and hot dogs.

Most stayed late into the afternoon. By the time the last guests left, Birdie and Aaron were exhausted.

"One more glass of wine," Birdie suggested.

They sat on the porch, she in a cushioned wicker rocker, he in his wheelchair, and watched the sunset sky over the algae-green waters of the colony's pond.

"It was a nice afternoon, Aaron. Such good people!"

Birdie wrapped a woolen comforter around Aaron and propped a pillow behind his head. After a significant pause, he answered.

"Yes, probably. But I'm not so sure that they really know what they saw there, in Russia. From what I heard today, it seems to me that each of you was limited by what you expected to see."

"What are you trying to say, Aaron?"

"The pinkos who went there expecting to see proud achievements of Socialism managed to find what they were looking for. The ones who felt that the Soviet Union was evil incarnate found evidence of how wise they had been. And the rest of them, from what I heard, mostly enjoyed the scenery and the food, but they hated the cramped showers in their cabins."

"You're a cynic, Aaron."

"No, I'm not. I'm just summing up what I heard today. Now you tell me, Birdie. You hardly talk about your own feelings. You nearly died over there. But first you saw your 'Promised Land.' You got to live it again. Did you learn anything?"

She surprised herself at how instantly the answer came—she knew not from where, and in words which she had never, until this moment, formulated.

"They threw it away, Aaron. They threw it away!"

"Don't start that again, Birdie. Don't say that they threw it away. It was *dreck*, shit from the start. Can't you see it yet?"

"You'll never understand, Aaron, because it isn't inside you. I saw how bad it was. I've always known it. I lived through it. Remember? I saw people starve while I ate royally. I saw the terror firsthand. You know all about my husband being sent away on trumped-up accusations. And still...you know what? None of it matters. When I hear the Red Army band playing 'The International' or when Paul Robeson sings the Soviet National Anthem—'Long may her crimson flag inspire'—my heart still beats faster, tears come to my eyes. Right away, I'm home. These are my people. And I'm not able to let go of the dream. Can you understand that, Aaron? Can you?"

"Sure I can. But first, bring me that blanket, would you...Thanks. You aren't really crazy, you know. There's a name for what you have. It's called 'cognitive dissonance,' the ability to believe two things at once, two diametrically opposed things. You're not the first person to suffer that affliction. Do you remember *Huckleberry Finn*?"

"I read it."

"Well, do you remember the dilemma Huck faced? Nigger Jim was his best and only friend. He was helping Jim run away from slavery. But he knew that Jim was Aunt Polly's property and that Polly had never done Jim anything but good. He struggled with it and decided on a course of action he knew was wrong and could send him to hell. He did it anyway. That's you, Birdie. You and Huck, you both got saddled with conflicting realities, and you hold onto them because they are a part of your being. That's why you can't quite deal with me, Birdie, because whenever, God forbid, we get back to politics, part of you knows that I'm right and part of you can't accept it."

Instead of answering, Birdie sat listening to the chirping of the crickets as the evening light faded. After a few moments of silence, she said, "It's a lonely world out there, Aaron, and it's a lot lonelier when I'm not with you." Using her arms to push herself out of the rocker, she stood. She kissed Aaron on the forehead, and after retrieving an additional throw rug, she wrapped it around his shrunken frame.

Birdie awoke the next morning after a good night's sleep. Sunlight filled the room. She smiled, and in her mind, she sorted the events of yesterday, remembering each of the guests, their faces, their quirks, and how they had behaved in Russia. Aaron was still asleep beside her. When, after a while, Birdie snuggled closer, wrapping her legs around his, he snorted and turned away from her.

"Aaron," she said. "It's time you were awake. I'm thinking about our conversation last night. There's one more thing I wanted to say."

"Don't start out my day with suspense, already. Just say it."

"You asked how I feel about the collapse of the Soviet Union. Remember? I figured it out. I know what I'm feeling. It's like what remains after a limb is amputated. It isn't there anymore, but you can still feel it. It itches, and you want to scratch it. Sometimes, it even pains you. Your eyes, your intellect, they assure you that the limb is gone. But another part of your being knows that it's still there. Do you understand me, Aaron?"

Aaron untwined his legs from hers, propped himself on one elbow, and looked at Birdie. "I can relate to what you are feeling, Birdie."

Aaron pushed back the quilt and slowly brought his feet to the floor. He sat for a moment and then ruffled what remained of his white hair.

"Here's how I experience what you're talking about. Before I was married, I spent most of my waking hours walking around with a hard-on. It wasn't easy to pry my brain loose, to think about anything other than sex. And now, I'm an old man. I probably spend as much time thinking about sex as I ever did. But nothing happens down there. Not a twitch. I can visualize what used to be. But it isn't there anymore."

With two hands, Birdie pushed Aaron back onto the bed. Snatching her pillow, she swung it, hitting him over the head.

"Now you're just baiting me, Aaron. You're not half as narrow-minded as you pretend to be."

FIFTY-SEVEN

They returned to Florida before the northern weather turned cold. Aaron had recovered from his stroke as much as he ever would. He could take only a few steps unaided, and he couldn't drive. Birdie was the family driver. Whenever they went out by car, she would first maneuver Aaron into the passenger seat and then fold his wheelchair, tip it onto the rim of the Buick's trunk, lean her shoulder against the two wheels, and using all the strength in her body, shove the chair all the way in and slam the trunk closed.

That winter, she had the first of numerous automobile accidents, none of which she thought were her fault.

In these years, much of Birdie's attention was occupied by the doings of her family: children, grandchildren, great-grandchildren, nephews, nieces, and all of their children. She managed to involve herself in the minutia of each one's life, remembering to send a card on every birthday.

She gave up her lease on the Broadway apartment as no longer necessary.

She still watched her investments attentively, continuing to buy, to sell, and to shift money from bank to bank, from fund to fund. It was clear to her that she was getting better returns on her investments than was Aaron, who still relied on his computer to indicate financial trends. He had developed a set of charts, which, according to his calculations, should tell him what to buy and what to sell. He followed his system faithfully, but his return was no better than the market average. Birdie, on the other hand, by listening to the advice and tips of those whom she trusted and then following her own intuition, continued to grow her portfolio at an impressive rate.

Birdie reached the age of ninety when she realized she could no longer care for both Aaron and herself. For a week, she struggled over how to tell him and finally said, "Sweetheart, I've decided. It's time for you to go back to your daughter in Queens. Yes, I still love you, but I haven't got the strength to care for you. Not for the two of us."

Aaron accepted the proclamation stoically.

Birdie was surprised that the sadness she had expected to feel was outweighed by relief. Aaron went to live the final year of his life with his daughter. During those months, Birdie and Aaron frequently talked by telephone but never saw each other again.

It was nephew Ernest's task to keep an eye on her in Florida. In the summers, Joy would find her mother a place to stay nearby but not in her home. Mother and daughter quarreled and snipped at each other too much to live together. Still, Birdie acknowledged to herself how dependent on Joy and Richard she had become.

The three of them sat outside on Joy and Richard's terrace. Birdie noted the tomatoes, some in pots and others in well-tilled soil, just starting to flower.

"It's too hot for tomatoes already back in Florida," she said.

She took in the view of the Catskill Mountains, some thirty miles away, seen vividly above the swamp maples beyond the backyard. A roll-up awning protected them from the bright sun. Joy had brought out iced tea and cookies. In front of Richard were a number of manila folders, bankbooks, and Birdie's most recent tax returns.

"Why do I feel that you're going to subject me to an inquisition?" Birdie asked, looking first at Joy and then at Richard.

"No, Mommy, it isn't that. We're trying to make life easier for you. You said yourself that you can't keep it all straight."

"Well," said Richard. "There's not going to be any inquisition, but still, I can't make the figures come out right unless there are some accounts somewhere that you haven't told us about. You want me to do this for you, but I suspect you aren't sharing everything with us."

A few moments of silence passed, with Richard looking puzzled and Joy fixing an accusatory stare on her mother.

Birdie thought she might cry but quickly regained control of herself.

"You're right," she said, angrily. "I haven't told you everything. I'm protecting my grandson, your son, Jeffery. I'm not sure you will take care of him after I'm gone, and there isn't anybody else."

"You know that isn't true, Mother," Joy exploded.

"Yes, it is true," Birdie responded. "When I bought him his house, you told me I was spoiling him, and he'd never be able to take care of it. Didn't you? That's why I haven't shown you everything I own."

"Mother, you bought him the house, what was it, three years ago? You told him, 'Go find a tenant, and you'll always be able to pay your taxes.' That's what you told him. Has he been able to keep a tenant?... Has he? You know he has lost every tenant he's had."

"See what I mean?" Birdie responded. "You're not going to take care of him. I have to keep myself alive so I can take care of him. You're living just fine, here in the country. His twin, Carlo, is rich. No worries there. But from the time when Jeffery was fourteen years old and you threw him out of the house, when I found him and took him in, nothing but struggle."

"Stop it! Both of you," said Richard, the peacemaker. If he didn't succeed in easing Birdie's worries, at least he did convince her to identify her still-hidden assets.

One day, in Florida, Ernest got a call from the local police department.

"We understand that Birdie Cantor is your aunt."

"Yes. What happened?"

"She's OK. She ran a stop sign and rear-ended a delivery van. No injuries, but her car isn't going anywhere again. You've got to tell her, 'Enough already.' Tell her, 'You're ninety some years old. Give it up!' The computer says this is her fourth accident in three years. She shouldn't drive anymore."

"I've been telling her that for years," Ernest answered. "You tell her. It will sound much better coming from you than from me, her nephew."

That was the end of her driving.

In June, Joy arranged a nearby summer rental for her mother. It was in an apartment complex that was student housing most of the year but catered to snowbirds in the summer. Birdie hated it. "Nobody is the least bit friendly."

The following year, she refused to come north. "I'm staying right here in my own home!" she insisted.

When the hurricane struck in August, Birdie wasn't worried. She had been through other hurricanes, but the woman living four doors down the open walkway was new to the development. She was alone and old, though ten years younger than Birdie, who considered her "somewhat scattered in her thinking." The storm arrived. The wind was ferocious. Electricity went out at four in the afternoon. Birdie's phone rang. It was the neighbor, asking if Birdie was all right.

"Of course I am. How about you? Do you need anything? Do you have candles? Did you save drinking water?"

"I'm fine. No. I don't have any candles. But that doesn't worry me."

"Stay there. I'll bring you candles."

Birdie hung up the receiver, went into the kitchen, climbed onto a stool, and, from an upper shelf, took down an unwrapped package of commemorative candles. She opened the front door. Immediately, the wind wrenched it from her grasp, flinging it fully open. The slap of wind threw Birdie to the cement floor of the walkway. The candles were gone. She was soaked by sheets of pelting rain. Still on her knees, Birdie crawled back into her apartment. The steel front door was beyond her grasp, and water was streaming into the living room. Birdie crawled to the couch and by reaching for the wooden armrest, pulled herself upright.

She sat there a moment, collecting her thoughts. *How do I block the opening? No way can I reach the wide-open door.* She looked around. *Ah...The dining room chairs,* she thought. *I'll pile them in the opening and cover them with blankets. That should do it.* By the time she had positioned three of her chairs, she was exhausted. She went into her bedroom to get a blanket, stopped a moment to regain her breath, and when she returned to the living room, her pyramid of chairs had been blown across the room.

Telephone service had long gone out. Birdie went back to her bedroom, shut the door, changed her wet clothing for pajamas, and climbed under the covers.

It was morning before Joy could reach her mother on the cell phone.

"Mother, now you see why we have to get somebody to live with you. I'm going to start looking right away."

"You certainly will not," Birdie replied. "I am still able to take care of myself. Ernest will come and fix the door. It doesn't close right anymore. But I am just fine. My poor old neighbor is, too."

It was months later that Ernest got a call from the resident manager in their section of Shelter Harbor. "Apparently, the neighbors say that your aunt has been getting into her apartment by climbing through the living room windows. Can you please find out what's happening?"

It turned out there had only been one such episode. Birdie had gone for the mail, shut the door behind her, and returned to find it locked.

"It was a totally reasonable thing to do," she told Joy, who called as soon as she heard about it.

"No, Mother, it wasn't reasonable. You are ninety-five years old. You aren't supposed to be climbing through windows. You really do need somebody to live with you, and I'm going to find you someone as soon as I can."

Joy located a live-in caretaker, a seventy-year-old West Indian woman, and called her mother to tell her they would be coming.

"Ridiculous!" Birdie said. "You can't tell me how to live my life. I'm fine. Just mind your own business."

"This isn't for you to decide, Mother. I've decided already. We are flying down on Tuesday."

Joy and Mimi Dinkens flew south. Joy introduced them and spent that afternoon and evening acquainting Mimi with the apartment, with her mother's needs, and with the neighborhood.

Birdie spent most of that time sitting on her couch glaring at both of them and refusing to speak.

Joy flew back north the following morning, and before the week was over, Birdie considered Mimi her best friend.

FIFTY-EIGHT

Summer came. Birdie and Mimi Dinkins flew north to a comfortable, two-bedroom manufactured home that Joy had purchased with her mother's money. The home sat on cement blocks and was not at all mobile, but nonetheless, Birdie always referred to it as "a trailer." It smelled of smoke from the previous tenants. Birdie had not smoked since Bryan's death, but she made her peace with the smell, which gradually diminished, but never fully left the unit. The town library was a three-block stroll, which Mimi and Birdie, arm in arm, took several times a week.

By their second summer in the unit, Birdie no longer had the energy even to walk to the library. Still, she remained a voracious reader. Also, she avidly followed the news, reading local papers as well as the *New York Times*. She watched television news several times a day although she could hear fewer and fewer of the spoken words.

When any of her numerous relatives visited, she would painstakingly examine the details of their lives, retaining every scrap in her memory. The next visitor, then, would be regaled with a detailed recounting of the previous visitor's life and the lives of various cousins, nephews, or children of friends whom her listeners hardly knew. It was easier for a visitor to let Birdie do the talking, rather than tell her things she could barely hear, and once she had an audience, she was able to go on for a long time.

Birdie and Mimi returned to Florida to find an impossible situation awaiting them. The state was responding to a heightened concern over illegal immigration. Papers were being checked in workplaces, in welfare offices, and any other place the politicians could think of, even the gate into Shelter Harbor. Before passing through the gate, anyone who worked there must be registered and show proof of legal residence in America.

Mimi had no such proof. There was no question of breaking up a relationship that worked so well, and one week later, Birdie and Mimi returned north, to the "trailer."

In the fall, Isaac visited. His knock was answered by Mimi, who, once Birdie emerged from her bedroom, excused herself, put on her jacket, and went out for a walk.

"I'm so glad to see you *milie moi* [my dear one]. It's been so long. Can I make you some tea?"

"Yes. I'd like that. Let me do it."

"No. Sit. Everything is right here."

The tea was prepared, and they took their cups into the living room where they sat side by side on the couch.

Isaac sniffed the air. "I see that the cigarette smell is almost gone by now."

"What? Say it again." Birdie listened carefully, and Isaac repeated the observation.

Birdie took out one of her hearing aids, examined it, struck it a sharp blow, and replaced it in her ear.

"Birdie, can you hear me now?"

"You know, Isaac, I can hear just as well without these things as with them. They really aren't much good, but they cost a lot."

Isaac nodded in agreement and sipped from his teacup. Birdie's cup sat, ignored, on the coffee table in front of them.

"Oh, Isaac!" She sighed. "It's terrible to sit and wait till I die. It should have happened a long time ago. But I can't die now. I have no idea what will happen to Jeffery if I die."

"Birdie..." Isaac spoke clearly into her ear. "That's not true, Birdie. Jeffery has family. He'll be OK. You have to have confidence in Joy and Richard. Can you do that? Please."

"What? I didn't listen to you. I was thinking."

"Birdie, I've been talking to my cousin Bridget, your niece. She's coming upstate next week, and she wants to see you."

"Bridget? I know who she is, Isaac. You don't have to remind me she's my niece. She's the crazy one. And I know why she wants to see me. She wants money."

"Birdie, that's ridiculous," Isaac shouted into her ear. "She wants family. That's what she wants. She's lonely. Her father, Christopher, stopped talking to her years before he died. You remember that, don't you?"

"Of course I do."

"She doesn't see her sister. Her mother is dead. She wants family. She doesn't want your money."

"You can tell her to come if you want to. I'll be nice."

Birdie went on and on, telling Isaac how Bridget's father was a tyrant. "He treated Bryan's sister, Lilly, like a servant. And she accepted it. Your mother, Belle, may have been tactless and mean, but she was never submissive the way her sister, Lilly, was. Come to think of it, their mother was that way too. Grandpa Morris treated his wife like a doormat. And Christopher treated his two girls that way. Lauren accepted it. Good! But Bridget didn't jump when he said jump and so he stopped speaking to her, his own daughter. Do you know where his arrogance came from? Tell me, Isaac, was it because he was one of the Communist Party's 'intellectuals' so, by definition, he could do no wrong? Or maybe it was his being a Negro and he never really trusted the rest of us?"

"I don't know about Christopher, Birdie. But I know Bridget will be happy to see you."

A month later, Bridget did visit. She and Birdie enjoyed a pleasant afternoon, which consisted of Birdie relating family stories, some already known to Bridget and some new.

After an hour of talk, Birdie said "Enough, already. I need to take my nap. Bridget helped her to her feet. They kissed, and Bridget left. As Birdie went down the hall, to her room, she had a feeling she had just done something good, but wasn't sure what it was.

One week later, Birdie awoke to the sounds of Mimi moving about somewhere in the house. The room was flooded with bright sunlight. Outside was bitter cold, particularly cold for New York's Hudson Valley. But inside, was snug. From her bed, she peered at the ceramic bust of Vladimir Mayerhoff atop her dresser. She had treasured the figurine for over seventy years. The familiar head of the Soviet theater director, with his elongated Jimmy Durante nose accenting his handsome Semitic features, and the vivid greens and blues of its glaze brought a smile to her face.

Birdie pushed back her quilt, brought her skinny legs over the side, and carefully stood up, feeling the stiffness as each of her joints responded, reluctantly, to the instructions that that they move. She put both her hands on the figurine and muttered, "You know what, Volodya? Jeffery will be OK. Isaac promised me he will be taken care of."

Then she turned and shuffled to the bathroom.

Emerging, she ignored the set of teeth soaking in a bowl of water. She paid no attention to the hearing aids on her night table. "The batteries are no good anyway," she muttered.

She dropped her frail body into the middle of the living room couch and smiled up at Mimi, who wished her a good morning in her lilting West Indian accent. Birdie's slender hands reached out for the proffered cup of coffee.

Mimi peeled an orange, divided it into sections, and put the sections onto a plate, which she set in front of Birdie, who had already finished her coffee.

Mimi took the empty cup to the sink, washed it, dried it, and returned it to the cabinet. She turned around and saw that Birdie's head had fallen to her chest. Birdie was dead.

About the Author

Karl Rodman is a retired educator who now lives with his wife on Sanibel Island, Florida, where they raise chickens and he remains active in the local historical museum. Throughout his extensive teaching career, he taught all grades, from kindergarten through college. And for a time, he and his wife also directed a children's summer camp, as well as a neighborhood school—an experience he describes in his book A School Named for Thoreau.

Rodman eventually went on to run a tour company that guided American teachers through the USSR. He went back to school, earning an EdD in Soviet studies, which enabled him to offer the tours as credit-bearing courses.

Rodman's novel Comes the Revolution, a fascinating fictionalized biography of his aunt, draws from his family history, academic studies, and the more than thirty trips he led to the USSR.

17142402R00179

Made in the USA
Middletown, DE
08 January 2015